Quell the Nightingale

PRAISE FOR MICHELE ISRAEL HARPER

"Quell the Nightingale is the perfect blend of everything I crave in a story: lush, expansive, fresh worldbuilding; witty, multifaceted characters and banter; non-stop action and adventure; a wonderful, lion-hearted heroine and swoon-worthy hero; and a hard-won, satisfying happily-ever-after.

In the tradition of *Once Upon a Time*, *Quell the Nightingale* weaves together fragments from some of my favorite fairy tales to produce an original and unpredictable tale I could not put down!"

~J. J. Fischer, award-winning author of *Calor*

"A delightful journey into a land of mystery and magic, where fairy tales collide and hope hangs by a thread."

~Annie Sullivan, author of *A Touch of Gold*

"Quell the Nightingale is a fun, delightful romp! Weaving several fairy tales into a seamless tapestry, Michele Israel Harper crafts compelling threads of family, love, and courage that will leave you smiling. This story treats readers to much-loved fantasy characters and is a quirky, magical tale that makes one wonder what truly is real and what's worth fighting for."

~Ronie Kendig, award-winning author of the Droseran Saga

"*Quell the Nightingale* is a masterful mash-up of many fairy tales, both popular and obscure. It's also an emotional narrative about a strong female character learning that love can only make her stronger."
~**C.O. Bonham**, author of *Runaway Lyrics*

"Such a fun fairy tale mash-up! I loved seeing all the unexpected connections and characters. There are also deeper themes woven into the story—silence, secrets, and stuffing your feelings only gives pain more power. *Quell the Nightingale* is definitely an adventure worth taking!"
~**C.E. White**, author of *Vincent in Wonderland*

"Prepare to be enchanted by this tale of a fiery huntress much better at facing magic beasts and evil spells than romance! Swoony heroes, a grouchy granny, and fun-loving family will warm your heart and keep you smiling. Ro's quest through dark forests and fairy tale kingdoms will have you turning page after page!"
~**Savannah J. Goins**, author of *Whisper of Weapons*

"The fairy tale medley I didn't know I needed! *Quell the Nightingale* introduces beloved characters at every corner in a new and fresh way. It balances high stakes and romance with a quirky and humorous—but strong—female lead at the helm. It's a tale that will keep you guessing until the satisfying end."
~**E. A. Hendryx**, author of the Xerus Galaxy Saga

Praise for other books in the Beast Hunters series:

"*Silence the Siren* is a fresh take on a classic fairy tale that I did not see coming! Michele Israel Harper weaves a wildly creative tale that will have your heart beating fast with excitement one moment and then breaking the next. Ro is the heroine we've all been waiting for. You'll be rooting for her as she takes on man and sea in this odyssey-esque adventure. Can't wait to see what Harper does with the rest of the series!"

~**Julie Hall**, *USA Today* bestselling author of the multiple award-winning Life After series

"An enjoyable retelling of the ORIGINAL *Beauty and the Beast*! Forget Disney—this is French inspired with delicious food, disappearing castles, and fairies. The lead character is tough, feisty, and not your traditional beauty. I stayed up (too late) reading this one. If you like fairy tale retellings, check out *Kill the Beast*!"

~**J.M. Hackman**, award-winning author of the Firebrand Chronicles

"*Beast Hunter* is an absolute must-read for those who love twisted fairy tales with strong female leads. Family drama, mystery, shadowy characters, and a heroine you can't help but root for, what's not to love? I was hooked immediately and now can't wait for the rest of Ro's story to unfold."

~**Dawn Ford**, award-winning fantasy author

Quell the Nightingale

Book Three of the Beast Hunters

Michele Israel Harper

Love2ReadLove2Write Publishing, LLC
Indianapolis, Indiana

ALSO BY MICHELE ISRAEL HARPER

Beast Hunters Series:

Beast Hunter: A Prequel Novella

The Lost Slipper: Cosette's Story

Kill the Beast

Silence the Siren

Quell the Nightingale

(Coming Soon)

Slay the Wolf

Stop the Snow Queen

End the Fey

Candace Marshall Chronicles:

Ghostly Vendetta

Zombie Takeover

(Coming Soon)

Vampire Feud

Mummy Resurrection

Wisdom & Folly Sisters:

Part One

Part Two

Wisdom & Folly Sisters:

The Complete Story

Coming Soon:

Elvish Duology:

The Elvish Queen

The Mortal King

Standalones:

Queen of the Moon

Dreamworld

Stars Collide

The Ravens

Altered Time Saga:

The Lady Bodyguard

The Lady Spy

The Lady Assassin

Altered Time Novellas:

Lady in Hiding

Making of a Lady

Lady Out of Time

Tales of the Cousin Kingdoms:

Ruby Dragon Kingdom

Diamond Unicorn Kingdom

Sapphire Griffin Kingdom

Emerald Pegasus Kingdom

Time of the Dragons

To my husband Ben,

This book wouldn't have gotten done without you.
Thank you for making dinner,
thank you for going on walks with me to brainstorm,
and thank you for giving me so many weekends to myself to write.
I love you!

PART I

THE ROYAL PALACE IN PARIS, FRANCE / LE PALAIS ROYAL À PARIS, FRANCE

"The Sleeping Beauty in the Wood"
La Belle au Bois Dormant
—Charles Perrault—

There was a very fine christening; and the Princess had for her godmothers all the Fairies they could find in the whole kingdom (they found seven), that every one of them might give her a gift, as was the custom of Fairies in those days, and that by this means the Princess might have all perfections imaginable.

Il y a eu un très beau baptême ; et la Princesse avait pour marraines toutes les Fées qu'elle pouvait trouver dans tout le royaume (elles en trouvèrent sept), afin que chacune d'elles puisse lui offrir un cadeau, comme c'était la coutume des Fées à cette époque, et que par ce moyen la Princesse pourrait avoir toutes les perfections imaginables.

Laura Hollingsworth

1

*H*untress Ro LeFèvre slid off her still-moving horse and took the palace steps two at a time. The intricately carved and inlaid-with-gold doors swung open as she reached them, and Cosette was there, tears in her eyes.

"Rose! You're home."

Her sister flung herself into Ro's arms, her sobs echoing down the palace hall.

Tears burned Ro's eyes, but she kept them at bay. She was fully aware of her audience: guards at her back and courtiers just inside.

Plus, Olt was around here somewhere.

Ro's eyes slid closed. It felt so good to have Cosette back in her arms. How could she have ever been upset they weren't truly sisters? This was home. This was right.

Footsteps hurried down the hall, and Ro lifted her head to see the king of France, her sister's husband, coming toward her, his own eyes swimming with tears.

King Beau Alexandre Trêve gave her a firm nod and struggled to speak. "Huntress. I am glad you have finally returned from your voyage."

Ro returned his nod and pulled away from Cosette, gripping her shoulders. "Tell me everything."

Cosette nodded, looped her arm through Ro's, and drew her inside.

Lovely as ever, Cosette strangled a handkerchief as she set a steady pace into the king's palace in Paris, France. Ro almost gawked at the sheer size and exquisite beauty of the French château, but she kept her focus on Cosette.

Right now, Allura was her priority.

Words poured from Cosette's mouth. "My daughter, Allura Aurore, your niece, won't wake up. It's been almost six months since she fell asleep, and she won't wake up!"

Six months? Ro gritted her teeth. The magical trail from the culprit would have faded by now. Still, she tried to reassure her sister. "Take heart, Cosette. We'll find whoever did this. And I swear to Dieu, I will do whatever it takes to break the curse."

Sharp movement caught Ro's eye, right at Cosette's back, and she spun around, fists raised, ready to take down whoever dared threaten her sister.

A noblewoman who'd slipped past their retinue of soldiers stared back with wide eyes, but she retreated at Ro's fierce glare. Behind her, a line of Mesdemoiselles-in-waiting and other nobles of the court eyed her, crowding close while pretending not to eavesdrop.

A soldier waved back the crowd, but Ro couldn't make herself relax. "Must they be so close?" she groused. "Can you not send them away?"

She wanted to be alone with her sister.

Cosette startled as if she'd forgotten they were even there. "The nobles? Rosette, it is an honor for those who help lead our realm to share in our daily lives. Of course I cannot ask them to depart."

Ro didn't know how to respond to that. She would've never made it as queen.

Cosette dabbed at her eyes. "I have missed you so. Why were you gone for so long? We couldn't reach you for three years!"

"My love," Trêve interrupted from her other side. "I'm sure the huntress had her reasons."

He paused, as if hoping Ro would answer Cosette's question. But Ro couldn't answer. She had no idea how she'd misplaced three years on her voyage to silence the sirens. Once Allura was well, it was the next item on her to-do list.

Ro focused on Cosette. "Can you tell me anything more? Anything that was not in your letters?"

Cosette launched into repeating everything Ro already knew. "We invited all neighboring royals to Allura Aurore's christening as an act of goodwill. You know, to show them France has recovered from her curse and we're viable trading partners again?"

Trêve gave a gentle laugh. "You *were* listening to me."

Cosette tossed him a flirty look, then went back to wringing her handkerchief. "Well, we may have slighted some visiting empress, from whom we received a furious missive." She traded a look with her husband. "It was only brought to our attention because of the threat within."

Ro recited quietly, "'For your insult to my honor, a curse shall rain down upon your heads such as you've never before seen.'"

Cosette nodded. "Exactly. We, of course, looked into it immediately, but Trêve has received a steady stream of threats or flattery since his crowning. The letter could not be traced, and our contacts who trade with the Far East did not know to which kingdom she belonged, if any. But then, when Allura Aurore fell asleep and wouldn't wake, I"—another glance at her husband—"*we* remembered the letter."

Ro knew every word. She'd memorized Cosette's letters on her way from London to Paris, and it seemed Cosette didn't have new information.

Their daughter, enchanted in a deep sleep. Unable to wake. No one knew how it had happened or why, or even who had done it.

And Cosette's true mother, the Queen of the Fairies, could not be reached.

A ripping noise caught Ro's attention, and her eyes settled on Cosette's handkerchief. One of its lace edges dangled. But then Cosette smoothed it out, and it was whole again. Ro blinked. What now?

Cosette, oblivious to what she'd done, continued talking. "How was I to know how important the letter would become?"

A torrent of words spilled from Cosette's mouth, and Ro studied her fairy sister's profile as she fretted and paced. She'd grown even lovelier, despite tears streaking down her face and worry creasing her brow.

If Ro had spent months crying, she'd be a shriveled old hag by now.

That's fairy blood for you, Ro thought to herself.

There was a clamor behind her. "I'm sorry, Monsieur, but you cannot enter here. The servants' entrance is that way."

The intruder's answer was obscured by a clattering of weapons. Thankfully, Ro had inherited her père's tall, willowy build, so she stretched up on her toes and peeked over the courtiers' heads.

Soldiers blocked Olt with their spears as they tried to shove him back out the door.

"Arrête!" She waved him forward. "He's with me."

The soldiers looked to their king, and they only moved their spears at his nod. Ro tried not to be offended at *that,* but it was all she could do not to growl. They were just doing their jobs, after all.

She intentionally focused on her traveling companion.

Tall, fit, and lean, the sailor had a ready grin, light-brown hair, and warm brown eyes flecked with gold. His unruly hair was currently trying to escape its queue, which might have had something to do with her tearing toward the palace at breakneck speed the moment they entered Paris's main thoroughfare.

Olt came forward with a sheepish grin, straightening his clothes. "You're fast," he said under his breath. "Took off like an arrow."

Ro raised an eyebrow. "Getting into trouble already, are we?"

She eyed his travel-worn clothes. He didn't look that much like a peasant, did he? He looked like the sailor he was, oui, but his clothes were sturdy and in good repair.

He gave her a quick grin, then turned to the king and queen. The lighthearted atmosphere Olt carried with him evaporated. He bowed and said, "My deepest condolences, vos Majestés."

They both inclined their heads regally, then looked to Ro for an introduction. Or an explanation.

Ro gestured his way. "This is Olt. He, um"—she eyed him, wondering how best to say this—"he helped me parley with the sirènes and asked to assist with Allura's sleeping curse. If you don't mind."

Cosette tilted her head, far too interested all of a sudden. She took him in from crown to sole. "Enchantée," she said, dipping into a curtsy and giving him a coy smile through her tears.

Ro rolled her eyes. She could see where this was going a kilomètre away. If Cosette had anything to do with it, she'd have Ro stuffed into a wedding dress and tied to an altar before she could escape. *Non, merci.*

Trêve stepped forward and offered his hand. "Bienvenue, Monsieur Olt."

Ro blinked in surprise. The king was offering his hand in welcome? He truly was a different person than before—when he'd been cursed to live as a beast until he put others before himself—but a handshake from royalty was unheard of.

Olt barely covered his surprise and returned the king's firm handshake. "Thank you very much, I mean, merci beaucoup. I am honored to meet you both. I've heard much about you from Ro."

Cosette's eyebrows shot up, and she turned to Ro with a mischievous smirk. "Have you now? My, that's interesting."

Leave it to Cosette to try to make a love match in the middle of tragedy.

Ro immediately changed the subject. "We have to find this empress. And I want to see the original letter, please."

Cosette threw her hands wide, a move Ro often made but her elegant sister did not. "No one knows anything about her! We've sent inquiries far and wide, but nothing." She strangled her handkerchief some more. "And I, uh, may have burned the letter."

Ro spun on her. "You *what*?"

"I know, I know. I shouldn't have. I was furious anyone would dare threaten my dear babe, so I tossed it right in."

Ro groaned and rubbed her forehead. "Cosette…"

"I know! But the scribe did make a note of it, thankfully." Her eyes filled with tears. "I was so upset I couldn't help myself, and then—"

Before Cosette could continue rehashing information they all knew, Trêve interrupted her. "My darling, surely our travelers are weary and wish for food."

Cosette whirled toward her husband. "How can you possibly think of food at a time like this! How could anyone possibly eat?"

Trêve's smile was patient. "The rest of us need to eat, dear. We'll think clearer and be able to help our daughter that much more."

Ro's stomach chose that moment to loudly agree, and she flushed. She'd been too focused on getting to the palace to eat, and now she was regretting that particular decision. "Désolé."

Cosette sighed, the sound weary and pained. "Very well, then. If you must."

Trêve slipped an arm around her, his look tender. "I'm afraid we must."

They shared a kiss.

Ro's gaze pinged away and landed on Olt. He too was busily looking away from the demonstrative couple. But unfortunately for her, he was studying her with a concerned expression.

In an unguarded moment, she'd told him of her past with the king, how he'd asked her to marry him to break his curse. How she'd agreed—how her sister had married him instead.

But it was *not* affecting her now, nor would it ever. She'd not wanted to be queen then, and she wanted it even less now after being shadowed by all the nobles in the realm. She flicked a glance at the courtiers filling the massive palace hallway to the brim.

Had more squeezed themselves in?

Deliberate footsteps echoed toward them at a brisk clip, and the crowd parted like a stream for a boulder. "I came as soon as I heard…"

The newcomer's deep, strong voice echoed in the vast space, and he quickly bowed to the king and queen. Ro smiled, glad to see her fellow huntsman, now captain of the king's personal guard, who had won her begrudging respect.

Liam.

"Vos Majestés. Pardon, but I came as soon as I heard the huntress had arrived." Liam turned a far-too-eager look in her direction. "Has she returned to set our fair princess free of the sleeping curse?"

He was grinning, actually, really smiling, his eyes alight, which made him look years younger. And mildly attractive. And not so much like the irritable grouse he'd always been.

Ro took a step back. What in all the realms?

They'd had an uneasy truce when she'd left, true, but they were rivals. Competitors. His reaction didn't make sense. Her eyes flitted over him, looking for signs of what could have changed his attitude toward her so.

Her rival huntsman—blond hair, brown eyes, a head taller than Ro—had settled into life at the palace quite well, it appeared. His tall, muscular frame had filled out with having enough food to eat. He'd lost his cagey look and instead exuded confidence.

It looked good on him.

The eager look he was currently directing her way? Not so much. Had the whole palace gone mad?

"At ease, High Général," Trêve rumbled out, an amused cadence to his voice.

Ro's eyes widened. High général now? Over the king's entire military forces?

Well done, Liam, she silently congratulated him. He'd done well in the past three years—even if to Ro, it had only been a little over a year. She really needed to find out how she and Olt had misplaced three years in the Caribbean.

"Won't you join us for dinner?" Trêve asked amicably.

Liam still had eyes only for Ro. "Merci, votre Majesté."

The king and queen resumed their trek, their line of peacock courtiers following, and Liam sidled up to Ro. "Huntress. Ro. I—"

"Congratulations on making high général, Liam. That's quite an accomplishment."

He looked far too pleased.

Olt sidled up to Ro's other side, the daggers he was staring at Liam so sharp, Ro flinched. Was the room a thousand degrees hotter? She tugged at her collar.

"Liam, Olt. Olt, Liam."

They looked at each other, the clash of their gazes like a thousand cymbals, and Ro slipped out from between them.

Let them be weird. She was going to latch herself to Cosette's side if she had to drag her away from her adoring husband.

Or worse. Watch it all up close.

Ugh. Could this visit be over already? She had a nice, quiet country home she couldn't wait to escape to. She frowned. If it were even still there.

Ro moved toward her sister and stopped. Trêve and Cosette had their heads bent close, whispering to each other as Trêve kissed her knuckles. Um…

Ro glanced back at the men. Still glaring at each other. Nope.

Trêve turned away to speak with a servant; Cosette noticed her then and held out her hand. Ro seized it and wasted no time dragging Cosette down the ornate hall to escape all the awkward.

Ro asked, "When did you move your court to Paris?"

Cosette waved her hand dismissively as if the topic wasn't important.

Well, it wasn't. But she was trying to get Cosette's mind off her heartache. And hers off her own embarrassment.

"Captain Liam, I mean, High Général Liam and his huntsmen came to Paris to clear the streets of lingering wolves and to ensure it was safe before we returned, oh, not long after you left for Angleterre and your voyage, actually."

Ro clutched her free hand behind her back, fighting hard to make small talk. It didn't come easy for her. "Did you have Allura before that?"

Cosette shot her a quizzical look, and Ro flushed.

"I wasn't asking when you had her. I mean, I can figure that out. But did you move here before or after she was born?" She held up both hands, trying to stem the onslaught of words. Her words. "I'm not asking anything of the birth. Not a thing. I just—" She blew out a huff of air, weary from her side of the conversation already. "I just want to know when you moved here."

Cosette gave her such a kind, sisterly, teasing look, Ro's embarrassment eased.

"Oh, Ro, how I've missed you."

They gave each other a side hug as they walked, then Cosette started prattling—something Ro was simultaneously grateful for and not sure that she liked. Cosette was much more settled before becoming queen.

Cosette winked. "Why do you think Trêve had Liam clear the city?" She smiled. "He wanted his child born and raised in Paris, a true heir to the French throne. She was born here—in her nursery, in fact. Which I will show you"—she slid her husband a begrudging look—"right after you eat."

Trêve finished his conversation, then the servant hurried off, frantically barking orders and sending a runner to the kitchens.

Ro watched the servant go, then asked, "Can you tell me more about Allura's christening?"

Trêve eyed her. "You think it had something to do with her curse?"

Ro nodded. "I do."

Cosette immediately obliged. "We invited all the neighboring kings and queens, but we never heard back from the king and queen of Prussia. I didn't think much of it. There were so many invitations sent, and so many had responded, the few who hadn't or had declined were no bother.

"But after the christening, we received that missive from someone who called herself 'the empress'—though the empress of what is anyone's guess—furious that we'd insulted her honor by not inviting her."

Cosette stopped in the middle of the hallway. "We have no idea who she is! No one at court knew of her. She gave no real name, no way to contact her. She could have been anyone, really."

"Did anyone try to identify her? List dignitaries who didn't attend, perhaps?"

"Oui," Trêve answered, "as best as we could. And we've sent inquiries, but there's just not enough information."

"May I see this list?" Ro asked.

"But of course," Trêve said promptly. "I will have it delivered to the library." At her surprised look, he said, "Where I assume you wish to set up your search?"

Ro tried not to smile. This was a serious situation, after all. "Oh, absolutely." Then she frowned. "You do not trade with the Far East, do you?"

Trêve shook his head. "Not yet. We have been busy enough with local trade, establishing ourselves as a trustworthy nation after twenty years of the curse making our borders impenetrable. It's been hard to convince merchants—and neighboring kingdoms—that they won't be trapped here after setting foot inside our kingdom."

Ro whistled. "Incroyable. I hadn't thought of that."

Cosette resumed her trek deeper into the palace. "Something else she said has stuck with me these long months. The letter said, 'For your insult upon my honor, you will lose your kingdom's most precious treasure. She will hear my sweet, sweet song and will never leave it.'"

Ro made a mental note. "What of your mère? The Fairy Queen? What has she to say about all of this?"

Cosette shook her head as tears spilled down her cheeks. "There has been no response. If she had only been here, this would've never happened. And now she won't speak to me, her own daughter!"

Cosette stopped right there and started sobbing all over again, and Ro looked to Trêve for help. Ro loved her sister, would give her life for her, but she didn't know what to do with all the tears.

Trêve hurried to his wife's side, took her into her arms, and rested his chin atop her head. He looked at Ro over his wife. "Can you do it? Can you break my daughter's curse as you did for me?"

Ro shifted uncomfortably. She'd learned a thing or two since Trêve had been a raving beast with a foul temper in a hidden château, but she still didn't understand how her magical hunting gifts worked.

Even so, she hadn't been given them for nothing.

She nodded at the king. "Oui, votre Majesté. I will."

She'd break the curse or die trying.

2

Ro entered the dining hall and stopped in her tracks. For a moment, she was back at the beast's château, recalling meal after meal with the fairy creature that had unwittingly held her hostage.

But that wasn't the only reason she'd stopped.

The long, ornate table was filled with familiar faces.

Bernadette, her eldest sister, whose looks were just like Ro's and their père's—tall, slender, dark hair, ice-blue eyes— was the first she saw.

The rest of the sisters took after their mère's fair looks.

Next came Reinette, the second eldest. She had honey-blonde hair and dark-blue eyes and was more reserved than people in her family were known for.

Lynette and Nicolette, the twins. They sat between another set of twins, a male set of twins, and leaned close to each other, whispering as they always had. Again, more blonde hair and blue eyes, but in different shades.

Yvette. She looked most like their mère. The lightest shade of golden-blonde hair and warm blue eyes—with a pang, Ro realized she also looked like Cendre. Almost exactly like Cendre, the girl she'd lost at sea.

Ro frowned. But how could that be?

Servants were hastily laying out additional place settings at the head of the table, on the far end.

Her sisters were surrounded by men. And children. So many children. Why were they here instead of at a children's table or with a governess? Ro and her sisters never would've been allowed at an adult's table were anyone besides their immediate family present. Especially not at a palace.

Ro searched for her brothers, Claude and Pascal, her best friends growing up. Well, besides Cosette. Though unfamiliar men were sprinkled among her sisters, her brothers were not present.

Disappointment crashed through Ro, though she tried hard not to let it show. Her sisters were like sharks, disappointment, like blood.

No need to give them something to use against her right away.

"Rosette! It's Rosette. Look!" Yvette cried, though Ro couldn't tell if she was happy or just surprised.

Heads swiveled her way, a plethora of emotions displayed there.

Curiosity from what Ro assumed were their husbands. Her sisters had all married while she was trapped with Trêve, and she had yet to meet any spouses.

Disgust from Bernadette, who stared at Ro's clothes as if they might come alive and eat her.

Ro would most likely encourage them if they did.

Her hunting gear, leathers, and red cape were like armor, and she never went anywhere without them.

The twins giggled behind their hands. That could mean anything. All they did was giggle. When they weren't bickering, of course.

Yvette turned cherry-tomato red, which led Ro to assume she'd just been talking about Ro, and perhaps it had been less than kind. Not that Ro expected anything different.

Reinette was the only one Ro couldn't read. More reserved than the others, no less selfish, Ro understood her least.

The children kept being noisy, doing whatever it was children did, their boisterous, bouncing selves often springing from their chairs and running wild all over the enormous dining room, giving Ro a headache, and terrorizing the wait staff, from the looks of things.

Maybe she'd just eat in her room…

Ro started to edge away, but Cosette looped her arm through Ro's and pulled her forward. "Sisters! I have such a surprise for you. Our dear sister Rosette has come home!"

If Cosette was expecting cheering or weeping in joy, she was to be severely disappointed.

All the men in the room immediately stood. Her sisters looked at their husbands as if they'd grown curling horns atop their heads.

Bernadette was the only one who voiced what they were all thinking. "For heaven's sake, sit down. It's just Rose. You don't need to stand for *her*." She tugged on her husband's dinner jacket.

Bernadette's husband flushed a little and spoke in a quiet, weary tone. "I seek to not only honor the huntress and her return, but our queen as well."

Bernadette looked uncertain, but only for a moment. The haughty look flashed back into her eyes the instant they landed on Ro.

Ro bared her teeth, hoping it somewhat resembled a smile. "It is lovely to see you again as well, Bernadette."

Bernadette just sniffed and turned away.

Cosette kept a firm grip on Ro's arm and practically dragged her to the head of the table. Ro kept looking for an opening to escape, but Cosette didn't give her one.

Trêve entered the room just then, and everyone who wasn't already standing jumped to their feet.

Except the children. One of them, a rather mean-looking thing with Bernadette's coloring, was using his spoon to flick peas at some of the other children, who were catching on to the game rather quickly.

Bernadette sighed. "Bernie, dearest, Maman really wishes you wouldn't."

Because that would teach him. Ro leaned over her place setting to give Bernadette a look, but she pretended not to see.

Ro craned her neck further. It looked as though none of the nobles or Mesdemoiselles-in-waiting would be joining them for this meal, thank heavens.

"Please, sit," Trêve said. "These are extraordinary circumstances. I do not expect anyone to stand on ceremony."

The moment the king took his place, chair legs squealed and squelched as everyone resumed sitting.

Trêve took the middle chair, Cosette to his left, and a chair to his right sat conspicuously empty. Dishes rested before it, whimsical with small pink rosebuds, with child-size utensils instead of the heavy ornate ones on the rest of the table.

Ro could only stare at it and think of the little princess, lost to sleep.

Though, once again, odd to see a child setting in a formal dining room.

Ro sat to Cosette's left, Liam next to Ro, and Olt sat directly across from Ro, next to one of the husbands. Ro quickly looked away so she wouldn't be introduced.

The man spoke up anyway. "I have heard much about the mighty huntress. It is an honor to meet you."

She flushed at the unexpected and unwelcome words and nodded.

Another husband leaned forward with an eager look. "I too have looked forward to this day for quite some time. Your exploits are legendary."

Yvette jerked her head in Ro's direction and scowled.

Ro swallowed. Yvette, the youngest of her elder sisters,

glared at Ro as if she'd spit in Yvette's tea—and then dumped it in her lap. Ro tried to deflect Yvette's husband's attention, but he carried on witlessly, unaware of his wife's glares or Ro's discomfort.

"The things you've done. The things you've seen. I would pay good livres to witness one of your hunts!"

Liam, steadfastly paying attention to his soup, smirked as if to say: *Been there, done that. Non, you wouldn't.*

Ro considered flicking peas at *him*. She wondered if they'd notice if she slid under the table and crawled down its length till she could flee to her room. Surely Cosette would be too embarrassed to stop her.

The sisters glanced at each other, then softened toward Ro, asking after her and if she was well and such.

Ro gave one-word, monosyllabic answers whenever she could. Even better was when others answered for her. She could've kissed Olt for fielding most of the questions about Angleterre, their voyage, and the sirènes.

Then Liam jumped in to answer further questions about exploits when they'd hunted together. Ro looked at him askance. He'd hated Ro then. He'd antagonized her nonstop, and she, him. Why was he making it sound like they were the best of friends?

Sure, they had each other's backs, but that was expected of a fellow huntsman.

Ro glanced around the table. At first her sisters had appeared interested. Impressed, even. Now annoyance was the prevalent glance passed around as stories focused entirely on Ro, as their husbands hung on every word.

Ro wanted to shout, "I'm not even talking about me! You can't possibly be mad at me about this."

But they continued to glare at Ro as though she was the cause of their problems. Ro sighed. Not much had changed, apparently.

Ro looked between Liam and Olt as both of their stories

included just a tad more camaraderie with Ro than was strictly true.

Oh good heavens, not them as well. Her sisters were enough to deal with. Ro shot a steady glare in Olt's direction until he noticed. He gave her a sheepish grin and took a sip of his wine.

Liam kept going until she kicked him, giving someone else a chance to say something. Olt almost spit out wine at that. He shook with silent laughter as Nicolette inquired after the sleeping princess, obviously trying to get attention off Ro.

Trêve's smile trembled. "It is our dearest wish that our Rosette will find the cause and return our daughter to us."

Ro felt the full pressure of that statement. What if she couldn't? What if Allura never woke up? Sleeping curses deteriorated quickly, trapping the person deeper and deeper within sleep, and if not broken in time, a sleep that lasted forever.

She'd done nothing but read about them on her way to the French palace from England, or Angleterre, though there was precious little information on such things, and much of it was speculation. Now to find something that told her how to *break* one.

She should be out searching, now, not forced to take part in this most dreadful of dinner parties.

Cosette waved a lace handkerchief in between dabbing at her eyes. "S'il vous plaît, I cannot speak of this. Talk about anything else, anything, I beg of you."

Ro reached over and squeezed Cosette's hand. She couldn't imagine the horror she was going through.

A man a few seats down from Olt immediately spoke up. "My dear huntress, is it true that during your first hunt, you defeated the Mesdemoiselles of the Mountain? That they were witches who were gathering France's wealth in exchange for food from their magical garden, so that they could further cripple France when the time came? That you defeated them, took over their garden, and provided food, gradually returning the wealth of France to her people?"

Ro froze, then her eyes swept the table to find the person who Just. Wouldn't. Shut. Up. The man sat between Reinette and Yvette, so Ro wasn't sure whose husband he was.

Oh. Reinette's cold stare said he was hers. Great. The last neutral sister was decidedly against her now.

Cosette gasped. "Ro, that was you? I mean, I knew you'd defeated them, the Fairy Queen said so, but I never knew the rest. Did you really? Oh, Rose!"

Ro squirmed as the pressure ratcheted up a few notches. If she'd defeated the Mesdemoiselles—cruel witches who profited handsomely from the curse—if she'd broken Trêve's curse and in turn France's, and if she'd negotiated with the sirènes to allow trade between the Americas and Europe—sans any slavery whatsoever—she couldn't fail little Allura.

It didn't matter that Ro was going into this situation like any other: blind, deaf, and dumb.

And Ro discovered her face could burn a new shade of embarrassed. Unfortunately, neither Olt nor Liam could help her with this one, and both men looked simultaneously impressed and curious.

Ro shifted awkwardly as she answered Reinette's husband. "I only defeated one of them. She'd already eaten her sisters for their power when I'd gotten there."

Shocked silence met her words.

And now she had the children's attention.

Lynette gasped. "Rose! How could you say that?" She had her hands over a little golden-haired girl's ears.

Cosette sat up, tears forgotten.

Mères all up and down the table gasped and exclaimed and waved for servants and nannies and whatever else they were to remove the children. They went with protests, dinners half touched or not touched at all, peas and other odd bits scattered across fine table settings.

"Well then, give them pastries," one of her sisters called as a servant protested that her charge hadn't finished his plate.

Liam was smiling, big time, his eyes riveted on the next course he was calmly eating.

Reinette's husband seemed impervious to the flutter around him. "But the rest is true? Oui?"

Desperately, Ro looked to Olt, to Trêve, to Liam, for help. She avoided Cosette, but even Ro could see her eyes were huge, shock making her speechless. For once.

"Aw, Maman, I want to hear about the witch eating other witches!"

Bernadette just pointed, and her servant dragged the protesting Bernie out with all the rest. The heavy dining room doors lumbered closed, cutting off the noise of far too many children. Ro breathed a sigh of relief. Thank goodness.

Reinette's husband waited patiently, not looking away from Ro.

Ro just shrugged, not knowing what else to do. "I suppose so…"

He took out a notebook and started scribbling. "Parfait!"

Ro eyed him suspiciously. "May I ask why you wish to know?"

He didn't stop scribbling. "I write for the *Parisian Weekly: A Journal for the Discerning Monsieur*."

Ro blanched. "And you're going to publish *that* in *there*?"

His pen froze, and his eyes lifted to meet hers. "With your permission, of course."

Ro just spluttered.

He smiled, a friendly, gentle thing, and spoke calmly. "There are many rumors about you, huntress. It is time the people knew more about their liberator. What is fact and what is not. I would love to run a series of articles on you, in fact, if you don't mind."

She most certainly did.

Reinette looked like she might faint.

Of course, Ro was about to join her. "I don't understand. Why me? Why would anything about me interest you? There are so many more fascinating people…"

Her voice trailed off as, instead of diminishing, his enthusiasm increased tenfold.

He set his notebook aside and grinned. "I have to admit my interest stems from a personal nature."

Reinette's head whipped toward him, her woozy expression vanishing as her deep-blue eyes narrowed. He kept speaking, oblivious to the danger he was in.

"When I was but a lad, and the Mesdemoiselles of the Mountains' wagon came through our village, we had nothing to barter. They turned us away. Our elderly neighbors shared with us, or we wouldn't have survived. When it came through again, the wagon master spoke of a huntress who had defeated the Mesdemoiselles. He gave us more food than we could eat, and we found gold hidden in our bags besides."

His eyes danced with excitement.

"I was visiting my mère in her little village just last week when Clement and Hamish came through, making deliveries."

Ro shot to her feet. "They live? Praise Dieu!"

She froze as all eyes swiveled toward her. She slowly sank into her seat, feeling rather lightheaded. Clement and Hamish had stayed at the cottage to tend the magical garden while Ro had traipsed off to defeat first the beast and then the sirènes.

Although she viewed it as their cottage instead of hers, she really should check on them. It had been years. More years than she'd realized.

"S'il vous plaît, continue." She slid down a little further. Would they notice if she kept sliding under the table and stayed there?

He smiled at her reaction. "I wanted to write about you before then, of course, but when I asked why they were still delivering when France could now grow food, they said the last thing the huntress asked of them before she left was to provide food and return any valuables, finding their rightful owners if possible, until there was no longer a need."

Tears filled Ro's eyes, and she quickly blinked them away. After the awful things both men had endured at the hands of the witches, they'd stayed, helped her people.

It meant the world.

"Now they travel through towns, teaching the best ways to plant and harvest, providing food and seed when needed. You have left quite a legacy, huntress. I am honored to have finally met you."

Ro started to duck her head, but movement from Olt caught her attention. He gave her a gentle smile and then winked. Ro lunged for her wine glass. In her haste, she knocked it aside, spilling red wine over the gold thread–stitched tablecloth.

A servant rushed over and cleaned up her mess.

She stuttered out an apology that got her strange looks. She hadn't meant to make more work for anyone. Could this meal be over already?

Cosette shook her head. "Rose, I had no idea."

Ro gave her a helpless, pleading look.

Cosette stood. "Oui, Gérard, I think Rosette would be most pleased to answer your questions. Later. For now..." She drew Ro to her feet. "I have need of the huntress. My daughter is under a sleeping curse, after all."

Ro kept her head down as Cosette spoke kindly to all on their way out.

Cosette didn't speak to Ro until they were alone in the hallway. Well, a few ladies of the court and several soldiers joined them and then followed at a respectable distance, but Ro was trying to get used to that.

"Ro, I know you were hungry. I'll have food sent up."

"Merci. But please, I do want to see Allura right away."

Cosette quickened her steps.

3

Cosette knocked gently on the nursery door, and Ro heard scraping on the other side before it swung open. A plump maid in a frilly cap and apron filled the doorway. She dipped a curtsy and opened the door wider.

Cosette swept past, and as Ro followed, she glanced back to see the servant fitting a bar over the closed door.

Ro's eyebrows climbed her forehead, and she gave her sister a questioning look. But Cosette was already by the bed, firing swift questions at a severely dressed matron who was struggling to her feet from a chair next to the bed.

"Has there been no change?"

"Non, votre Majesté."

"Nothing? She hasn't stirred, sighed, awakened, nothing?"

"Rien, votre Majesté. I am sorry."

"Have you played her music box for her?"

The maid dipped a deep curtsy. "We save that for when you are present, ma Reine."

Ro's gaze followed Cosette's to an ornate music box next to the child's bed. A little bird wrought of pure gold and encrusted with jewels perched on the lid.

Cosette wound the little box, and the most beautiful music Ro had ever heard tinkled out of it. She closed her eyes briefly, savoring the exquisite music.

Whoever had built that was a master craftsman.

Cosette leaned over the little lump in the bed, studying the child's face closely. Ro craned her neck, but she couldn't see past the blankets, and she didn't feel right intruding just yet.

Cosette frowned, then visibly struggled, bowing her head in grief. She said in a whisper, "You may both go." The servants shot each other surprised glances, and Cosette's voice turned sharp. "I said go!"

The servants bustled away, unbarred the door, and shut it softly behind them. Soldiers stood sentry on the other side.

Ro was rather startled to hear Cosette raise her voice. She hadn't done that before. Not in Ro's presence.

Cosette took several deep breaths, then turned to Ro and smiled through her tears. She held out one hand. "Come."

Ro took it and was pulled to the side of the little sleeping beauty.

She stared down at the three-year-old in awe. Allura was even more beautiful than Cosette had been at that age, and that was saying something. All of Cosette's and Trêve's best features were wrapped up in one angelic little face, perfect golden curls spilling onto the pillow.

Soft blonde curls lay against cheeks flushed in sleep. One little fist rested beside her cheek, and the child took a shuddering breath.

And Ro's heart was no longer her own.

Swept up in cascading elation, Ro wanted to cry, to weep, to throw herself over the prostrate little body and promise never to leave her, never to let anything bad happen to her. Her heart belonged completely, irrevocably to her darling little niece.

Ro struggled against the onslaught of so many emotions at

once. She would do anything for her. Anything. Even give her life for her.

Even take lives for her.

"You said she's three?" Ro whispered.

"Oui." Cosette's broken reply nearly undid Ro as well. "We'd just had her birthday fête when the…curse…fell. My little girl…" Cosette wiped her eyes and nose.

"Why is she so beautiful?" Ro whispered, struggling to keep her voice from trembling.

Cosette sniffed. "Rosette, really."

It was all Ro could do to tear her eyes away from the little angel. But she forced them to settle on Cosette and stay there while she waited for her question to be answered.

Cosette shifted a little, wouldn't look her in the eye. "Some of Mère's…friends…came to the christening ceremony. They gave her a few…gifts."

Even though Ro knew Cosette spoke of the Fairy Queen, her true mother, Ro's heart broke to hear her sister call anyone but the mère who had raised them that.

Ro's mère. The one who'd given her the red cape, her companion in every hunt. Ro would give anything to feel her mère's arms around her one more time.

Ro pushed past the pain and raised an eyebrow. "Gifts such as beauty this world has never before seen?"

Cosette, once again, shifted uncomfortably. "Perhaps…"

"What else?"

Cosette looked embarrassed, as if she didn't want to say.

"It's important. What else?"

"Oh, a few things." Cosette waved her hand dismissively. "Good nature, charm, kindness, sweet disposition, unparalleled singing voice, as well as a few trinkets, like that music box."

Ro barely spared a glance for the ornate music box with the jeweled nightingale perched on its lid. A music box was hardly as important as the rest.

"It's her favorite, you know. You simply wind it up, and… she smiles." Cosette dabbed her eyes. "It's the only reaction she gives. Ever. Just…not this time. Not for the past few times, actually."

Although Ro found herself reaching for Cosette to comfort her, she steeled herself and jerked her hand away. "You allowed the fey to give a human-born child gifts?"

Cosette blustered a little. "Excusez-moi, but I am half-fey myself!"

"Yet your child is human born. Born to *this* world. Fey gifts—they attract the worst of humanity, Cosette. They stand out on humans." She pierced Cosette with a hard look. "She won't have your glamour. She won't be able to hide it."

"Don't you think I know that?" She slid resentful eyes toward Ro, then deflated. "Oh, Rose. Don't you think I *know* that? If only I would've said no…"

Cosette dissolved into sobs, and Ro opened her arms. Cosette fell into them and hung on for dear life, strangling Ro just a little bit.

As she did, Ro took several deep, calming breaths, and turned her eyes to the little girl. The effect was immediate—adoration, devotion, love that nearly drove her to her knees and made her pledge herself to the girl's every whim—but the girl needed a huntress, not an addled devotee who wouldn't leave her side.

Ro made herself stare at the girl until she could look at her without falling apart.

Cosette never should've let so many fey gifts converge upon one child. Men would fight over her, die for her, try to kidnap her, beg for her hand, kill others just for a glimpse of her face. Women would flock to her side, vying to be her friend, her confidant, her serving maid, her courtier. She'd never know who was a true friend or who simply wanted to use her, to be near her for her glory to enhance theirs.

Her parents had better lock her in a tower, and fast.

But of course Cosette couldn't have known. In the moment, she would've been flattered, pleased, wanting the best for her daughter, wanting to honor the mère she was just getting to know.

Ro rubbed Cosette's back and studied the little girl. "Speaking of which, what of your mère? What of the Fairy Queen? We never did finish that conversation."

Cosette pulled back. Tears slipped down her face. "I have been unable to reach her. She hasn't tried to contact me, not once since little Allura Aurore fell asleep. Not once! I don't know what to do. I don't understand."

Ro didn't either. How could the Queen of the Fairies not care about her own granddaughter? "Has she met Allura?" she asked quietly. "Besides the christening, I mean. Has she accepted the little girl as her own blood?"

Ro knew it was the reason the Queen of the Fairies had hidden Cosette in the Reynard family in the first place—the other fairies wanted to kill her for being half-human.

Now that she was queen of the Fey Realm, and her daughter was queen of France, the Fairy Queen had publicly claimed Cosette and threatened any who came against her with sudden and swift death.

Perhaps the queen had changed her mind now that there was more human blood in her lineage? Although, she and Trêve's royal mère had arranged Trêve and Cosette's marriage from birth…

Cosette's eyes widened as she realized Ro's implications. "But of course! She dotes on our sweet little Allura Aurore, cannot get enough of her. She's a wonderful grandmère." Cosette hiccuped another sob and wailed, "I do not understand why she'll not answer me!"

Ro rubbed soothing circles on her sister's back, but it just made Cosette cry harder.

"I couldn't reach you because you were on that horrid boat across the ocean. Beau does nothing but brood and pace his library, seeking a cure and muttering why you aren't back yet—"

Ro blinked at that. Cosette had a hand in breaking his curse as well, not just Ro. Why was he adamant *she* come to the rescue?

"And I can't even reach my own mother!" Cosette's sobs grew louder, on the verge of hysteria, and she ran a hand down the drenched handkerchief, drying it instantly. "Claude and Pascal and their wives try to comfort me, but they don't understand what I'm going through. How could they? They don't have children yet. And our sisters…"

Ro raised an eyebrow. She couldn't even begin to imagine what they'd done now.

Cosette's cheeks flushed the loveliest pink. "I yelled at them, Rose. I told them to stop being so unkind and so unfeeling and to comfort someone else for once, or they could simply pack their bags and leave. I've been hiding in here ever since. Well, until dinner tonight, of course."

Ro snorted, then laughed outright. Cosette's face colored a deeper shade, and a smile crept onto the corners of her mouth.

"Now that I would've liked to see. I didn't know you had it in you."

"Rose…" Cosette chided, then sighed. "I guess it was a sight to behold. Me, losing my temper."

"Believe you me, they had it coming. Did you zap them with your newfound magical powers?" Ro teased.

Cosette blinked. "How—how did you know?"

Ro smirked and said, "That drying-your-handkerchief thing you did just now? Mending it earlier in the hall? Oui, I noticed."

Cosette blushed. "It only ever works on the silliest things, like clothes and shoes and hair." Her tone was dismissive. Apologetic. "Nothing important."

"Cosette. It isn't silly. Nor unimportant. Not if it means something to *you*, as I know it does."

Her sister looked almost hopeful, before the light went out in her eyes. "It hasn't helped me get my daughter back."

Ro sobered instantly. She lowered her voice, leaned close. "I promise you, Cosette, I will do everything in my power to find the enchantress responsible. To set your daughter free. Even if it means giving my life for her."

Cosette gasped. "Oh, don't let it come to that! I…I need you."

Ro wrapped her sister gently in her arms. "I need you too, Cosette. I will do everything I can to get back to you. But only once Allura wakes."

"Rosette, please. Her name is Allura Aurore. Both. At the same time. Not simply Allura."

Cosette said it with just enough exasperation that Ro got the feeling she explained this quite often. Ro tried to squash the smile lifting her cheeks and was only mildly successful.

Cosette didn't miss a thing. She scowled, and as with everything else she did, the expression was lovely. "You of all people should know that names have power. And her power is in her full name." Her eyes fell on the bed. "She can hear us. I know she can."

Ro's mirth evaporated, and she studied her sister. "I didn't realize it was so important to you. Désolé."

Cosette continued to stare at her daughter. "Her name means awakening dawn." She lifted tear-filled eyes to Ro. "She is a herald to a new age, a new France. She must awaken, she must. Or all is lost."

Cosette's eyes overflowed again, and she laid her head on Ro's shoulder and sobbed her heart out. Once again, Ro took Cosette into her arms and let her cry as much as she needed to, but she didn't voice her conflicting opinions.

Dawn didn't always awaken to better things.

Ro smoothed her sister's curls and spoke low and fervently. "Cosette, listen to me. I promise you that no matter what—no matter what, you hear me?—I will find a way to lift the spell. I will find a way."

Cosette sighed a shuddering breath. "Oh, Rose, if anyone can do it, it's you."

Ro's jaw tightened. At least one of them had confidence in her success.

4

t the first possible moment, Ro disentangled herself from Cosette and went in search of the palace library.

She made it four steps within and found she couldn't move. Every length of wall that wasn't a window was covered in bookshelves. And those bookshelves were mostly covered in *books*. Heart fluttering in her chest, she slowly turned, lips parted, soaking it in.

It rivaled the beast's library in his summer château. And that was saying something.

But shelves were only half-filled. Dusty books, stacked in towers all over the room, were in the process of being inspected, repaired, and sorted into their new homes. They must've come from all over the kingdom, since the palace had been raided, much of its contents burned for fuel, after the curse had fallen.

Little glass doors that swung upward covered each shelf, promising to keep the books dust free and to frustrate anyone who wanted to grab a stack of books quickly.

Ro loved every bit of it. If she wasn't careful, she might never return to the real world. She shook herself and got to work.

33

Later. She'd lose herself in book worlds *later*.

Seating herself at Trêve's massive desk, Ro spread Cosette's letters before her, as well as her list of books that mentioned enchantresses or curses of any kind. She started making notes of anything that might be helpful.

While Cosette had sobbed in her arms, she'd tried to get a feel for the curse, reaching out with her senses, as she'd done with the sirènes. But something stopped her. It felt like a heavy, wet blanket smothered the little girl, and Ro couldn't get past it.

The more she drew near it, tried to manipulate it, to figure it out, the harder it was to breathe. She didn't know how the little one could bear it.

Ro tapped a letter's edge on the desk.

An empress no one had heard of. Numerous fey gifts. Had one of them gone bad? Or been given with ill intent? But Cosette could reach no one from the fey realm, and Ro wouldn't even begin to know how to try.

So she scribbled down a list.

- *Inquire after so-called empress*
- *Her name? Where is she from?*
- *How did she learn to wield her power?*
- *Try to contact the fey realm and ~~Cosette's m~~—the Fairy Queen*
- *Find anything, <u>anything at all</u>, that mentions breaking sleeping curses*

She chewed on her featherless quill, dyed ebony with a metal nib, the kind Trêve preferred. What was she missing?

Not getting anywhere with her thoughts or her notes, Ro jumped up to dig through stacks of books not yet catalogued and put away. Soon she was covered with dust and sneezing loudly enough to disturb the entire palace.

She dusted off her hands and went to the shelves. She'd return to the stacks tomorrow with a cleaning rag or three.

It wasn't long until she had a jumbled collection of old wives' tales and fairy stories spread around her. Which, in her line of work, were helpful if she could make sense of what was true and what wasn't.

Lighting several candelabras to ward off the coming night, Ro read until lines were crossing and she couldn't make sense of the text anymore. She rubbed her face.

These fairy-tale authors had such conflicting tales and wild imaginations. If only more of them agreed. She found bits of truth in each one, bits of the fey realm bleeding into reality, but still nothing on sleeping curses.

She prowled the library once more, candelabrum held high.

Why were there no books on sleeping curses?

A sign that read "Rare Collection" caught her eye. She looked everywhere but could find no rare or first editions. She opened glass doors and moved books and tried different things until she discovered the back of the bookcase sounded hollow when she tapped it.

No matter what she did, no matter which book she moved, she couldn't get it to open. Never accused of having much patience, she set off to find Trêve.

A servant directed her to one of the gaming rooms. Utterly exhausted, Ro marched in before the servant could announce her.

Trêve, Liam, Olt, and her brothers, Claude and Pascal, glanced up, then immediately stood. With a cry, her fatigue forgotten, she ran to her brothers and threw her arms around them both.

"We came as soon as we heard you were here," said Pascal.

Claude added, "Yeah, but we were told we couldn't disturb the great and mighty huntress, so we came in here like the undeserving supplicants we are."

"Not even worthy to be in her presence."

"Oh, truly not," Claude agreed.

Ro punched Claude's arm playfully, and when she stepped

back, he ruffled her hair. Then he dusted off her shoulders and pulled a cobweb from her sleeve.

"Playing in attics again, mon petit chou-fleur?"

Ro mock-scowled at him and pushed his hand away, her shoulder-length dark hair half out of its queue. "The library, actually, and I am *not* your little cauliflower."

Years later, and it still drove her to distraction. It was *the worst* nickname. Why would anyone use that as an endearment? If only Claude didn't know how much she hated it.

He just grinned. Oh, he absolutely knew.

Trêve took her in, his expression mortified. "My dear huntress, my deepest apologies. I hadn't realized so much work still needed to be done. I shall have it cleaned at once."

But no one heard him, for the three siblings had begun speaking to each other at the same time. Within minutes, they'd covered Ro's voyage, the brothers' marriages, how they felt about domestic life, and her hunting successes since she'd last seen them.

No one gave each other room to talk, yet they all heard each other and got their stories out in a matter of minutes.

They laughed at the same time, then Pascal and Ro began comparing the best books they'd read while Claude and Ro discussed the best hunting spots during her travels throughout France and what the Caribbean was like, the conversation flowing and weaving together flawlessly.

"What," Olt asked the room at large, "is happening right now?"

Liam shook his head and took a sip of his port. "I have no idea. I can't keep up with any of that."

Trêve just relaxed and smiled, as if enjoying the siblings' reunion.

After the madness seemed to be slowing, just a little, Trêve interrupted. "Would you like to join our game, huntress? At least while the servants clear out the dust and cobwebs."

Ro smiled gratefully and sank into a chair. As soon as the

men sat, she bolted to her feet. "Oh! Désolé, but I cannot. I came to ask for access to your private collection, mon Roi."

Trêve waved his hand. "None of that 'my king' business here, s'il vous plaît." He withdrew a key clipped to his waistcoat, his matching blue frock coat hung over the back of his chair, and held it up. "You'll have to climb the ladder to find the keyhole, I'm afraid. It's behind a volume called *The Water Trading Routes of France*."

Ro's heart skipped a beat. That was the first book she'd read to him when they were trapped together in his summer château, when he was a beast and wooing her nightly for her hand in marriage.

She schooled her expression not to give her traitorous emotions away, but she did *not* like the reminder of her then hopes and dreams being crushed. Or the fact that he had kept —and treasured—such a volume.

Still, she couldn't hold it against him. Trêve and her sister had found something precious together she'd never had with him.

To be clear, she did *not* still have feelings for him. She wasn't sure she ever had. It was simply that a voice in her head tended to jump up and down and scream, while pointing, "Wasn't that the most humiliating moment of your life? Remember every second. In great detail!"

If she could shoot that voice with one of her arrows, she would. Gladly.

A small smile touched Trêve's mouth. "Hold on, for the ladder spins rather quickly. I told my library architect to have fun with its construction, and, well, he did."

The Messieurs at the table chuckled, and Ro belatedly joined them as her mind scrambled to catch up with the conversation.

The king gave them a mock glare. "I trust you all to keep my secret, oui?"

They agreed as Ro moved to take the key.

"Non, Mademoiselle, I must insist you stay," said the king. He eyed her far too perceptively. "I believe your mind will be the better for searching if you allow yourself a small diversion. My servants won't be long, and you can rest while they do what I should've asked them to take care of months ago." He gave her a self-deprecating smile. "I fear I have not been as observant as usual lately."

Ro wanted to disagree, but she nodded, a little uneasy. What would Cosette say if she found Ro sitting here, playing games, while Cosette hovered at her daughter's side, watching her wilt away under a sleeping curse?

Non, she couldn't disappoint her sister so. "I assure you, this was enough of a reprieve." She sent a fond look her brothers' way. "I will keep searching, merci beaucoup."

Trêve gave her a look that said how much he appreciated her dedication, then contradicted it with his words. "Then let's make it interesting, shall we?" He placed the key in the center of the table. "My key in exchange for your taking the break you need."

Ro was torn, and from the looks on their faces, so were her brothers.

Before the curse, their family had lost everything to gambling—their home in Paris, their status as nobles as they fled in disgrace, everything—which was likely why the game she'd interrupted had no livres on the table.

"Besides," the king continued, "your traveling companion, Olt, has brought a rather interesting game with him." He turned to Olt. "What is it called again?"

Olt grinned, pulled out a velvet bag, and scattered game pieces across the tabletop. "Ever play Strategists and Dreamers?"

Ro just raised an eyebrow. He well knew she avoided most games.

He grinned at her. "It's easy. I'll teach you."

She knew they were trying to take her mind off the puzzle

she couldn't solve so she could come back to it fresh, and she appreciated it, but she couldn't do it. Not for a wager.

"Non," she said. It came out rather sharper than she'd intended.

The others looked up at her and grew still.

She smiled to soften her words. "I will play a few rounds, if that is your wish, but then I will take the key and return to my research, oui? But I will not play for the key."

The king of France inclined his head, and Ro settled in.

Interest sparked as Olt began setting up a complicated spread, and she studied the board, game pieces, and intricate cards. She clapped her hands. "All right. Teach me." Then she pointed a stern finger at each in turn. "But after I best you, I'm going right back to my research, non?"

The teasing began immediately from all quarters, and Ro found herself smiling. She'd missed them all so much, and Trêve was right. This was exactly what she needed.

Still, a little worry and a lot more guilt filtered in, and she couldn't help peeking over her shoulder for Cosette.

She would understand, wouldn't she?

few hours later, Ro was feeling warm and happy and filled. It'd been far too long since she'd been surrounded by people who cared for her, and she, them.

She'd forgotten how no one else in the world could make pastries as well as the French. She popped the last of another fresh-fruit tart into her mouth. It was divine.

And she'd eaten far too many.

Chasing the bite with a sip of perfectly crafted café, Ro eyed Liam's game piece, which looked like a chess set's bishop, as he moved it in front of her. "I commandeer a squadron of your soldiers for the king of Angleterre."

Ro smirked and slid a card in front of his game piece. "Ah, but your squire's head is filled with the *Jack and the Beanstalk* story he just read, so he missed his road marker and went to the wrong town. The troops will be gone by the time he realizes his mistake."

A book was painted on the thick card, open with all kinds of fairy-tale elements spilling out of it, including vines that reached to the top of the card.

Liam quickly shuffled through his cards, then laid a card with neat rows of soldiers painted on it, as well as one with the word "arrête" or "stop" on it. "I double the requested troops, and cancel your last action."

Ro searched through her cards. "Aha! But a wagon broke down right in front of the sign, and when the lad stopped to help, he missed the sign entirely and still went in the wrong direction. Doesn't matter how many troops you commandeer if no one's there to pass on the order."

She slid another ornately painted card on top of Liam's. A wagon was painted on it, filled with lush produce of all kinds. Nothing else. It was up to her to dream up the story.

But it was a countermove card, all the same.

Olt slid his own game piece in front of Liam. "And the emperor of the Orient asks that you make good on your trade agreement and send soldiers to see the current shipment arrives safely."

Liam's jaw tightened infinitesimally. His soldiers were dwindling, no matter how many troops he requested or how many cards he threw out to countermand their moves.

Ro smirked. "All that strategy, Liam, and the dreamers best you every time. Told you storytelling would come in handy one day."

As she was speaking, Ro glanced at the mantel above the fireplace and the clock ticking there. The game had gone on longer than she'd intended.

Liam threw back his head and laughed, the sound rich and full, hearty and deep.

Ro froze. All she could do was stare. Her comment wasn't that humorous, was it? Surely he was overreacting. But…his laugh touched something deep within her that craved approval. Craved making someone laugh.

And she'd just made Liam laugh.

He looked at her, eyes twinkling. "My storytelling was just as dry and dusty as yours. Admit it."

His words had the opposite effect they normally would have. She was rather testy about all the teasing her stories had taken as a child, and as such, was rather defensive about her storytelling ability. And Liam knew that.

But this time…this time, Ro couldn't stop staring at the man who didn't chuckle, didn't tease, didn't know how *not* to take anything seriously, who was now doing all three.

Gameplay continued around the table, banter tossed about at a steady pace, but it left Ro behind. Who was this agreeable person in the huntsman's place? This…this…*fun* person.

Liam noticed he still held her attention and sobered slightly—returning her stare. Something uncomfortably like attraction leaped to his eyes as others took their turns. "Ro, mighty storytelling huntress, it's your move there."

He winked at her. She flushed. Olt stiffened.

Ro slapped the table and stood, her core hot, face burning. "I believe it's far past time I return to the library. I thank each of you for the blessed respite."

She nodded to the table at large, then snatched up the key and fled the room. Liam's parting look seared into her soul. What was seriously happening right now?

Liam's deep voice rumbled his own goodnights, then Ro heard footsteps and spun.

Liam was trailing her, an indecipherable look on his face. She gave him an aloof nod, as if it were any normal day and he, a passing acquaintance. Then she bolted for the library.

She'd almost reached the library doors when he grasped her elbow and expertly guided her into a nook on the other side. One that was completely concealed when curtains fell into place.

Ro's eyes went wide. She didn't know if he backed her into a corner or she backed herself, but she squeaked when she hit solid wall. "Liam, what on earth?"

But he was grinning, and with a smooth motion, he plunked an arm right above her head.

If Ro were short, this wouldn't have been a problem.

Probably. But she was tall. Almost as tall as Liam. And he was crowding her space.

And then there was the way he was grinning down at her. As if he saw something he liked. Not an expression she was used to seeing on his face. At all.

He reached out and brushed his fingers down her cheek. "Huntress…Ro. Dare I think something might be happening between us? Something, perhaps, more than companionship?"

His words tangled and twisted in her mind, and Ro desperately tried to make sense of them.

His breath smelled faintly of port. Although he didn't seem inebriated, Ro didn't trust spirits or the men who drank them. She'd lost too much to both.

And although her père had made the choices that led to his downfall, he'd been a savvy businessman and merchant. It was only once he'd started drinking and gambling that he'd made poor decisions — costing them their future and home.

But those were past dangers, and a very real one stood right in front of her.

His fingers continued down her neck and across her collarbone, out to her shoulder. And her traitorous self responded with a shiver.

To be clear, she didn't feel threatened, just…discombobulated. Off-kilter. Like he was taking everything right in the world, turning it upside down, and shaking it around a bit.

"Liam, this is madness!" Ro tried to back up another step but was rudely reminded she didn't have anywhere to go.

"Is it? Your feelings about me have changed, haven't they?"

He smiled, in such a self-satisfied manner, Ro would've normally had some kind of retort. Now she found herself at a loss for words.

He lifted her hand and kissed it. Ro's knees went weak.

"Liam…" She couldn't retreat any more, and the worst part was, she wasn't sure she wanted to.

She just wasn't thinking clearly. That was all.

Liam didn't know what he was saying. He'd had too much port. And the late hour and strong café had heightened her senses so that she was too easily rattled. That was the only reason her breath was coming in short gasps.

He dropped his voice and leaned close. "I can see it in the way you look at me. The way you react to me. You've changed. I've changed. I think we should explore that."

She didn't know what to do with this new Liam. But if she wanted to retain any self-respect, she needed to stop this *right now*.

She jerked herself away from melting and blurted, "Are you feeling all right?"

She said it as he was leaning forward, his lips almost on hers. She didn't dare move or take a full breath, in case their lips touched.

He pulled back, looked into her eyes. Blinked. "I beg your pardon?"

She lifted her hand and placed it on his forehead, removing it instantly, as if burned. "Are you feeling well?"

"Of course I'm feeling well. Why do you ask?" A slight pucker formed between his brows.

"You seem like you might be feverish," Ro babbled. She put her full concern in her voice, even if it was embellished.

"What? Non. I'm simply expressing—"

"Because you should probably see a healer right away. Right now, in fact. Before it gets worse."

He stared at her, hard.

Ro did not squirm. She kept her expression completely innocent and stared back with the greatest concern.

He moved his arm away from the wall, and Ro could breathe again.

"May I ask why you refuse to have this conversation with me?"

Leave it to Liam to cut right to the heart of the matter.

"You're not thinking clearly," she said, feebly.

"Ro, for the first time I am thinking clearly!" He rubbed the back of his neck, agitated.

Ro wilted against the wall. At least he wasn't trailing fingers of heat over her skin anymore or about to *kiss her*. She wouldn't have been able to look him in the eye for the rest of her life. Not that she'd be able to after this.

Ouf! One touch, and she'd nearly lost her head. Was she truly so starved for attention?

According to Cosette, oui. And tightly wound. And all sorts of other things that simply weren't true. But that was something to worry about another time. Or never.

Ro didn't try to gentle her voice. The Liam she knew could take her honesty. She hoped. "Us, Liam? Really? We've spent most of our acquaintance at odds. Bickering. Arguing. Trying to best the other. We would murder each other in less than a fortnight." She shook her head. "It wouldn't work."

"Ro, you're not being sensible…"

She threw her hands in the air. "I'm the only one of us *being* sensible! Liam, think of it. We would despise each other after a month. A week, even."

His stare was incredulous. "Is that really what you think?"

Ro blinked. Was it? "Y-yes. Of course. We're not a good idea. At all."

A muscle in his jaw tensed, and he backed up a step, allowing Ro even more air. "Thank you for so clearly stating your mind."

He straightened his dark-blue officer's jacket firmly, turned, and strode from the little alcove.

Ro stared at the curtain as it settled, the question swirling over and over in her mind. She was sure—wasn't she? And what about Olt?

Oh, dear merciful heavens, Olt!

What would he say if—non. She wasn't going there.

Ro slipped out of the hideaway, certain it had oft been

used for the purpose Liam had just cornered her for, and yelped when she came face-to-face with Olt.

Face burning, she lifted her chin and nodded at him, pretending nothing was amiss. "Olt."

He took one look at Ro's flushed face and rumpled shirt and disheveled hair, then Liam's retreating back. He snapped out, "Monsieur Liam! A word?"

Liam stilled at the end of the corridor, shoulders tense.

Olt marched over to him, and from all the hand gestures and Liam's crossed arms, scowl growing darker by the second, things were not going well.

Ro wanted to intervene, but she needed space. From them both. Olt glanced over Liam's head, scowled, and poked him in the chest. Ro tilted her head. Wha—?

That's right. He could see colors over a person's head that told him what they were feeling or thinking or something. He'd said it looked like a miniature Aurora Borealis, changing color with mood or intent or emotions, though it wasn't always accurate.

She wasn't exactly clear on the details, just that she couldn't hide a thing from him. He'd glance over her head, smirk, and tease her out of whatever mood she was in. It wasn't even a little bit fair.

Ro groaned and moved toward them. Could they not leave each other—and her—be?

Liam's low voice grated as Ro drew near. "Are you challenging me to a duel, pup?"

Olt straightened. "Over the huntress's honor? Oh, most definitely."

Ro froze, mouth parted. She could honestly say this had never happened to her before.

Liam schooled his expression to reveal nothing of what he was thinking. "What's it to be? Pistols or swords."

Olt couldn't hide his feelings if he tried, apparently. He

scowled harder. "Staves. I'll not take a life needlessly, whether that scum dishonored the huntress or not."

"Now wait just a moment…" Ro tried to insert.

"Fine." Liam cut her off. "Dawn. South training yard."

"Fine."

Olt stalked off one way, Liam the other.

Ro rubbed her temples, and after a moment of indecision, went back to the library.

Perhaps she'd fallen asleep hunched over an old tome and would wake tomorrow with a terrible crick in her neck, finding this nothing more than a horrible dream. *Please?*

At dawn, on the southern training yard, Olt and Liam glared at each other. Ro, unable to sleep at all, had wandered that way out of morbid curiosity, still hoping it had been a misunderstanding.

"This is not necessary, I assure you."

Neither man listened to her.

"My honor was not compromised, not even a little."

They still prepared to face each other.

"I make my own choices."

Not even a reaction.

Ro looked between the two men and wanted to scream.

Before her return, Liam had not shown an iota of interest in her—Not. One. Iota—and now Olt was challenging him for that very thing. And Liam, for some reason, was letting the challenge stand. Even though *he knew* nothing had happened between them. Even though *he knew* they weren't a good idea. Didn't he?

Olt shrugged off his frock coat and swept his hand wide. "After you."

Jaw ticking, Liam swept up a staff, eyed it, then met Olt's gaze deliberately. "Gladly."

The two men strutted off, shoulders back, chests out, march rigid.

Ro stared after Olt and Liam in disbelief. What on earth? They weren't going to *hit* each other with those stupid sticks for no reason, right?

They shrugged out of their shirts—Ro's face flushed an uncomfortable degree of hot, for no reason whatsoever—and they readied their staves to pound each other.

The first *crack* snapped through the air, Olt taking the offensive and Liam soundly blocking him. They started to parry, thrust, circle. Soon, a fine sheen of sweat coated their shoulders and torsos.

Although both men were all hard muscle, Olt was leaner and all grace, spinning and dodging as if he were turning the fight into a dance. Liam, on the other hand, had settled into a fighter's stance that complemented his bulkier frame. His strikes were wicked fast, and he wasn't moving around as much, saving his strength for devastating blows.

Ro wanted to strangle them both.

Cosette touched her elbow. "I came as soon as I heard. Olt and Liam, then?"

Ro jumped, then growled a little to cover how flustered she was. Both from Cosette sneaking up on her and their ridiculous contest. "What is wrong with them?"

"Why, I do believe they're fighting over you, dearest." She looked as if she were trying to hide a smile. "As is our way."

By that she meant the French way. Well her country could keep its silly duels and flirting and intrigue to itself. Did Ro's opinion have no weight? She grumbled under her breath, tossing Cosette a disgruntled look.

Cosette laughed. "Oh, don't look at me like that. And why wouldn't they? The mighty huntress is rather a fine prize."

Ro scowled. "I am no one's *prize*." She eyed the sweaty, vein-bulging men, each trying to kill himself to outdo the other. "It's repulsive."

Though she had to admit they both looked rather fine with their shirts off. Ugh. When had she become *that* female?

The sun hadn't even fully risen, and already Ro was feeling uncomfortably warm.

Cosette slipped her arm through Ro's, her voice turning positively coy. "Come now, it's me. You mean to tell me you aren't enjoying this the teensiest-tiniest bit?"

Ro's mouth fell open. "Cosette!"

"What? You know you are. Admit it." Cosette beamed.

"I'll do no such thing. They're both behaving like children, they won't listen to a word I say, and I can't fathom in the slightest why they would care one whit about *me*."

Ro snapped her mouth closed. Oops. She shouldn't have said that.

Cosette's demeanor instantly changed, a fierce look upon her cherubic face. "Because you are the most wonderful person in the world, worthy of love and of someone defending your honor, and they both see it." Her riled expression softened to hurt. "They can see it. I can see it. Why can't you?"

Ro looked away and swallowed, not bothering to answer.

Cosette settled in to pout at her side. Ro truly hated that her sister always took offense on her behalf—Ro wasn't one for word games or pretended feelings. Couldn't she say what she thought, truly, without anyone telling her she shouldn't feel that way?

Ro wasn't a prize. She was grumpy, preferred to be alone, and although she was confident in her hunting skills, her grasp on her protectress powers was rudimentary at best. She simply could face the truth without lying to herself. She wasn't seeking approval or someone to defend her or…

She eyed her beloved sister. And here she was arguing with herself, and her sister hadn't said another word. Ro sighed. Cosette had probably done that on purpose.

After an eternity of traded blows, Ro's temper mounting by the second, she turned to leave.

"Where are you going?" asked Cosette.

Ro spoke without looking back. "If they want to act like children, fine. But I don't have to be here to watch it. I have better ways to spend my time."

A smack then a subsequent yelp almost had her turning around, but she gritted her teeth and hurried away. She had a curse to figure out how to break, even if everyone at the palace was set on distracting her from the only reason she was here.

❧

Ro hurried to her sanctuary: the library. A measure of calm wafted over her as she stepped inside. She really could live here forever and be perfectly satisfied.

Ro carried over a new stack of tomes and settled behind Trêve's desk.

A few hours into her task, she realized someone had said her name several times.

"Mademoiselle LeFèvre?"

Ro jumped and focused on a servant decked out in high-ranking livery. "Oui?"

"Monsieur Gérard to see you."

He bowed and stepped back, and Reinette's husband, Gérard, stepped in.

"Mademoiselle, forgive my impertinence, but—"

Ro held up a hand as an idea struck her. "Hold on."

She fumbled for blank parchment and a quill and almost knocked over the inkpot twice in her haste to scratch out her idea.

Gérard waited patiently while Ro wrote.

Mesdames et Messieurs:

> *A reward of fifteen livres to anyone who can provide valuable information about the empress who cursed the little sleeping princess,*

or regarding sleeping curses in general, and how to break them specifically.

Please remit all inquiries to the palace, in the care of Huntress Ro LeFèvre, and rewards will be delivered to those missives of a helpful nature that do not waste our time.

Huntress Ro LeFèvre, Defender of the Realm

Ro couldn't remember all the other titles she'd earned throughout her time as huntress, but since Trêve had bestowed that one upon her at his crowning ceremony, it would have the most impact.

The moment she finished, she bounded up, blowing the ink dry, and held out the page to Gérard. "Can you print this? In your journal?"

He took the square of paper, settled a pair of spectacles on his nose, and carefully read the letter. He faltered a little at the last line, but Ro was nothing if not direct.

He turned a broad smile on her. "Exactly what I came to suggest."

"Is it…too direct?"

"If I may, Mademoiselle." He scratched out a few changes, then held it up for her to read.

Please remit all inquiries to the palace, in the care of Huntress LeFèvre. Rewards will be given for missives of a helpful nature, not those of gossip and hearsay.

Ro wilted in relief. "Merci."

She didn't go about trying to offend, but she often did so anyway. She tilted her head. Rumors, though…they often held a hint of truth…

"May I also interview you?" he asked.

Ro glanced around at the mess she'd made, seeking escape. "Perhaps after Allura…she is my priority…"

He held up both hands. "But of course. I meant, may I

interview you about your attempts to break the curse? Though I must point out, if we remind the people of your past successes, it will give them that much more hope for the future."

That's what Ro was afraid of.

Ro's mind went blank, and she desperately wished someone would walk through that door and rescue her.

But nooooo. Her would-be rescuers were beating each other senseless on the southern training yard.

At her wide-eyed look, he continued. "We'll print your letter full page, of course, but if we include an interview as well, it should stick in our readers' minds that much more." His smile turned him from a scholarly looking fellow to someone who might have an impish streak. "I'm sure I don't have to tell you how valuable such printing space is."

Not to mention, Ro thought sarcastically, *if they have an interview with the mighty huntress, that particular edition will sell rather well.*

Ro tried to squish her uncharitable thoughts. An interview could only help Allura. Their interests aligned. "You'll ask for people's help foremost?"

He bowed slightly at the waist. "But of course, Mademoiselle."

Ro squirmed, uncomfortable. She didn't know what she could possibly say that would be useful. Or worth reading. "If you think it will help…"

His notebook and pencil were out in a flash, and he gave her a warm smile as he settled into one of the chairs before Trêve's massive desk. "Now, tell me what you know about sleeping curses and what you plan to do to stop this one."

And so began the most uncomfortable interview of Ro's career.

6

early a week later, at the end of another long day, Ro stumbled into the room she was shown, yet again, weariness leaving her swaying on her feet.

Splitting her time among studying in the library, scanning stacks of unhelpful letters—more coming in each day—and sitting at Allura's bedside with Cosette had left precious little time to use her suite of rooms.

She flicked a glance around the sitting room. Not that she minded. The place was huge. And stodgy. A bit pompous. But she would never admit that to Cosette.

Her eyes settled on the fainting couch with an oval café table before it and a blanket draped over one arm.

That would do.

Ro plopped onto the damask-covered settee and groaned. Every part of her ached. Who knew sitting hunched over old tomes, squinting to read minuscule print, and rarely moving from that position could be so physically draining?

She picked up one heavy boot at a time, her legs protesting, and dropped them onto the low table in front of her. Her second boot toppled a stack of letters.

The off-white squares and rectangles scattered all over the floor, making a gentle shushing sound, and Ro groaned again.

Great. More of them. Would someone's cousin's third aunt twice removed have yet another home remedy or potion guaranteed to break a sleeping curse?

As loath as she was to ask servants to do things she was perfectly capable of herself, maybe they could clean up her mess this time?

Before the thought had fully formed, she flinched, her père's sharp words from years past, his hand raised, coming to mind, and before she knew it, she was on her knees, frantically picking up letters.

She paused, took several deep breaths to calm her racing heart, and spoke to herself. "You are no longer a child in your père's home. He cannot hurt you."

She nodded to herself and finished picking up letters, stacking them haphazardly on the marble surface. They teetered, but at least they stayed.

She fell back on the settee and pulled off her boots one at a time.

As thankful as she was for Gérard's influence at his paper, most of the letters pouring in were filled with unhelpful tips that only wasted her time. She wished she'd kept her original, harsher wording. Could nothing go right?

No sooner had she propped up her feet than a knock came at the door.

With a groan, she called out, "Come in!" not even caring who would see her in such an unladylike state.

A moment later, a knock came again.

"Oh, by all the saints!" Ro dropped her feet to the ground and dragged herself upright. Stupid giant rooms!

She grumbled the whole way to the door and yanked it open.

Olt stood there, hand raised to knock again.

"Olt!" She hadn't seen him in a week!

Not that she hadn't been using every alcove in the palace to hide from him or Liam, but that was beside the point.

She launched herself at him, wrapped her arms around his waist in a bear hug. He winced a little. She started to pull away, but his hands came up and held her gently to him.

"Why, it's good to see you too."

"I'm so glad you're not dead!" Ro said without thinking.

"I'm glad to hear you have such faith in my sparring skills, huntress," Olt said wryly.

At the laughter in his voice, Ro's eyes flew wide, and she jerked back, smoothing her hair. "Oh, ah…" She stared past him at the wallpaper, counting fleur-de-lis in the pattern, wondering how she could ever recover from throwing herself at him. "What are you doing here?"

At his smile, her eyes wandered back his way.

"Not going to invite me in?" He mock-shivered. "It is rather cold and lonely and dark out here, you know."

Ro rolled her eyes and turned away. "Close the door behind you."

Ironic that Olt would call Liam out for backing her into a corner then seek her out in her rooms. But she was staying out of the whole mess.

Actually… "Was the fight all you hoped it would be and more?"

She headed straight to the settee, grabbed the blanket, and plopped in the same position, feet on the table, blanket draped over her.

Olt shuffled his feet. "Yeah, well, about that…"

Ro waited impatiently.

He combed his fingers through his hair. "Cosette had… words…with us after you left." He grinned. "And I thought you were a firecracker."

Ro's eyebrows shot up. What had happened to her calm, sweet sister, and who was this assertive person in her place? Probably had to do with fairy blood. Or being queen. Or running a country, raising a family, and protecting her daughter. Probably all the above.

He tried to look apologetic. "She said if we wanted to win you"—he spoke right over Ro's spluttering—"it wouldn't be from beating each other senseless, but from treating each other, and you, with respect. And allowing you to make your own choices."

Ro crossed her arms. "Well, she's not wrong." Not that she'd allow anyone to "win her." "So this is your apology?"

He grinned. "This is my apology."

It had certainly taken him long enough. She nodded toward the settee across from her. "Have a seat. I'm listening, I swear."

And she leaned her head back and closed her eyes.

Olt chuckled, and the settee across from her groaned as he sat. "I feel like such an honored guest. You going to fall asleep on me?"

"I hope not," Ro mumbled. "And you should feel honored. I don't relax like this in front of just anyone."

"High praise indeed." After a moment, "So I just wanted to say I'm s—"

Another knock interrupted him.

"Oh, for the love of all that is holy!"

Ro whipped off her blanket and started to stand, but Olt stopped her.

"I'll get it."

He settled the blanket back over her and dropped a light kiss on her forehead.

All tiredness fled, and Ro's eyes popped open. She watched his retreating back—all lean muscle, and that confident stride—all the way to the door, knowing her face had to be five times its normal color.

She needed this mission to be over so she could go hide in her cabin from all the unwanted attention being thrown her way.

But is it unwanted, really?

She shushed the clearly delirious voice in her head.

If the messenger was surprised Olt opened the door instead of her, it didn't show on his face. "Is Mademoiselle LeFèvre within, Monsieur?"

Olt pointedly didn't look at her all sprawled out on the settee, stocking-covered feet splayed for all the world to see. "Aye, she is. Can I help you? She's exhausted and needs to rest."

Ro had to smile at that. She could get used to someone deflecting unwanted visitors.

"I have more of her letters. From Monsieur Gérard?"

Ro sat up, and the blanket slid off her shoulders to pool in her lap.

"I'll take those for her, merci." He took a thick packet tied with silky rose-red ribbons from the messenger and started to close the door.

"But Monsieur Gérard said—"

Olt flipped a coin at the proper young man and shut the door in his face. Then he came back whistling. Ro jumped to her feet and tackled him for the letters, her feet tangling in the blanket. He held them out of reach.

"Now wait just a moment. That was a lot of work, getting up and walking over there and *talking* to someone for you. What will you give me for them?"

Ro blinked. "What? They're mine. I don't need to give you *anything*—"

"Well if you don't want them…" He shrugged and started to turn away.

"You wouldn't dare." She jumped, but even as tall as she was, Olt was that much taller, and he held them just out of reach.

His grin was too delicious, and she tried hard not to stare at his mouth. She apparently wasn't doing such a great job by the way his grin stretched wider.

He licked his lips, and she smacked him.

"Olt, seriously! Let me see them. They could be important."

He pointed at his lips, then ran his finger over to his cheek and tapped it twice. "Right there."

"What?"

"A kiss. Right there. And then they're yours." He waggled his eyebrows, then shot her a wicked grin at Ro's horrified expression. "Surely that's not *too* terrible an idea."

She snapped her mouth closed, giving him a solid glare, but even she could tell it lacked its normal spice. She swallowed, hard, as her pulse pounded in her ears.

When she didn't move, he shrugged and turned away. "Or I can always bring them back later."

"Don't you dare!" Ro grabbed his arm and yanked him around, nearly falling into his chest, her legs being held up as they were. She kept trying to detangle them, but the blanket held fast. Stupid blanket.

That delicious, delicious grin nearly undid her. "You know what to do." He drew his finger closer to his mouth, then back up his cheek in a circular motion. "Just a kiss. A measly little kiss, right here, and these precious letters, Mademoiselle, are yours."

Ro gave an aggravated huff and shoved him. "Go on, then. I'll just ask Gérard what they say."

As she tried to step out of the blanket, she tripped, and Olt caught her just as she would've toppled over. She froze, against his chest, staring up at him. He stared down at her, his teasing expression morphing into something—serious. And scary.

She was having trouble breathing again. His warmth seeped into her, and it was all she could do not to melt against him. He felt just right, and smelled even better.

Ugh. *That's* where her mind went? How good he *smelled*?

Just as suddenly, Olt stepped back and held out her

letters. "Désolé. Votre lettres, Mademoiselle. I should not have kept them from you."

Thrown off-kilter from his sudden change, Ro accepted them, and he put some distance between them. Then he turned away and started running his fingers through his hair, which he only did when he was agitated. But he didn't leave.

Why that was a relief Ro would never know.

She fumbled with the ribbon as she kicked off the blanket. The ribbon wouldn't cooperate, so she yanked harder. She had no idea how she was supposed to concentrate after *that*.

The ribbon came undone, the top two letters stuck together. She pulled them apart with a vengeance. What was he thinking, talking about respecting her one moment and trying to tease a kiss out of her the next? He seriously needed to…

One dingy, gray, ancient square of heavy paper hit the floor with a smack.

Ro sighed and scooped it up.

As soon as she touched it, she stilled. Something tingled through her palm. Something familiar. But the folded paper was fused shut.

"Ro…"

She jumped, startled to find Olt at her elbow.

"I'm sorry."

Her eyes flew to his. "For what?"

His face colored slightly. "For…that. I shouldn't have…I wasn't thinking." He raked a hand through his hair. "I shouldn't have tried to force you to kiss me in order to get your letters. I'm sorry."

She rolled her eyes and pushed past him, not wanting him to see how flustered she was. "I have brothers, Olt. It's not like I haven't ever heard them brag about stealing kisses. Seriously, not a big deal."

He followed her. "Ro, I mean it."

A bit of temper tried to make an appearance, but Ro

squashed it down with every stomp of her stockinged feet across the parquet floor. He was seriously damaging her calm. And she would not be held responsible if she exploded at him.

"I'm sorry, truly. I came here to apologize, and I just made everything worse. I shouldn't have…"

She stopped and huffed, inches from her goal, an ornate letter opener. She wouldn't be able to read in peace until she addressed this, would she?

She spun around, hands on hips. "Out with it. Do you regret trying to get me to kiss you?"

She hated how her voice hitched without her permission.

His eyes flew wide. "What? Never! I mean, I wouldn't, not if—you—I—um…"

"Then you *do* want me to kiss you."

Now his face was suffused with color. "Well, ye—I mean, if you—only if *you*…"

Had she seriously just asked him that? She rubbed her face. "Never mind," she said, regretting every word.

"But I—"

"I said forget it," she said too sharply. She turned away and fumbled with the letter opener, unable to focus on a blasted thing with Olt so close to her and his words swirling in her mind.

Blast him and his misplaced chivalry! She had half a mind to spin around and end the discussion once and for all. By kissing him till he couldn't breathe.

She smirked. Now wouldn't that shock him into silence?

Not that she'd ever be brave enough to do it.

Her eyes fell on a note from Gérard.

Mademoiselle:

Although I include all missives per your request, I still try to filter them for you, arranging them from most important to least.

I do not know why, but this missive stood out above the rest.

*Neither I nor my colleagues can open it, and although the note has
passed many hands, its import has stuck out to all.*
   I hope it will shed light on that which you seek.
   M. Gérard

Blood pounded in Ro's ears. Was this it? The clue she'd
been looking for?

She turned it over again. A square of heavy paper, soft to
the touch. Folded in half and sealed with something she
couldn't identify.

She slit the folded square open. It made a slight hissing
noise as the paper separated, and her fingers tingled.

Her eyes widened. The note was written on heavy vellum.
Not just any vellum—a title page from a family Bible, edge
jagged where it had been torn out, ink scratched across its
velvety surface.

She didn't care how religious someone was or not—
tearing a page from a family Bible simply wasn't *done*.

She glanced around furtively, as if Père Guise, the priest
who hated her, would round the corner any second and set
her aflame in the town square for even holding it.

Shielding the page with Gérard's letter, just in case, she
took in every detail. The handwriting was terrible. Barely
discernible. She tried to make out the chicken scratch–like
letters, all badly misspelled.

Huntress:
   *Let's hope ye 'ave some gud sense, unlike the rest of that sorry lot
   at the palase. I know wer the witch be that cursed the wee prinsess.
   Come find me.*
   Protectruss of the Forêt

She couldn't make out the signature, which was just a
squiggly line across the bottom of the page. And good heavens. Which forest?

She flipped to the top part of the title page and tried to make out the filled-out lines, the ink worn with age. It was a marriage record. Someone whose last name started with an *R* married someone named…Ro gasped. LeFèvre.

She squinted. Jacqueline Rose LeFèvre, her mère, wed to Monsieur Michèl-Pierre Reynard the third, her père.

This was from her family Bible! But…who had come by it? What did they mean by ripping out a page? And *writing* on it? Was this a threat?

She didn't know she was shaking until Olt stilled her hands, his voice full of concern. "Ro, what is it? You're trembling. What does it say?"

She handed him the letter. "Read it." Then she marched toward her bedroom without another word.

He whistled. "A bit cheeky, don't you think?" he called after her.

"Sacrilegious, more like," she muttered, then started grabbing everything she'd need for her trip.

He was still staring at it, forehead creased, when she came out and dumped a pile of clothes next to her bag.

She stuffed her feet into her boots, then started rolling clothing in the smallest bundles possible, wishing he would hurry up and be done already. She didn't bother mentioning it was *her* family Bible, not that she remembered having one, and she wondered if he'd be able to tell with how faded the writing was.

Then she caught sight of his pale face. She froze. "Olt? What is it?"

He gave her a wooden smile and tried to hand it back. "Looks like the old mother of the forest knows something."

Ro snatched the letter, nearly shouting as she shoved it under his nose. "You know who this is?"

He nodded, straining away from the letter as if it would bite him. "She's the old woman who lives in the Black Forest. In Prussia? You call it Prusse."

"I know what I call our neighboring country," she snapped. "What of it?"

He swallowed. "She was ancient when I was a child, so I can't even imagine how old she is now. Lives alone, wields an axe, chases off anyone who sets foot on her property. Legend says she lures children in with candy and then eats them, but I think it's a tale to frighten children from getting lost in the woods." He shuddered. "The Black Forest is friendly to no one."

Ro stared at him a moment more, mouth open, before she threw the letter on the low table, grabbed her bag, and started stuffing it full, heedless of making anything tidy. "Why didn't you say so earlier? We need to find her. Now."

After a slight hesitation, Ro shoved in the clothes she'd meant to have mended or washed. That would have to wait. Gross.

"Ro, this is one letter out of hundreds."

She clenched her jaw, still stuffing. "And it's the only one we need. I know it."

"Are you sure you can trust it?"

His unsaid words echoed loudest. They didn't know how much time Allura had. If they went after the wrong clue…

Ro's jaw tightened. "What else can we do? Sit here and wait some more?"

She didn't mention the letter's personal connection. How could she? She was still reeling, still raw. And Olt hadn't noticed.

She set her pack next to her. "I'm going. This is too big to pass up."

As if there were any other option.

"Of course you have to," he said, as if every word pained him.

Ro froze. Lifted her eyes to his. "You're coming with me, n'est-ce pas?"

That was the whole reason he'd insisted on dogging her

steps from Angleterre. No way would he leave her to find the old woman by herself. Especially since *he* knew who she was. And hopefully where.

A muscle in his jaw ticked. Olt took so long responding, Ro almost gave up on waiting for what he was struggling to say.

But she was a huntress. She could outwait anyone.

"I don't know..."

Ro blinked. "You don't know? What could you possibly be doing that is more important?"

"I might return to England and set sail with another ship..." he said weakly.

Ro struggled to keep her raging emotions under control. "You said you wanted to come, remember?"

He glanced away, unable to meet her eyes. "I don't think that's such a good idea anymore..."

Ro reared back, the words like a slap. "What? You said you wanted to help me. Do you know where this woman lives or not?"

"I do."

"Then show me."

Another long stretch of silence graced the room.

"Ro, you don't know what you're asking of me," he said in a low voice.

Ro's jaw went hard. "I'm asking you to save a little girl's life. I know exactly what I'm asking."

Still, he hesitated. And he wouldn't meet her eyes. "I'm sorry, but I...can't."

Stunned, Ro tried to make sense of his words. "What, because you have so much to do? New places to explore? What happened to helping a damsel in distress?"

"That's not it."

"Is it because you hate Liam so much?"

He looked uncomfortable—and annoyed at her mention of Liam. "Ro, I'm sorry, but I can't explain. I just...I can't go with you. I'll try to help you find her, I will, but I can't be the one to show you where she lives. I'm sorry, I truly am."

"And I don't have time to waste seeking her out, when you can take me to her doorstep!"

Rage, hurt, abandonment, fear—that she'd done or said something to drive him away—it all boiled up inside of her. She grabbed the letter and marched up to him.

"What, we have one adventure together, and you decide that's enough for you? What happened to helping my niece? Helping me? You're abandoning me after the first solid lead we receive!"

"Ro, it's not that. Please, I swear to *Gott*, it's not that. You don't understand."

Angry tears burned the back of her throat. "Then make me understand."

"I—can't."

"Can't or won't?"

Olt seemed to struggle. "Ro, I promise you, if there were any other way…"

Fury exploded, and Ro poked his chest. "You said I could trust you! You said I could come to you for anything. You said that if I ever needed help, you were the one to ask. Well I'm asking now. My niece—whom I didn't even know existed—is being crushed under a sleeping curse, and I don't know what to do!"

Olt didn't say anything, wouldn't meet her eyes.

"Non." Ro stepped close, her nose inches from his, forcing him to look at her. "This is how it's going to be. *You* followed *me*. You flirted with me and hounded me and insisted I include you in this adventure, so guess what? I'm including you. You can pack your bag and saddle your horse and come with me, or you can walk out that door right now and never come back. Do you hear me? Do not *ever* come back."

Olt grabbed her face in both hands with an urgency that took her breath away and kissed her. Hard.

Ro didn't know what to do. She stood there, frozen, completely conflicted and out of her depth.

It was sheer heaven.

Just as she was starting to melt into the kiss, to raise her arms to slip around his neck, he released her, his breath ragged, and caressed her face so gently she wanted to weep.

Her eyes drifted to his lips, and Dieu help her, all she wanted was another taste.

He leaned his forehead against hers and closed his eyes. "Ro, you have no idea what you're asking me. I can't. I *can't*."

Every muscle in Ro's body coiled tight, and she stood there, rigid, not allowing herself to sink into his embrace. Horrified she almost had.

She ground out, "I'm asking you to keep your word and save a little girl's *life*."

Her voice cracked on the last word. Their eyes caught and held, and he didn't say anything for a stretch of eternity.

He swallowed a few times, then glanced down, breaking their intense gaze. "All right. I'll do it. For you. I—I'll do it."

Ro, prepared to argue as hard as she could, deflated a little. "Really? I mean, are you certain?" A hard edge sharpened her words. "I would hate to inconvenience you."

Olt winced, but Ro wasn't sorry. He was just like every other male in Ro's life. Unreliable.

"I'm certain," he said quietly. "I'll go with you." He licked his lips. "Like I said I would."

Ro frowned. Why did he sound like he was going to his doom? Did he truly not want to go with her so badly? But then that kiss—argh!

Romance complicated everything. And it was so blasted confusing.

He released her, and she stumbled back a few steps, desperate for distance between them.

"Bon," she said simply. "Be at the stables, ready to go, within the hour. We're leaving straightaway."

Olt left her room without another word, a shadow of his boisterous self.

Ro finished gathering her gear with jerky, trembling motions, then left it all bundled and ready to go by the door. She'd tell Cosette their plans, then she'd grab her things on her way to meet Olt at the stables.

If she could find her way back to her rooms, that was.

Ro slipped on her red cape, then dropped her face into her hands. She wanted Olt to come with her because he *wanted* to, not because she'd goaded him into it.

She'd only insisted he keep his word. She'd only insisted he help save her niece, as he'd told her he would. So why did she feel so guilty for forcing him to do the right thing?

And what did that say about his character that he was reluctant to do so in the first place?

7

*A*llura's door was cracked open, so Ro peeked in. Cosette was within, in an elaborate gown and recently done hair, coils of ironed blonde curls springing over her shoulders.

Ro slipped inside. "Cosette, I—"

"Bon, you're here. Come quickly. The priest has summoned us."

Cosette bustled around the room, barely tolerating the maids who followed her and were attempting to make her even more presentable. One carried a jewelry box while the other kept trying to powder Cosette's face.

Ro tried to explain what she'd discovered. "But I—"

"We mustn't keep him waiting," Cosette interrupted.

She shooed the maids away, only concerned with making Allura comfortable, fluffing pillows and repeating instructions to the little girl's caretakers several times over.

Then she swept out of the room, tugging Ro in her wake.

Ro and the servant girls followed a bit helplessly, the girls stopping just outside the door as it was barred behind them all. Ro sent them a commiserating look as their mistress hauled her down the stairs.

King Trêve waited for them at the bottom of the staircase. He searched his wife's eyes, and she gave a little shake of her head. He lowered his head and adjusted a cuff that didn't need adjusting.

Ro took them in as the couple took a moment to compose themselves.

Light-brown hair recently powdered and tied back in a queue, Trêve looked every bit the regal king with white ruff at his neck and wrists and a vibrant-blue frock coat that shimmered in the candlelight and reflected the color of his eyes. White hosiery separated matching breeches from heeled blue shoes with proud bows that moved when the king did.

Cosette was resplendent in a crème-colored gown, her bodice and underskirt a pale peach that complemented, and was lighter than, the crème that made her skin gleam like silk. Her blonde curls, though obviously ironed, coiled over her shoulders in a fashion Ro envied, never having any such luck with her own straight-as-a-board dark tresses.

Ro fingered her short queue self-consciously.

Cosette eyed her while Ro wasn't paying attention. "Ro, why are you in your red hunting cape?"

Ro started to explain, but this time, Trêve spoke before she could. "My darling, we mustn't keep the priest waiting. He may know—he wishes to speak to us without delay."

"But of course, mon amour. Shall we?"

Cosette gave him a forced smile, as if she didn't smile with all her might, she might crumple and start crying and not be able to stop. Ro's heart ached for her sister.

Trêve held out his arm for his wife, and they set off at a brisk clip, Ro trailing behind. Liam joined her, not looking her way, for which she was grateful.

She couldn't handle *two* romantic confrontations in as many hours.

They cut through the garden, torches lit against the oncoming nightfall.

Only four other guards accompanied them, instead of the flock of courtiers normally present, and they took up posts outside the building the moment they reached the chapel on the property. Liam held open a side door.

Ro followed Trêve and Cosette inside.

And stopped dead in her tracks.

Candlelight and incense may have given the cathedral an ethereal, smoky glow, but there was no mistaking the man who stood at the front of the room.

Père Guise bowed, pleased to see the king and queen, then lifted his head and froze when his eyes landed on Ro.

I will remain calm, she told herself sternly.

He pointed at her, fury in his eyes. "She cannot be in here."

Ro quirked a grin. "Surprised I haven't gone up in flame for stepping on holy ground?" Oops.

Cosette looked furious herself, only it appeared she didn't know to whom to direct it. "Père Guise, you forget to whom you speak." Under her breath, she said, "Rosette, really."

Ro dipped her head in apology. To her sister. Not the priest.

Père Guise seemed to remember his audience and visibly struggled to control himself. His eyes swept over Ro. "I only seek to keep order and decency in the church, votre Majesté. She is not dressed modestly, and as such, shouldn't be here."

Ro looked down at her leathers and laughed. Being covered head to toe in hunting gear wasn't modest? Her clothing covered more than most women's dresses!

They especially covered more than Madame LaChance's ever had, and she was an intimate of the priest's. That said something about him right there.

Cosette shot her a look. "Be respectful."

Unfortunately, Ro didn't hold even a glimmer of respect for the priest. That man had whittled it away every time he'd reprimanded her over complete and utter nonsense.

Cosette's eyes flicked over Ro's attire as well. "Her clothing befits her station, as does yours. I would remind you to keep in mind your role here, Père Guise."

He bowed low. "As you wish, votre Majesté."

King Trêve took control of the room. "You called us here, Père Guise. Have you news?"

Père Guise's glance to Ro clearly said he hadn't called everyone present, but he answered the king anyway. "I believe we have found a way to slow the princess's decline. Keep her from slipping away."

Cosette choked on a sob, her hand flying to her mouth. King Trêve stepped up to his wife and cradled her in his arms, resting his cheek against her temple.

The old priest shot a tired look her way, thinly veiled in respect. "Votre Majesté, perhaps the queen will do well to retire and leave the planning to us?" His eyes settled on Ro. "To the men?"

Ro bristled.

Before Trêve could answer or Ro could assault the priest and be carried by angels straight to hell, Cosette straightened and regained a measure of composure. "That will not be necessary, I assure you, Père Guise. Please continue."

"As you command, votre Majesté." He addressed the room at large. "I suggest she be taken to a place where the magic oppressing her can be slowed to give us time for a solution to be found."

Ro stilled. Not magic. Where *time* could be slowed…or stopped.

Trêve's deep voice filled the room. "Where could we find such a place?"

Père Guise tilted his head, the respectful move smacking of pride. "We could take her to an abandoned, out-of-the-way church. I would oversee an order of monks myself to ensure she comes to no harm."

"Absolutely not!" Ro blurted the same time King Trêve asked, "Oui, but would you be able to slow the magic?"

The priest gave Ro a sour look even as he answered the king. "Our prayers would be all she needs, Majesté."

Ro spluttered, the old priest shushed her, and King Trêve turned to her.

"Speak, huntress. I know you have much experience in these matters."

That earned another glare from the priest, but Ro took a moment to pull herself together and wrangle her jumble of protests into coherent thoughts.

"With all due respect, Majesté, the priest only hopes prayers will work. I am not one to discount prayer"—she'd certainly had her own prayers answered, but most of the time she had to act to make it happen, to step out in faith, as it were—"but she needs to be in a place where magic cannot penetrate. A safe place, one with a barrier to magic."

An idea sparked in her head, and she stopped abruptly, sorting through the many things she'd read in the past week.

The priest sneered. "Which is exactly why she should be protected in a house of Dieu. What magic would dare enter?"

Ro shot him a look, not bothering to mention the fifteen-plus years the curse had brought all organized religion to its knees.

"As a man of Dieu, I must insist—"

Ro hissed through her teeth. "If you were the man of Dieu you claim to be, I would not hesitate to put my niece in your care, no matter how I might feel about you."

A few gasps echoed in the open space, leaving a shocked silence in its wake. Liam sighed, Cosette covered her face briefly, and Trêve raised an eyebrow. But Ro did not repent of or retract her words.

She'd met a true man of God once, one who was kind and helped the poor without a thought to himself, and this priest wasn't worthy to sit under that monk's tutelage.

He drew himself up, breathing heavily, face turning red. "You are in danger of hellfire, young Mademoiselle—"

She gritted her teeth. "The only hellfire I am in danger of—"

"Rosette, please…"

Her sister's quiet words were enough to snap her out of her fury and back to the task at hand. "Oh, Cosette, forgive me. As I was saying"—she quickly added, so Cosette wouldn't make her apologize—"she needs to be in a place no one can enter, so if the enchantress seeks her, she cannot find the child."

"Where do you suggest, huntress?" Trêve asked.

Ro started to answer, then held her tongue. "I have an idea, but I will only speak of it to the king and my queen. I-I want to make sure it can be done, first."

Père Guise looked like he was preparing to have a stroke right then and there, but both King Trêve and Queen Cosette nodded, which was all the authority she needed.

Ro felt a flash of regret. Her mère had loved the Church so…

She tilted her head toward the priest. "But I would welcome your prayers that my mission might succeed."

There. She'd taken a stab at civility.

"Votre Majesté…" the priest tried to protest.

"Thank you, Père Guise," the king cut in. He swept his hand to the aisle. "After you, my dear."

Cosette made the sign of the cross, genuflected, and left in a flurry of skirts, and Ro copied the movement and strode down the aisle in her hunting gear, leaving a sputtering priest in her wake.

Smug, she flicked one glance behind her and was decidedly unsettled to find Père Guise smiling after them, looking less like a raving lunatic and more like the conversation had gone exactly how he'd wanted it to go.

He gave her a nod that seemed to say, "Your move."

Ro nearly collided with the wall, but Liam tugged her out of harm's way at the last second. She gave him a grateful nod, and he returned a cool look.

Great. Now Olt *and* Liam were upset with her. Not to mention Cosette and possibly Trêve and definitely Père Guise. Not that she cared about that last one.

And Père Guise was hiding something. And perhaps not at all what she'd thought him to be.

She couldn't wait to be done with palace intrigue and on her own where things were simple and direct once more.

8

o's mind churned with plans as they made their way back into the palace proper.

The moment they stepped inside, Trêve grasped her elbow and pulled her into the first room they came to. Claude and Pascal glanced up in surprise, pausing from a game of chess before a welcoming fire.

Cosette and Liam swiftly entered, the latter shutting the door and putting his back to it so that no one else could.

Trêve didn't seem to care that Ro's brothers were within. He grasped Ro's shoulders tightly. "What is it? What's your plan? Where will you take her?"

Ro couldn't help the joy that bubbled up within her. After being so lost for so long, everything was falling into place. Finally. "Why, le Château des Roses Noires, of course. There was quite an impenetrable barrier there before, remember? I just need to raise it, like before."

Trêve released her as if burned.

Cosette gasped. "Rose, is it even possible?"

Ro nodded, trying not to let his reaction sting. "I think so. It will take more research, but hopefully not much, now that I know what to look for. I know we haven't much time, so I will be swift."

Trêve looked unsettled. "What of soldiers?"

Ro shook her head. "We do not want to draw attention to the château." She flicked a glance at Liam. "A contingent of huntsmen in the woods should be enough to alert us of any danger."

Liam nodded once. He would see it done.

Cosette's eyes flitted between them, a frown creasing her brow. "But what of servants? Surely Allura Aurore will need someone to tend her. *I* could tend to her…"

Ro was already shaking her head. "No servants. No one else on the premises whatsoever." She met Trêve's eyes. "I'm going to freeze time within the château's grounds. Create a barrier that magic cannot penetrate."

Realization streamed into his eyes, and he took a step back. "Huntress. Are you certain?"

She begged him to understand without saying so. "It's all I can think to do to save her until I can bring her out of her enchanted sleep. The château can be set outside of time, thanks to Marie, the witch who trapped you. What I don't know yet is how to manipulate a sleeping curse."

Others in the room kept talking, but Trêve kept his eyes on Ro. "Have you found a way to…do such a thing?"

To lay such a curse.

Although he didn't say it, Ro felt his meaning down to her marrow. "I believe I have, votre Majesté."

She knew exactly which books to pull the moment she stepped foot in the library. She just needed to repeat what his enchantress had done, but on a much smaller scale.

He looked as if she'd just slapped him.

She started talking fast. "It will not harm her. It will not harm anyone else either, but the priest is right. I must slow her decline while I find the empress. Which I may be able to do shortly thereafter." She looked at Cosette. "That's what I was coming to tell you. I believe I've found a clue to the empress's whereabouts. Olt and I were preparing to set out."

Liam cleared his throat. "With all due respect, huntress, I should accompany you. As should a contingent of soldiers. The empress is a threat to us all."

"Non." Ro met his eyes. "No soldiers. We ride hard and we ride fast. Besides, soldiers won't be much good in a magical battle. I'll not have good men harmed because they can't protect themselves."

Claude and Pascal exchanged a look.

"We'll go too," Claude said with far too much enthusiasm. "We can certainly protect ourselves."

Pascal's grin matched Claude's. "We'd be honored to go with you."

"We can guard the camp while you fight the, uh, magicky stuff."

More like they were thrilled to get away from their responsibilities. She didn't even care what they were up to. All that mattered was Allura.

Trêve was still staring at her with a glazed look. "But…"

He looked as if he didn't know which of his protests to give voice to, as if he still staggered under the weight of her words.

"It must be done," she said quietly, gently. "I give you my word that I will be as…meticulous…as possible. I will ensure what befell you will *not* befall her."

She'd be placing the same curse on his daughter that had been placed on him, one he'd been trapped under for years. And if she couldn't find Allura's attacker, if she were killed during her mission, his daughter would be trapped for the rest of her life.

Only she wouldn't know it.

"How long…will it last?" he asked with difficulty.

Ro swallowed, remembering the few facts she'd gleaned

from her research. "It will not diminish, possibly for a hundred years, if I do it right."

Not that she was at all certain she could do it right. The pressure ratcheted up a notch. Ro took a deep breath and didn't look away, waiting for his consent.

"Do it." Trêve held Ro's gaze. "Do what you must."

Ro nodded and spun, her red cape swirling around her. Liam stepped out of her way, and she headed toward the library. Cosette followed her out, took her arm.

Ro slowed her pace, but only a little.

"Do you really think it can be done?" Hesitant hope tinged her voice.

"Oh, I hope so, Cosette, truly. When the priest said the magic attacking her needed to be slowed—ideas simply exploded in my mind. I finally know what I'm looking for."

Ro thought of the books she needed to pull, the ones that could be shoved off her desk…

"Darling, I wish you wouldn't aggravate him so."

"Hmm?" Ro's swirling thoughts and plans were interrupted, and it took her a moment to focus on her sister's words. "Who?"

"Père Guise." Cosette sent a somewhat exasperated smile her way. "Whom else?"

"Oh, I don't know…" Ro ticked off the men she knew well on her fingers. "Claude, Pascal, Trêve, Liam…" Her voice trailed off. *Olt.*

Cosette chuckled, but it was strained. "Yes, well, he was assigned to our palace chapel here by the Church, and he does mean well."

"Mean well?" Ro rounded on her, halting their progress. "That pompous, prattling, boot-lick…"

Cosette made a shushing noise in her throat. "Chut! That is quite enough of that."

Ro cleared her throat, choked back the rest of her tirade.

"My apologies. But you can't mean he'll be overseeing the chapel *here*—"

"Oui, I do, and you should also know the import of presenting a united front to the people. Squabbling undermines everything we're trying to do for our kingdom."

Ro tried not to scream how this was such a bad idea. "But Père *Guise*…?"

Cosette looked mildly uncomfortable, possibly for Ro's sake. "He is overseeing the reconstruction of our personal chapel. It was badly damaged in the fires and riots that swept the city. He has connections, selflessly cared for others during the curse, and has many wonderful plans for rebuilding. The Church thought he would be a perfect fit, and…I agree."

Ro's frown deepened. Trêve didn't trust Madame LaChance. Why would he allow her confidante to be assigned to the palace? Besides, their personal chapel rivaled most churches in Paris for size. Except for Notre Dame on the Île Saint-Louis, of course.

They could have any priest they wanted.

"Cosette, you know I respect the Church—our priests— but that man…" Ro dropped her voice. "As an intimate of Madame LaChance, I would be cautious of giving him any foothold in the palace. You know how much sway she held during the curse."

Cosette pulled Ro along to keep them walking. "You can't fault her for making her own way in a terrible situation. Besides, you were going to send me to her, remember?"

"Of course I do. And I don't fault her—she employed me, after all. But there are…concerns…" Ro frowned, thinking of the rumors. Olt's dislike for her. The same dislike she held for the priest. "Can you not appoint someone else to the role? Ask for reassignment?"

Cosette stretched up on her tiptoes and kissed Ro's cheek. "I appreciate your concern, but you have much more important things to worry about right now. Let me see to the running of the palace?"

Ro sighed. "You're right. Désolé."

Cosette forgave her in an instant, as she always did, and then hurried to Allura's room while Ro stepped into the library.

Ro sincerely hoped the plan she'd formed in a moment of panic—not wanting the priest anywhere near the child—wouldn't get them all killed.

Ro immediately went to the king's rare collection.

It was locked up for more reasons than one—one of those being that it held books on the curse.

Ro pulled out the books she'd noted earlier, but dismissed, because they had nothing to do with sleeping curses, and carried them to Trêve's desk.

She went back to make sure she hadn't missed anything, and as she did, another tome near the back wall caught her eye. This one was decrepit. Ancient. Falling apart. She could've sworn it hadn't been there before.

But the slight ring of dust on the shelf when she pulled it free said it had been. Odd.

Ro carried it with her, ignoring the other volumes, and sat on the library floor in front of the fireplace, books spread around her. Hesitant, unsure why she was hesitant in the first place, she cracked it open somewhere in the middle. And frowned. Latin.

Her mère had made certain she'd learned it, due to the priests often reading Latin Scripture instead of French at Mass, but she hadn't studied it, read it, heard it in an age. She struggled a little, but the poem soon became clear.

It was a spell. On how to make one's hair grow longer, faster, fuller, thicker.

Ro gasped and dropped the book. Flung it from her, more like. She'd seen this book before. She'd *burned* this book.

Once, long ago, she'd battled the remaining Mademoiselle of the Mountain, a witch who'd asked for the Fairy Queen's heart. On a platter. Ro had defeated her, then cleaned her cottage of every poison, animal part, and spell book, burning the vile things in a massive pile. They'd been crawling with evil: dark, vicious, and full of death.

Now here was one back again, as if Ro had done nothing to it at all.

Too curious to keep away, Ro reached out and lifted the worn clothbound cover with one finger. And peeked at the name scrawled on the front end paper in elegant loops.

Marie Camille Louise Gabrielle Chauvineau.

Marie. Magic.

The sorceress who'd trapped Trêve.

It wasn't the book she'd burned after all. At least, not the same copy.

Reluctantly, she thumbed through a few more pages, finding spells for becoming a better cook, making one's garden grow faster and healthier, and attaining comfortable beauty that would catch the eye of the village sheepherder.

Yet…unlike those other books, this one didn't singe her fingers. This one didn't feel oily, vile, full of evil and all things dark. Though evil things didn't always, did they?

This one seemed to be a primer, more of a beginner's manual, things that were harmless, simple—that would make people's lives better.

Then she stopped cold. "How To Sleep Peacefully" lifted from the page and smacked her in the face. Across from it? "How To Bend Time (or How To Capture Extra Moments for Your Day)." The second title was a handwritten note next to the first. Alone? Seemingly harmless. Together? The beginnings of a formula to place a curse.

Panic beat rapid hummingbird wings in her chest.

Had Père Guise secretly placed this book in the king's collection for her to find? She wouldn't put it past him.

Nonetheless…

She flipped to the beginning. And read the whole thing.

At the end, she sat motionless, the beginnings of a plan sitting like a cold stone in her gut. She wasn't about to cast a spell like some sorceress! There was a reason she fought to undo their magic: to protect people.

When she'd thrown out her plan to Père Guise, she thought she'd just pull the magic of the place around Allura, placing her in a cocoon, using what was already there. According to this, it was far more complicated than that.

Sifting pages through her fingers, she started noticing a pattern. Bits and pieces of spells stood out to her. Perhaps woven together, rearranged…

Was she truly considering this?

Ro set the tome aside and rolled onto her back, stretching and releasing tight muscles. Her entire back screamed in pain. But her mind was so close to grasping exactly what she needed to do.

She needed to freeze time so Allura stopped fading, so the sleeping curse stopped sucking the life right out of her. Ro sat up. Just like how time seemed frozen inside the beast's château while they were both trapped there.

She bounced to her knees, throwing books aside. Somewhere in here, someone had transcribed the curse. If she could use parts of it…

Her hand found the book, and she yanked it toward her. Soon she was flipping pages. Finally, the curse rested before her bleary eyes. She read a portion of the chant aloud, then paused. Nothing.

The power wasn't in these words. That had already fled. Been used up.

She pulled the ancient tome onto her lap and compared the two, finally seeing what her brain was trying to tell her.

Marie hadn't made up the curse when she'd turned the crown prince into a beast.

She'd taken bits and pieces from various spells, woven them together to make her monstrosity. Dread dropped low in Ro's belly. Marie had spliced together more than she could handle, perhaps done it poorly as well, and it had backfired to curse all of France.

Incroyable. All Ro needed to do was take pieces of the same spells, following Marie's example, and limit it to Allura and the château. Not too much, not too vast.

Did she even know how to do that?

She wracked her brain to remember everything Marie had done to entrap the beast. She'd used blood. Her blood. She'd used an enchanted dagger…with a ruby hilt.

Ro frowned. She could've sworn she'd seen one of those lately. But her mind brushed off that information as unimportant, and she moved past it.

Marie had used a single rose to grow thorny vines that encircled the château. A boundary to contain the magic.

Her head came up slowly. Was she truly considering using magic—dark, deep, *wrong* magic—like the most vile and evil sorceresses?

Her heart felt like it was trying to beat right out of her chest. She fought sorceresses for a living. Kept them from harming others. Hunted them.

She often gave them a choice to stop harming others, but they were usually too far gone, too embroiled in the evil they wielded, to want to do more than eat hearts and ensnare children and kill any who opposed them.

Would she be any different than the witches who'd used such things for their own gain?

But she was doing it to save Allura's life!

Everything in her stilled. And Marie had done the same first to save her daughter's life and then to avenge her daughter's death. It was no different. *She* was no different. All it took was that first step. Then another. But what else could she do?

Ro put her head in her hands, and her dry eyes burned with unshed tears.

Everything she'd worked so hard to undo…and she was considering putting the same curse on her niece. If she did it wrong, who knew how far-reaching the effects would be this time?

Marie's curse had exploded out of her control and had trapped all the land Trêve was to be king over, all of France, not just his summer château as she'd intended.

Ro could plunge France into another curse. She could be trapped alongside her niece, unable to leave or help her.

But she must do something to save Allura's life! If dark magic were the only way…

Could she do it? And if she did, would she ever come back from it?

❧

A solemn group waited for Ro outside the library. Several paced the stretch of hallway.

Cosette barreled toward her the moment Ro stepped foot outside. She'd been crying. Again. "Well? Did you find it? Did you find a way to save my daughter?"

Ro nodded, once. As her hand strayed to the parchment in her pocket, her heart bled and shriveled up and died inside of her. Cosette would never allow her to do it. Not if she knew. She could never find out the truth.

Ro's eyes met Père Guise's. Did he have to join them right now? His judgmental look speared her. It was as if every horrible thing he'd said about her was coming true.

Ro hesitated.

"Speak," Cosette said. "I do not care who hears it."

"Oui, I have found what I was looking for. But I will need to take Allura to your summer château right away."

Cosette stared at her a moment before hurrying away. "I will have her nurse prepare her to leave first thing in the morning."

"Non. Now. This very moment, in fact."

Cosette stopped and glanced out the darkened window to the dead of night beyond. "Surely not, Rose! There are still wolves."

"*Now*, Cosette." Ro gentled her tone. "It's better if we leave under the cover of darkness." She gave Père Guise a fierce look. "Secrecy is of the utmost importance."

Père Guise gave her a smirk, which was more riling than all the glares or snide remarks in the world. "You couldn't possibly be suggesting that *I* would—"

"Enough, both of you," Cosette snapped.

Ro took a deep breath, let it out, and looked away. Cosette was right. Her feud with Père Guise wasn't important right now. Allura was fading too fast. Besides, if Ro didn't act now…she wasn't sure she could go through with it.

Trêve stepped up. "I will go with you."

Liam immediately protested. "Votre Majesté, it would be best if you were to stay here. I can see the princess safely transferred to your summer château."

Trêve started to protest, but Père Guise cut in, respectfully. "I must agree with High Général Liam, votre Majesté. Who will run your kingdom while you're gone? If you're trusting the huntress with this mission, then trust her."

Liam nodded in agreement.

Wolves could've burst into the hall and eaten Ro's face, and she wouldn't have been more shocked. Père Guise was agreeing with her?

"I will see that no harm comes to the wee princess," Liam said in a gruff voice.

Trêve didn't look convinced.

While the priest and Liam continued to dissuade the king from going, Claude and Pascal sidled up to Ro.

Claude fingered the leather jacket under her red cape. "I see you kept my jacket."

Ro raised an eyebrow. "*Your* jacket?"

She flicked a glance at Pascal, whose jacket it actually had been, but instead of taking offense or teasing as she'd expected, he looked pleased. A little embarrassed.

He eyed the shabby thing. "We really should get you another, you know."

Ro tugged it tighter around herself. "You will not. I keep this jacket in perfect repair, thank you very much. It's just fine how it is."

Again, Pascal looked pleased, but Claude snorted. "Then you clearly need your eyes checked. There're enough holes in that thing to be considered indecent."

Ro shook her head. "Are you going to help us or not?"

Pascal seemed to recover as he arched one eyebrow. "Hold your horses steady, there, little Rose. We still have to consult our wives."

Claude guffawed. "Right, you run along home to the Madame and tell me what she says when you tell her you want to go gallivanting around the country for weeks on end."

"It would actually be several countries, potentially…" Ro snapped her mouth shut. "Never mind."

Pascal didn't look too pleased at that. "Non, please do say. We need all the facts." He turned to Claude. "I'll just stop by and see your wife on my way. You say she'll have no problem with it?"

Claude visibly paled. "Don't you dare, mon frère, or there will be hades to pay for us both. I'm the only one who gets to tell her that kind of news."

Pascal studied him. "You will tell her, oui?"

Claude grinned. "Actually, I was hoping Trêve would give

me a letter saying I was drafted into the army and being sent on a secret mission. Much easier."

Pascal smacked the back of his brother's head. "Just tell her the truth, dimwit."

Claude rubbed his head, wincing more than the situation called for. "Easy for you to say. All you have to do is make doe eyes at your wife and kiss her a few times, and she'll go along with anything you say. My wife wants it to be her idea before she agrees to anything."

As much as Ro didn't want to think about her brothers kissing anyone, she was pleased to no end that they were married and happily so.

She studied Pascal. He shared her and her père's looks, with his tall, lanky build, dark hair that curled around his collar, and crystal-blue eyes. And although he could tease as readily as Claude, he was the quieter, more thoughtful of the two.

Claude not only had the twins' honey-blond hair and twinkling periwinkle-blue eyes, he always had a joke on the tip of his tongue and could take any serious matter to levity in a moment. It was easy to tell whom he liked best by whom he teased most.

She'd missed them so.

Would she lose them too if they found out how she was going about this?

Ro couldn't think about it a moment longer. She interrupted a lively discussion: Trêve insisting he should go and everyone else insisting he shouldn't.

"We really must leave right away." She glanced at her brothers. "You'll have to send word to your wives if you intend to go with me — be vague."

They nodded and hurried away to do so.

Trêve and Cosette followed her to Allura's bedchamber while Liam went to clear the stables and ready horses. Ro hoped Olt was already there. She half wondered if he was on his way to the closest port to book passage away from her and her demands.

As with every time she entered the room, Ro stretched out her senses, feeling for the curse. If it were possible, the curse smothered the little girl just a little more.

Ro hissed and drew back. It hurt to be around the oppression too long. How was the young princess bearing it?

Cosette spoke to the young girl's nanny. "Please prepare her for a carriage ride—"

"We will take her on horseback," Ro cut in.

Cosette gasped, eyes wide. "Surely not!"

Trêve wrapped his arms around his wife. "She will be safe with your sister. I will carry her to the stables myself, my love."

"And I will guard her with my life," Ro said fiercely.

Cosette turned her face to her husband's chest as sobs shook her shoulders.

Ro rolled her eyes. She stilled when Trêve's eyes met hers and he raised an eyebrow. "Désolé," she mouthed.

She usually didn't feel animosity toward her sister, but she was so incredibly tired. And heartsore. And right now, they needed to take action. Not cry. Not object. Take swift and sudden action before they lost Ro's niece and Cosette's only daughter.

The nanny bundled the little girl's things together as Trêve lifted the wee one in his broad arms. Ro tracked the movement, and it broke her heart. Would their daughter have looked like that?

Ro jerked her head and her thoughts away. She was beyond exhausted and too tired to be awake right now. She had no business wondering things that could never be.

"We must go." Her voice was gruffer than she meant it to be, but she was angry with herself.

It was time for action, nothing else.

9

*O*lt was waiting for them at the stables.

Ro hated to admit that she was surprised, but, well, she was.

He didn't meet her eyes as she tied her horse alongside his. Everyone else had their tack ready and were getting gear onto their horses.

Ro readied Fairweather, tethering everything she would need for the journey on his back. At one side, Claude and Pascal did the same, and on the other, Olt mirrored their movements.

Liam was already ready, waiting somewhat impatiently, if his horse's stamping and his frequent perusal of their progress were any indication.

Claude and Pascal were more subdued than normal, and Liam kept throwing suspicious little scowls at the stable door. The stable was off-limits at the moment, but that didn't mean he didn't trust someone to wander in accidentally and throw their carefully laid plans to the wind.

Plus, Allura's nurse stood nearby with the child's things, shivering and looking frightened and setting Liam even more on edge. They were still waiting on Allura.

89

Ro just hoped the five of them would be enough to protect the girl.

Her eyes were drawn back to Olt. She studied him over her horse's hindquarters, the scent of dust and hay and horse-hair strong in the barn, making Ro feel right at home. She thought back to how Olt had reacted while confronting Liam, glancing over his head then challenging him to the sparring match.

Olt and she moved between their horses at the same time, adjusting saddles and tightening saddlebags. With the jangling harnesses, Liam's horse's stamping, and her brothers' nonstop verbal sparring, Ro thought she might be able to have a conversation with Olt without being overheard.

She bumped his shoulder with hers, trying to regain some of their familiar levity. She couldn't bear to lose this friendship, even if she was the cause. "All right, handsome, spill. What colors do you see about Liam that you don't like?"

Olt frowned, and not just from her use of "handsome" to goad him. She'd called him that once without meaning to, and not only had the pirate who'd overheard teased him relentlessly, it had flustered him to no end. And so rarely did anything fluster him.

No matter that he fit the descriptor to a T, though rugged and dashing could be thrown in there too—all things Ro needed to stop thinking about right now.

He seemed to debate telling her.

She pressed just a little harder. "I saw you looking at whatever colors you see over a person's head," she said quietly so the others wouldn't hear. He didn't want anyone to know he could see such things. "Does he plan to murder me in my sleep? Overthrow his king and queen? Does he sip tea and read romance novels in a foaming bubble bath"—an image she quickly snuffed out and regretted conjuring—"like a foppish gentleman? What?"

Olt looked disgruntled. "He's attracted to you."

Ro snorted. "Is that all?"

Olt's steady gaze didn't waver.

"You're joking."

Still no help from the grumpy sailor.

"Oh, please. He can't stand me. I should know—we worked together for years. He's just glad the queen didn't lose her sister, that's all. He's loyal to a fault." She paused. "Of which he has many. Plus, he was drinking and wasn't in his right mind. That night."

Ro bit off her next excuse. Was she trying to convince herself or Olt?

She waited, but Olt didn't elaborate. "Well? Was there more?"

Olt's neck went a dusky red.

Ro's mouth fell open. "You mean you challenged the head of the king's guard to a duel because he was *attracted* to me? That's it?"

Olt wouldn't meet her eyes.

Ro huffed and started to move away, then paused and peeked over her shoulder. "What color would that be, anyway?"

He came up close behind her and spoke next to her ear, his voice low and intimate. "A glittering, shining diamond that picks up silver light and refracts it everywhere. And when attraction turns to love? True love? Unprecedented love?" His warm breath fanned over her neck, and Ro couldn't breathe. "The light is so blinding, I can hardly look at it."

Just when Ro thought she would pass out from lack of oxygen, when she couldn't pull her gaze from his, when she thought he was going to kiss her, again, Olt turned, his skin brushing hers, and retreated.

Ro sagged against Fairweather and sucked in a quiet gulp of air, trying to calm her racing heart.

And their quest had just started. Heaven help her if things got awkward or anything.

A man in commoner clothing and a dark forest-green hood entered the stable, holding a tightly wrapped bundle. He uncovered Allura's face, handed the little girl to the nanny, then began readying a horse.

Liam was on him in a hot second. "Votre Majesté! You shouldn't be here…"

Trêve's low, commanding tone filled the stable with its presence. "You bear my daughter. But of course I am coming with you."

"Mon Roi, you cannot…"

The king turned dangerous eyes on the high général. "Finish that statement."

Liam snapped his mouth closed, and even Ro reared back at the whip-sharp words. Everyone else stilled, their preparations forgotten.

Liam checked himself, stood rigid.

The king waited half a heartbeat past uncomfortable—for all of them—then turned back to his horse. "I'm going."

Liam swallowed and tried again. "If you do not trust me—"

Trêve turned on him. "It is not a matter of trust, High Général. It is a matter of a father's love for his daughter and his wish to see her safely conveyed to her resting place with his own eyes."

"But the affairs of state, the secrecy…"

"That is all I have to say on the matter." His commanding tone brooked no argument. Trêve saddled his horse with efficient if unpracticed movements, then tied on the items the servant had gathered for his daughter.

Liam's jaw ticked, but he bowed, deeply, and relented. "As you wish, mon Roi."

Ro winced on his behalf. She understood why the king wanted to come, but she also understood Liam's reaction—the perceived slight to his competence on a mission that was to be his responsibility.

King Beau Alexandre Trêve mounted his horse as Liam held it steady, then held out his arms for his daughter. The nanny visibly wilted in relief and handed her charge over quite readily before fleeing.

Trêve wrapped the little girl in the folds of his cloak, effectively burying her from sight. "I suggest you call me Alexandre for the remainder of this journey. Not many know me by that name."

Liam nodded. "As you wish it."

At Liam's insistence, two more soldiers in nondescript clothing joined them. He'd already sent word for huntsmen to meet them at the summer château.

Ro almost protested, but Liam cut her off. "I'll not have the king ride back to Paris alone." He met Trêve's eyes. "I intend to go on with the huntress to find the sorceress."

Claude and Pascal glanced at each other. "Yeah, so do we," Claude put in.

"We'll keep Ro safe so she can complete her mission," Pascal added quickly.

As if she couldn't keep herself safe.

Liam continued, though somewhat hesitantly, as if he feared the king might protest just because he suggested it. "And I believe the queen would be better settled if the king were to rule at her side, giving the courtiers a glimpse of normalcy while the little princess is hidden away without their knowledge."

The king finally nodded his agreement.

Liam seemed to deflate with relief, but he checked himself and gave a firm nod in return. Not that Ro doubted for a moment they'd be having this same argument in a few days.

One by one, the rest of them swung up into their saddles and headed out into the adjacent courtyard in the darkness. A somber evening greeted them, as somber as the riders about to embark on their journey.

Liam immediately moved to flank the king and flicked his

head so Ro would do so on the other side. She urged Fairweather forward to comply.

The two soldiers, those of Liam's elite guard, filtered into their group seamlessly, also in the same hunter-green clothing as their royal commander.

Ro glanced up at the window belonging to Allura's nursery, a single candle lit within. Cosette watched them, keeping up the pretense of being unwilling to leave her daughter's side, one hand splayed on the glass.

❦

They'd ridden hard, knocking the three-day journey into two.

The little girl hadn't stirred in all that time.

Ro stared up at the king's summer château. White stone reflected sunlight, giving the castle a glowing appearance, while rich-blue peaks made the roofline appear to soar into the sky. Well-groomed grounds morphed into well-kept garden mazes and fountains, something Ro was loath to destroy.

It was just as it had been before she'd left to silence the sirens.

And she'd turn it back into a thing of nightmares.

"What now?" Trêve asked, close to her side.

Ro jumped a little, then looked down at the sleeping girl in his arms. He'd barely let her go for two days. In a moment of tenderness—directed at his daughter, not her—he'd told Ro he imagined if he held the girl close to his heart, she'd know he needed her and would hold on longer. It was hard not to be moved by such words.

"We find a comfortable place for her to rest," Ro said finally.

Trêve nodded and urged his horse up the long crushed-shell drive. Orange trees in full blossom stood sentry on either side, their warm scent invading the air and encouraging deep breaths.

Ro would hate to turn them curse-blackened again.

She forced her thoughts away from what she was about to do. It was necessary. For Allura.

They dismounted at the front doors. No one came to open the doors.

"Where are the servants?" Claude asked.

"I sent them all away," Trêve answered. "Just as you requested, huntress."

Ro nodded. "Bon." She didn't want any more servants trapped here. She turned to everyone but Trêve. "Please stay with the horses. We will join you as soon as we can."

Liam looked as if he were going to object. Again. Ro gave him a hard look, and he backed down.

Her eyes went to Olt, but he hadn't said a word since the stables. Just kept to himself, withdrawn and looking as if something pained him. She ached to ask him what was wrong.

Not that he would actually tell her. Besides, she needed to stay on mission here.

She followed Trêve to Allura's room, decorated in alternating pink and blue, as if the designer couldn't make up his or her mind, ethereal drapings everywhere.

Trêve adjusted his daughter on the bed just so.

Ro gave him time, looking away as he kissed her forehead and brushed blonde hair away from her face. "Come back to me, little one."

He straightened, tears dripping into his beard. He didn't even try to hide them. "What do I do now?"

"I need you to take everyone and get off this property. Outside the gate."

Suspicion darkened his gaze. "What are you going to do?"

Here came the hard part. "I'm going to place a curse on this château, the same one Marie did—I'm going to freeze time."

He didn't argue. He took one long look at his daughter, rested his hand on Ro's arm, and gave her a single nod.

She hadn't been expecting that. Not after how opposed he'd been to the idea in Paris.

Ro waited for his heavy footsteps to recede, and the moment she felt the front door shudder closed, Ro drew the heavy book from her satchel, her heart sore and aching.

She had no choice. Just like Marie.

Laying the book aside, she took out a hardened case, pulled moist towels from within, and carefully unwrapped them.

A perfect blood-red rose lay in the midst of the off-white cloth, still damp, still fresh from when she'd cut it from Trêve's rose garden, releasing its perfume in the air.

She took it over to the iron-wrought table and lay the rose in its center.

Then she took a deep breath, opened the book, and began the spell she'd written. The words rumbled from her chest, deepening with every syllable.

The magic was foreign. Cold. Tight.

Wrong.

She jerked back, away from the words, and the magic dimmed.

Ro dropped her head. It wouldn't work like this. She was either all in, or she might as well give up now. It wouldn't work unless she was willing.

"Creator, forgive me."

Resolve hardened her features. She lifted her head and began anew, no stammering or halting or hesitance this time.

Her words rang through the chamber with a power all their own. And as the spell wove out of her mouth and started snaking throughout the château and grounds, twining around everything like ribbons, Ro adjusted a few words here. Redirected a few strands there.

She didn't even realize she was doing it, just that the spell needed adjusting as she followed her instincts.

She cut her palm and dripped exactly three drops of blood on the cut rose.

Slowly, the rose lifted from the table, hovering midair. It started to glow, red glittering motes sprinkling from it, just as the enchanted rose had in the beast's château. When this place used to be the Château des Roses Noires. The Castle of the Black Roses. A place of nightmares.

As it would be again.

As her tongue twisted around unfamiliar words, the rose's stem plunged through the table, shooting straight down into the marble floor and the many floors below it, rooting deep underground. Marble dust sprayed into the air with each crackling explosion of broken stone.

With a flick of her wrist, Ro kept any dust motes from touching Allura.

The iron table grew up around the rose in a cage, sheltering it from any who might wish it or the little girl harm. A window shattered elsewhere in the château, and vines added shards of glass to any openings in the iron dome to keep the rose safe.

The ground deep below trembled as roots worked their way under the entirety of the château grounds, steadily climbing toward the outer walls.

They paused there, waiting for her final command to shut the château off from the rest of the world.

Dust motes slowed. Stilled. Allura's chest paused midbreath, suspended in time.

Ro felt time's slowing tug at her.

She walked backward out of the room, word upon word building, weaving a tapestry of spell upon spell, not allowing anyone or anything entry, not allowing time in. Freezing the little princess in one single moment of time.

She didn't even realize she'd left the book behind. That she no longer needed it.

She made it to the bottom of the stairs when a bell tolled, the deep sound vibrating through the floor and nearly knocking her from her feet. Right where the curving staircase split toward the east and west wings, a giant clock appeared, slightly wavering and transparent.

It clicked once, backward, and stayed there.

What did it mean? But the magic Ro was wielding came for her, and she stepped back, not wanting to be caught in its flow and held captive.

She made it to the front doors, walked backward along the drive. Trees blackened and died. Grass withered. Flowers curled in on themselves. She made herself look at what she was doing. Made herself remember this moment.

It mirrored what was happening to Ro's soul.

The gate creaked open behind her. She stepped back, trusting her companions to have her back, to do as she'd asked.

She stepped through the gate. Two of them held it open. Ro was so deep in the spell, she couldn't tell who. She could tell, dimly, that they struggled to hold it open, as if the gates were trying to shut themselves.

But Ro wasn't ready for them to.

The words built into a crushing crescendo, and she wavered under the power of it. The pressure built and built and built—until it snapped.

The gates flew closed of their own volition.

The château's extensive grounds dropped away. Nothing but a rickety stone bridge spanned over nothingness. Wild, thick, ropey vines shot out of the ground and wrapped around the entirety of the château's boundary, whether fence or imagined line. Huge thorns grew and pointed out and up, keeping any who might find this place from getting within.

And then, for the pièce de résistance, the château disappeared from view. Unending forest stretched out before them, no hint that the château had ever existed.

Those behind her gasped. Trêve was completely silent, though it was an aching silence that keened with pain in her enhanced state.

Ro sat down, hard, on the ground right there outside the château. She'd done what she came to do. No one was getting in. Or out.

The castle had…vanished…just as when it held the beast.

Only this time…she stared hard through the glamour she'd so carefully placed. Her illuminating eyesight flared to life. She could see the château's outlines, hazy and indistinct, but there.

Ro's eyes drooped, then slid shut, exhaustion claiming her without her knowing it did so.

10

Ro came to with Olt's and Liam's worried faces above her. Then Claude's and Pascal's worried faces above them.

"Is she awake?" demanded Trêve.

Ro groaned and closed her eyes. She just loved being the center of attention. "All right, all right, I'm awake. Move back."

No one scattered.

"Seriously?"

"You did it." Claude's voice was awed. "You brought back the curse, just like before."

"Not *just* like before," Trêve was quick to add.

Everyone looked at him.

He flicked a glance around the still bright-green forest before returning his gaze to Ro. "It feels different."

Ro nodded. "That's because it is different."

She'd been careful with the magic. Treated it delicately. Made it anew. After all, she didn't want to be the next raving lunatic locked in the château's highest tower.

She tried to sit up and immediately had five eager helpers.

She grumbled at them but let them help her up. Her head felt like it wanted to explode.

"What now?" Olt asked.

She gave him a hard look. "We travel on, see if that note means anything."

He looked away.

Ro couldn't understand it. Why didn't he want to help? Why was he so reluctant to travel to the Black Forest, to help her niece?

Her throat burned as she refused to ask. If she knew, she might not insist he go, and if she did that, she had no hope of saving Allura. He was the only one who knew where to find this mysterious keeper of the forest.

So she kept her questions to herself.

Trêve looked uncertain, glancing between where the château used to be—where it still was, just cloaked from view—and the two soldiers who waited to escort him back to Paris. "Perhaps I should go with you…"

Liam stiffened. Although Ro didn't show it, she felt the same way.

Head aching, Ro spoke before Liam could object and make Trêve want to go with them that much more. "Mon Roi, go back to your wife, to your kingdom. Leave me to my task, and pray the Creator speeds me on my way."

Still, he hesitated. He studied the space where the château had been—what looked like forest but would lead any wanderer in a wide berth around it—as if he didn't want to leave. "I feel I should do more."

Liam spoke before Ro could think of what to say. "Running your kingdom, undoing the damage of the curse—that will help Princess Allura more than anything else, mon Roi. Make sure the kingdom she will inherit is back on its feet. Dieu will speed us on our way, and we will not return until we have found what we're looking for."

Liam was more right than he knew. Ro certainly wasn't coming back until she'd found a way to break Allura's curse.

Trêve nodded, resigned. "You are right, of course."

Liam looked surprised, as if he'd been expecting the king to argue.

A wry grin touched Trêve's lips, not making it to his weary, sad eyes. "I do value what you think, Monsieur Liam. That's why I placed you at my side, as one of my advisors, and as leader of my forces. Thank you for seeing this task through to its conclusion."

Liam inclined his head, and Ro let out the breath she'd been holding. One less worry. On to her next task.

She quickly mounted Fairweather and gathered the reins, ready for the long journey.

Trêve stepped forward. "Ro, I cannot thank you enough for all you have done and are about to do for my daughter."

Ro held his gaze, steady and sure and strong and with far too much faith in her. "I will do my best to succeed."

He closed one of his hands over hers. "I have no doubt you will."

Ro was extremely proud of herself for not flinching when his hand touched hers.

She instinctively flicked a glance at Olt, who gave her a sympathetic look, which Liam caught as his eyes darted between them, which would likely open a whole mess of problems Ro didn't have the capacity to deal with.

Her eyes settled on Trêve, that familiar ache at looking into his crystal-blue eyes only slightly less than before. Thank goodness his journey with them ended here.

She chose her words carefully. "Thank you for your confidence in me, mon Roi. I pray it is…well placed."

"But of course it is." Trêve smiled, the action warm and familiar. "And how many times have I said to call me Beau, huntress? You are my family, and you always will be."

Ro's heart jerked at that. She doubted he'd feel that way if she failed his daughter. Nor would the rest of the kingdom.

Although the little princess's sleeping curse had been made known, especially as they desperately sought a cure, they'd kept the extent of the princess's fading a secret. The people couldn't know how close they were to losing the little girl.

The country couldn't take such another blow. Neither could the royal family.

So far there were no revolts—surprising considering Trêve and now his daughter had been cursed—but murmurings and fear and suspicion had grown. The people did not want to spend another twenty years under a curse. Something Ro understood completely.

So it was simple: Ro couldn't fail.

She nodded once, and the two soldiers and their king mounted and turned their horses toward Paris.

Ro scanned the woods. True to his word, Liam had huntsmen spread out and keeping an eye on the summer château. Her eyesight picked out and illuminated the men just enough for her to pinpoint their locations.

Once again, she was awed when her fey-given eyesight surprised her and functioned like it was supposed to. Heaven forbid it always work when she wanted it to.

Her gaze fell on Olt, who stared after the king as if he wanted to follow him back to Paris. She tightened her jaw and started forward, pulling Fairweather to a halt after only a few steps. The others had started to follow her, but Olt hadn't moved. How she knew was a mystery, the way she could sense his mood or where he was in a room the moment he entered or came near her, but she stopped all the same.

She turned toward him. "Olt?"

He met her gaze with difficulty.

"You will lead us, non?"

He tried to smile. "When we get to my country, oui."

Ro blinked. His country? But he spoke English so well, she'd assumed…

Olt went a little green, and Ro feared he was ready to jump off his horse and either hurl the contents of his stomach all over the trail or run till he found a ship to take him back to Angleterre.

Ro nodded briskly and dug in her heels, making Fairweather lurch forward and canter a few paces before settling into a steady pace. She wanted to say more but didn't want to draw attention to his obvious discomfort. Or scare him off.

Which was entirely possible, because it was her.

Liam drew his horse alongside hers, her brothers followed, and Olt trailed behind. Although she and Liam quietly discussed what lay ahead, her senses, maybe even her heart, stayed behind with Olt.

He still hadn't told her what this journey meant for him, but she could tell it wasn't anything good. And she'd forced him to come anyway.

But it was the right thing to do, wasn't it?

As they delved deeper into the trees, Ro settled into Fairweather's cadence, beginning to enjoy her ride and the freedom a wide-open trail brought.

The road turned at a sharp angle, and she turned her horse's head away from the château, away from Paris, away from the village of Champagne, where she'd once lived.

And toward the Black Forest.

PART II
THE BLACK FOREST / LA FORÊT NOIRE

"Rapunzel"
Raiponce
Jacob Grimm and Wilhelm Grimm

Rapunzel had magnificent long hair, as fine as spun gold, and
when she heard the voice of the enchantress, she unfastened
her braided tresses, wound them round one of the hooks
above the window, and then the hair fell twenty ells down,
and the enchantress climbed up by it.

Raiponce avait de magnifiques cheveux longs qui brillaient
comme de l'or filé, et quand elle entendit la voix de
l'enchanteresse, elle détacha ses tresses, les enroula autour
d'un crochet au-dessus de la fenêtre, et puis les cheveux
tombèrent de vingt aunes, et l'enchanteresse les utilisa pour
grimper.

<h1 style="text-align:center">11</h1>

It took far too long to reach France's border and cross into Prussia.

Eight days. Eight days that slipped away without there being anything Ro could do about it. Then two more to reach the forest.

They'd ridden at a grueling pace, camping only when the light failed and stopping only when the horses needed a break. At long last, they urged their horses to the top of a grassy knoll, and a mass of twisted, gnarled trees rose in the distance.

The Black Forest.

Ro grinned in relief and leaned back in the saddle, ready for the gently sloping descent. Olt's horse ground to a halt. Not expecting it, Ro pranced forward a few steps before she reined in her mount. She eyed him, but Olt didn't budge.

"Halt!" Liam called a brief moment later.

Ro and Liam glanced at each other, then Olt. He didn't move.

Ro sighed and turned away. Great, another long pause in which Ro was certain he'd bolt. They observed the long line of trees while they waited.

The border to the Black Forest, still quite a few paces away, was distinguished from the rolling field they were in.

When the vegetation of France had sprung back after being dead for so long, it had grown more lush and beautiful than before. This field seemed to be a part of that. Flowers blossomed and vibrant grass grew right up to the wood, then changed.

In fact, the greenery on the other side looked a bit—sickly. Or perhaps just a darker shade of green?

"It does look rather ancient, doesn't it?" Ro mused.

"Oui," Liam answered.

Ro turned her head to look at him, but her eyes went to Olt. It didn't seem to matter where she was, what she was doing—she sought Olt first. Liam tracked her gaze, and Ro turned away.

"We should move on," Liam said. "Not much daylight left."

Ro nodded. "Agreed."

Still, no one moved, the thought of entering the ancient forest that held so many secrets, that housed so many evil creatures, overwhelming. Ro could feel its weight pressing down on her.

But time frozen for her or not, little Allura didn't have the luxury of their taking their sweet time. She was still being smothered, even if the curse was in a holding pattern, unable to finish her off.

Ro had done her best, but what she'd done could break at any moment. And then there was that clock, whatever it meant. They needed to hurry.

Ro waited impatiently for Olt to go first. To choose to lead them into the Black Forest. Liam sent her a glance, but Ro gave a little shake of her head. He needed to do this. He could do this. He *had* to do this.

The moment stretched on, and Ro considered pushing Olt down the hill herself.

Coming to a decision, Liam scanned their surroundings and dismounted. "If we are not moving forward, then we should make camp. Get an early start."

Claude and Pascal started to get off their horses, but Olt's voice stopped them.

"I disagree."

They paused. Ro raised one eyebrow. Disagreeing with Liam? This would not go well. Also, she was going to enjoy this.

Liam's quiet glare for Olt was just blistering enough to singe those nearby as well. "Noted."

He continued preparing to set up camp.

Olt didn't budge. "It's not safe out here."

Now Liam was listening, but by his clenched jaw, he wasn't happy. He waited for Olt to elaborate, arms crossed over his wide chest and tapered torso, honed from years of surviving a hard life and forging a new one.

Ro eyed Olt's leaner physique and slightly shorter height. Though Liam was more thickly muscular and Olt more scrappy, both had strengths that made them rather evenly matched in a fight.

No matter—she wasn't going to stand by and watch them beat each other up again. If they tried, she was taking them both down, tying them to their horses, and deciding for herself where they would spend the night.

As the men squared off, Ro sighed, raised her eyes to the heavens, and prayed for patience.

Olt, his back to the forest, nodded to Ro's right. "There's a village just over that rise. Wolves attack nightly, trying to get within for their livestock and any villagers foolish enough to be outside their homes after the sun dips below the horizon."

First of all, it was the most Ro had heard him speak since leaving the château. Second, how did he know all this?

Liam took out a spyglass, much like the ones the sailors

had used on her voyage, and scanned the tree line. "And you think camping where the wolves come from will be safer?"

Olt kept his eyes on the weathered huntsman. "We'll have more of a chance if we stay away from that village. The last thing we want is to camp in the open where we'll be spotted immediately and attacked."

Ro waited somewhat impatiently for Liam's findings, studying him while she waited.

Since Trêve had left with his soldiers, her brothers had teased and laughed for most of their journey, goading Ro into joining them every once in a while, while Liam mostly watched with an amused smile, his standoffishness not much different than when he and Ro had the same hunting jobs together.

Ro smirked at the memory. Even though they were near each other's age, Liam had thought he was taking the brand-new huntress under his wing, protecting her, disabusing the fool girl of the notion of becoming a huntress.

Instead, she'd turned it into a competition. A rivalry. She excelled at hunting, knew what she was doing, thanks to her training with Hamish and Clement, and soon drew ahead of the other huntsmen. Something Liam didn't handle very well.

Their competition was fierce—and benefited Gautier greatly. The only thing Ro regretted about it.

Then again, Ro wouldn't be where she was now if not for Gautier, so she was grateful for that time in her life, too. Even if the memory of working for such a monster sickened her.

Liam made a noise of surprise. "Well, I'll be. There is a village. Look, huntress."

He handed her the spyglass, and she scanned the forest's edge.

Ro couldn't help her whistle. "Looks robust, well stocked." She drew the glass away from her eye and smiled at Liam. "Fortified too."

Her brothers crowded her to get a look for themselves.

She handed the spyglass off and glanced at Olt. He stared at the tree line in dread, oblivious to the bustle around him.

Liam tracked the sun's descent. It was sinking rapidly. "Then we should stop in the village for the night. I'd rather be in there than out, if the wolves in this area are as much of a problem as you say."

Ro shrugged. "Might be good to get a feel for the locals. See what they know."

Liam nodded, decided. "All right. Ro, lead the —"

"No," Olt said forcibly, surprising them all once again. "We shouldn't."

Ro was the first to recover. "Surely those walls will keep any wolves at bay."

Liam got that obstinate look to his face. "We should make camp while it's still daylight. It's too dangerous otherwise. As Ro said, it would be good to talk to the locals."

Olt just shook his head, not bothering to glance in the direction of the village with the enclosed, wooden-pike walls and matching gate. "They are barely surviving. We cannot afford to get caught up in their fight."

Ro's mouth fell open, and for once, Liam didn't have any words to throw back in Olt's face. Pascal was silent, studying Olt thoughtfully, and Claude whistled.

"Waouh. How can you know a thing like that?"

Liam jutted his chin toward the trees. "Again, how will we be any safer sleeping in the forest, on the ground, in the wolves' path?"

Ro felt her heartbeat quicken, her blood surge for the fight, for the hunt. She took a steady breath to calm herself. They weren't deep in the fight yet.

"Then perhaps we should help them this one night," she said quietly.

Ro's voice had more effect on Olt than any other. His shoulders tensed, then he forced himself to relax while letting out a slow breath.

"Believe you me, huntress. They would not allow any to leave who could fight wolves such as you and Monsieur Liam can do."

Ro's heart tugged her toward the village. The wolf attacks on her own village had been few and far between during the curse. They mostly picked off those who wandered into the forest, and most of the creatures had converged on the fallen city of Paris, taking it over and driving the humans away. Hence why Gautier had ruled elsewhere.

She couldn't imagine wolves attacking nightly.

Liam scowled at Olt. "Again I ask why you think we would be safer *inside* the forest? Without a wall for protection?"

Olt spared him a glance. "Because they'll be attacking the village. They sleep during the day, attack at night. As long as we wait for the howls, we can press forward or camp in the dark without fear."

Liam didn't look convinced. And for good reason. It was odd behavior for a wolf.

Wolves hid in the day, yes, but they were mostly scavengers, stayed away from people, and only attacked when threatened or starving. Seeking out the same villagers night after night? Attacking a well-fortified village? Odd behavior indeed.

Liam's jaw went hard. "I won't ask again. How. Do. You. Know we'll be safe?"

Olt continued. "Because you have me with you."

That got a reaction from all sides, but Olt clammed up and wouldn't say another word.

Ro shuddered at how dead Olt's eyes looked, as if he were walling himself off from every emotion. She steeled herself against compassion for Olt and for the village. Allura first. *Then* she'd see what other wrongs she could right in the world.

Dieu, help them. Protect them, she prayed silently.

Ro interrupted the questions being thrown at Olt's unresponsive self. "Then lead the way. Right now. Before the wolves cross our path."

Still, Ro couldn't help flicking a glance toward the village. If not for Allura…

As if reading her thoughts, Olt spoke softly to Ro, ignoring the others. "Finding and stopping the source of the attacks would help them more, huntress."

Ro blinked when their eyes connected, and she could hardly breathe. His eyes drowned in so much turmoil, he looked like a completely different person. Not the carefree sailor she'd met on the *King's Ransom*. Who'd annoyed her with his perpetual cheerfulness.

She'd give anything to have that Olt back.

She cleared her throat, tried to take control of the dread spreading through her bloodstream. "After Allura…"

He nodded once. "After Allura." And turned back to the Black Forest.

Liam had watched their exchange with an unreadable expression. "How far away is this old crone?" he asked Olt.

"Three to five days, if we make good time. Her cabin is in the heart of the forest."

Non, her cabin is *the heart of the forest,* insisted a voice she didn't recognize. Now where had that come from?

Liam only debated a moment more. "Since you know this area better than I, I'll trust your judgment." He tied back on his bedroll and mounted. "After you."

Olt nodded and urged his horse toward the forest. They followed him to its edge. And Olt stopped just outside the tree line.

Ro held back a sigh. This was getting old. She didn't know how much longer she could hold her frustration in check. The others lined up beside her, waiting.

Taking a deep breath, Olt dismounted and started forward, leading his horse. Ro didn't know why, but no one moved to follow. Like an unspoken agreement among them.

Olt crossed into the trees with small, steady steps, and Ro held her breath. She knew it was significant; she just didn't know *why*. But she would be there for Olt if he needed her. That's what friends did. Besides, it was the least she could do after forcing him to come.

He hesitated, then forced himself over the boundary, wincing as he did so. Ro leaned forward, ready to help if he needed her.

After he crossed into the thick foliage, he stopped. Just stopped. Didn't move, didn't turn around. Ro's anxiety spiked. Should she go to him? Did he need help?

He paused for so long, Ro finally blurted, "Well? Do you know where this old hag is or not?"

Ro winced. She didn't mean to snap, but he was scaring her here. And she wasn't good with people as it was. Churning with emotions she didn't know how to deal with? It was a wonder they hadn't left *her* behind already.

He looked down at himself, ran his hands down his chest, and patted his thighs. Then he turned, eyes wide. "I'm all right!"

Ro cocked her head. "Excusez-moi?"

What did he think was going to happen?

He rubbed his hands down his linen shirt again, as if checking himself over to make sure the statement was true.

Liam nudged his horse forward first. "All right, then. Lead the way, *Olt*."

Ro's head came up at the tone of Liam's voice, at the way he said Olt's name, with derision, mocking. Would they never leave the other alone?

Not that she hadn't thought Olt's name was ridiculous a time or two, but such things couldn't be helped.

Olt stiffened, then mounted and urged his horse on. The beast was a deep-brown color with a golden sheen, mane and tail a brilliant golden blond, called a Black Forest horse. Ro had chosen it for Olt, not only for its origin, but because Fair-weather liked the horse so much.

As she followed Olt, she realized with a jolt that the horse's coat was the same color as Olt's eyes.

She'd picked his horse based off the color of his eyes.

Ro dropped her head back and groaned, which earned concerned glances from her companions. "I'm fine," she assured them. She tilted her head, studying Olt. "Are you?"

Olt nodded, once again pale, withdrawn. His jaw tight, he turned away. Without a word, retort, or teasing of any kind, Olt urged his horse deep into the forest's twisting under-growth, now leading the way.

Ro's heart broke all over again. What was wrong with him? And how irreparable was the damage she'd done to their friendship?

She steeled herself against compassion. Served him right for wanting to abandon a little girl to a curse.

You don't mean that.

Her mère's gentle voice nearly undid her. Non, she didn't mean that. But a little girl was relying on her, and Ro still didn't know how to break a sleeping curse.

And she'd just passed up a village that needed their help. She couldn't help feeling if any were lost this night, their lives would be on her as well.

She felt Liam's gaze on her, stiffened, and prodded her horse after Olt. Fairweather balked. "Fairweather! Forward."

The huge draft horse swung his heavy head toward her and gave her a sardonic look that said, "You sure you want to do this?"

"It'll be fine. Go."

He shook out his head, his last objection, and lumbered forward.

As she pressed on, the branches seemed to swallow her whole and whisper, "You, too, shall never leave us."

Ro lifted her chin and sat straighter. Well that was just

ridiculous. She would too be leaving, and she'd be taking her entire party with her, thank you very much.

Liam caught the look she flung at the forest, one of defiance, and he winked at her when their eyes met. Then his look lingered. A heated look. One that spoke of no good.

She couldn't help the glare she sent his way. That drew out his infernal grin—the one that turned plain, steady Liam into a rather devilishly handsome individual—and she turned away at the smug satisfaction on his face.

Curse him. Curse them all. Was he planning to flirt with her the entire way through the Black Forest? Because she wasn't going to stand for that for one blessed moment.

12

"Time to stop for a break."

Liam's voice intruded upon the dream Ro was having, and she jerked her head up, coming to. She blinked rapidly a few times. Had she seriously fallen asleep on her horse?

How had she not fallen off and died?

Ro gratefully slid from Fairweather's back and stretched and twisted until she felt more like herself. Liam's gaze lingered on her, but she couldn't decipher it. She frowned his way, and again he gave her another smoldering smile before turning to see to his own gear.

It didn't make her heart leap as Olt's smiles did, but Liam's attention was rather flattering, if she had to admit that to herself. Which she'd rather not.

She'd worked so hard, fought so long to prove herself—to be seen as his equal—to have any attention from him flattered her on a level she couldn't quite comprehend.

What was it about all the right things happening at the wrong time? Had her life been normal, had she not become a huntress and been forced to provide for herself and her family, she would've welcomed the attentions of two such handsome men, both good men.

But she was independent. Took care of herself. And she was determined to rely on no one else ever again.

Yet the question nagged at her: Could she accept, even pursue, love and keep her independence? Or would she simply be left for someone better suited for marriage, relationships, love…again?

It was confusing, disconcerting, and a problem she never even considered she'd have to face. Best to stuff it somewhere deep and ignore it. Forever.

Ro focused on her task: setting up camp. After she'd done all she could—leaving the cooking to Claude since he enjoyed it and Ro was bound to destroy any meals she touched—Ro made her way over to Olt.

Liam perked up, like all his senses went on alert. Ro knew the movement well enough to guess what he was doing. He would try to listen. And she'd make sure he didn't hear a thing.

She sat on a fallen log next to Olt as he messed with his tack. "Hey."

"Hey." He didn't look up.

She bumped his knee with hers. "Is everything all right? Are you all right?"

He still didn't look up, but his movements paused. He tried to say something, but hesitated.

"Olt? Talk to me. You're scaring me here."

This elicited a halfhearted grin. "Didn't know you cared."

Ro bumped him again, this time harder. "Hey. None of that now. You know I do. I *am* ready to dunk you in the nearest stream, however, if you don't start talking."

Olt laughed outright, as if trying to be his teasing self but couldn't quite manage it.

That got everyone else's attention. Especially Liam's. He

frowned, but Pascal grinned and Claude winked. Ro's face burned as if a thousand suns had heated it all at once.

If her brothers started making kissing faces, as they used to do when they were children and Ro would shyly talk to a certain lad at the market, Ro was going to kill them both. On the spot.

Olt chuckled again, then glanced at her. "No need to worry. All good."

Ro read his eyes in an instant. "Liar."

He ducked his head and offered nothing more.

"Know that I'm…here for you. If you need me."

He nodded without lifting his head, not saying another word.

Ro studied him as he fiddled with his tack—she didn't even know what he was trying to do with it—then stood and made her way to her own campsite for her small satchel of personal items.

She couldn't help Olt if he wouldn't let her.

As she dug through her pack, she steeled herself for the inevitable. She wasn't looking forward to wearing something soiled, since she'd been through all her clean clothing. But under what she'd packed—and used the last few weeks—she found clean clothes and more personal items.

Ro couldn't help her smile. Count on her sister to take care of Ro, even when consumed by her own daughter's needs.

It just made Ro love her all the more.

Ro marched toward the woods, soon stepping into thick foliage until camp was no longer visible. She stepped back through quickly, only to find Liam a few paces away, Olt watching after her anxiously, and her brothers looking completely oblivious. On purpose.

She pointed at all of them in a great, sweeping gesture. "Don't follow me. Any of you. I'll be back when I'm good and ready and not before."

Liam got that familiar obstinate look, the one that said he didn't like a particular decision Ro made, then settled in as if he would listen to her. Not likely.

Ro made her way back into the foliage, spending some time exploring the area before picking a friendly bush, then a spot near the stream to clean up. If Olt or Liam followed her, or Dieu forbid, her brothers, then heaven help them all.

She slipped off her red cape and hung it on a tree nearby.

&

Ro came back to camp much later, as the sun was beginning to disappear and paint their world dark, to find Olt pacing, her brothers gulping down food—typical—and Liam watching the forest with a calm expression.

A practiced calm.

He nodded at Ro, and Ro nodded back. She'd stayed close enough to ensure Liam could pick out her louder movements —ones she made on purpose to let him know she was still alive—but far enough away for some privacy.

She felt more herself for being away from people for a while. And being clean. That helped too.

Besides, Olt said the wolves waited to come out until after dark. Liam kept scanning the forest, not letting their impending emergence fall far from her mind.

Olt looked less and less like his confident, assured self, and he startled at nearly every noise, especially if it was a bird call. Which made absolutely no sense.

Ro watched him, hoping he would joke or tease or do anything else Olt-like, but he kept to himself. And didn't say another word for the rest of the night.

The rest of them ate, made plans for the next day, and one by one, curled up in their travel blankets or cloaks. Ro couldn't help but notice that Liam gave everyone a shift to watch over the camp—except Olt.

Claude woke her for the final shift before dawn.

Ro didn't think she'd be ready to wake so early, while the chill was still on the air, but her eyes opened what felt like seconds after she'd closed them, and she sat up, wakefulness streaming through her for the start of a new day. As well as deep satisfaction over a night spent in the forest.

Life as she knew and loved it.

She got up, wrapped her red cloak tighter around her, and followed Claude to the perimeter. Then he fell into his bedroll and didn't move. Ro grinned and scanned the forest, prowling around their camp in the near darkness.

She'd been so tired, she was out before the wolves had started howling, and they hadn't roused her. Interesting. It was hard to miss wolf calls while sleeping outside.

As if her thoughts had summoned them, something rustled nearby.

Ro froze.

Then something rustled on the opposite side.

They came from the direction of the village.

She slowly scanned the woods, her eyesight lighting everything slightly. Dark shadows, voids of light, slipped around their camp, coming close but not stepping one foot inside.

But she couldn't see them. Her eyesight wouldn't touch them. It was almost as if—they sucked in the light.

Adrenaline thrummed. Every muscle coiled tight. She rested her hand on her bow and readied herself to grab as many arrows as she needed.

But as if the dawn was driving them on, whatever they were slipped away, and it felt like the forest lightened at their absence.

She didn't know how long she stood there, motionless, but the world awakened on a sigh, and Liam stirred behind her.

He got up and touched her shoulder briefly before doing his own perimeter sweep.

Ro sat down on a stump, suddenly weary from standing there, muscles coiled tight, for who knew how long. She jumped when Liam touched her shoulder again.

She'd been focusing too hard on the forest in case the light wells came back.

Ro gave him a sheepish grin, which he returned before moving off. She stretched and yawned and bounced up, then fed and watered the horses while Liam got breakfast going. Ro started whistling, which soon roused her brothers. They got up with moans and groans and trailed off into the forest to take care of early morning business.

Normally, that was her, but maybe having time all to herself in the dark made a difference? She didn't know, but it was nice to be the morning person for once.

When they got back, they scarfed down the hot gruel Liam handed them and set about haphazardly throwing their things on their horses.

Pulling Fairweather forward, Ro glanced over her shoulder and faltered when she realized—Olt still hadn't woken up.

Liam looked at her, apparently the same thought on his mind, and tilted his head in Olt's direction, then went back to cleaning and packing up dishes and pots.

Guess it was up to her to wake him.

Ro dropped the reins, made her way to Olt's side of the fire, and shook him none too gently. "Olt, wake up. It's time to go."

He just curled tighter into his blankets. Ro glanced at the pot in Liam's hands, full of water from the stream, and Liam grinned and offered it to her. She sighed. He'd like that, wouldn't he?

"Olt, so help me, wake up right now or you are getting a full pot of water on your head. Seriously! How are the situations reversed? You're usually waking me up and all cheerful in the mornings."

Liam's smile died. Her brothers looked horrified—well, Pascal looked horrified, but Claude, just mildly surprised. She swallowed. Oops? Maybe she should've worded that differently. They'd spent close quarters on a ship. Then traveling. Not *together*.

She prodded Olt's side with her boot, not wanting to go near Liam with that look on his face. Or that pot of water in his hands. "Olt, I mean it. Get up."

He groaned and climbed out of his blankets, rubbing his face. Ro's eyes widened. Face pale, dark half-moons under his eyes, bloodshot eyes—as if he hadn't slept a wink.

He mumbled something and wandered off, Liam following just far enough behind to help if needed. Ro gave Liam a grateful look, which he didn't see. Or possibly ignored.

Something was wrong with Olt, and it was scaring her. And if something happened to him because she'd forced him to come, it would be entirely her fault.

13

*I*t was the morning after their fifth night in a forest that seemed to watch them, to confuse their trail, and to come alive at night. Ro kept the last watch before dawn, and the creatures passed their camp on either side each night. They came no closer, made no move.

But she felt their eyes on her.

And though no one had said so, they weren't the only ones watching Ro. No one had objected yet, but they were all thinking it. How much longer would Ro drag them through the woods, answering the call of a letter that could be false?

It felt like they were wandering endlessly, and Olt had withdrawn so far into himself, they could only get the occasional "just a little farther" out of him.

Ro felt the weight of their expectation, their doubt, and it was all she could do to remain calm. She knew she needed to be here, that it was Allura's only hope, but she wished she could explain what every fiber in her being told her: this was the correct path.

She needed the old woman to explain how she'd come to possess Ro's family Bible. How she knew the empress. If it was the *right* empress.

Weary, Ro trudged away from the campsite for her early morning cleansing ritual. She had plenty of time before they set out, and she was close enough to call for help. The wolves wouldn't be out till dark. And the shadow creatures had already passed by.

Ro hung her red cape on a dangling branch so it wouldn't get wet in the stream that always seemed to be near wherever they stopped for the night.

But first, her coffee mug needed cleansing. Then herself.

Ro scoured her mug with gritty sand from the bottom of the stream, then rinsed it in the cold water.

"Well, that's as clean as I'm getting that."

She scowled at the pottery her sister had included in her bag. It just wasn't practical. It wouldn't take much to shatter. And Liam's disgusting café left stains that no amount of sand could eradicate.

But it was so much better than her tin cup, and wrapping her hands around its warmth each morning and evening quite possibly made the added weight, bulk, and fragility worth it.

Her skin prickled. The hair on the back of her neck stood up. A twig snapped.

In one swift move, she released the mug into the stream, pulled an arrow, and fitted it to her bow.

She faced the noise. Nothing was there. She was alone.

Still, she kept her bow out and arrow ready, scanning the trees for movement.

Sounds came from camp, mostly her brothers teasing each other, trying to break the relentless tension that hounded them every step of the way, but nothing else presented itself to Ro.

Yet she was being watched. She was sure of it.

She held the arrow steady, trusting she was aiming in the right direction. Something was there. Something hunting her. She just couldn't see it. Couldn't sense it as she did other creatures. Her eyesight wouldn't touch it.

And the moment she called a warning, it would be upon her.

She focused wholly on the emptiness stalking her, whatever it was. Her travel mates needed to be warned. But she couldn't help them. Yet.

"Steady," she whispered to herself.

Her arms burned, adrenaline coursed through her blood, and she took a calming breath to aim true.

The thing raced toward her the same moment that there was a rush of movement toward the camp at her back.

"Wolves!" Ro called just as Olt cried, "Ro!"

The thing sprang from the bushes directly across from her, front paws spread, monstrous teeth aiming right for her face.

She moved the tip of her arrow to its heart and let it fly.

Swords being pulled from their scabbards rang out in the camp behind her.

The arrow buried itself deep in its chest, but still the wolf came at her, tongue lolling, a wicked doggy grin on its face.

It was unlike any wolf Ro had ever seen. Deep brown, mostly hairless, rippling muscle, hunched form—bright-silver eyes. And jumping as it was—taller than a man.

Just then, before she could dodge it, a bell toll sounded, shaking the forest around her and nearly throwing her from her feet. In her mind's eye, a giant clock ticked once more, backward. She stumbled back instead of to the side.

Her fingers brushed the fletching of the next arrow as the creature slammed into her. They both went down.

Ro screamed as the wolf sank its teeth into her shoulder and shook her.

"Ro!" Several voices called at once from the midst of their own battle.

She abandoned arrows for her long knives, but her left hand refused to grasp the handle. She raised the other knife and stabbed again and again, but the wolf wouldn't release her shoulder.

It just shook her and growled, saliva streaming everywhere.

Ro flopped like a homemade rag doll. She'd never felt so helpless. The overwhelming pain made her cry out, but still she stabbed.

Nothing. Her blades, her arrow, they did nothing. Meaty flesh squelched as it was impaled, but when she removed the knife, no wound marred its skin, no blood coated her knife.

What was this creature?

The sing of a blade near her head swept the air, and Ro flattened herself. It found its mark, and the wolf released her with a howl, gone before she could whip her head around to see what weapon had struck it.

She readied herself to fight again, but the other wolves in the bushes scattered, away from her. Away from their camp.

Ro scooched herself to a tree, pressed her back against it. It hurt to breathe. Grunting, she grasped her torn hem with her right hand and pulled. It didn't want to give.

She cursed well-made tunics and slashed out with her knife, then yanked again, this time getting a rip. She tore a long strip from the material that came to her thighs, each movement sheer agony.

Putting her knife between her teeth, she tried to wrap her shoulder. Sweat poured down her face at the effort, and she couldn't remember whimpering so much in her life.

She grumbled at herself for being so weak.

Growling, snarling, scampering came from a lone wolf nearby, in the direction that blade had come from.

The attack nearby faltered, that same singing noise driving the creature away. Ro frowned. What kind of weapon could make such a clear and distinct sound in the middle of such growls and cries?

"Find the huntress!" Liam bellowed, and they scattered— in the opposite direction.

Ro sighed. Of all the times not to remember she'd said she

was going to the stream. She paused. She'd told them she was going to the stream, hadn't she?

She fumbled again with the strip, but she just couldn't make it work. Giving up, she pressed it to the wound. Hopefully the bleeding wasn't too bad on the back.

Her senses prickled, and she dropped the cloth. Retrieved the knife from her teeth. Tried again to grasp her second long knife. She couldn't.

The wolf must have damaged nerves.

She pushed to her feet, using the tree for support, gritting her teeth to bite back a cry of pain. Her eyes took in the scattered arrows and bow. She couldn't use them if she wanted to. The knife would have to be enough.

She reached out with her senses to find where the attack would come from, but she stilled. Something was different. It was focused elsewhere.

Keeping her back to the tree, she rounded it and found an axe buried deep.

And on the ground, in a little clearing, a little old woman lay on her back, weaponless, as a wolf took slow, steady steps in her direction.

And smiled with every step.

Its shoulder had been hacked into, the hairless skin gaping open, dark blood dripping on the forest floor. A curl of steam rose from each drop, whether from extreme heat or something acidic, Ro couldn't tell.

It paused. Pranced a little. Readied itself to leap, its grin stretching wider.

Then it leaped.

No weak, helpless little old lady was going to be killed on her watch!

Ro dropped her knife, spun toward the axe. Ripped it from the tree with a well-timed spin and a surge of strength and sent it hurling toward the wolf in one smooth motion.

It buried itself deep in the wolf's skull, and the force of it slammed the wolf to the side.

Unlike her weapons, the axe worked. The wolf crumpled in a heap and lay still.

Ro rushed to the old woman, holding her own shoulder against the blood drenching her clothes in an ever-widening circle.

She held out her hand anyway, not really noticing how much blood coated it. "Here, let me help you. Are you well, Madame?"

The old woman slapped Ro's outstretched hand away, eyes blazing, and wobbled to her feet. "I had it, fool girl!"

Ro's mouth dropped open. "I just saved your life!"

Finally, the old woman settled on her feet, and she raised her chin a notch. "You could've ruined everything. Everything!"

Oh, that was quite enough of that. "What, were you going to wait till he gobbled you all up and I had to cut you from his stomach?"

The old woman heaved the axe from the wolf's head and settled it over her shoulder. "Been listening to children's stories, have you?" She snorted. "Such creatures haven't breached our world. Yet."

Ro's retort died as she tried to come up with a response to *that*, but everything was going hazy. She glanced to her throbbing shoulder. Maybe it was the lack of blood?

The old woman's gaze rested on Ro's wound. She sighed, deep and heavy, as if Ro's injury was a major inconvenience. "I suppose you'll want help stitching that up?"

Ro stretched to her full height, which was considerably taller than the old woman's shriveled frame. "I would rather die."

The old woman rolled her eyes. "Rather dramatic, you are. Very well. Come."

And she grabbed Ro's uninjured arm and started dragging

Ro behind her—in the opposite direction from camp. She had the grip of a mule. Or maybe the stubbornness of one.

"Who are you?" Ro demanded, trying to pull away and hold her shoulder at the same time.

"Never mind that now." Her eyes seemed to memorize Ro's face. "Come. The Black Forest is no place for clueless wanderers."

Ro stiffened, starting to object, but the woman cut her off with a sharp hand gesture.

"Not here. The woods be full of things much worse than wolves."

Ro's eyes widened, and she shot a quick glance behind her, her eyes coming to rest on the spot where a dead wolf should have lain.

It was gone. Only a faint outline remained.

Ro gasped, and the old woman answered Ro's questions before she could voice them.

"The creatures return from whence they came and regenerate anew. When they intrude once again upon my forest, they bring with them many more besides. And that, O foolish girl, is why we do not kill the wolves in this forest. We must send them back in such a way that they cannot regenerate nor return." She turned just enough to give Ro a solid glare. "And that is why I said I had it handled. Next time, listen."

Ro blustered, unable to get a word past her lips, and the woman once again started dragging Ro away.

"Wait! My huntsmen…"

The old woman spun on her. "Huntsmen? You brought huntsmen into my forest?"

Ro hedged. Well, one, besides herself, but was that a bad thing or a good thing?

Thankfully, Liam and Olt chose that exact moment to burst into their little clearing.

"Ro!" Olt was at her side in an instant.

Liam forced her to the ground. "You've lost a lot of blood.

Here, lie down. Heart level with the rest of you. Olt? Pressure here."

Olt was already putting pressure there.

Liam grunted. Ro's brothers burst through the trees. Claude looked a little faint; Pascal looked as if he might be getting choked up.

Liam turned to Pascal, whose face had gone considerably pale. "My pack. Immediately."

Pascal took off running. Claude followed a moment later, and Ro hissed as Olt also applied pressure to her shoulder blade.

The old woman propped her fists on her ample hips, a move Ro could barely take in through the haze of pain. "Well, they're not huntsmen, but they're swift to act."

Liam gave her a cursory glance as he tore Ro's tunic away from her shoulder, revealing puckered and torn skin and entirely too much blood.

Ro groaned and dropped her head back. There was nothing glamorous about being wounded. Just pain, misery, and extreme embarrassment. How had she let this happen?

As if time skipped, Pascal was back with Liam's pack; Claude with a handful of packs. "The horses bolted," he said. "I brought what we hadn't tied to the horses yet."

"Never you mind that," the old woman said. Her eyes pierced Ro's haze of misery. "You got a Black Forest horse with you?"

Ro frowned as Olt answered in the affirmative. How could she know—?

"Then he'll lead 'em to my place. If they ain't all ate up already. Don't you worry about that now."

Olt propped her up a little, and Ro hissed, forgetting what she was about to say.

"Ro, bite this." Liam placed something hard and leathery between her teeth. His belt.

She did.

And bit down harder around a scream of pain as Liam poured whatever alcohol he kept in his pack all over her wound.

Ro promptly passed out.

❧

Ro came to in a bed. Wasn't she just in the woods? Her fingers grasped scratchy wool blankets. Voices hummed in the background, low and respectful. But all male.

She peeled her eyes open and squinted up at a wood ceiling. Plank walls, and…it hurt too much to look further.

She closed her eyes and let memories stream through her.

Had she really passed out like a wee babe?

Some huntress she was.

"Well? Are you awake? Or are you just going to lie there and pretend to be asleep all day?"

Ro cracked an eye open to find the old woman standing over her and scowling. Frizzy gray hair sprang up all around her head like a frazzled halo, a long silver braid draped over one shoulder like a sturdy rope coming out of a cloud, and her skin was leathery and wrinkled like, well, a piece of leather someone had neglected…for a long time.

A little fire trickled into Ro. She pointed at her shoulder. "Wounded. Remember?"

The old woman snorted. "Hogwash." And ripped the blanket from Ro.

She gasped as freezing air rushed over her.

The male voices in the room went silent. Ro panicked. What was she wearing?

Her head shot up, and she winced against the wash of pain. Same pants, different shirt—smelled like Olt's—boots on, completely covered. She let her head fall back with a sigh. Thank Dieu.

She shivered as panic filled her once more. Her cape! Her

mère's red cape! The last thing she had to remember her by. And she'd left it dangling off some tree!

Before she could ask about it, the old woman pulled her up—she was uncannily strong—and swung Ro's feet out over the edge of the bed. "There we are. Now we can be of some use around here. Earn your keep."

"She is wounded, Grandmère," Claude said kindly, calling her the respectful "grandmother" most young men used for their elders, whether related or not.

Ro wouldn't have been so respectful.

"Posh. We can rest when we're dead. She needs to be active to get that wound healing."

Ro gritted her teeth as she was hauled from the bed. She rather thought this one required rest and hoped to promptly pass back out. On the bed.

She had no doubt the old woman would simply leave her sprawled on the floor should she faint now.

The old woman seemed to read her thoughts. She grinned a little. "Believe me. These wounds only get worse with inactivity. You need to work the poison out."

Ro's eyebrows climbed her forehead. "Poison? What poison? It was a wolf, not some rabid creature."

Then again, it was unlike any wolf Ro had ever seen…

The old lady rapped her hand with the handle of a wooden cane Ro hadn't noticed she carried. "Watch your sass, young miss. Do as I say, and no backtalk."

Ro yelped and jerked her hand back. Who was this demon they'd found in the forest, and could they put her back?

"What do you say to your elders?"

Ro blinked. The old woman waited.

"Ah, um, oui, Madame?"

"In English. You are Frenchmen in Germany. Well, most of ye are, anyway. Speak the common tongue."

Ro gritted her teeth. Her English wasn't spectacular. "Yes, ma'am."

"Good. Now, you can help me around here."

Ro kind of wanted to scream. Instead, she walked the few steps to the fireplace and huddled close. She was going to get warm first, then she'd help.

The fire wasn't big enough to break the chill of the room.

She shivered again and glanced around her. Such a tiny cabin. Seriously, how did they all fit? The rest of her group watched her with concern, but not one of them objected to anything the old woman said or did. Ro would've been mad about that if she wasn't so cold. A chill wracked her body.

Olt and Liam moved as one toward her pack along the wall, but Olt got there first. He pulled out Ro's red cape and settled it gently around her shoulders.

Ro relaxed as its warmth surrounded her, and clutched the fabric as emotion welled in her. She hadn't lost it.

Olt stepped back—as far as he could go in the small space—and the old woman's eyes riveted on Ro's cape. Her lips tightened, and her voice came out on a whisper. "Where did you get that?"

A little unsettled by her reaction, Ro's voice came out uncertain. "It was my mère's?"

"Your mère's?" Her watery eyes flew to Ro's, and Ro tried not to cringe, she really did. But the hag was just so homely. She snapped gnarled fingers in Ro's face. "Her name, girl. What was her name?"

Ro couldn't help her jump, and she grumbled at herself for it. She hesitated giving the old woman her mère's name, but what could it hurt?

"Jacqueline Rose Reynard."

Now the old woman wobbled on her feet, but Ro was afraid to steady her. Would she take a swing at Ro or thank her?

"Her maiden name, fool girl!" Although the words were sharp, the tone was hoarse, and Ro wondered if the old mother were about to faint.

"LeFèvre."

Now the old woman sat down, hard, on a split-log stool directly behind her. "Jacqueline Rose LeFèvre."

"Oui, as I have said." Ro couldn't help adding, "What's it to you? Did you…know her?"

The questions reminded Ro of…something…one of the reasons she was here, but her befuddled mind couldn't quite grasp it.

Instead of answering, the old woman toddled to her feet and headed toward an old iron cookstove. The oven looked large enough for a child to play hide-and-seek in.

How on earth had they gotten something so monstrous through a forest their horses could hardly pass through?

Not important right now.

Ro snuggled deeper into the red fabric, crossing her legs and seating herself on the floor. She was done with mysteries. If the old woman didn't want to tell her what the red cape meant to her, that was fine by her.

She tried to pull warmth from it, as she'd always been able to do no matter how cold it was, but it wasn't enough. "Can we please build up the fire? It's freezing." Ro caught a few exchanged glances. "What?" she demanded.

That's when she noticed the sweat on Olt's upper lip. Her eyes flew to his.

He gave her a kind, though concerned, smile. "Ro, we'd have the fire out and the windows open if we could. It's overly warm in here."

Her eyes flew around the room, the other men's discomfort apparent. "Ah, désolé."

The old woman stirred something in a giant pot. "It's just the poison flooding your system. You'll warm as it leaves." She flicked a glance at Ro. "If you want to build the fire, go get more firewood."

Ro's mouth fell open. Was she serious? All she wanted to do was fall back in bed!

Claude and Pascal moved toward the door.

The old woman spun on them, spoon pointed threateningly their way. "Not one more step! If I say she'll get firewood, then she'll get firewood." She turned to Ro. "Now, shoo! Off with you! You'll find it in a pile at the back of the house."

Ro looked from her arm tied to her chest to the old woman and again to her arm. "But, how…?"

"Bring it in one log at a time, for all I care. Just fill the woodbox."

Ro's eyes fell on the crate by the door. It dwarfed the fireplace. She rose to her feet and wobbled over to it, then lifted the lid and peeked within. A giant crater waited to be filled. "Are you kidding me?"

The spoon came Ro's way, and she ducked out the door. She stumbled down the steps, then stomped toward the back of the small cabin.

Some group of strong, handsome warriors she had. They were so scared of the little old lady, they hadn't even defended Ro.

Not that she'd defended herself, but still.

She found the firewood, tried to pick up more than one, and ended up dropping them all with the use of only one arm. Gritting her teeth, she grabbed one log and marched back around the house. This was going to take all day!

The face of the little cabin came into view, and she stumbled to a halt with a gasp. It was beautiful!

Tucked into a perfectly circular clearing, the forest seemed to keep its distance, but that only served to make it all the more beautiful. Constructed simply but with a decidedly German flair, its whitewashed walls were crisscrossed with dark-brown planks.

Embellishments were carved into the shutters and front door—the front door! Ro leaned closer to admire the intricately carved wood, glossy and rich.

Two children skipped through the forest, baskets swinging, a smiling father watching them while he swung an axe — seriously dangerous — as they skipped toward an old woman who had a long, beakish nose with an exaggerated hook and wart. She handed them candy from a cabin strikingly similar to this one.

How did an entire story fit on a door? And who was the master carver? The story had come to life under his touch.

Ice crept back into her veins, and Ro jumped forward and opened the door, suddenly irrationally afraid that if she stopped moving for long, she'd freeze solid.

The old woman shot her a quelling look, then her gaze slid down to Ro's one hapless, pathetic log. She sniffed.

Ro glared and tried to wedge open the woodbox to drop it in. Liam, who was now smoking a pipe, stretched forward and opened it for her.

Ro flushed, dropped in her measly little log, and headed back outside.

And so she spent the rest of her afternoon, till stew was ready, filling up that stupid box one log at a time.

14

Olt hung up her cape for her, and Ro fell to the stew with all the grace of a dog, ravenously hungry. The bread, the stew—it was almost more than she could take. She'd never been so hungry, never tasted food this good.

She stuffed in bite after bite, and stew spilled down her chin and onto her leather jerkin and white blouse as she took bites bigger than her mouth could handle. She couldn't get it in fast enough.

Four of them had squeezed at the little table meant for two, while Claude stood and Pascal sat in the rocking chair. The old woman took turns serving and sitting at her little table, its surface straining to hold four bowls and a loaf of bread.

Ro's spoon hit the bottom of her bowl. She scowled at it. How could it be empty already?

The old woman reached to take it, but Ro snarled and snapped her teeth at her.

All movement in the room froze.

Well, except for the old woman's. She calmly rapped Ro's knuckles and took her bowl to the stove to fill it.

Ro's face filled with heat, and she grabbed her cloth

138

napkin, wiped her face, and dabbed at her shirt, wishing she could melt into the deepening dusk and they could all forget they knew her.

"Oh! Oh, I have no idea what came over me—I am so sorry."

Her rushed apology did nothing to wipe the concern—the fear—off her companions' faces.

She didn't blame them. It was pounding within her own heart.

The old woman set the bowl before her, and Ro forgot everything as she dug back in, the call of more food too much to resist.

It was a while before anyone joined her, but they didn't stop watching her.

Ro felt their stares, but she didn't care. All she cared about was stew. Carrots. Potatoes. Hunks of *meat*.

The old woman replaced her bread, and Ro attacked it.

"Madame, is she…well?" Liam's hushed voice did nothing to dissuade her as she tore apart bread with her teeth, to slurp the stew, now using her hands, her tongue.

The old woman sounded bored. "Oh, she'll have a few of the wolf's characteristics until she fully heals. It'll be worse at night. But don't worry. I've seen this before, and as soon as she's fed, I'll get the rest of the poison out of her before it can taint her permanently."

"As soon as she's *fed*? What does that even mean?"

Pascal sounded panicked, but Ro couldn't imagine why. Why were they talking? Why weren't they all devouring this glorious meal alongside her? Flavors exploded on her tongue, each one divine.

Much better than the tasteless gruel they'd consumed on the way here.

"Do not worry yourself, young man. It will pass, and she will be herself again. Tomorrow ere the sun rises, or I'm not the protectress of this forest."

"What do you mean by permanently?" came Liam's quiet voice again.

Liam reached for his drink as he awaited an answer, and Ro snapped her teeth at him and hunched over her bowl, turning herself and it slightly away.

His startled look didn't even bother her.

"You are certain she will return to normal on the morrow?" Liam questioned.

The old woman shrugged. "Certain as I'll ever be."

"Bon." Liam finished taking a drink and set it back down.

Ro growled and moved her bowl as far away as she could manage on the small surface.

He watched Ro, his expression guarded. "Because if she is not, protectress, you will answer to me."

Olt bristled at that.

Ro couldn't make herself care. Or be annoyed. As she should've been, she knew. It just didn't seem to matter.

The old woman cackled, sloshing her drink over the rim. "Ooh, I like you! Brains *and* beauty." She cackled some more, then leaned forward.

Ro jerked away.

"You have my word, General. Your huntress will be her miserable self come morn."

Ro picked up her bowl and licked the bottom. Why was it empty again?

❧

Ro sagged, regretting everything about last night.

Not the food. Non, she'd had several more bowls, until her belly was a soft mound and she had to loosen her jerkin, but she was still ravenous. The old woman had finally cut her off and forced her outside, under full moonlight.

Ro had never felt so alive.

Then the old woman had begun training exercises, making her run, spar, fight, crawl. Anything and everything Ro did to stay fit and more. She hadn't even noticed when her bandage had fallen off, letting the moon shine full upon her creamy-pale skin.

The edges of the wound had started to close, whether from her unusual healing ability or the moonlight, Ro wasn't certain. She'd just felt better bathed in the moon's glow.

The old woman hadn't let Ro stop once.

The others had watched out the little cabin windows in turns, but their host had been most clear that not one of them was to set foot outside until the sun was at its apex, shining full and straight down into the clearing.

Now that it was midday, Ro could feel their restless movements inside. They wanted to be outside as much as she wanted to rest. As much as she wanted to eat—but not like a ravenous woodland creature this time.

The dawn brought relief to most of her cravings, but it wasn't until the sun hit her full-on, rested above her, that she felt them melt away.

Now Ro sagged against the rail as she guzzled water, dumped a bucketful over her head, then guzzled again.

She checked her wound. It was still puckered, still sore, and still pulled when she moved, but it was nowhere near as painful as last night.

Ro felt someone behind her. She put her head down. Fiddled with her bucket. "Was last night really as awful as I remember?"

"Worse," Pascal said with a chuckle. "You all right, sis?"

Ro swiped at her streaming-wet face, hating how ridiculously close to tears she was. "I think I am. Now."

"Your shoulder—how is it?"

She flicked a glance at the angry, puckered welts, then rolled her shoulder. It twinged, but she had full range of motion. Somehow.

She shrugged, feeling the uncomfortable pull. "Fine, I guess."

The woman insisted she was fine, anyway. She might have phantom pain, but that was all.

It would have killed her had she stopped moving for too long last night, or so the old woman had said. According to her, the moonlight burned off the poison from her skin as it churned through her system with activity, then the sunlight finished it off.

Ro couldn't even argue—she knew nothing about those wolves, this forest, or the crazy old lady.

"Is she—is she asleep?" Ro asked.

Pascal chuckled. "Out like a candle. She didn't bother to shoo us out or anything. Just nudged Claude out of the bed and fell into it." His voice turned more serious. "But I'm more concerned about you."

Ro lifted her head and looked at him. He studied her face a moment, then opened his arms. Ro dropped the bucket and walked into them, burying her face in his shoulder and bursting into tears.

She wasn't a loud crier. Nor a demonstrative one. Silent tears tracked down her face, and she let them all out with quiet, shuddering breaths, her brother holding her until they were spent.

She was glad it wasn't Claude. He'd tease or tweak her short dark queue or dunk her in the well to get her mind off her woes. Claude didn't handle emotions so well.

"I've never been so embarrassed in all my life." Ro's voice came out on a pathetic wail she couldn't help. That didn't even touch how she felt about last night, but she couldn't put it all into words. It was too awful.

Pascal pulled back, eyebrows high. "Oh really? Worse than Lynette or Nicolette throwing themselves at all those noblemen who were *not* interested? Making fools of themselves at every ball across Paris?"

Ro allowed herself a small smile. "You forget Cosette and I were too young to participate. We watched from the banisters above and laughed."

"What about when Reinette was asked to play the pianoforte for our guests, but she forgot her lessons and couldn't make two notes go together? Then Yvette tried to save her by singing, but she ended up crying instead, and they both ran from the room to the laughter of our guests?"

Ro couldn't help her grin, though it was rather weak. "You forget I was the one who started the laughter, even though Cosette did everything she could to shush me."

"All right, then." He folded his arms, thought a moment. "Worse than Bernadette making fun of all the stories you wrote when you tried to read them to us in the garden?"

Ro flushed, but with anger. "I was young, and my stories were ridiculous, but she had no right."

"Even if she was correct?"

Heat flamed on Ro's face, and she took a step toward her brother. She didn't even know her fists were raised until he laughed and caught them in strong hands.

He tweaked her nose. "And there's my sister. Good to see you again, ma sœur. Now, if you will please calm Olt about your well-being, Liam might not kill him. His pacing is driving us all mad."

She glanced to the little cabin. Olt stood on the porch, one hand on a support to the deck, watching them. She could feel his tension all the way across the yard.

All her memories from last night came flooding back, and she turned away. "I can't…"

Pascal groaned. "If you don't, I'm going home. I'd rather take my wife's endless requests to improve our house than his worrying, especially after all that moodiness on the way here." He pointed toward the porch. "Go. Talk to your Olt. He's unbearable when he's worried about you."

Ro grumbled as Pascal prodded her toward the cabin. "He's not *my* Olt…"

How many times did she have to say that before anyone believed her? Including herself.

She stayed on the ground, below the three steps leading up to the porch, as Pascal passed her for the front door. She watched him go, avoiding looking at Olt for as long as possible.

Pascal winked at her before he went inside, and her face flushed and her eyes flew to Olt's to check if he'd seen.

Olt looked like he was ready to jump off the porch and wrap her in his arms.

She couldn't have that. She backed up a step and stammered out, "So, um, Pascal said, um, are you well?"

"Am I well?" He rubbed his hands over his face, and his eyes came away red rimmed. "I think the better question is if *you* are."

Ro ducked her head and scuffed her boot on the hardy grass. "Oui. Embarrassed, but well."

"What *was* that? I've never seen anything like it."

Ro shook her head. "I have no idea. I just hope it never happens again."

"You and me both."

Still Olt didn't move toward her. He watched her as though he was concerned at any moment she would shatter, but at least he wasn't trying to kiss her or hold her or do anything else to damage her fragile nerves.

Ro blushed at the thought and glanced away. "Um, I'm starving, so…"

Olt jumped toward the front door. "I'll make breakfast." And he was gone.

Ro stared after him, mouth ajar. Was he—was he scared she'd tear him to pieces if she didn't get food fast enough?

She huffed and marched back into the yard. Well, he needn't worry!

Ro picked up the staff the old woman had smacked her with again and again, whenever she'd started to falter or wanted to give up and go to sleep right there, standing.

She wasn't used to a staff, but its weight felt right in her hands. Ro began twirling it as a blush stained her cheeks. Did she really have to act like a starving wolf in front of them all?

With a yell, she brought the staff around in a wide, sweeping arc, stopping it inches above the ground. Then spun it the other way. Then twirled it side to side till it was a blur.

Her muscles burned, sweat coated her, yet she pushed herself harder. She wasn't going to think about what had happened, and she wasn't going to stop until exhaustion pushed her to sleep.

If only she could make herself forget.

&

Olt stopped her to eat. She ate normally, even slower than normal, actually, as every male in the room watched her every move, then she wrapped herself in her cloak and fell asleep sitting in the corner.

When she woke, the old woman was still sleeping, so she slipped outside, guzzled water, nodded to Liam and Claude, who had their own weapons out and were sparring, and grasped the staff once more.

She whacked herself a few times before she found her rhythm, but soon she and the staff were caught in an intricate dance as it taught her its moves.

Ro felt someone watching—besides the occasional glances of her companions, all of whom were outside with her—and turned to the porch.

The old woman, eyes gleaming, gave Ro a firm nod. "I taught you well, if I do say so myself."

Ro couldn't believe the woman's audacity. All she'd done last night was hit Ro! It was all she could do to defend herself. Besides, Ro had plenty of weapons training on her own.

Taught her well, indeed.

The old woman jerked her head toward the house. "There's warm water on the stove and a shallow tub in the shed. You're welcome to bathe."

Ro barked a laugh. "Let me guess: If I draw it myself?"

She grinned. "You're catching on to how things are done around here."

The old woman hobbled back inside. Ro gritted her teeth and nearly decided not to bathe, but then she moved and caught a whiff of herself.

Oui, she was bathing.

She marched toward the house, slung her bag with a change of clothes over her shoulder, and heaved the heavy pot of water off the stove with the two thick wedges of cloth the old woman kept there for that purpose.

She growled as she strained to lift it. Her shoulder protested, and her muscles reminded her they'd taken a beating, but she forced herself to lug it out the door and around the house to the shed.

She was going to get clean if it killed her.

"Don't forget to hang the sheet over the window! I don't run a peep show around here."

Ro froze as the woman's words washed over her—in front of the men.

Liam barked a laugh, Pascal and Claude made gagging noises that devolved into laughter, and the old woman turned away with a smile. Olt was the only one not in Ro's periphery, and she wasn't about to turn and find out his reaction.

She resumed her trek, sprinkling muttered curses every few steps. How quickly could they leave this place—and that awful woman—behind?

<h1 style="text-align:center">15</h1>

The old woman loudly sniffed the air at Ro's return. "You smell better, I'll give you that."

Mortified, Ro went beet red, heat washing from her head to her toes. Claude and Pascal took one look at each other and burst into laughter. Olt turned away and rubbed his face, and Liam looked down at the table's surface with a smile.

Yep. Ro was going to kill her.

"Come," the old woman told them as Ro took a step toward her. "You must learn something of this wood."

Ro tried to rein in her anger, but it was kind of hard to do with her brothers' mirth. They were hanging off each other now, tears streaming down their faces.

"But my niece, Allura—that's why we've come…"

The old woman cut Ro off mid-sentence. "We'll get to that. For now, a walk is in order."

Ro's mouth fell open as the old woman marched over, uncovered her own red cloak buried under some furs that should've been stored away for winter, and toddled out into the day.

Fury started to stoke a fire within Ro. Could the old

protectress not listen to her for half a heartbeat? She didn't have time to take a leisurely stroll through the forest. She needed to break the sleeping curse and get her niece back. For Cosette.

Plus she needed to find out why the old woman had sent the title page to Ro's family Bible, and why they had matching capes. How she knew Ro's mère, for that matter.

She couldn't be delayed a moment longer!

Liam spoke quietly from nearby. "I think this relates, huntress. Don't discount her too quickly."

Ro met his eyes. At his concerned look, she took a deep breath and gave him a steady nod. She could be civil. She could.

As the huntsman moved to follow, Claude and Pascal, mimicking Ro from the other night, snarled and kept pretend-food away from her and each other.

Ro rolled her eyes. Apparently they'd given her time to recover and had moved on to teasing her relentlessly. No doubt they'd keep all their sisters and their husbands entertained for the rest of their lives with that bit.

They traipsed after Liam and the old woman, each trying to outdo the other.

Olt came right next to her and stopped. "She's something, isn't she?"

His grin was a welcome sight.

"Does she live up to all the stories you heard about her as a child?" Ro asked.

His light expression held some of the carefreeness from before. "Even better."

Ro gave him a tentative smile. "For your sake, I'm glad. For mine…well, I might just get lost in these woods. On purpose."

Her words wiped away his smile as effectively as if she'd shot it down with one of her arrows. He stepped close, touched her shoulder briefly, as if to reassure himself of her safety. "Please…don't. Stay close to the old protectress. Do as she says."

Ro frowned. "D'accord…" She tilted her head. "Aren't you coming with us?"

He ducked his head and shuffled his feet. "Ah, well, not yet."

The familiar frustration started to build. "Olt, you said…"

"And I will." He attempted a smile, but it fell flat. "When it's time, I will. For now"—he glanced around the little cabin—"I'm going to straighten up in here."

Straighten up? The old woman had barely anything but the basics, and those were neat as a pin, if worn.

She studied his face. "Will you be here when I get back?"

A look came over him, as if he might kiss her again, and Ro shied away. He stretched one hand toward her face, and Ro went still.

Just when she thought he was going to cup her cheek, draw her closer, maybe unleash that devilish promise in his eyes, he tucked a few strands of loose hair behind the shell of her ear and trailed his fingers briefly down her jaw.

Heat instantly seared Ro's insides, burning low in her belly. What was it about him that could do such a thing to her? And was it more than attraction? Attraction she could deal with, shove away. Like with Liam. If it were something more…

"Aye. I'll be here, huntress."

Ro blinked, having forgotten she was waiting for his answer. She nodded, backed away. "Bon."

Then she fled.

❧

Her head came up as she neared the trees. Liam stood there, watching with arms crossed. The old woman leaned on her staff, eyeing the forest, seemingly in no hurry at all.

Claude snickered and elbowed Pascal, making some joke Ro couldn't hear, and Pascal frowned a little, though it lacked the ferocity of Liam's scowl.

Ro gestured toward the forest, the movement pulling at her shoulder. She hissed and clamped her hand over it. The pain was sharper than it had been before her nap. Perhaps she'd strained it?

Apparently something in the wolf's bite slowed her healing ability.

Besides, she hated wounds that looked like nothing but made her appear a weakling. Like cuts from the pages of books when one was reading a bit too enthusiastically.

Something that happened to her far too often.

She bit out, "Well? Are we going?"

The old woman snatched up her walking staff with a half-smile. Without another word, the protectress turned and plunged into the trees.

Her brothers took a moment to eye each other, and at Pascal's shrug, they followed. Liam waited for Ro. The moment she reached him, he fell into step beside her.

Ro glanced back just before the forest swallowed her.

Olt stood on the porch, and her eyesight flared, just for a moment, giving her a clear view of the fear on his face. But he wasn't looking at her. He was staring at the forest as if it might come alive and eat him.

What was Olt hiding, and why wouldn't he just tell her what was going on already?

Ro stumbled a little, and Liam righted her, then kept walking.

She grumbled to herself.

The old woman spun on her so quickly, Ro almost fell over her as her brothers stepped to either side.

"You call yourself a huntress?" she hissed. "Keep your grumbling to yourself!"

Ro blinked. She thought she had.

And then the woman took off like a crossbow bolt, and Ro grumbled—inside, of course—and hurried after her.

§

It didn't take Ro long to realize they followed a well-worn path, almost invisible in the forest's undergrowth. Yet as she followed the old woman, it opened to her like an old friend welcoming her to its secrets.

That would've been nice the five days they'd struggled through the nearly unsurpassable old wood.

They came to a particularly thick copse of trees and stopped.

The old woman nodded toward their right. "Just past there is where the kingdom of Prussia begins. Now up here. Climb."

They blended in well with vines covering them, but a system of ropes and pieces of wood strategically placed all over the massive tree made for easy climbing. Ro grinned. It had been years since she'd visited her own treehouse, her sanctuary as a child.

Claude and Pascal came up on either side of her.

Claude's grin was as wide as her own. "Nice."

Pascal eyed the system in appreciation. "I might have to take notes."

Claude chortled. "What, because you're going to build yourself a treehouse? Going to invite your fellow soldiers up for afternoon café and macarons?"

Ro turned her grin upon her brother and stilled. His face was a little flushed, but he looked more pleased than embarrassed, his eyes shining.

Ro bit her lip, not sure what it meant.

Claude's mouth fell open, then he slapped his brother's shoulder, nearly sending him headfirst into the tree. "You old rascal, you. Why didn't you tell anyone?"

Pascal's smile nearly split his face. "We weren't going to say anything until…later. When the danger had passed."

Ro tilted her head, but Claude grunted like he understood. "I hope it works out for you both this time, mon frère."

He clapped his brother's shoulder again, but before Ro could say anything, he moved toward the tree, and Pascal followed.

Was Pascal's wife…pregnant? And how could she ever find the right words to ask such a personal thing?

"Well, what are you all waiting for? Up the tree!"

The old woman rapped Ro's calf with her staff, and Ro spun on her. The old woman just poked her in the stomach, prodding her closer to the tree.

Truly, it only stung a little, but Ro *hated* to be punished. Especially if she hadn't done anything wrong.

"I can't show you the rest if you ain't up there."

Ro gritted her teeth and made herself climb, hoping she'd get a chance to talk to Pascal later. She'd missed so much in her family's lives while away, hunting magical creatures.

Although Ro thrilled at the rough bark under her fingers and the familiar sensation of scaling a tree, tightness gripped her stomach and squeezed. Curse the mast that had splintered under her and given her this new fear of heights!

And the pain growing in her shoulder wasn't helping. Wasn't that supposed to be mostly healed now? Yet spikes of new agony reached down her shoulder blade and tightened her stomach. She took deep breaths and kept climbing. She could do this.

The tree wasn't going to fall out from under her, after all.

She hoped.

Liam followed her, off to the side to be respectful, but close enough to grab her should she slip. Ro gritted her teeth and climbed, forcing herself to use both hands, no matter how much her shoulder protested.

Dizziness swamped her, and she paused and leaned against the tree.

Liam was next to her in an instant, his hand at her back.

Curse those wolves! How long until she could fight? How long until she could use her bow again? She couldn't be wounded. Not when Allura needed her.

Taking deep breaths until her racing heart calmed, she finally nodded at Liam. Yet he didn't move from her side as she resumed climbing.

They came to a layer of boards wedged between a split trunk, and the five of them squeezed onto the boards, lying next to each other.

The old woman grunted. "Thank the good Lord that boy stayed behind. I thought ye'd all fit, but boy was I wrong."

Liam gently lowered himself beside Ro, careful not to bump her shoulder.

The old woman passed a spyglass down the line. "If ye look due northeast, you'll find a dark-green tower rising above the trees. See it yet?"

Pascal shook his head. "I don't. Désolé."

He started to pass the spyglass to Claude, but Ro plucked it from his fingers and brought it to her eye. She gasped as the distance fell away, and her eye was drawn to a pagoda-type building from East Asia, China specifically, elaborate decorations and squat stone birds decorating its roof.

"What do you see, huntress?" Liam asked in a low voice.

Wordlessly, she handed him the spyglass and looked to the old woman for an explanation.

She happily obliged. "The Kingdom of Prussia is but one of a group of warring kingdoms, all trying to rule the other. It's the largest, and its king and queen often oversaw the others, settling disputes and the like. They've been talking about uniting into one country for years now."

She nodded toward the foreign building.

"About six years ago, complete silence. From all of them.

There, the king, an emperor over the rest of the nobles who called themselves kings, was a kind and generous and boisterous ruler. All who knew him loved him, and he held his people's loyalty."

Liam shifted beside her, his side and thigh to hers, and Ro couldn't help wishing Olt were there instead.

And she was being ridiculous. Again.

"After the kingdoms went silent, this fell tower loomed over the land. Do you see the forest surrounding it?"

Before she could ask, Liam handed Ro the spyglass. Ro turned to thank him, and his face was inches from hers. Her smile fled and she snatched up the spyglass to her eye.

Scanning the area, she gasped again. "Why, the trees are all shriveled and blackened and dead looking, just like how France used to look!"

She turned her gaze to the old woman.

She nodded sagely. "Rumor has it that a sorceress has moved in from a foreign land. See there? Her pagoda lies where the emperor's palace used to be. You can just see the crumble of stones at its base. I've sent word to her people, asking for information, but the good Lord knows how hard it is to get a response of any kind from the Forbidden City."

Ro didn't know, actually. Her tutors were long gone by the time she would've learned such things. Every foreign country had been cut off from her for most of her life. Her education had been focused on surviving.

Which was why she'd read every book she could get her hands on.

Ro asked, "And this is the sorceress who cursed Allura? The one who calls herself the empress? Is it the same woman?" At her nod, Ro asked, "How do you know?"

The old woman gave Ro a wink. "I have an inkling."

Ro's mouth fell open. "You mean you don't *know*? Haven't you investigated?"

She shot Ro a disgruntled look. "I can't get close to it.

Something tells me you might. Besides, my hunches have never led me astray before, huntress. Just you remember that."

Ro gave her the side-eye. She didn't know the woman well enough to put that kind of faith in her.

"Besides." The old woman shrugged. "Rumor has it that this one hands out sleeping curses, and the reason the nobles ain't been heard from for so long is because they're fast asleep at her feet."

Ro's mouth parted, and she sucked in a breath. She'd found her. The empress that had cursed Allura. She was sure of it.

Ro's brothers exchanged a glance, and Liam shifted, letting out a grunt. Apparently he was relieving pain from how he was lying, but the movement placed him closer to Ro, and she started to sweat. She was about done with this arrangement.

"So she deals in sleeping curses, then," came Liam's quiet voice, a deep rumble that Ro felt through the board they were on.

"Aye. That she does, General. That she does."

"Then what are we still here for?" Ro pushed herself up.

A nice loud crack sounded beneath her. She froze.

The old woman grunted. "Off o' here, nice and easy now." She started grumbling, "Come into my forest and start breaking my things…"

Liam slid off first, then his warm hands were around Ro's waist as he helped her ease off the boards.

Ro's face felt a whole galaxy of suns hot. He'd never treated her like this before. So kind and gentle and…*caring*. She rather preferred his condescension and her heated retorts.

Before she could push away from his hands, the ground taunted her from a million kilomètres below, and a wave of dizziness left her reeling. She slumped into his embrace without meaning to do so.

"Don't just stand there holding her, for heaven's sake," the old woman barked. "Get her to the ground!"

Liam was already moving, and he guided Ro swiftly and safely to the ground, pretty much holding her with one arm while he climbed single-handed. Then he held her upright as the dizziness faded.

She eyed the tree she didn't remember climbing down and swept a speculative gaze over him. "Merci beaucoup, Liam."

He nodded. "It was my honor."

It was said with just a bit too much huskiness for Ro's liking. She dropped her gaze and pulled away. Liam let go reluctantly as the others scrambled down from the tree.

Claude was the first to reach her. "Waouh! I thought we'd be picking your bones out of the surrounding treetops."

Ro just rolled her eyes. "I was never in any danger. Not with Liam there."

A pleased look crossed his face, and he glanced away.

Heat suffused Ro. She couldn't take it back—it was true, and she'd meant it—but she wished she'd stop encouraging him without meaning to.

Pascal was helping the old woman down the tree in his quiet, unobtrusive way. He eyed Ro when the old woman finally toddled on her own two feet, hanging off his arm. His concerned expression asked if she was all right, and she gave him a single nod.

His expression eased.

"Well don't just stand there gawking at each other! Help me back to my cabin. We have some planning to do."

Before Ro could say anything, her brothers were off, Pascal lending his arm and Claude lending his wit.

She started after the trio, but Liam was there, taking her hand, placing it on his arm. Ro almost pulled away, but lingering dizziness and the solemn nod he gave her changed her mind.

But then she caught the jump in the pulse at his throat, the gentle tension between them, and the way he deliberately kept his attention off her to set her at ease.

Ro swallowed—she didn't know how to deal with all these emotions and drama and subtext people kept throwing at her—and grumbled all the way back to the cabin.

Hopefully she kept it to herself this time.

Ro couldn't help admiring the little cabin as they came out of the woods and into the clearing. It was quaint. And old. And rather charming, for its occupant.

Trees didn't grow near it, which was odd since it was smack-dab in the middle of an ancient forest. They hadn't been cleared, either. No stumps, nothing. It was as if the forest had taken a giant step back.

Ro smirked. Made perfect sense.

Then she noticed…everything was quiet. Too quiet. No movement in or around the cabin. She reached out with her senses, trying to determine what was wrong.

Then it hit her.

No Olt.

Ro bolted toward the cabin. Footsteps rushed to keep up. Her heart nearly flew out of her chest, it beat so hard, and she burst into the cabin. Nothing. No one. Quiet, tidy, and…deserted.

She gave a cry.

A soft noise made her spin. Olt jerked awake from the rocking chair with a little snort, a brightly colored quilt falling from his shoulders, and Ro stood there, frozen.

Then she sagged against the doorframe in relief. He hadn't left. Now for her heart to stop pounding like it was thundering alongside horses in a race.

Blinking away sleep, he smiled the moment he saw her and stood. "You're back."

The light in his eyes said his dreams had erased the heaviness in his heart.

Just as Ro was returning his smile, Liam and her brothers tromped in after her, and Olt seemed to realize where he was. Gravitas surrounded him like a cloak.

Ro felt the change like a loss, but she didn't have time to dwell on it.

Dizziness slammed into her, and Ro wavered on her feet. Before she knew it, Liam was there, holding her upright. And she just had time to see panic suffuse Olt's face before she closed her eyes, concentrating on staying *awake.*

"The bed," Liam said, just as Olt blurted, "She can have my chair. Here."

"I don't want to be any trouble. The chair is fine," Ro mumbled, but she was pretty sure no one heard her, for she was soon being swept into the bed and fussed over by a gaggle of Messieurs.

"Out of my way," a wretched voice demanded. "I'll see to her. You lot wait over there. Except you, handsome."

Efficient hands pulled back Ro's shirt, and her wound was prodded and inspected. Waves of pain roiled through her, and Ro vaguely wondered what twisted part of her was keeping herself awake for this torture.

"I don't understand it. The wound should be healed already," the old woman muttered to herself.

"After one day?" Claude demanded from the door, sounding more than a little upset.

"What can I do to help?" came Liam's quiet voice from close by.

She rattled off a list of herbs. "From my garden. Do you know them by sight?"

"I do," Olt said instantly.

"Bon," she said. "If they aren't in season, I'll have them dried and hanging in the shed. Go. Quickly."

Footsteps rushed away.

The old woman leaned close. "Let's take a look-see at what could be causing this."

Just as Ro was making an effort to open her eyes, fingers invaded her wound, bringing excruciating pain and, finally, blessed oblivion.

Ro woke to a quiet cabin and a stench that made her want to retch.

She lifted her head, searching for its source—it was coming from her. From her shoulder, specifically.

Wrinkling her nose, Ro pulled back the square bandage held on by a single wrap to find a green, oily poultice filled with crushed herbs and...wild garlic...if her nose could be trusted.

"Grandmère, she's awake," Olt said quietly.

The old woman's head came up from her knitting, and she offered a toothy grin. "Well now, I told you all she'd be just fine, didn't I?"

Olt leaned against the fireplace's mantelpiece, Claude and Pascal sat at the small table, and Liam stood back, arms crossed, and watched them all.

No one agreed or disagreed with her, but Ro was certain she was still somewhat delirious. Surely she'd imagined the relief in the old woman's voice.

Ro forced herself up the wall, leaning heavily against it and wrapping herself in the blanket. "What happened?"

The old woman went back to knitting, her giant wooden needles clacking together. "It seems we didn't get all the poison worked out. That should do the trick."

That's when Ro noticed the pain in her shoulder wasn't

just wounded flesh from a wolf tearing into it—the pain trailed in tendrils into her chest cavity and down into her belly, as if the poultice were chasing down the poison and burning it out of her.

It was not pleasant.

After a pause of no one saying anything, Ro quietly asked, "And if it doesn't?"

"Oh, pish posh. No use worrying about that now. If need be, we'll get to it when we get to it."

Her words were not reassuring. Or useful in the least.

"Now," the old woman continued in a matter-of-fact voice. "You have questions for me?"

Ro sat up straighter. Finally! She leaned forward, ignoring the pull in her shoulder, more than ready to move on with her hunt. "What do you know of the empress? How soon can we reach her? What do you know of her sleeping curses? What do we do to defeat her? How do I wake my niece?"

Her eyes riveted on Ro, and Ro forced herself not to shrink back. But she wasn't done yet. She had more questions.

"Where did you get a page out of my family Bible? How did you know my mother, and why does your cloak match hers? I mean, mine?"

Liam, Olt, and her brothers exchanged surprised glances.

The old woman gave her a secretive smile. "All good questions, all will be answered in time, but I'll start with this: How did I come to be in possession of your family Bible? Why, your mère gave it to me. You see, Rosette Jacqueline LeFèvre Reynard, I am your grandmère. Your mère was my daughter."

Ro fell back against the wall, hard. The cabin was quiet a moment, then Claude burst out with, "Why, that makes you our grandmère too!"

He beamed at Pascal.

"Clever boy, you are," she said with enough hidden sarcasm that Claude missed it.

Ro did not.

"Over there, boy." The old woman, Ro's actual *grandmère*, pointed with her staff to a cedar chest at the foot of her bed. Pascal jumped up to open its lid. "The Bible is just there, on top."

He reverently removed the ginormous, decrepit tome, and he and Claude took a look before passing it to Ro.

After wiping her fingers on the bedclothes, Ro placed it on her lap and lovingly ran a hand over it, hardly daring to breathe. Her mère had touched this. Read from it. Loved it.

She vaguely remembered it resting on a pedestal in their family room, but the memory was there and gone again in a flash.

Closing her eyes, Ro tried to picture her mère's face, but it was fading. Just feelings remained. A brush of a hand. Petal-soft lips kissing Ro goodnight. A gentle voice she'd give anything to hear again.

Ro swallowed against the burn in her throat and smoothed its cover. Opened it, ran her hands over illuminated pages. Took Grandmère's note out of her pocket and fitted it to the jagged edge from where it had been torn.

Suddenly angry, she said in a tight voice, "Why did you desecrate it?"

She raised furious eyes to her grandmère's.

"Oh, pish posh. It got you here, didn't it? If it makes you feel any better, I still have some paste from the traveling peddler. You can glue it back in after this is over, yes?"

Ro scowled. Like that would repair the damage. Might make it worse, actually. What she needed was a book repair kit…

The old woman continued like she didn't care. She probably didn't. "Upon your mère's death, it was sent to me, with a note saying she wished me to have it. O' course, I'd already felt her spirit pass on."

Ro thought she might throw up, grief swept her so hard, like she was a ship, battered against rocks, unable to move upright as wave upon wave of grief rolled over her.

"Why didn't you come to the funeral?" she barely managed to ask. Ro would've remembered her if she had.

"I had my reasons. Your cape," she suddenly demanded to the room at large, "bring it here."

Liam started to move toward it, since he was closer, but Olt was already there. He gently carried her red-satin cloak, its white wolf–pelt lining safely stored away till winter, to the rocking chair.

The old woman ran wrinkled hands down the seam of Ro's red cape. "I see your mère kept my cape. In rather good condition, too." The old woman cackled. "I knew it would work."

Ro started to ask "What would work?" when a portrait in the still-open chest caught her eye. Her parents, young and eyes shining, done in surprising detail with watercolors.

Why wasn't it proudly displayed on the crumbling little cabin's wall?

Ro reached for it, but another portrait—a smaller, newer-looking one—commandeered her attention instead. She plucked out the charcoal sketch with shaking hands. "Who is this?" she whispered.

The crabby old woman heaved herself to her feet and peered over Ro's shoulder. "My other granddaughter—your younger sister, Cendrillon."

Ro dropped it, but the old woman was quick for her age and plucked it from the air before the glass could shatter or the frame could crack against the wooden floor.

"Be careful, girl!"

"Cendre? You mean..." Ro lifted tear-filled eyes to Olt's,

and he gave her a look filled with so much empathy, it almost undid her. "My sister," she mouthed for him only.

He nodded, looking positively miserable for her sake.

"Oh, buck up and stop your blubbering. She ain't dead."

Ro spun to her. "What do you mean she's not dead? She was lost at sea! She died in battle. The sirens took her."

Shame washed over her, and Ro dropped her head, unable to face the old woman after she'd failed the girl—her little sister. The one the Fairy Queen had taken and replaced with Cosette, her own daughter.

At nothing from the old woman, Ro raised her head to find her studying Ro, a speculative look on her face. "Uh-huh. Anyway, the fool girl had it in her mind to go see the world, so she left me high and dry, the only caretaker of the forest. Fool girl!" she repeated.

Ro's eyes widened, temper swift to follow. She'd just told her Cendre was dead, and the woman went on like nothing was amiss? What was wrong with the cruel old bat?

Yet the old woman squinted at her in a way that made her squirm.

Ro couldn't quite look away from the spike of scraggly, white hair on the woman's chin. Ugh. Would Ro look like that when she was that old? She sincerely hoped not.

"The Siren Queen let you go, didn't she?"

Ro nodded.

The old woman shoved her cane in Olt's direction and poked his chest. "She gave that one back, didn't she?"

What else could Ro do but nod? And how on earth did she know all this?

The old woman nodded, decided. "Then Cendre's still alive."

Ro wanted to scream her frustration to the rafters, but she was afraid the old cabin would fall down around their heads. It was the only thing that kept her temper in check. That and respect for the woman who was her grandmother, whether she deserved it or not.

"What are you talking about, old woman?"

The old crow slapped her hand. Hard.

"Ow!"

"Be respectful of your elders, ye old sauerkraut!"

Ro snapped her mouth closed. Her cheeks burned. It didn't help that Olt choked on a laugh and stared at her with twinkling eyes, looking half amused and half like he was debating coming to her defense. She raised her chin.

"There's that LeFèvre spirit," the old woman crooned.

Ro blinked. Her mother's maiden name rolled so easily off the old crone's tongue, the name Ro had used to distance herself from her family—the Reynards—to keep them safe from the dangers of her hunting life.

"Listen closely and listen well, for I shall only say this once. The Siren Queen does not let those promised to her go. She offered you her pearl combs—"

Ro sucked in a breath. How in all the realms had she forgotten? She reached deep into her sewn-in pocket and touched the combs, their smooth surface like silk under her fingertips.

She was supposed to deliver them to Madame LaChance. Why hadn't she?

Their presence winked out of her mind the moment her fingers moved away.

"—and in exchange, you were to join her in the sirens' quest to wipe out all men who crossed the great ocean." She jabbed a cane in Olt's direction. "She would've killed that one had you joined her."

Olt swallowed. Now Ro shot him a look of sympathy, and his expression said he appreciated it.

His time spent in the prison deep underwater hadn't been pleasant. He nearly hadn't recovered. She shuddered to think of him being dragged to the ocean depths and drowned, as so many of the men on their ship had been. Thank the Creator he'd survived.

"That's not the bargain I struck with the Siren Queen, Grandmère."

"Are you sure about that?"

The old woman studied her while Ro doubted everything. Why *had* the Siren Queen let them go? And why couldn't she remember?

"The fact remains." The old woman hobbled over to the cast-iron stove, stoked the fire, and checked on the boiling water she'd made Claude and Pascal get her. "The Siren Queen would've never let you go had someone not taken your place. And who else would take your place but a sister who loved you dearly?"

Ro needed to sit down. Like, right now. It took her a moment to realize she already was. Then Olt was there, by her side, squeezing her other shoulder. She hung on to his hand for dear life.

Liam, Claude, and Pascal lurked in the background, crowded into the little cabin, all trying to remain unobtrusive, yet listening intently.

"And," the old woman continued, "I would know in my heart if she'd left us." She shook her head. "*Nein*, I felt it when she changed into a daughter of the sea."

Ro couldn't take any more vague statements. "Changed into a daughter of the sea? What are you talking about? And how on earth could you possibly know such a thing?"

The old woman gave her a toothy grin. Ro tried not to shudder, she really did, but she wasn't quite successful.

"Because I was once a daughter of the sea myself." Her eyes took on a dreamy, far-away look. "You see, I loved every-thing above the ocean, and I wanted to live in this world so badly I could hardly stand it." She shrugged. "So I made a bargain with the sea witch, got my legs, came ashore, and never looked back. Oh, close your mouth. 'Tisn't as shocking as all that."

It most certainly was. Ro snapped her mouth closed. Then a thought struck her. "Does that mean I'm part siren too?"

"Don't be a fool. Once I changed, I was as human as the rest of ye."

Ro eyed her. The old woman really had no way of knowing that, did she? The Siren Queen had asked Ro to stay underwater…how else could she unless she had siren blood?

Ro frowned at a third portrait, one edge frayed as if it had been torn, and touched the frame. "Why do you have a picture of my sister Yvette?"

The old woman scowled at Ro. "Fool girl. That's me. Before I got with child and my body betrayed me by getting all old and wrinkly."

Ro's eyebrows shot up. Yvette—and Cendre, for that matter—most looked like Ro's mère. Both were stunning in their beauty. Her grandmère had once looked like that?

The old woman grunted. "Don't look so surprised, girl. I gave up my siren powers when I left the sea. No immortality for us. We'll age and wrinkle to death with the best of them."

Ro gritted her teeth as the old woman carefully repositioned the picture in its spot in the chest. No wonder Cendre had run as far and as fast as she could from the old hag.

Then something Llyr, a siren who had been kind to her, had said came to mind. She'd helped because Ro reminded the siren of someone. She'd said, "You have our Darya's eyes."

Ro swallowed. "Your, uh, name wouldn't happen to be Darya, would it?"

She shot Ro a sharp look. "Who told you that?"

Unsure how the volatile old woman would react, Ro said somewhat timidly, "Llyr? One of the sirens who helped us."

The old woman's entire demeanor changed. Her face softened—wiping away so many years and so much hardness, Ro could believe she'd quite possibly been beautiful in her youth.

Then came that grotesque, toothy grin. "Now there's a name I ain't heard in an age." Sadness touched the old woman's eyes. "Dear girl. Heart of gold and a tail to match. How I miss her."

Ro's eyes widened. "Her tail was the color of pitch, just like the rest of them."

Her grandmère's eyes widened. "Were they now? The curse must've gotten more out of hand than I thought."

Ro rubbed her forehead. Another curse? Just thinking about it made her head ache. Where were they all coming from?

Her eyes drifted toward her brothers. She tamped down the grin that wanted to break free. Ro couldn't let this opportunity pass her by. "Now that would've been something—seeing you both with tails. Had our family stayed in the sea, of course."

She snickered at the looks on Claude's and Pascal's faces. Both boys—men now, really—shifted and squirmed like they used to do during their lessons Ro tried to help them with.

Tried being the key word there. Her lack of patience never made her very good at teaching.

Ro grinned. "My brothers. The mermen. What a shame to have missed *that*."

Grandmère sniffed down her long, regal nose at them. "Mermaids are quite different than sirens. Flighty little brightly colored things, always flitting around warm water and laughing and playing, leaving the heavy magical work to us. Quite annoying, really. But what can you expect from creatures who weren't meant to rule the sea?"

Pascal elbowed Claude. "Um, firewood…"

"Yes, um, behind the cabin…"

"We should go…"

"…get some."

They looked at each other and nodded.

The old woman grumbled under her breath, "'Bout time you made yourselves useful—"

They were already out the door.

Ro couldn't help her chuckle. She sincerely doubted they needed more than a few logs after all her hard work last night. Then again, the old lady kept the fire going constantly.

Olt spoke quietly from next to her. "I'm sorry about Cendre."

Ro's heartbreak came flooding back. "Thank you, Olt. That means so much." She flicked a glance at him. "How well did you know her, really?" She flushed a little—something she did far too often around Olt. "I mean, besides the time she was on the same ship we were. For months."

He rubbed the back of his neck. "Well, she worked at an inn I frequented while in London. She looked so sad, so jaded, so hurt, I couldn't help but try to befriend her."

Of course he couldn't. Then another thought struck Ro. Oh no. Not again. "You weren't—you and she—she didn't..." She blurted, without meaning to, "Did you like her?"

A curious look came over his face, one that made Ro wish she could snatch her words back.

"Not like that," he said finally, his gaze serious. "I tried to befriend her, but she wouldn't let me close. But it was nothing like that. Promise. She needed a friend, and I tried to be one."

Ro glanced away, not liking where this was going. Being vulnerable. That he saw so deeply into what she was asking. Not in front of her grandmère and *Liam*, of all people.

Curse her moment of weakness when she'd told Olt about Trêve and Cosette.

"Ah, but she liked you."

Both of their heads popped up at the old woman's pronouncement. Ro hadn't realized how close they'd gotten to each other. She sat up straight.

The elderly woman nodded emphatically, her eyes twinkling as she took in Olt. "She didn't just give herself up for the sister she'd grown to love, she gave herself up so the man she loved could be with the woman he loved. The ultimate selfless act, and the only thing that could satiate the Siren Queen's desire for the huntress to join her ranks. Can you imagine a siren with Rosette's talents?" She cackled like the crazy old lady she was. "I can't believe the Siren Queen let you go!"

Ro's gaze slammed into Olt. He kept his eyes on her grandmother, but dusky red crept up his neck. It was kind of adorable.

Ro couldn't imagine her own face was any less red. Though embarrassment was the least of the emotions churning within her.

He most certainly didn't love her. He couldn't. Not really.

His kiss burned in her mind, and now a different kind of heat took over. She wrestled with the covers, jumped to her feet, and took off for the door.

That spoon pointed her way. "Halt, young lady. Dinner's not ready yet, and we have a passel of young men to feed. You." Now the spoon swung toward Olt. "Get out and do whatever needs doing. I got some nice veggies in the garden that would do well for a salad." She gave Liam a sweet smile. "And you, handsome, can stay right here and keep me company."

Liam bowed slightly at the waist. "It would be my honor, Madame."

Flicking one last glance at Ro, Olt obeyed, and Ro stomped to her grandmère's side, feeling wrung out. She hated to cook and burned everything in sight. Olt loved it and could make something edible out of nothing, but kitchen duty it was.

Another loud sniff, and her grandmère said, "Maybe clean up first. We don't want to be smelling that while we're making food."

Ro scowled at her.

Her fingers got rapped once more. "And ye can leave that scowly attitude outside with the wolves!"

Ro gritted her teeth and did not shout a thousand insults back, though she dearly wanted to. She hastened to clean up, then to get everything her grandmère asked for. Before she had permanent bruises.

She would never get used to the old woman, not as long as she lived.

And Ro was *related* to her. No wonder she and her sisters were the crabbiest people alive, if they all came from this old crone's line.

It made sense why Cosette was the angel of the bunch.

As the old woman flirted and chatted with Liam, Ro clumsily tried to help her grandmère cook something—without burning down the cabin.

❧

Grandmère eyed her, one excruciating meal later. "Ya weren't teasing. You really can't boil water to save your life, can ya?"

Liam coughed, her brothers laughed outright, and Olt covered a smile by rubbing his face.

Ro was heading toward the door with a mumbled, "I'll go chop more firewood" when she heard Olt say, "Let me help you clean up, Grandmère."

Suck up. Leave it to Olt to wrap every person he met around his finger in a few spoken words flat.

Ro paused, stuck her borrowed axe in a chunk of wood, and straightened, holding her back. Maybe she shouldn't have jumped into so physical an activity right away? Cutting wood was exhausting.

For once she was thankful her brothers had taken care of that particular task at home. She frowned. If she wasn't so desperate to get away from the old woman, she'd march back in there and hand off her axe to one of them.

A smile found its way to her face. Bon, but it was good to see them again.

"Show me what you can do."

Ro yelped and tripped over a log while spinning to face the old woman—her grandmère, she reminded herself. Darya. She could remember that name. Probably.

Ro sat down hard on one of the logs and held her aching foot.

Darya eyed her dubiously. "You sure you're a huntress?"

Heat filled Ro's entire body. "I'm sure. Have you been kind a day in your life?"

The old woman looked like she wanted to rap Ro's knuckles again, but she grunted and leaned heavily on her cane instead. "Don't be impertinent. Show me what you can do."

"You want to watch me chop wood?" Ro eyed the axe.

This time, the old woman wielded her cane like the weapon it was and smacked Ro's thigh.

"Ow!" Ro gritted her teeth and restrained herself from ripping the cane away and showing the old woman how it felt. She would be respectful. She would.

Whether the old hag deserved it or not.

"Stupid girl. Show me your powers! Your hunting ability. Show me what you can do."

Ro stared at her, mouth open. How did she know Ro had magical hunting capabilities? True, they rarely worked, and only when Ro was least expecting them, but she'd never told anyone. Not a soul.

"Flies will start landing any moment now."

Ro snapped her mouth closed. Why couldn't she have a nice grandmère who liked to go to the opèra and spent her days picking out chandeliers and new wallpaper for her château?

"I know what you think you can do," Darya snapped. "Show me what you truly can do."

"Do you mean…?" Ro bit her lip, wondering how to word it without sounding like she'd lost her mind.

"Yes, yes, the things you can do that no one else can. Those eldritch and mysterious abilities that give you an edge over your common, and ordinary, fellow huntsmen."

Ro shook her head. "I can't. I mean, I don't know how. It just…happens…sometimes."

Her grandmère stared at her, aghast. "You mean…you haven't been trained?"

Ro was getting tired of explaining herself. Of defending herself. She sighed. "And who would train me, Grandmère? My père? He was too busy roaming the countryside, drowning himself in drink. My brothers? They had no idea I even had powers. Gautier?"

Her jaw tightened, and it was difficult to keep speaking.

"He of all people I didn't want to know I had powers. My fellow huntsmen?" She shuddered. "Just no. Earning their respect was hard enough as it was. Prince Trêve? He couldn't even break his own curse, let alone be bothered with mine."

"Are you finished yet?" the old woman asked dryly.

Ro glared. "Non. I'm not."

Darya sighed and settled herself on a stump. "Fine. Pray continue."

Ro lifted her chin, determined to finish now that she'd practically been challenged not to. "The Fairy Queen? She may have given me my powers, but I left to defeat the sirens right after learning about them. And then I came here. So who, may I ask…"

The old woman started cackling, and she bent over her knees, wheezing, as her mirth grew.

Ro planted her fists on her hips. "What's so funny?"

"The Fairy Queen?" Darya gasped between cackles. "The one who gave you your powers? Oh, that's rich." She let loose another string of cackles until her laughter rose to the treetops.

"What are you saying?" Ro demanded, just wanting her to *stop*.

Once she controlled herself enough to speak again, Darya pointed to her own chest. "Any powers you have came from me, ma chère."

Ro choked. "From…you. What was that about leaving your siren powers behind when you became human?"

Darya waved her hand. "Oh, I did, but that's not what I'm talking about. No, your powers stem from the forest, from being a protectress. Special powers endowed by the Creator for our kind, though there be precious few left, to hold back the things that hunt humans. I find it laughable the Queen of the Fairies tried to claim credit for such a gift."

Ro blinked, having trouble taking in all the new information. Besides, she'd come out here to clear her head, not to have it stuffed full of things that didn't make sense. "But—but she said—*you* said—"

Her grandmère didn't even let her finish. "She said, I said. Who cares what anyone said! Now, show me what you can do."

Ro shook her head, frantic. What else had she been lied to about? "I can't. I don't know how."

The old woman sighed and rose wearily to her feet. "Then it looks as though your quest is doomed from the start."

"But of course it isn't—"

"Nein!"

Ro jerked back.

"Do not question me on this matter! You cannot go against a powerful witch with nothing but a hunch and a hope that your powers will save you when you don't even know how to use them! You must know what you're doing. You are foolish to think otherwise."

"But, but…"

"'But, but' what? Spit it out. The beast? How did you defeat the sorceress and help shed the beast's skin from the prince?" Ro's grandmère waited only a moment. "Very poorly, if I do say so myself."

Ro was too offended to do more than splutter, and Darya kept right on talking.

"It has been rumored this witch has done away with an entire family of nobles, just so she can rule the Black Forest and the magic that resides here. She just wasn't counting on me. She has already placed your niece in an enchanted sleep not even the Fairy Queen can awaken her from. And you think you'll just walk in there with no plan, no control, and simply defeat her?"

Ro couldn't have said two words together if she'd tried.

"Fair warning: You can't. You have to *know* what you're doing to defeat a power such as hers." Darya settled herself once more, her glare firmly on Ro. "So again I ask you: Show me what you can do."

Ro climbed to her feet and stood there, not a clue of what to do next.

So she peered into the forest, trying to get her eyesight to lighten creatures bathed in shadow. When nothing happened, she closed her eyes, listening for sounds that seemed to reach out and tap her shoulder, letting her know to pay attention.

Everything just sounded normal.

Scents had never been particularly strong for her, but she breathed in anyway, trying to parse various forest smells for anything important. Musky animal pelt. The stench of humans too long in the forest. That clear, crisp, sharp scent she couldn't quite describe, preceding anything with a fey nature. Or the rotting stench from a fey creature who'd recently feasted on someone, whether body or soul or spirit.

Nothing.

She tried to sense Olt nearby, in the cabin, or even her grandmère, sitting across from her. How someone else's presence seemed to intrude and let her know they were close by, especially if they were watching her or her quarry.

She gripped the axe harder, but magic didn't sizzle her fingertips, as it sometimes did when she touched an enchanted object.

Once, so very long ago, she'd used lightning to destroy a witch trying to kill her, and more recently, the lightning during the siren battle had followed her movements, as if it mirrored her and wanted to obey her.

But she felt nothing from the sky. Absolutely nothing.

She was broken! She didn't work. She didn't know how to make any of it work. And she wished anyone, *anyone*, other than her grandmère was here to witness her humiliation.

After an excruciating, awkward eternity, Ro shook her head, and humiliating tears filled her eyes. "I can't do it. I can't. I can't save my niece, I can't help my sister…I can't do anything right."

At the woman's sharp look, Ro stuttered out a correction.

"M-my…other sister. Cosette. The Fairy Queen's daughter. I fumbled my way through every magical hunting job I've taken on. I couldn't even save my real sister!"

Ro choked on a sob. Dead or no, Cendre was at the bottom of the sea, a siren, taking Ro's place when *she* should've been the one to sacrifice herself for her sister, not the other way around.

Cendre was no longer human, and that meant she was as good as dead.

The old woman reached out and flipped over Ro's wrist. "Look at the mark, child. How can you not know your sister lives in peace? Happy in her choice to save you?"

Ro blinked. "I don't understand…"

"Had your sister not saved you from the poison, you'd be a siren right now, the best part of yourself erased, preying on ships to capture men's hearts and break them and their bodies at the bottom of the ocean, using those pearl combs for yourself."

Once again, Ro knew exactly what the woman was talking about for a brief moment, before the knowledge of the combs winked away.

Ro felt sick. "But…how do you know Cendre isn't that way right now? A monster in my place?"

"You and all your questions! Think, girl. What did the siren do to you?"

Like a flash, the memory resurfaced, and Ro gasped.

When she'd stood before the Siren Queen, one of her sirens had scratched Ro. The ichor, the poison that flooded their veins, had entered Ro's wrist, had hurt excruciatingly, had made the sea start to sing to her. To call to her. To speak of its delights.

How had she forgotten?

"And what did your sister do, eh?"

Ro searched her memory, but ended up shaking her head. "I can't—I don't know…"

The old woman sighed as if everything about Ro pained her. She closed her eyes and reached out her hands. She didn't touch Ro, just held them on either side of Ro's head, and after a moment, her eyes popped open.

"You have no memory of it, buried or otherwise. But you've had many memories repressed."

Before Ro could even ask what that meant, her grandmère changed the subject. "Now, show me what you can do. Like this."

And a wash of magic barreled into Ro and toppled her over backward.

18

Thankfully, Ro didn't land on the wood pile or slice herself open with the axe she clutched.

No thanks to her grandmère, of course.

The old woman had somehow harnessed Ro's powers and had dragged them out into the open like a runaway horse dragging a cart on its side.

And Ro felt like the driver trapped under the cart, scraping every rock along the way.

Her grandmère finally released her and sat back on her little stump, not even a little exhausted. "You've had much repressed, young one. Some from past trauma, most by someone else. Almost as if you've been muzzled. Silenced. Repressed."

Muzzled? Ro couldn't even begin to think of the implications. Or who'd done it. The Queen of the Fairies? The Siren Queen? The three witches, called the Mesdemoiselles of the Mountain? Or perhaps Marie, their apprentice who called herself Magic? Gautier even, who'd delved into strange magic himself?

And there was a long line of magical creatures she'd faced between all those as well.

"Can you…do anything about it?"

If Ro didn't know better, she'd have thought Darya looked slightly worried. "Not without knowing where the anchor is and how to break it." She shrugged. "I do it wrong, and the memories are either gone forever, or the repression will rebound and take your mind with it. It's best not to mess with such things till I know more." She gave Ro a stern look. "But I suggest you protect yourself against such things in the future."

Like Ro knew how to do that.

Ro wanted to argue—everything about this woman made her want to argue—but she was sweaty and shaky and she'd had more power pulled through her than a lightning strike. She collapsed on the log she'd sat on earlier, sweat sticking her tunic and breeches and long boots to her skin.

Who knew that something completely invisible that took no physical strength whatsoever could be so exhausting?

Wearily, she asked, "And how would I even do that, Grandmère?"

Darya got a faraway look in her eye. "I'll think of something."

Ro barely kept herself from rolling her eyes. Sure she would. Was it too much to hope it would be before Ro faced the empress?

She wiped her face on the small towel her grandmère wordlessly handed her and took deep breaths, ready for a quick bath and a long sleep.

"You have more questions for me."

Ro glanced up and frowned. Well, she did, but was that important right now? More important than a warm bath and a good night's sleep?

"Go ahead and ask them."

Ro debated. She felt wrung out, like this sweaty rag, wanting nothing more than to be laundered and put to rest. Couldn't her questions wait till morning?

She eyed the woman's tapping toe. Apparently not. "What —can you tell me more about my mère? About…you. Coming to live here?"

Darya looked inordinately pleased, and as she settled in to talk, Ro settled in to listen. A breeze swept the clearing and cooled Ro's heated skin.

"After I became human and left my world for his, my prince became betrothed to another, one with better connections and incredible wealth, unlike the beauty who came from the sea and had nothing and knew no one."

Ro gasped.

The old woman barked a self-deprecating laugh. "Didn't stop him from taking what he wanted from the young, foolish siren throwing herself at him. So he married someone else, and I had to find my own way, make a life for me and my babe. His child."

Ro nearly fell over. "His child—?"

Grandmère waved off her words. "Yes, yes, your mother."

Ro couldn't believe what she was hearing. "But—Grandmère! A child out of wedlock?"

If her père had known…well. She wouldn't be here right now.

"Don't you think I know that?" Darya snapped. "Do you think I enjoyed giving birth to his child while the fireworks announcing his wedding were going off all around me? I've shed more than enough tears over him."

"What kingdom?" Ro demanded. She was going to find him and…

"Never you mind that now. Some bratty-nosed prince with a seaside palace all to himself ain't got no claim on my family, no matter that he sired a fine specimen such as yer mother. Just leave it be."

But Ro couldn't leave it alone. She might have more family. The thought spiraled through her head, over and over. Just who in the world of royals was she related to?

"You are as much a part of his family as you are a part of the mer. One no longer has anything to do with the other, and that's that."

Ro completely disagreed. But she was too stunned to say anything else, and her grandmère continued with her tale.

"Thank goodness my girl was a looker. I'd kept my voice, so I sang to support us, and after I married a wealthy artist who had many patrons and could provide for us both, she had no problem finding a suitable match and taking care of me after my husband died. Well, until Cendrillon."

Ro gritted her teeth. "What about my sister?"

Her grandmère eyed her as if taking her measure. As if searching her out to see if she could handle what she was about to tell her. Ro gazed steadily back.

It seemed to be enough for Darya. "As an heir to the Siren Queen's line, it is the next queen's duty to be ready in case she is called upon to rule. It was unforgivable that I sought the world above."

Grandmère glanced away, fleeting embarrassment on her face, enough to penetrate the spell woven around Ro as she listened, enraptured, to a history she hadn't known existed.

"When I chased after my prince, when I abandoned my birthright to live above the sea, it changed everything." A dusky red tinted Darya's cheekbones, out of place on her weathered skin. "I didn't realize how much until France was cursed and fey creatures began pouring into our land, but I set things in motion that day I'd do anything to reverse."

Ro nearly fell off her log. "What things? You caused the curse? How?"

"Silence, girl!" her grandmère snapped. "How can you hear anything while blathering on? I'll tell you when I'm good and ready and not before."

Ro bit her lip until she tasted blood.

Her grandmère eyed her for an excruciating moment, then nodded, satisfied, when Ro didn't speak. "My daughter had five daughters, and then the strangest thing, two sons. I was fascinated. Sirens are made, not born, and as the second siren ever created, and young too, I knew nothing of children. I assumed she'd have only one, just as I had. But they were the most delightful things, full of energy and wet kisses and so much dirt. I was enchanted."

Grandmère's eyes fell on Ro and stayed there.

"And then there was you. An eighth child. An eighth! I'd never seen such a thing. People marveled that your mère gave birth to so many healthy children, but I never wondered at that part of it. Sirens are robust, healthy. And at that point, I was certain I'd retained at least some of my powers, passed on something of my heritage to my offspring." She barked a laugh. "Something the years have more than disabused me of."

Ro tried not to squirm as she almost couldn't take wanting to know the rest of the story.

Darya's voice dropped to a whisper. "And then there was Cendrillon. She was not to live. She did not breathe. She did not cry. Her face turned purple as she struggled to breathe the strange air you humans take in, but not once did I consider what it meant. What it might mean. We stayed with her all the long night, watching her struggle to take every little breath. Trying to take each gasping breath with her. For her. But then, as humans are often weak, we fell asleep."

Her grandmère ducked her head, looking so miserable and ashamed of herself, Ro couldn't help but feel sorry for her.

"I was the first to wake, and I knew instantly, that child was not my Cendrillon. Your mère woke and was overjoyed, calling her Cosette over and over, as if she'd forgotten her own daughter's true name. I left. I followed the trail left by the fairy."

Ro held her breath. This dream had plagued her often during her voyage, details just slightly different each time. Here came the most painful part. The part where her dream cut off every time, leaving agony in its wake.

"It was hastily done, the switch. And because of it, I was able to follow the fairy's trail quite easily. You see, fairies will spend time planning the switches, yet this one had all the marks of haste. I found her, I found your sister, nestled in the roots of an enchanted tree, just past our world."

Ro bowed her head. It was too much. Tears dripped onto her lap as she listened.

"Her chest lay perfectly still. Not a breath passed her lips. But when I placed my hand on her heart, the faintest fluttering, like butterfly wings, greeted me. You see, had the fairy waited a moment longer to switch the fey child and my Cendre, the fairy tree would not have had any life left to hold on to. But my Cendrillon lived."

The old woman sniffed and dabbed at her eyes, her dingy handkerchief flashing in the dappled sunlight.

"Well, I couldn't bring her back to our land, now could I? She'd already been traded for a fey creature, so I had to keep her as close to the Land of the Fey as possible." She looked around her. "So I chose the Black Forest, near a rift between our worlds. I could nurse her back to health and keep her close to the magic keeping her alive."

So many questions exploded in Ro's mind, she made a half-strangled noise, trying to voice them all.

Her grandmère simply nodded, acknowledging what Ro couldn't say. "Oh, yes, she grew quite strong. So strong, in fact, that she left me and the miserable existence she claimed she had here and went searching for her family. I kept track of her, of course. A robin here, a jay there, each telling me where she was and of her well-being."

Ro frowned. "But what about her breathing problems?"

"Oh, she struggled, but the forest kept her strong. I worried for her, away from the magic. And she always got sick near her birthday, always so sick she lost her voice."

Such a random thing to say, yet Ro felt it was on the cusp of explaining so much.

"It wasn't till she boarded a ship that I lost track of her. Then the waiting. The not knowing. And no matter how hard I tried, the gulls refused to fly this far inland to share any news. And I couldn't leave my forest, not if I wanted my girl to live. Not if I wanted anyone to live."

Ro tried to puzzle it all out. "So you were keeping her alive, tied to the magic here, and the farther she got from you, the worse she became?"

"Sharp one, ain't ya? Yes, she grew worse. All things I didn't know until she became a siren. Until she took my place, as it were."

Ro jumped to her feet. "She what?"

This time, the old crone grimaced. "You heard me. Now, this is just me speculating, but I think the ocean was taking back what I owed it by leaving. The Siren Queen had no direct heirs after I left —"

"What happened to them all?"

Darya's rheumy eyes twisted Ro's stomach into knots. It was hard to picture her as a beautiful young siren, ready to throw away her long life as a siren for a short one with a human prince.

"The sirens fought back for good reason, young huntress. The men in ships did a rather thorough job of trying to wipe them all out. Yet men also created them by being their worst selves. I'm surprised it took so long for Zarya to declare war on the humans."

"Wait. Wait just a moment." Ro stilled, just now remembering something. Then she turned and ran to the cabin. She burst through the door, startling her brothers, and started digging in her satchel, muttering to herself. "It's got to be in here somewhere…"

She hadn't left it at the palace, had she? "Aha!" She seized the clutch of papers triumphantly and spun toward the door.

Darya was hobbling in just then. "What's got you in such a snit, girl?"

Wordlessly, Ro handed her grandmère the stash of papers. It could explain better than she could. Somehow she'd known —just known—that tale needed to be written.

After the hopelessly romantic story she'd written about a beast and his beauty, she'd felt this mermaid story needed a tragic ending.

Not that it reflected her experience with failed romances or anything.

But the little mermaid wishing for the prince, not getting him, him falling in love with someone else…well fine then. It reflected her and her grandmère's stories more than she cared to admit.

"You, young man. Help me to my chair," her grandmère demanded the moment her eyes landed on Olt.

Olt dutifully obeyed, helping her sit comfortably in her rocking chair as though she were a kind, fragile creature.

Ro stood awkwardly next to the table while she waited for Olt to settle the old protectress in. And fetch her a blanket. And put the tea kettle on. And build up the fire. And fetch her reading spectacles. And then the page she dropped.

Liam stood back, arms crossed, watching them all.

While her brothers sent looks her way as if *she* should be the one doing all those things. Not on her life. She wasn't the kind, caring, nurturing type.

And finally, after an eternity of distractions, the old woman began reading.

Ro started pacing. On a pass close to Olt, he grabbed her hand and pulled her down to sit next to him. Her thigh burned where their legs touched, but she didn't dare pull away. He was her lifeline to sanity.

He kept her hand in his.

She grasped his hand tightly, buried it between both of hers, hanging on for dear life. Liam stiffened, and Claude and Pascal glanced at each other, then tried to pretend they hadn't.

Darya kept reading, but it wasn't long until she was cackling and wheezing, then gasping for breath, tears rolling down her cheeks.

Not the reaction Ro was hoping for. Ro's face flamed brighter with every wheeze, and she darkly wished the old woman would lose her voice altogether.

"Well if that isn't the biggest load of tripe I ever did read!" The old lady slapped her knee and wheezed some more.

She held the papers out to Ro, and Ro snatched them away and buried them in her bag, face burning.

Olt, who'd read it and done his own share of teasing, took pity on Ro. "Was any of it accurate?" he asked the old woman.

"Turning into sea foam? Kids need better stories than such tales. No, the whole kit and caboodle weren't nothing but a fairy tale. And a rather pathetic one at that."

Olt got up and blocked Ro's advance. "What parts were true?" he asked affably as Claude and Pascal snickered and elbowed each other.

Ro could see them scheming to get their hands on the tale and shot them both a glare. They grinned back innocently.

Ugh. How had she forgotten the annoying parts of having brothers? She either needed to lock away her story or burn it. Her vote was on the second.

She eyed the fireplace.

The old lady scratched a few places. "Well, now, let's see. I did fall in love with a prince with a seaside palace, I did make a bargain to become human, and I did leave the underwater world thinking I would marry him, but that's where the similarities end."

That was practically the entire story!

Ro elbowed her way past Olt. "Now wait just a moment!"

Olt dropped an arm around Ro's shoulders, again to hold her back, as Liam shouldered his way inside with a load of wood Ro had chopped.

She hadn't even noticed when he'd left. His cold look met

Olt's smug one, and he wordlessly turned to stack wood inside the box.

"Little neater, there, boy! This ain't a pig's swallow."

Liam paused briefly, then continued to stack his neat rows without changing a thing.

"Did you marry your prince?" Olt sent a wink Ro's way, and with a roll of her eyes, she shrugged off his arm and sank back in her chair, arms crossed. Olt sat next to her.

"Naw. He married some princess, and I went off to make my way in the world and raise his child."

A stunned silence followed her words, but Ro just felt sick.

One thing at a time. First, Allura. Then, a visit to whatever prince to put the fear of Dieu into him. If she could figure out who he was. And if he were still alive.

Olt swallowed. "And Cendre? You started telling us about her?"

But Ro had already heard everything she needed to. It was too much. She needed air. To breathe. To process…

She jumped up and stormed out of the cabin.

"Take yer weapons, girl! There be wolves about!"

Out of habit, Ro grabbed her bow and arrows, dropped them into place, and had her hand on the door when her grandmère barked, "And the axe!"

Ro swiped up the closest one, the extra axe she'd just been chopping wood with, and once again tried to escape.

"And yer cape! My goodness, do you want to be visible to every fey creature who prowls this forest? Have you learnt nothing?"

I've learned nothing because you've taught nothing, Ro flung into the ether, not giving voice to her frustration. She gritted her teeth to keep the words at bay and swirled her cape around her shoulders.

She wasn't planning on going far past the clearing, anyway. She just needed to clear her head.

Her grandmère made a sound of disgust. "If you learn to control that temper of yours, ma chère, things will go much better for you in this life."

Ro almost couldn't form words. Had the old woman ever even learned her own lesson? She fled before her grandmère could witness just how much of a temper she had.

Or break down into tears. Which would be a thousand times worse.

Olt followed her out, and Ro wished he hadn't. Couldn't he see that she needed to be alone? She made straight for the trees.

Olt nervously cleared his throat and called out, "Ro, can I…talk to you?"

She stopped, and although Olt didn't press, Ro felt the weight of his stare like an anvil in the middle of her back. It wasn't pleasant.

Now he wanted to talk? When she least wanted to listen?

Taking a deep breath, calming her roiling emotions—mostly—she turned.

Olt looked so serious, Ro could only nod. She didn't know what to make of his somber mood. Or how to fix it.

She crossed her arms, steeling herself for whatever he had to say. "So…what's going on?"

Olt paused. Looked at her. Opened his mouth, then snapped it shut. "Give me a minute."

"All right…"

A few more paces, and he spun on Ro so suddenly, she stumbled back a few steps and raised her hands in defense.

"Ro, I need to tell you something."

That never boded well. Ro straightened, glad he hadn't noticed she'd almost throat-punched him. She braced herself, preparing for the worst. It wasn't like her life had been all roses and fairy tales up to this point, anyway. How much worse could it get?

Actually, she didn't want to know the answer to that.

"Ro, I know her."

Ro blinked. "Who?"

"The witch. I—she—I think she's my—my—I think I know who she is."

Ro just stared at him. She couldn't think, couldn't speak—just gave him a gape-mouthed stare that spanned the ages.

"She, well"—he swallowed—"she's not a very nice person."

You think? Understatement of the year, right there. Especially if she was slinging sleeping curses on innocent little girls.

He rubbed the back of his neck with a vengeance. "I may have had some experience with her curses, too."

Ro pressed her lips together to repress her scream of *Why didn't you tell me?* She'd learned so much, so fast, she didn't want to lose control in front of Olt. She wondered who close to him had been put to sleep.

Again with the rubbing. "I don't quite know how to say this…"

"Then just say it."

"Right. So. She cursed my family too. A long time ago. I can't go home—without dire consequences."

Ro squinted at him. "Like what?"

He paced some more before answering. "I can't say."

Not this again. "Can't or won't?"

Frustration filled his face, and Olt took to running his hands through his hair, over and over. Ro had never seen him so agitated.

She went up to him and put her hand on his arm, stilling his frantic motions. "Olt, what is it? You can tell me."

He only stood still a few seconds under her touch before grabbing her arms in a death grip. "That's just it. I can't. I can't speak of it, or my family will be in danger." His pleading eyes met hers. "You believe me, don't you? You have to know if I told anyone, it'd be you, right?"

Although it took everything Ro had to remain calm—all the information she sought was right there, at her fingertips— she spoke quietly, reasonably. "I do believe you. It's just…" A pause.

"What?" Olt's demand that she continue jumped into the space between them as though it couldn't be held back.

"Olt, don't you think she's had control long enough? Don't you think speaking about it—telling someone—would ease your burden? Give someone the opportunity to help you?"

He slid his hands down her arms and took her hands in his. "You don't understand. I can't. *Gott* help me, I can't. One word spoken, the wrong word, and I have condemned them— us—all. I can't." He dropped his head in shame.

Ro's eyes narrowed. She'd heard almost those exact same words years before—from the beast.

What was it with witches and sorceresses and enchantresses threatening everlasting curses if the spells they wove were mentioned? Was it a lie to further solidify control? Or was the curse made more ironclad with each mention?

She needed to look into that…

"Olt." This time, she lifted his chin with her fingertip and waited till his eyes met hers. "I promise to help you. Whatever you need. Whenever you need it. I promise. Just…please. Help me rescue my niece. And who knows? Perhaps we can…solve both problems at once? Please."

Olt stared at her a long time before answering. "How could I do anything less?" He tried to smile, but the motion was false. Didn't even reach his eyes.

"Merci," Ro whispered, her heart breaking. She felt like the worst kind of traitor to force him to do something after he'd begged her not to.

But what else could she do? Her niece was in danger, and she would do whatever it took to set the precious little girl free. Hopefully she could make it up to him after this whole mess was over.

Before she knew what was happening, Olt pulled her into his arms and rested his chin atop her head. And for once, Ro didn't pull away. In fact, she took a deep breath, let out her pent-up frustration, and settled deeper into his arms.

It felt like heaven.

Ro's eyes started to slide closed when his arms tightened, and everything shifted. Ro's senses came alive, thrumming through her, feeling every inch of where his body rested against hers like lightning. Like fire. Like the most intense bliss she'd ever experienced.

All she wanted was another kiss, but she had no experience in these matters.

And no way was she asking for one.

As if reading her thoughts, Olt pulled back and looked down at her. Eyes warm yet intense, he brushed his thumb down her bottom lip, settling it on her chin. He gently guided her face toward his, but she was already leaning toward him without meaning to do so.

Both of them paused right before their lips touched.

Ro couldn't breathe. The wait was agony. The anticipation excruciating.

Someone cleared his throat behind them, and Ro jumped away from Olt like she'd been stung. She whipped around, and her eyes met her brother's. They weren't friendly.

Pascal said, "Rosette, may I have a word?"

Ro swallowed and shrugged, trying to sound unflustered. "Sure, um, why not?"

He marched away into the woods, clearly expecting her to follow, and Ro took her burning face after him, not daring to look at Olt.

Once they'd gone far enough into the woods not to be overheard—with raised voices, Ro couldn't help but note—Pascal spun on her. "What were you thinking?"

Ro stared at him, dumbfounded. "Excuse-moi?"

"Oh, I think you know exactly what I mean."

Wrong tone. Ro lifted her chin and glared back. "I think it's none of your business."

Whatever it was. She whirled to stomp away, but he caught her arm and spun her to face him.

"Look, I get that you're the only one of us unmarried. I understand you haven't had much experience with men. But Ro, throwing yourself at him like that... He's gonna think... Well, any man would think..."

Ro yanked her arm away. "Think what? Say it."

He took a deep breath and blew it out. "Rosette..."

"Say. It," she growled out.

He gave her a sorrowful glance. "He'll think you're a loose woman, Ro. I know you've lived differently than any of us. I understand you've been in situations most Mesdemoiselles have not. Seen things I can't even comprehend. But this, Ro, throwing yourself at him like that..."

Ro reeled back a step, putting more distance between them than just a step. "It isn't like that. You don't understand. Not a thing, Pascal. You have no idea what we've been through. You have no idea what's between us. You have *no right* to judge."

He winced. "Ro, men like that..."

Rage burned hot in the pit of her stomach. "Like *what*, Pascal?"

"Men like him don't settle, Ro. They take and they take, they dance through life thinking everything's a game, a big joke, and all the while they leave a path of devastation in their wake. Broken hearts. Lost virtue." He ducked his head. "Making promises they never intend to keep."

Ro blinked, and her retort died on her lips. He looked so guilty, her temper fizzled out just a little. She really had no idea what had been going on with her brothers since she'd run away, did she? What they'd been through.

What they'd done.

Ro gentled her tone. "I'm not exactly a blushing maiden,

Pas. I'm well past old-maid status. Was even before I started working for Gautier all those years ago." She spread her hands. "What do I have to offer a husband?"

She'd been disowned by her father, had no dowry to speak of, and although she could live off the land with the best of huntsmen, she wouldn't know what to do with a house or a kitchen…or a man. She huffed. It was just a hug, for heaven's sake!

And, well, an almost kiss.

Most girls she knew were married with a babe on the way by eighteen. Or younger. Marriages arranged by their pères. Places set firmly in society.

Her père wanted nothing to do with her.

Pascal shook his head. "Still, I would not wish that life for you. Not ever."

Ro didn't quite know what to say to that. She could see where he was coming from, his good intentions, but his concern was…misplaced. Olt was a good man. He would never hurt her. In fact, she was much more likely to hurt him, and the thought stung.

Before Ro could find the words to defend Olt, Pascal straightened his shoulders. "I'm afraid I must ask you to keep to yourself for the remainder of our journey. To keep your distance. Do not be alone with him."

She raised both eyebrows. "Excusez-moi?"

"Furthermore, if you need to go into the woods, please ask Claude or Liam or myself to accompany you. Someone you're not romantically entangled with. I wouldn't want you to ruin your reputation beyond repair—"

"Absolutely not!" Ro exploded.

Pascal froze, as if he hadn't expected her to object. Seriously, had he not remembered a thing about her? "Uh…"

Ro stepped forward and poked him in the chest a few times. "No one tells me what to do, least of all you."

He batted her hands away. "As your elder brother—"

"Elder brother be hanged! You are not the boss of me. Haven't been for eight years, or for any time before that, I might remind you."

"Surely you must see the wisdom —"

"All I see is someone who's had no say in my life for years trying to tell me what to do! I'll spend my time with whomever I please."

A mutinous look crossed his face. "And I say you won't."

Ro's temper exploded, blinding in its intensity. "How dare you? You are nothing but a bossy, pigheaded imp, and I want nothing to do with you!"

Shouldering him aside, Ro stormed past him, and he called out behind her, "Now wait just a minute!"

She spun and shouted at him across the little clearing that separated them. "Don't talk to me. Don't even look at me! I'm not speaking to you right now."

Feeling like a foolish child and not even caring, her temper broiling so hot she could barely see the trees around her, she stomped off. Even with all the crashing she was doing through the underbrush, she didn't hear him follow.

Maybe her infuriating brother had some good sense after all.

❧

She plowed through ferns and bushes and around tree trunks until she'd calmed enough to stop and take a deep breath. Where on earth had that come from? Pascal had been the more protective brother, sure, but he'd never tried to boss her around once.

In fact, it had always been the other way around.

She scowled. Was this what she had to look forward to, should she never marry? Every male relative trying to tell her what to do? Trying to decide what she should or shouldn't do with her life? Whom she could *speak* to?

The fire was back, big time, and she stormed farther into the trees, certain she could follow the obvious trail she was making, crushed leaves underfoot and broken branches in her wake, and return to the cabin whenever she wanted to. *If* she wanted to.

After she'd gone quite a ways, the foliage's color started to change around her, and Ro wondered if she should turn back. Wolves still roamed the Black Forest, after all, and she had no desire to meet another. Or get scolded by Grandmère for wandering off.

Grandmère…her mother's mère. Who'd raised Cendre, Ro's true sister.

Who was now a siren at the bottom of the sea.

Thinking of Cendre made her think of Olt, which made her think of Pascal, which made their argument swirl through her mind again.

Nope, she needed to cool off some more.

As she was taking her next step, pounding footsteps reached her ears.

"Ro, don't! Stop!"

But she'd already taken half a step, and the world around her flashed bright white the same time someone barreled into her. She felt more than heard what sounded like a rush of feathers, then nothing.

PART III

THE GIRL IN THE TOWER / LA FILLE DANS LA TOUR

"The Wild Swans"
Les Cygnes Sauvages
Hans Christian Andersen

The nettles she must use grew in the churchyard. … There she saw a group of hideous vampyres sitting in a circle on one of the large gravestones. … With skinny fingers they clawed open the new graves. Greedily they snatched out the bodies and ate the flesh. She had to pass close to them, and they fixed their vile eyes upon her, but she said a prayer, picked the stinging nettles, and carried them back to the palace.

Les orties qu'elle doit utiliser poussaient dans le cimetière. … Là, elle vit un groupe de vampires hideux assis en cercle sur l'une des grandes pierres tombales. … Avec leurs doigts maigres, ils ouvrirent les nouvelles tombes. Goulûment, ils arrachèrent les corps et mangèrent la chair. Elle était obligée de passer à côté d'eux, et ils la fixaient de leurs yeux mauvais, mais elle récita une prière, cueillit les orties piquantes, et les rapporta au château.

Laur
Hollingswo

<h1 style="text-align:center">19</h1>

When Ro slowly came to, a completely different forest surrounded her. Where the trees had once been dark green, with foliage, now they were blackened and spindly and bare of leaves, as if they'd been burned. But no scorch marks touched anything.

Even the undergrowth lay shriveled and dead, like in winter, only no snow covered the ground.

But it wasn't completely dead, was it? Ro squinted at the canopy above her head. There, at the very top, at the tips of most branches, even, a brush of leaves fought to survive.

Survive.

Someone had attacked her.

The moment she remembered, she frantically looked everywhere. No one was there.

She could've sworn the voice sounded like Olt's, but surely Pascal wouldn't have let him pass without a fight of some kind. Also, she could've sworn a blanket of feathers had slammed into her just before she went down, but that sounded addled.

A loud honk brought her head around.

Her eyes caught on all-white against the darkened backdrop of dead forest, and when everything stopped spinning and she could focus, a swan stood there, squawking and flapping its wings and ruffling its feathers.

What was such a beautiful swan doing in the middle of the forest? Was it lost? Was there a homestead or a pond nearby?

She slowly made her way to her feet, wondering how to capture it or drive it somewhere safe. Left to itself, it wouldn't survive the night. Not with wolves about.

And she hated to admit it, but the thing made her nervous.

Ever so slowly, so she wouldn't startle it, she gathered the arrows that had splayed over the forest floor from her fall and carefully slid them back into her quiver.

The swan spread its wings and gave a mournful little bleat. Ro almost felt sorry for it.

She clucked and rubbed her fingers. "Here, ducky, ducky."

The thing stopped flapping and gazed at her, cocking its head. Ro could've sworn it looked puzzled.

She gave a self-conscious laugh. "I guess you're not a duck, are you? And you're quite far from home, non? Can you show me where you live?"

Ro felt utterly ridiculous talking to a bird, of all things, but she couldn't in good conscience leave it on its own. It studied her with a dubious expression.

"Won't you show me? Wolves are about tonight, I'm afraid, and I don't want to leave you here."

At the mention of wolves, the swan startled and swung its neck from side to side. Ro blinked and took a step back. Was it intelligent? She reached out with her senses, but no fey magic presented itself.

Good thing, or she probably would've kicked some dead leaves at it and taken off, leaving it to fend for itself.

A howl punctuated her words, and Ro flinched—perfect timing. The swan shuddered and looked all around, as if searching for the noise.

Ro found her axe sprawled nearby. She cinched it to her belt with a strap, adjusted the cloak around her shoulders, and scanned the groundcover, but she couldn't tell from which way she'd come. She scowled. She'd left a trail the most rudimentary of trackers could follow, and she couldn't find it?

She searched for boot marks, bent twigs, crushed undergrowth, anything, but as if her path had been erased, it looked as though no one had been through this part of the forest in quite some time.

With another ruffle of feathers, the swan waddled away. It moved out of sight, and when Ro didn't follow, it came back around the corner and honked at her.

Ro jumped and moved quickly after it, feeling chastised… by a swan.

But as she followed the creature, Ro wondered if she should. Who knew where it was leading her? But that was ridiculous. She'd just see it safely home and look for her missing path along the way.

She truly hoped she wasn't making the biggest mistake of her life.

§

Some time later, as Ro was following the swan, still looking for something familiar, still unsettled by the state of the once-lovely forest, a bird call sounded. The note was sweet and high and pure of sound, and Ro paused to listen.

She hadn't heard a nightingale in ages. Surely that's what it was—the depth and diversity of its song couldn't compare to any other. Although she couldn't recall being quite this enchanted by its song before.

Without warning, the swan went ballistic. It started squawking and flapping its wings and biting at Ro.

"What the—have you lost your mind?" she shouted at the bird, trying to shove it away with her boot.

The swan kept nipping at her, flapping all around her, in a way herding her faster down the path. Still Ro tried to push it away, not comfortable with hurting it, even if it had turned into a demon bird all of a sudden.

The other bird trilled again, in the trees right above them.

The swan froze, wings extended.

Ro's whole body relaxed. Such sweet music! She took a moment to look for it, forgetting the crazed swan.

Exploding into motion, the swan ran right at the tree, flapping its wings but not getting more than a mètre off the ground.

The nightingale continued to sing sweetly, and Ro couldn't help but close her eyes. How could any birdsong sound so beautiful? It was bewitching, it was unearthly, it was…

Ro's eyes snapped open.

Magic.

As soon as she'd thought it, a swirl of smoke turned the little unremarkable brown bird raven-black in hue, glistening iridescent in the light, shimmers of dark purple, deep blue, and forest green undulating in its wings.

A bright-red eye homed in on her. The forest seemed to dim around her, casting shadows. Emerald tendrils of fog drifted from the creature, reaching for Ro.

Ro backed away. The ground dipped behind her. She stopped, one foot hovering over nothing, and brought it back to solid ground slowly.

Just before the tendril got to her, Ro snatched up her bow, drew an arrow, and flung it at the bird, all in one smooth motion.

It struck the nightingale, which gave a cry and flapped its wings, rising off the branch in a lurching, drunken motion. Then it flew away, trilling and fluttering in a panic. Arrow stuck through it at an angle.

What in all the realms…?

Before Ro knew what was happening, the swan ran right

at her, launched itself into the air with a massive effort, and slammed its orange feet right into her chest.

Ro's bow and arrows went flying, and she tumbled down the hill, hitting every rock along the way, one with her head. Ro hissed and curled in on herself, trying to protect herself.

The moment she passed through the magical barrier, it snapped closed behind her, impossible to feel except for when Ro was past it.

She tumbled to the bottom of the hill and lay sprawled in the most undignified position, cloak up and over her head and legs spread wide and still partly up the incline. She lay still, dazed, bruises throbbing and head pounding.

She needed to move, needed to get up, but everything hurt so much.

The swan squawked from nearby, and Ro found her feet in a heartbeat.

She wrenched the cloak from her face, her shoulder-length hair springing every which way, out of its queue, and the swan stood there, calmly looking at her from a well-kept path.

A path that was surrounded by vibrant greenery and foliage and undergrowth, just as a forest should be in summer.

She felt for her axe, found the hanging strap, and saw it just then. Her axe lay at the bottom of the hill, past the swan, too far away to reach. Thankfully it was inside the magical barrier.

The magical barrier!

Ro spun and tried to push up the hill, toward the shriveled and dead forest, but something sizzled and her hair stood on end. Pain traveled through her body, so she took a hasty step back.

It lessened. She tried again, but she couldn't take a step in that direction without discomfort. Something blocked her, something she could feel but not see. No matter where she moved, it was there, stretching across her path. Like a shield or invisible wall.

And there lay her arrows, scattered down the hill, and at the very top, her bow. On the other side.

Great. Just great.

At a great squawking, she spun around. An entire flock of swans swarmed her way, heads lowered, white wings flapping, orange beaks snapping and hissing.

Ro turned and ran right at the magical barrier, but it flung her back with a hiss, as if batting her away.

Unfortunately for her, it hurled her right toward the swans. She sprawled again, this time into some low shrubs. Every part of her ached, especially her teeth. Which was just weird.

Ro's vision filled with flailing white feathers and her ears with harsh honking. A huge white swan hovered over her, flapping its wings in her face and pecking at her. She raised her arms in defense and wished the shrubs were just a little deeper.

Now that she was within whatever barrier this was, the magic surrounding the swan nearly soaked through her pores. What had she been thinking, following a magical swan through an enchanted forest?

She stumbled to her feet and put her back to a tree. It was just the one swan, the one she'd followed here. The others hadn't reached her yet. But they were coming. Sweat slid down her spine.

"Shoo, you crazy bird. Shoo!" A hefty branch caught her eye. Ro lunged for it.

The moment her fingers closed around the branch, the swan slammed into her, knocking her over in a tangle of limbs.

Ro scrambled away on hands and knees, but the thing flew at her, trying to bite her, snapping its beak just shy of her each time. She rolled to her feet, reluctant to hit the bird, even if it was trying to eat her.

No matter how many times she dodged its strikes, it wouldn't leave her alone.

So she turned and ran.

It seemed to herd her, flying into her path if she tried to go a certain way, moving her away from the other swans.

Before she'd gotten far, the five white swans surrounded the single swan, honking and pecking and twining their necks around him in strangleholds. The single swan shied away, ducked its head, tried to cover itself with its wings.

Ro started to flee, but against her better judgment, she glanced back. And stopped.

What was she doing? She needed to get out of here while she could!

But…the poor thing was being attacked.

Cursing herself for her weakness, Ro swiped up another fallen branch and ran forward, yelling, "Get away from him! Get off, shoo. Stop hurting him!"

Then she noticed—they were snaking their long necks around their fellow swan as if greeting him, not attacking. She stopped, branch half raised, wondering what to do next.

Then the other swans saw her, and they lowered their heads and hissed.

"Now wait just a minute," Ro said.

But it was too late. They ran at her, biting, snapping, making a terrible racket.

And after years of training to remain calm in stressful situations, to meet her attackers head-on, to hunt with skill and dexterity and patience like the huntress she was, Ro threw her measly little stick and ran as if hellhounds themselves were after her.

It wasn't long until she burst out of the forest onto an idyllic little scene she might've enjoyed at any other time. Peaceful lake, a barn that had seen better days, a single tower behind it all, wrapped in woody vines, and a little enclosed garden behind that.

Ro headed straight for the barn.

Shelter, plus, hopefully they had a pitchfork or something she could use as a weapon. She'd just left her axe behind like an imbecile.

Ro didn't bother calling out. The birds were at her heels, nipping, and she doubted anyone in the entire forest couldn't hear the flock of them scolding her.

A shovel leaned against the barn, so Ro snatched it up and turned on the swans with a yell. Wrong move.

The whole flock of giant swans flew at her head. She slashed out wildly, trying not to shriek like a banshee, trying to protect her face, trying to get inside that barn.

After batting them away a few times, swinging wildly but rarely making contact, she made it to the barn door, heaved it open, and fell inside, just as the first bird slammed into it. Ro jumped to her feet and hurled the door closed. Then she leaned against it, breathing heavily, clutching the shovel to her chest. Stupid birds!

A smaller door within the barn door itself flapped open, and a swan started to push its way through. Ro yelped and dove at it, trying to block it from getting in, but before she could, someone tackled her from behind.

The shovel went clattering to the ground, out of reach.

The pair landed on several stacks of hard flour, the cloth bags so firm and full, the landing was hardly gentle. A grunt escaped Ro.

The person who'd tackled her was small, short, and decidedly female. Ro peeked at the fiery woman who now rained blow after blow upon her—all of which Ro easily deflected—while yelling her head off.

Ro's eyes widened. She'd never seen so much hair in all her life! It cascaded around the room in white-blonde strands, coiled tight and springing every which way, and Ro was surprised to see it tangled around her leg from their scuffle. It was partially braided, as if Ro had interrupted the girl's attempt to contain it.

And it smelled of sunshine and wildflowers, as if it had just dried in the sun after being washed.

Ro opened her hands in a calming gesture, still using her forearms to block the wild and ineffective blows. "Easy now, easy."

Ro tried to soothe the woman like she did her horse, but it just seemed to enrage her further. She threw her whole body into the attack, even though her punches were hardly worth the effort.

"Look, calm down, will you? I don't even want to be here! Those stupid birds attacked *me*." Ro *oofed* as a fist found the soft part of her belly. "Can't we just talk about this? I just want to talk!"

"No one comes here to talk," the young woman screeched. "Only to cast spells, or weave magic, or steal my swans."

At the last word, fury seemed to shake her, and she heaved her whole frame at Ro. Ro rolled out of the way, and the girl hit the flour sacks hard.

Ro disentangled herself from the coil of tangled hair and staggered away, holding up her hands. "Wait."

"For what? You to attack me?" She shot Ro a glare. "I don't think so."

The girl retrieved a heavy rolling pin lying nearby, heaved it upright with both hands, and ran for Ro with a wild yell.

Just as the girl nearly reached Ro and Ro was readying herself to dodge that rolling pin and hoping if it grazed her it wouldn't hurt as much as she knew it would, one of the white swans fell through the little door.

Amazingly, it kicked the door shut, and it stuck fast. Then it flapped between them.

Ro shrieked and tried to duck away, but the bird turned on the girl and flapped at her, kicking with its bright-orange feet and snapping with its bright-orange beak.

Ro straightened, relieved it wasn't coming after her, and looked for another way out. Solid wall met her eyes, one curved stone—the base of the tower—and two of solid wooden planks. She needed to get past them to the door.

"Odin, you're back!" the girl gasped. "Go outside, you dolt. I'll protect you."

She tried to lunge around the bird, but it once again got between her and Ro. All Ro could do was hunch by the flour sacks and watch the mad girl talk to her mad swan.

"What is wrong with you? Get out of my way! I've got to get her out of here, you know that."

Poor girl. It was clear that she'd been trapped here for quite some time. All alone for who knew how long, it was no wonder she'd started talking to birds.

"Odin, get out of my way!"

Now the girl heaved her rolling pin at the swan, so Ro leaped forward and grasped her arm high above her head, mid-swing. "Arrête! I understand you aiming that thing at me, a stranger and intruder, but leave the bird alone."

The girl's eyes widened, with the same surprise Ro felt, before she sneered. "Says the girl who was swinging a shovel at the lot of them."

Ro flushed. "They bite. *Hard.*"

The swan chose that moment to shove its way between them, and it gave the girl a hard push that sent her sprawling. Ro lost her grip on the girl's arm, but before Ro could react, the swan came up to her and nuzzled her leg with its long neck, as if wrapping her in a hug.

Ro went rigid, not daring to move. Could she kick it away without getting bit? Maybe toss an empty flour sack over its head and dart outside?

Without tripping over the girl's hair?

The girl's face went white. "Traitor," she whispered. Then, after a heartbeat, she threw a handful of hay at the swan and shouted, "Traitor! You brought her here, didn't you? Is that why you abandoned us for five years? So you could bring a stranger here to discover our secrets? It's been five years, Odin. Five! What if the sixth had passed and you hadn't returned?"

Now the girl was shaking and crying, her face red with fury. She picked up a measuring scoop for flour and hurled it at the bird. It hit the swan, and the thing winced, tucking itself closer to Ro.

Against all common sense, Ro felt sorry for the creature. "That's not necessary, n'est-ce pas?"

"Quiet, you!" the girl snapped. Her angry eyes flew back to the swan. "Well if we didn't need you so badly, I'd tell you to get out and stay out. Is that what you want?"

She collapsed into angry sobs, a pathetic mess on the straw-strewn floor, her hair now matted and filthy. Ro's heart went out to the girl. Even if she was blooming mad.

The swan unwrapped its protective stance from around Ro

and waddled through the girl's snarled hair. She sat sobbing, head in her hands, and after the swan prodded her gently, it wrapped its long neck around her when she didn't respond.

After a moment, the rolling pin fell from her fingers, and she slipped her arms around the creature. "Oh, Odin, I've missed you so."

Ro stood there frozen, scared to move or draw any attention to herself. If she could just slip past them…

At that moment, the barn door burst open, and the other swans fell through in a tangle of wings and snakelike necks, hissing and squawking and trying to look threatening.

In an instant, Ro jumped on the flour sacks and swung herself up on the rafters, arms and legs clamped around exposed beams, her cape dangling below her like a waterfall. But this time, the swans didn't fly at her. Non, this time, they surrounded the girl and the other swan, though they seemed to be hugging the swan more so than the girl.

Ro counted them. Six white swans, all huge, all muscular, all with dangerous, snapping orange beaks.

She wasn't coming down anytime soon.

After their strange little gathering or reunion or whatever it was, the girl dried her tears on her apron and caught sight of Ro hanging there like a bat.

The girl rolled her eyes. "Oh, come down from there. They're not going to hurt you."

Not going to hurt her? The girl was a raving lunatic! And so were her birds. But it wasn't like Ro could say that.

"I just don't like birds, okay?" Ro shouted back, not sounding the least bit calm. She clutched the wood tighter.

The girl rolled her eyes again, grabbed a staff with a large hook on one end, and gently herded the flock out the door. All but the one she'd called Odin.

Though she left the door wide open, Ro couldn't help but note.

"Shoo. Stay," she demanded several times before the giant birds listened to her. She propped one fist on her hip. "Happy?"

Ro hesitated, then swung her legs down, then dropped. She stood out of her crouched landing and dusted off her hands, pretending a calm she didn't feel.

Swans and geese and ducks *bit*. And it *hurt*. And they liked to swarm helpless young girls who were just trying to feed them and make friends and thought the world was all happiness and sunshine.

And it didn't matter that the little girl was all grown up and killed predators for a living. One swarm and she was back in that pile of geese, screaming and being bit and clutching bread and crying.

All things Ro didn't say in her defense.

The swan, the one that had protected her, turned and looked right at her.

She stepped back. Ro was certain she was just taking on some of the crazy of the place, but she could've sworn she'd seen those eyes somewhere before.

The girl studied Ro with ice-blue eyes. After a moment, she gave that shuddering sigh that came after a storm of tears. "I suppose you'll want to eat, won't you?"

Ro couldn't imagine anything this girl would make to be very pleasant or very poison-free. She jerked her chin toward the forest. "I can forage on my way"—she almost said *home*, but that cabin was definitely not her home—"on the way back."

But that didn't keep her stomach from rumbling and betraying her. Sigh. How was she forever getting caught up in what she was doing and forgetting to eat?

The girl scowled. "I take that as a yes."

Without another word, the girl gathered armfuls of hair and made her way out of the barn. Most of it still trailed behind her in a frightful mess, and Ro watched in fascination. How on earth had she gotten it to grow that long?

Still, Ro wasn't sure what was expected of her. Did she follow? Stay here? Attempt escape? She went outside, and the swans stayed far away. All but the one.

He rested his head against her thigh as she stood in the clearing and took in the area in more detail.

An exquisite circular tower stood off to one side, somewhat behind and to the left of the barn, with a wooden gate and a stone fence just beyond that. A wild garden was trying to climb its way over the fence and escape.

But that wasn't what held Ro's attention.

The clearing's center was filled with the most beautiful sparkling lake Ro had ever seen. A stream fed it from one side and trickled away on the other. It made her want to go for a swim, or perhaps find a small craft and bob on its surface while she read a book.

It was peaceful, the little lake. And it looked completely out of place in the dark, mystical Black Forest, like a fairy-tale setting in the midst of a wicked witch's lair.

Ro shook herself out of her imaginings and turned to the woods. She needed to focus on escape, not taking a vacation in the middle of a mission.

Ro heard a grunt and spun.

The girl rounded the tower, threw her hair on the ground, and swung the gate closed behind her. Then she picked up two steaming bowls from the stone fence and carefully made her way toward Ro.

Her hair streamed behind her in a lumpy mess, and Ro couldn't help but stare. Part of it was still over by the fence when the girl reached Ro.

She held out both bowls of stew, letting Ro choose, then settled on the ground, far enough from Ro to jump to her feet and run if necessary. At least, that's what it looked like.

Ro stood there, then blew on a steaming mouthful and prayed it wasn't poisoned.

Why don't you check if it is?

Ro froze. Waited. But the voice didn't come again.

She stared into the bowl. How could she check it?

Ro closed her eyes, forgetting her surroundings, forgetting the girl who sat across from her, forgetting the one swan that stayed close and the other five that only came close to show their displeasure at her being here.

An image of the soup solidified in her mind, and she could tell its contents. The words that came to her mind were mostly foreign and held no meaning for her, things like lipoids and carbohydrates and amino acids, but one thing was clear: they were all things nutritious for her body.

Ro's eyes popped open, and she stared down into her bowl. Now how could she know that? And was that why at times she ate what was offered, then at other times, declined?

And how did she grasp this gift of hers that seemed so far out of reach? Her grandmère had been significantly unhelpful in that regard. Trained her, indeed.

The girl huffed. "It may be humble fare, but if you're going to turn up your nose at it, give it back. I'll make sure it won't go to waste."

Ro startled, having completely forgotten her audience. She dropped the spoon back in the bowl and laughed uneasily. "Ah, pardon. It has been so long since I had…stew…"

Except for the other night in her grandmère's cabin…

Ugh. She shouldn't be allowed to talk without giving careful thought to what to say first. She didn't know where to go from there, so she shoved in a bite. And moaned. And closed her eyes.

It truly wasn't anything spectacular. Nothing exquisite such as what her sister's chef had served for their every meal at the palace, but it was warm and hearty and well made, and

Ro was starving. Which made it better than what kings served.

Ro shoveled in the remaining bites until her bowl was empty. The girl hadn't touched hers. Wordlessly, she stood and handed it to Ro.

Ro took it hesitantly. "But—are you not, what is the word, famished? Will you not eat as well?"

The girl offered a phantom of a smile. "I already ate. *Danke*."

Her thoughtfulness in bringing a second dish, just in case Ro wanted it, warmed Ro's heart. "Merci beaucoup. Ah, I mean, thank you very much."

Ro didn't know much German, and the girl didn't seem to know much French, so they settled for an uneasy and stilted English. Of course, they'd screamed at each other well enough in a jumble of languages just a few moments ago. Maybe her German lessons hadn't completely deserted her.

"*Bitte*. You're welcome."

The girl edged away, and Ro dug in, keeping her eyes on the stew in the hopes that the girl would be more at ease and perhaps talk to her. "So…what is your name, *Fräulein*?"

The girl started pulling at knots in her hair, running her fingers through the strands, starting at the top and working her way down. "Odette. You?"

Ro swallowed the bite she'd just shoved in her mouth. "Ro."

They said nothing for a little while.

"Have you been here long, Odette?" Ro asked. "In your protective barrier?"

She started to take another bite when her senses prickled. She didn't even hear what Odette replied, she was concentrating so hard on what had arrested her attention.

Voices. There. At her back, in the wood.

Her bowl clattered to the ground with the rest of her soup. Then she took off running for the barrier.

There! Just through the leaves. It sounded like…

"Grandmère! Grandmère!" Ro shouted. Her voice seemed to bounce right back at her.

The sound of talking came close and faded away. A whisper on the wind. Ro came right up to the barrier, and it sizzled in response to her. She held out her hand, just shy of the boundary, afraid to touch it. She'd already been slammed back once, a feeling that set her teeth on edge and left a metallic taste in her mouth.

Ro wasn't looking forward to experiencing that again.

She could hear her grandmère and male voices—Claude, Pascal, Liam—but she couldn't see them. She tried calling a few more times, but nothing.

Then they came out of the darkened trees, following the path she'd taken.

Liam stopped and hunkered down. "The trail ends here."

More like he needed to take a few more steps and look down the ravine to see where she'd tumbled down it. Well, been pushed.

Her face burned that a *swan* of all things had bested her.

He looked at his companions. "Spread out and see if you can find anything."

Faces grim, Claude and Pascal moved away and examined the ground at intervals. Grandmère just leaned on her staff and watched them with bright eyes, like she knew something they didn't.

Ro followed them, the barrier placed in such a way that it passed close to the top of the ridge where she'd fallen.

Liam, the best tracker she knew, moved closer to the invisible barrier separating him from Ro by mere inches.

"Liam, I'm right here."

He didn't respond, concentrating on the ground at his feet.

Ro took a deep breath. This was going to hurt.

Reaching out, not wanting to at all, she tapped the barrier with one finger. It arced and popped and shot out a milky haze that illuminated the barrier briefly before fading away. Her hand bounced off and went numb.

Liam's head came up. Ro froze. He stared just past her, like he'd heard a branch snap. Shoulders hunched against the pain, Ro gritted her teeth and started to try again.

"Hey! Over here," Claude called.

Liam turned away from her. "Found something?"

He went off to investigate, and Ro cried out, "Non! Wait!"

But he didn't hear her, and he didn't return.

Ro's eyes settled on her grandmère, who was staring at her. Ro blinked.

Then the old woman looked down at the bow that Ro just now realized she'd been blocking from Liam with her body. Ro's bow. That she'd dropped. And her grandmère shoved it under rotting leaf cover with her boot.

Ro's mouth fell open.

Darya smiled right at Ro, then turned and hobbled off.

Ro snarled. Why that dirty, rotten old lady! "Grandmère! I know you can hear me. Don't you dare leave me here!"

The old woman kept going.

Blinded by anger, Ro slammed both fists against the barrier, and the moment they came into contact, a burning smell met her nose and she was flung through the air.

When she came to and could see again, Ro raised her head with difficulty. The forest was quiet, her companions, gone. She lifted her hands, stared at them. They ached, bone deep, not a mark on them.

She dropped her head back, frizzy hair spread all around her.

Long-lost relative or not, Ro was going to *kill* her grandmère the next time she saw her.

21

o tried calling out a few more times, but nothing. No one responded, and no one came back. Dejected, she made her way back to the girl, who now leaned against the barn, brushing out her hair with long, firm strokes, watching Ro warily.

Curious, Ro started to ask about the white-gold tresses, but at a fierce glare from Odette, she changed her mind.

Instead, Ro eyed the spilled soup and regretted throwing the bowl. After years of scrounging for every bite, she hated to waste even a morsel. "Désolé."

The girl kept brushing, her furtive glances clearly saying the tangled mess was all Ro's fault. "She can't hear you. Nothing gets past the protective spell." She dropped her voice and muttered, "Nothing's supposed to get in, either."

Ro started to retort, but Odette kept speaking in a normal tone.

"The enchanted wall was the last thing my mother left me —us—before she died. A place for us to go if we had need of it. I never thought we would. Need it, that is. The magic built upon her love makes it impossible for evil to penetrate."

The words tugged at Ro. No evil? Perhaps…

She headed back for the barrier, and after a moment, foot-steps came up behind her. As well as a soft susurrus of sound that could only be Odette's hair trailing behind her on the path. So weird.

Ro really didn't want an audience for this, but what choice did she have? She gathered power in her palms, just as her grandmère had done to her, just as she'd said Ro could do as well, until it felt ready to be released.

The one thing her grandmère had taught her—besides how to be incandescent with rage at being struck over and over with a staff and not break it and the woman striking her "in practice"—and she hadn't even been taught. Just shown.

Hoping it would work, she sent a rush of invisible magic barreling toward the wall. As soon as it hit, a spray of reddish sparks swept up the barrier before fizzling into nothing.

The girl gasped and scrambled back, almost losing her footing in the strands. "A sorceress! Odin, you've brought another sorceress? You stupid, brainless—wasn't *Vater's* example enough?"

The swans squawked and fled in all directions, all except Odin. Ro watched the girl bound toward the tower, climb a pulley system of ropes to the only visible window, and pull them and her hair up after her—the coils were fully the length of the tower when she was at the top, the tips just barely brushing the ground.

She shut herself inside while the other five swans took to the air.

Ro gave a heavy sigh and looked down at the swan the girl called Odin. It gazed up at her with intelligent, mournful eyes.

"Don't look at me like that. You're the one who brought me here." Ro rubbed her temples. "What I wouldn't give to talk to Olt right now." She lifted worried eyes to the sickly forest she could see but had no hope of accessing. "I hope he's all right."

He hadn't been with the search party. Was he still

sequestered in her grandmère's cottage, afraid to go past the clearing?

She about jumped out of her skin when the swan touched her side. She yelped and leaped back, but the swan just waddled closer. Ro froze, ready to send it flying with one swift kick if it tried to bite her.

With a sigh of its own, the creature rested its head against her leg, and after a moment, she reached down and placed her hand on the bird's neck. It nuzzled her.

With a smile, she stroked its neck and marveled at the soft feathers under her fingertips. Maybe getting lost in the woods and finding this dreadful place wasn't too terrible after all.

Her gaze moved from the swan to the forest.

If it wasn't for Allura.

She didn't have time for this. She needed to get free and go after the sorceress who'd cursed her niece.

Her jaw hardened. Anyone who would do that to a child didn't deserve to live.

The slightest of sounds jolted Ro from a light slumber. Her eyes flew open, and she picked out the girl coming toward her in the predawn light. Her eyesight illuminated Odette clearly, and Ro blinked at the mass of braided hair behind the girl.

It no longer touched the ground, coming just about to her ankles, but the many braids looped over and around themselves and resulted in a creation that was almost as thick as Odette's shoulders. It must've taken her all night. It had to be heavy.

And it made Ro incredibly grateful for her own short hair.

Ro waited where she'd been curled up in her cape sleeping, every muscle coiled tight and ready to spring.

The swan was no longer beside her. Ro tamped down a

flicker of worry. The girl may have been upset with the swan, but surely she wouldn't have harmed it. Right?

Odette paused not far from Ro, studying her form where she lay. She spoke to Ro as if she knew she was awake. "Odin says you're not a sorceress. Or a spy. That you've been training with the old mother in the woods and you're here to help."

It sounded like every word pained the girl.

"And you believe…your swan?" Ro asked carefully.

"Of course I do," she snapped.

Because that made sense. Ro spoke kindly, gently, so she wouldn't upset the unhinged girl. "Of course you do. Do you want to tell me about them? Your swans."

"*Nein,*" the girl said succinctly. But she didn't move away.

"All right. Then can you help me? I need to get out."

"You can't. Not until the summer solstice."

The summer solstice? That was weeks away. Ro bit back frustration. "I don't have time to wait that long!"

She decided to be frank with the girl. Perhaps that would make her more forthcoming herself. Ro propped herself up on her elbows.

"My niece has been placed under a sleeping spell, and if I don't break it in time, she'll sleep forever. I've slowed it, but not enough. I may not have weeks."

As if her words had called forth the clock, it tolled and clicked once more backward, shaking everything around Ro and nearly sending her tumbling off her elbows. Yet Odette stood firm, not reacting to the tremors.

Ro's eyes widened. Three clicks. Nine more to go. It wasn't—counting down how long Allura had, was it?

Whatever she'd just seen brought forth the panic Ro had been trying so hard to suppress. She jumped to her feet. "I have to get out!"

Ro dug her axe out of the fir branches she'd piled to make a bed—having retrieved the axe after yelling herself hoarse

the day before, when her grandmère had just left her there —
and headed for the barrier at a sprint.

Allura needed her! She didn't have time to just…sit here.

Ro heaved her grandmère's spare axe at the magical
barrier. It bounced off the clear shield, jarring her hands and
shuddering her bones. But the magics fought each other, not
repelling the axe as harshly as it had done her.

"Ack!" Ro heaved it in her hands and swung again. "For
the love of pâtisseries, let me out!"

It had been a long time since she'd lost her cool. But panic
was strangling her chest, moving up her throat, making it
impossible to be rational. She was trapped. Her niece needed
her. Her *sister* needed her. And she was failing them both
spectacularly.

Ro traveled the full inner perimeter of the barrier, testing
it for weaknesses all the way around. She swung the axe until
her arms ached, until she was having trouble holding it. Back
at her campsite, she threw the weapon down in disgust.

What good was an enchanted axe if it didn't work when
she needed it?

Odette came stomping down the path closest to the lake.
She was yelling before she'd even rounded the bend. "What
are you trying to do? Lead the sorceress to our very
location?"

Ro eyed the girl who might weigh ninety pounds soaking
wet. Ro could take her in a heartbeat. "Are you yelling
at me?"

Odette hefted the heavy axe in her arms, bending under
its weight. "If you don't know how to use a magical weapon,
then you shouldn't have one!"

Ro jumped toward her, but she was too late. The short
girl was already hurtling the axe into the nearby lake, an
impressive feat for one so small. It rotated, end over end,
before landing with a great splash in the middle of the
water.

Ro might've been impressed had she not been ready to throw the girl in after.

"How dare you!" she yelled in Odette's face. "That was my weapon, my only means of defense, and you washed all the magic off with that water!" Ro took control of herself and drew back, her voice cold with fury. "Go get it."

"Go get it? What, so you can scale my tower while I sleep? Tear my swans to pieces? Kill me in my sleep? I don't think so."

Odette spun and marched down the path. Ro grabbed her and hauled her back. Three steps, and the girl was dangling over the water, feet scrabbling for the bank.

"I said go get it," Ro said in a low, calm tone, one that said she felt anything but.

And the girl's large, scared eyes weren't making her feel any better. Worse, in fact. Like a bully, which just made her angrier. The girl had no right to throw away Ro's weapon!

Odette looked panicked, then lifted her chin. *"Nein."*

Ro heaved her in the lake.

She hadn't meant to—but then there was a giant splash, water hit Ro in the face, and remorse splashed her at the exact same time. Good grief, what had she done?

All the swans let up a great honking, loud enough Ro was surprised this sorceress wasn't calmly waiting outside the shield. The girl flailed for only a moment—in which Ro *knew* she'd have to go in there and rescue her—before she took off swimming for the other side.

Ro watched her go, relieved to see such strong strokes. At least the young Mademoiselle could swim. If only Ro didn't feel like an absolute monster for throwing her into the lake in the first place.

When Odette reached the shore, the swans honked and flapped and made the girl fall back in the water twice before she could get out past their swarming her. Which was a feat in and of itself with all that hair.

Then the swans lowered their heads and hissed threateningly at Ro. Even the one who'd tried to be Ro's friend looked at her with accusing eyes. That stung a little.

Which was just pathetic.

The girl pointed at Ro across the lake, her shouted words echoing across the expanse. "You stay away from me, or I'll—I'll—you just stay away from me!"

She wrung out her unraveling braids as best she could, eyes full of fire, and Ro took a swift step forward, like she was ready to follow Odette across the lake.

The girl shrieked and took off, swiftly climbing her tower and disappearing inside, her ridiculous hair slinking after her in a soggy, writhing mess.

The swans fanned out at the tower's base, daring Ro to follow. She just laughed, the sound defiant. No way was she going near those beasts, but still. She was at least going to *act* like they didn't bother her.

Then she eyed the lake. Yeah, she'd be going in after it. The axe was the only weapon she still had, after all. Unless she could get to the other side of the barrier.

Stupid girl for throwing her only weapon into the stupid lake.

Ro took off her cape, kicked off her boots, and shed her leather jerkin. She slid down the bank and eased into the water, surprised at how pleasant it was, and then pushed off for the middle of the lake.

Once she'd gotten approximately to where the girl had flung her axe, she eyed the swans. They still watched from the base of the tower, not friendly in the least.

Ro made a motion like she'd be watching them, to which one of them ruffled its feathers and another pretended to sleep by placing its face under its wing—almost like these swans had a sense of humor—then she dove deep.

It was too murky to see anything.

She hadn't reached the bottom by the time she needed to

return for air. She burst through the surface, ready to dive fast if the swans were waiting to attack her.

They all watched from shore, far more interested than they should've been. They glanced away in various directions when Ro's eyes landed on them.

Stupid birds. Stupid tower. Stupid girl! Who kept a flock of attack swans as pets?

Ro took several deep breaths, preparing to dive once more. Then she paused. "I wonder…"

She sank slowly below the surface. Willing a bubble to form, as the sirens had shown her, she fitted it carefully over her mouth and nose. It pushed the water away from her face, and she took several deep breaths and smiled. Perfect.

And then, because the water was so murky she could hardly see, especially as she stirred up the silty bottom on her way in, she shaped the bubble to cover her entire face.

Weak sunlight barely penetrated the first mètre of water. She doubted even full sun would penetrate more than three.

She took a deep breath. Then another. Then dove deep.

The bubble held, fresh air in abundance. But it was pitch black. She couldn't see a thing, and her eyesight refused to illuminate anything.

Ro squeezed her eyes shut and kept going, relying on other senses to take her to the little lake's floor. It was rather impressive, how deep it was. Once she reached the bottom, silky dirt covered her skin, and her hand sank deep. She jerked it back. Opened her eyes.

Which just made it worse.

She closed her eyes again and felt for her axe. She rummaged around longer than she meant to, shifting her posi-tion by degrees, certain she was close to where it was flung.

But her hand couldn't reach the hardened bottom through the silt, her eyesight wouldn't light up her surroundings, and the lake refused to give her back her axe.

She let her body rise a little. Once she caught the direction of the surface, she swam straight up. As with the sirens, the air grew more stale as her frustration built.

As she burst through the surface, suddenly white wings and flapping and honking were her entire world.

Ro shrieked and waved her arms and tried to shoo them away and went under, choking on lake water. Hoping she wasn't about to drown, she bobbed to the surface.

"You can't finish me off that easily, crazy birds! Shoo. Shoo!"

Most of them eased away, though it took a while for all the bluster to die down.

They eyed her; she eyed them, then she started to swim backward.

When they stayed where they were, and when she was far enough away, she flipped over and swam with hard strokes to the shoreline opposite the tower. She scrambled up the bank, glancing behind her once or twice.

The swans stayed where they were, bobbing on the surface.

Ro stood on the shore, soaking wet, eyeing the blasted birds. They really had tried to drown her!

After scrounging in the garden for both lunch and dinner, and exploring the woods to see just how big her prison actually was, Ro tried for the axe again. For hours.

She eyed the sinking sun, no closer to finding her weapon, and admitted defeat for the day. Tonight would be miserable if she didn't get her only clothes dried out in time.

After climbing out, a shiver wracked her body, so she grabbed deadwood and fallen branches and began building up a fire. Summer or no, these woods were downright chilly in the evenings.

Taking her flint from the jacket she'd left on shore—along with a small bit of string and a paring knife she kept there at all times—it wasn't long until she'd made a few sparks. She cupped her hands and blew gently, bringing the tinder to life.

She stacked a wood tower around it, building it bigger and bigger until it roared into the loveliest bonfire. Then she added several large, dry pieces of wood to keep it going well into the night.

Ro huddled close, turning on all sides to dry herself.

Still, the wind was cool. And her clothes were still wet.

Just as she was considering putting her jerkin and cape over her still-wet clothes, honking and flapping came from the path. Ro rolled her eyes. If they were coming to attack her now, she would seize them and throw them into the fire.

She wondered what roasted swan tasted like.

The swans fussed and made a racket, and Ro moved to the other side of the fire so she could see when they came out of the trees. The first one came—backward.

Ro blinked. What in all the realms?

Its head was strained forward, out of sight, and every once in a while, it would rush away, honking and flapping. Ro couldn't imagine what the stupid things were up to now.

Then the swan, the one waddling backward, pulled a blanket into view.

Well. She hadn't been expecting that.

The other swans rushed it, making it drop the blanket, then tried to pull it the other way. It was rather pathetic, how the one swan kept trying to fend off the other five.

Ro sighed and grabbed a long branch, one she hadn't broken up yet, and marched toward the birds. "Shoo! Off with you. Shoo!"

The swans honked and flapped, trying to look intimidating, but Ro went after them with her stick. Once she'd driven the five down the path and they were well on their way to the tower, she came back to the swan waiting for her, measly little blanket at its feet.

She smiled at the bedraggled thing. "That's for me, huh?"

The swan snaked out its long neck and pushed the edge toward her.

Ro laughed and picked it up between her fingers, dirt clinging to it. "I would say merci, but it's quite a mess, non?"

The swan lowered its neck and gave a sad little bleat. Ro chuckled and ruffled the feathers on the bird's back, careful to go along the grain so she wouldn't cause pain. It perked up at her attention.

"Oh, come now, it's the thought that counts." She eyed the portion that had been dragged through a puddle. "We can let it dry while my clothes do the same, oui?"

The bird flapped its wings, honked happily, and trotted over to the fire. Not too close, but turning its back to Ro. Rather trusting. For a bird.

Ro spread the blanket over some branches. "There. Now it'll be ready when I am." She raised an eyebrow. "Or do you plan to roll me in the lake while I sleep and drown me for good this time?"

If a bird could look horrified, this one did, and Ro laughed.

"Of course you wouldn't want me thinking that, would you, mon ami?" She held out her arm. "Come. You can tell me the secrets of this place and help me find a way of escape. After we climb the tower and turn out all her clothes into the lake."

The swan gave her a reproachful look.

"What? You have brothers or sisters or friends or whatever they are." She waved her hand in the general direction of the other swans. "You're telling me you've never been tempted to pluck out their feathers? Not ever?"

The bird ducked his head, and Ro laughed harder.

"Ooh, look at me! I can't believe I'm talking to a swan. Tell me, friend, how long have you enjoyed the water in these parts?"

Ro kept up the ridiculous one-sided conversation as her clothes dried, giving tips from surviving her own brothers and sisters, sharing things she'd learned while working with

France's greatest huntsmen, and telling all about annoying Liam and endearing Olt.

And the swan placed its head in her lap and just listened as she stroked its feathers and talked, probably more than she had in her life.

As Ro chattered, she realized she'd never missed Olt more. She wondered if she'd be brave enough to tell him so if she ever got the chance.

She liked to think she would.

Her voice turned sad. "I just hope he's all right. That… he'll be able to forgive me for making him come with me."

The swan nuzzled closer, and Ro's eyes began to close on their own.

The next morning, the girl nowhere in sight, Ro decided to make herself useful. The barn's roof needed patching, weeds had decided the garden was theirs, and Ro discovered animal pens behind the barn that needed mucking. And repairing.

When she took a break to guzzle water from the well and then dump a bucketful of cool well water over her head to refresh herself from the day's heat, she found a simple meal laid out for her in the barn.

Ro fell to it almost in the same manner as when she'd been tainted by the wolf. After, she called up a "merci beaucoup" to the tower's window, then went back to work when there was no response.

Several times, she tested the barrier for weak spots, for a way through. And she never could find her axe, no matter how many dips in the lake she took.

The next two weeks went by in much the same manner. The girl avoided Ro like the plague, leaving food but disappearing inside the tower before Ro could thank her. Or apologize.

Only one bell toll had sent Ro careening off a ladder, but

at nothing worse than a bruised hip, she got up and went back to keeping her body strong for when she faced the enchantress. What else could she do?

The swans lowered their heads and hissed anytime she came around, all but the one, who'd become her shadow.

She was becoming fond of the thing, and unless the other swans startled her when she rounded a corner or came through the wood, her heart didn't try to beat itself out of her chest every time she saw them.

Odette spent most of her time in her tower, and Ro couldn't help but be puzzled by the sad state of affairs around the homestead.

The barn had been well-built, but tools were rusting, and hay left to mildew. The state of the garden was almost a crime. It looked as though the girl did the bare minimum to grow food, but nothing else. Weeds were healthier than vegetables.

Ro still tried to get past the barrier every single day, and by now had mapped out the entire inner perimeter, but she also sharpened and oiled tools, weeded the garden, and cut away vines climbing the tower and starting to eat the barn whole.

She replaced the hay with a wagonful she found near the tower, and dumped the molding, stinking hay in a scrap pile near the tree line.

The girl had a milking cow, a roost of hens with one rooster Ro was coming to hate, and two goats that liked to head-butt Ro every time she entered their pen.

It seemed the animals shared their owner's disposition.

Even with the rooster making every morning miserable—that and the sun, which came up far too early, in Ro's disgruntled opinion—Ro always found the cow and goats milked and the eggs gone before she got there.

Not that she was complaining. Mornings were the worst.

Ro half wondered why she was doing so much for the girl who had thrown away Ro's weapon, but she'd go crazy not doing *something*. She was already talking to the birds like they were human. Now if she could just get Odette to speak to her again, she could get out of here. Probably.

Ro was currently hoeing the garden, coaxing more food out of the soil, wondering how on earth they ate as well as they did with the garden and animals neglected so.

"I guess you aren't going anywhere, are you?"

Ro shrieked and threw the garden tool. She spun on the girl, heart pounding, chest heaving, and stared at her with wide eyes.

Odette giggled, the sound far too girly for her no-nonsense homespun clothing and tight braids she used to manage all that hair. She looked far too pleased with herself for scaring Ro.

She glanced around the garden. "And I have to say, I'm enjoying all the free labor I'm getting around here."

Ro's brows lowered, and she scowled at the impertinent girl. Forcing her tense muscles to relax, Ro picked up the hoe and leaned on it in what she hoped was a laid-back manner.

"You'll make your animals sick with rotting hay. Rusting tools might break and wound you when you use them, and this garden won't feed you much longer in this state. Nor will you have anything to put away for winter." Ro's gaze turned intense, though secretly she was glad to have something to do. "Someone had to do it. Why weren't you?"

The girl shifted uncomfortably, then shrugged. "I have better things to do."

Ro couldn't form words. In a magically enclosed homestead, caring for one's animals and food source somehow ranked lower than shutting oneself in a tower all day?

Ro was trying to think of how to respond when Odette said, "Since I can't get rid of you, not till the summer solstice, you're welcome to sleep in the barn." She held up a finger. "But only if you keep doing what you've been doing." She turned to leave.

Ro threw down her hoe. "Non, I'm done."

Odette stopped but didn't turn around.

"My niece is trapped under a sleeping curse, and I need to confront the sorceress who did this and set the little girl free! I don't have time to weed your stupid garden."

Odette's shoulders hunched. "I understand, I do, but…you can't. No one can leave. Not until my family is free from the witch's clutches."

"See, you keep saying that, but I couldn't help but notice we have fresh meals and plenty of bacon and ham and pork" —which Ro didn't care for; something about the sweet-salty taste of pig wasn't pleasant—"that isn't preserved in salt, by the way, yet you have no sty."

Odette seemed rooted to her spot.

"If no one can get out, and no one is supposed to get in, where is the food coming from? It sure isn't coming from this garden and your milk cow."

When Odette didn't reply, Ro took a step toward her. "Please, I am begging you. If you can't help me—and that's just fine—please let me go. Let me do what I came here for. I need to stop this empress from hurting anyone ever again."

Odette didn't move. Ro tried not to let her heart swell with hope, but that was like telling the sun not to shine on the clearing. She stayed quiet with every fiber of her being, waiting on Odette.

"This spell your niece is under." Odette glanced at her, then away. "Tell me about it?"

Ro chose her words carefully. The last thing she wanted was her lack of people skills to send the girl huffing back to her tower, not to be seen again for several more weeks. "We think someone calling herself the empress placed it on her, and we think that empress is here, in the Black Forest. Why do you ask?"

"I think…I think…your empress may be my sorceress. The same person."

Ro's eyebrows climbed her forehead. She was just now realizing this?

The girl eyed her before wilting a little. She jerked her head, her words soft. "Wash up. We'll talk over brown bread and soft cheese." Odette hurried away.

Hope not only filled Ro at those words, it burst forth like a ray of sunshine. Could she find a way past the magical barrier with the girl's help?

Ro put away her hoe, slung her cape over her arm, and cleaned up as fast as she could.

Smelling and feeling much better, though her clothes were still damp, Ro sat across from the girl, watching the spread and Odette in turn.

They were at a rickety wooden table the girl had pulled from somewhere and placed between the tower and the barn, close to the lake. A bright-yellow tablecloth and sky-blue napkins made the setup cheery, and hearty loaves of brown bread and bright yellow cheese wedges sat next to a pitcher of beer.

Ro stayed away from alcohol as much as possible, but she had to admit she was curious about the warm, yeasty smell coming from the pitcher.

It was a deep-brown color when Odette poured it into her mug, and Ro sniffed then sipped tentatively. She held off a grimace by sheer willpower.

It might take more than she was willing to give to get used to that.

Trying to be polite, she did her best not to guzzle well water.

Although this was a spread made with hearty German fare, she missed her café au lait and pâtisseries of her own country. Then again, she wasn't one to turn down good food.

But also, where was it *coming from*?

At any other time, Ro would've found the setup lovely. Right now she wanted to help Allura so much she ached with it.

"You said my empress and your sorceress are the same."

The girl nodded.

"Go on."

The girl fidgeted, touching everything on her plate but not eating it, and wouldn't quite look at Ro. Something about Odette's hands looked odd, something she couldn't quite figure out. As if the skin was stretched too tight. Or perhaps a little waxy?

Maybe burns that hadn't healed right?

But that wasn't important. Ro needed answers *now*. "Odette. I'm running out of time. If you have answers for me, I need them. I need to know who this empress is, what she's doing here, and if she has any weaknesses. If you have anything to tell me, anything at all, I beg of you—please don't let me waste another minute."

Odette stared at Ro with wide eyes all through her little speech, then turned to the white swan hovering nearby. "You're sure about this?"

The swan gave an urgent bleat.

Begrudging, reluctant, and looking as though the mere thought of what she was about to do pained her, Odette turned back to Ro. "I dislike this story, so I won't say it more than once."

Ro nodded her agreement.

"Well, then. It all started when the empress married my father."

Ro sat back, stunned.

"You see, the empress hails from a faraway land. She came to entertain us with her dancing dragons and fireworks and paper lanterns. But then she fell for my father—well, his position and land, really—and soon their engagement was announced."

Ro blinked. "Your père? Who was he?"

The girl gave a bitter little smile that aged her enough that Ro thought she might be even older than Ro was. Though it was hard to tell with her blonde hair and blue eyes and flawless skin that had seen little sunlight. No wonder with staying in the tower all day.

"Why, the king of Prussia, of course." She shrugged. "Well, this portion of Prussia, anyway. Something the witch did not realize until it was too late." She gave a humorless laugh. "The witch had her eye on another part of the Black Forest and assumed she'd get it all."

Ro took another sip of the dark, yeasty beer before she realized what she was doing. She swallowed with difficulty. Then shoved in a few bites of bread and cheese.

"Our land is divided into seven kingdoms, one for my father and each of his brothers. The eldest rules over the others, overseeing his own kingdom, mostly, but acting as a liaison for the other six and any disputes that may arise. There have always been seven sons born to the eldest of the royal line, and only ever daughters to the rest of the brothers.

"It was part of the agreement, the bond, my family took upon themselves when given the land for safekeeping. My father was always trying to unite his brothers, trying to get them to rule together, to make decisions together, instead of apart.

"My father was also the first eldest to have a girl."

She swallowed hard and looked away, and Ro's heart went out to her.

In other words, she'd been reminded her entire life how being a girl was a blight on her father, who was apparently supposed to have seven strong sons. Only.

If Ro had a livre for every time someone had told her a woman shouldn't be a huntress…

Odette went on, her voice not as steady. "I was the eldest, and it caused quite a ruckus. It was the first time that had happened since the kingdom had been placed into our family line to care for it." She shrugged. "That's all we were. Its caretakers, yet the people made us kings and queens."

When she glanced Ro's way, Ro nodded for her to continue.

"Well, after me, six more brothers came, but no more. My father and uncles were beside themselves. English queens may rule, but that was for the barbaric English, not the noble Germans. Yet one kingdom would be leaderless if they did not let me rule." Her voice grew tight. "They didn't know what to do, but as it turns out, their choice was taken from them."

Drink and cheese and brown bread forgotten, Ro leaned forward, hanging on every word.

"One by one, my uncles got sick and died. No explanation. No reason for it. They didn't have children yet, and rumors circulated about why all their queens were barren. Then... then my father..."

She looked down, hands clenched into fists on her lap.

After a moment, Ro ventured, "He died too?"

Odette glanced up, her gaze pinging away from Ro's, and laughed, though the sound held no mirth. "You know, I don't know. He must have. My brothers and I were certain our stepmother had something to do with our uncles' deaths, but when we tried to investigate, she cast a spell and banished us all."

She wrung her hands and fidgeted, but Ro could think of nothing to say. What would be comforting and not...trite?

The girl finally looked around her. "So we came here—well, *I* came here—and I await the day my brothers join me."

The empress must've put them to sleep as she had Allura. "And when they do?"

That hard look descended over her face. "When my brothers join me, we will defeat the witch and take my kingdom back. And if my father does not yet live, I will rule his kingdom, and I will do an excellent job."

The words looked like they gutted her, and a harrowed look came over her face, probably from hearing all her life that she was worthless.

Ro could relate. "I am sorry, Odette. I am so very sorry."

Odette jerked her chin, acknowledging Ro's words but still not looking at her.

Ro ventured one thing more: "Perhaps…perhaps you were born for such a time as this. To rule. To defeat her. To…unite them as your father couldn't."

Odette sat back, stunned, as if she'd never heard such words in her life. Never considered such a thing.

"What's your plan? For taking out the witch. And how do we find your brothers?"

This broke Odette's astonishment, and she studied Ro with a frown. "Someone has to break the spell holding my brothers captive before they can join me."

Yep. Just like Allura. Ro nodded. "I can do that. Well, if I get out. What do I do?"

Now Odette studied her so hard, Ro did squirm. After an excruciating eternity, Odette finally said, "You would do that?"

"But of course. The witch holds my niece under the same spell. The longer she sleeps, the firmer it becomes." Ro ducked her head and swallowed. "If I do not break it in time, she'll not wake." She lifted pain-filled eyes to Odette's. "I'll do whatever it takes to defeat the empress."

After a moment, Odette's eyes started sparkling. "I think I may come to like you after all, huntress."

Ro shrugged. "I don't really care if you do or do not. I just want to finish this and get back to my niece. And sister."

The girl inched closer. "She keeps her spells in a secret chamber at the heart of the mountain. If you break the globe that contains them all, she won't be able to hold on to them.

They will, in essence, float away and grow weaker and weaker until they dissipate altogether."

Well that was one of the strangest things Ro had ever heard. But if it worked… "Including the spell that holds my niece?"

Odette thought for a moment. "I'm not sure, but I think so? I know where my brothers' spells are held, because she was going to use me and Odile as its guardians, chained nearby to keep it safe."

Ro blinked. "She was going to…chain you?"

Odette just shrugged. "I escaped, but not before she trapped Odile." Now pain laced her face, so much so that she nearly folded under its weight. "My own sister, and I couldn't even keep her safe."

Ro was having trouble keeping up. "Wait, a sister? I thought you were the only girl…"

Odette waved away Ro's words. "She was my best friend from childhood, like a sister to me, and she married my eldest younger brother, Oberon."

Ro squinted, trying to keep it all straight.

Odette huffed a breath and held up a hand, ticking off names with each finger. "There's me, then Oberon, Odysseus, Odwin, Olov, Orbart, and O—"

She cut off the last name abruptly, then gave Ro a tight smile.

But Ro was nodding absently, certain she'd never remember any of that. Names tended to run like water in one ear and out the other.

"I understand." She copied Odette's movements for her own family. "There's my eldest sister, Bernadette, then Reinette, Nicolette, Lynette, Yvette, then my brothers, Claude and Pascal, then me, then my youngest sister—"

Ro faltered, unsure of what to say next.

"Your youngest sister…?" Odette prompted, eyes filled with curiosity.

Ro blew out a breath on a laugh. "Yeah, well, I guess I had two but didn't know it? The sister I grew up with, my best friend, was Cosette. The sister I never knew, the one who lived near here, actually, was Cendre."

Odette raised an eyebrow, a hint of a smile playing around her lips. "A sister you didn't know you had? Now that sounds like an interesting tale."

Ro shrugged but didn't expound.

Odette didn't press. "Cendre…that name sounds familiar. You say she lived near here?"

Ro sat up straighter. "Did you know her? She lived in a cabin in the woods with our grandmère. Um, the old protectress of the forest?"

Ro held her breath, waiting so hard for her answer.

Odette huffed a laugh. "The old mother of the woods? We were kept in constant fear of her my entire childhood. Told if we found her and she offered sweets, we'd be stuck there forever, then she'd eat us." She chuckled at what sounded like a fond memory. "I'm almost certain that wasn't true. Anyway, *nein*, I didn't know her, the girl Cendre, but her name certainly sounds familiar. Perhaps one of my brothers met her once? I don't know."

Ro had met—and rescued children from—an old witch who lured children in with sweets and then ate them, but that witch was most definitely dead.

Ro's mind went to little Allura. Another child she would save. "Do you have a plan? For taking down the empress?"

Odette seemed to wilt. "I was hoping you would?"

Ro closed her eyes. "Of course you were."

Her grandmère's words echoed back to her. She couldn't enter a situation such as this blind, deaf, and dumb and just hope it would turn out. She needed as much information as possible.

Ro opened her eyes. "Tell me everything you know about this empress."

Odette recounted—in great detail—every interaction she'd had with the empress, which mostly consisted of state dinners and sitting far away, as if she were the youngest and not the eldest.

The empress was easily offended, fiercely possessive of those she'd claimed as hers (such as the German emperor), and readily attacked instead of talking anything out.

With a vague promise to leave in the next day or so, Odette went back to her tower, and Ro prepared to depart.

She decided to grab more food, since she hadn't had much while they'd talked, but their leftovers had been set upon by the six swans. Odette had just left it all there, not bothering to put anything away, and Ro regretted having no more than a few bites.

Since Ro had been in a state of readiness to leave since she'd been trapped, it didn't take her long to prepare, so she did her daily perimeter sweep, just in case. As she went, another bell toll sounded, nearly sending her to her knees.

What did it mean? There was no rhyme or reason to it. No set length of weeks or days or hours. The clock simply showed up, let her know the hand was now pointing at the Roman numeral seven, then disappeared.

Frustration built, and she walked faster and faster around her path in the woods, but it wasn't helping. She was nowhere near calm.

A few laps should do the trick.

She took off running, traveling the perimeter of her prison several times before a measure of sanity returned. She dropped to the ground, exhausted, and wiped her sweat-slickened neck and forehead with her sleeves.

What did the clock *mean*? Would she be trapped here with no way to find out until it reached the one?

Something nudged her arm, and she yelped and jerked away. Oh. Just one of the swans. Odin. She eyed it warily. It studied her, and if Ro didn't know any better, she'd say it almost looked…concerned. Now who was going crazy?

Ro huffed a laugh. "Oh sure, come over here after the run is already over."

It honked a response.

"You want to get out of here too? You and me both, mon ami. You and me both."

She lay back and stretched out on the grass. Dappled sunlight played through the leaves, and Ro closed her eyes and just enjoyed its warmth on her face. The swan nuzzled beside her, and before she knew it, she was asleep.

Ro woke to complete darkness. A darkness so tangible, fear immediately swamped her. The swan at her side nuzzled closer, and peace settled around her shoulders like a blanket. Or her mère's cape.

For once Ro was thankful for the beautiful bird.

She settled and stared at the few stars she could see through the canopy of trees. She smiled. One of her favorite parts of the hunt. She should've been chilled, but the massive swan warmed her and made the cool night bearable.

After a while, one thought wouldn't leave her mind. She'd fallen asleep sweaty and gross, and good heavens but she wasn't going to sleep the rest of the night that way.

She sat up and spoke. "Come on, swanny."

The swan dutifully rose and followed her to the lake. She took in the tower, then eyed the grounds for movement. Nothing but the rest of the swans on the other side of the lake, heads tucked under their wings, sleeping.

Hopefully that meant the girl was in bed too. She eyed the sparkling water, cleansed by the stream trickling in one side and out the other, one of the few places the moon shone through the dense foliage, and was thankful it wasn't a scuzzy, scum-filled pond. She'd try not to kick up the fine silt on the bottom.

She started talking to the swan as she took off her tunic. "You won't mind if I share your little lake to clean up, will you? Don't want to wake Her Highness pumping water from the well, not with the squeaky handle…"

She started peeling off her undershirt when a great squawking interrupted her. Ro nearly fell into the lake as she yanked her shirt back down over her head to see what was going on.

The swan glided past her, skimming the water and aiming right for the rest of the birds. It took some doing, but Odin drove off the rest, and Ro just stood there and watched them climb into the sky, outer shirt clutched to her chest.

As soon as he'd driven off the other birds, Odin waddled off, disappearing behind the tower and into the garden there, somehow swinging the gate closed behind him.

The other birds turned into tiny dots before they banked then flew far enough away to disappear altogether.

What in the name of heaven?

She scanned the woods. No wolves or any other predator

that she could sense—not that there were any within the barrier—and glanced up at the tower in time to see a curtain fall back in place.

Ro couldn't be sure, but she thought she heard faint laughter.

She eyed the water next. A monster wasn't lurking under its surface, was there? Surely not. The swans wouldn't live here quite so peacefully if so.

After waiting a while—they never came back—Ro stripped the rest of the way and stepped into the cool, refreshing water. It was just the right temperature. Like everything else about this place. Just right.

It was a comfortable prison, but a prison nonetheless.

But she couldn't relax and enjoy herself, not with the swans' reactions, not with the mirror-finish of the calm lake reflecting moonlight, not with the silent wood watching her and the too-cool breeze dancing across any exposed skin.

She hurried through her bathing, dressed in the too-small clothes Odette had lent her, and scrubbed her clothes clean. Next she draped her clothing and cloak over branches to dry during the night.

Then she opted to spend the rest of the night outside, under the canopy of familiar and welcoming stars.

❧

Ro sat with her back to the tower, grinding the rust off a second pitchfork she'd found in the loft, seeing if the metal underneath were salvageable.

She ignored the footsteps that timidly approached, focusing on her task as if there were nothing else in the world that could possibly interest her. She knew better than to startle creatures that might bolt.

Odette nervously shuffled her feet. "You'll need new weapons. If you're going to face her?"

Ro's brows lowered into a scowl directed at the pitchfork. "I wouldn't need new weapons if you hadn't thrown my axe into the lake."

She hadn't meant to say it, but no matter how hard she'd tried, she couldn't find it. As if the lake were hiding it from her.

Odette winced. "About that…I'm sorry, truly."

Ro nodded once, kept grinding away at the rust. "And I apologize for losing my temper. Think there's any way to get it back?"

Odette's expressive eyes widened. "With how deep it is? I don't think so."

Ro huffed a breath. "Didn't think so."

She glanced up. Odette stood decked out in furs, which had to be sweltering in this weather, her monstrous amount of hair coiled into thick braids that wrapped around her head and still almost dragged the ground. It looked heavy.

As did the curved blade peeking over her shoulder. Ro craned her neck just slightly. Was that a Germanic war axe?

She almost looked like a warrior princess, if not for the uncertain look on her face.

"But, well, what I meant was"—Odette twisted her fingers —"you'll need new weapons for fighting the empress. To find her, even."

Ro tilted her head.

"I can—I'll have to show you. How to get new ones."

It took Ro a moment to figure out what she meant. "You mean, *outside* the barrier?"

Odette bit her lip.

Ro let out a curse. Then two more. "I knew it!" After jumping up to pace so she wouldn't be tempted to wring the smaller girl's neck, Ro noticed Odette was staring at her with a quizzical look on her face. "What?"

Odette jumped, then stammered a bit before getting out a

coherent answer. "I was just wondering—you really mean to help us?"

"Oui. It has the added benefit of helping my niece as well."

"And if helping us didn't help your niece?"

Ro's jaw tightened. She sincerely hoped she wouldn't find out at the end of all this that she hadn't helped Allura one whit. "If you've been lying to me, so help me—"

Odette jumped back, her hands raised. "*Nein, nein,* nothing like that!"

She was probably scared of being thrown in the lake again. Ro sighed. She really needed to learn to control that temper of hers. "Then why are you asking me this?"

Odette shrugged and, again, wouldn't meet Ro's eyes. "I just need to know. Please."

Ro immediately thought of the village, nightly attacked by wolves, that they'd bypassed to get to the decidedly unhelpful old lady of the woods. She sucked in a breath at the pain of not being able to help.

She rather preferred to jump in and help first, figure out consequences later. If she stuck around for them.

She let out her breath in a big gust. "I would go help my niece, and once that was done, return and help you. If I could."

Odette eyed her skeptically.

Ro shrugged. "You did want my honesty."

"I guess I did."

Odette wrestled with her decision for so long, Ro almost snapped her fingers in the girl's face, but restrained herself. Best not to get on the girl's bad side.

Well. Any *more* on her bad side.

After a moment, Odette finally managed, "Fine. Let's get this over with."

Hope flared to life, and Ro settled her red cape over her shoulders and retrieved the pitchfork that was mostly sound.

The girl eyed Ro's cape and improvised weapon. "*Nein.*

The pitchfork will do you no good, and the cloak is too...bright."

Ro gritted her teeth. "My mère's cloak has special...properties. It protects me from the fey."

Odette raised her eyebrows. "By calling them toward you like a beacon?"

"Non. By making me unseen." Or so her grandmère had said.

Though the beast had seen her just fine. Although, he was technically cursed, not a fey creature, so perhaps her grandmère was right?

Odette eyed the cloak begrudgingly, a hint of envy in her eyes. "Well, I don't know if the empress is fey, but her birds certainly are." She nodded at a homemade bow and arrows she'd brought from somewhere and laid on the wooden table they'd eaten on yesterday. "That's the only use you'll be to me out there."

Ro eyed the poorly made bow. "I have my own bow and arrows. Outside the barrier." *If they're still there.*

Odette gave her a strange look. "Still, I'd feel better if you had something." She eyed the pitchfork. "Other than that."

Ro sighed and leaned the pitchfork against the barn. Then picked up the bow.

If this thing snapped and got her killed—or took out an eye—she was going to personally haunt Odette. She hesitantly drew, then committed. The draw was shorter than she liked, but the wood bent easily, no creaking or cracking, and the draw held just enough power that she should be able to shoot a fair distance.

"Not bad. Not bad at all."

Odette smirked. "What? You think I'd make something I can't defend myself with?"

That's exactly what Ro thought, but she'd better not say so.

"What about that?" Ro jerked her chin to the blade

peeking over Odette's shoulder. "That would go a long way toward replacing my axe."

If nothing else, she wanted a better look at it. Ro knew weapons, and this one looked exquisite. Odette pulled it into her hands in a deft and well-practiced move, and Ro sucked in a breath.

A double-headed battle-axe, blades sharp and gleaming, intricate scrollwork carved into the blades and handle, and wicked-looking pike atop it for stabbing made for one of the most gorgeous battle-axes Ro had seen in her life.

She was halfway in love already.

She'd taken a few steps forward, hands outstretched, bow deserted and forgotten, when Odette pulled it away from her grasp.

"*Nein*. This was my father's, and only to be wielded by one of his line. Not that he would've expected that line to include me," she grumbled to herself. And then, as if clarifying, "You cannot have it. You may use it, if I allow, but you cannot take ownership."

Odette lifted her chin and looked as if she'd fight Ro for it. Or toss the battle-axe into the lake herself rather than let Ro touch it.

Ro sighed, stepped back, and glanced at the bow that looked as if it'd been made by a child. She decided to leave it where it lay. "Understood."

Odette nodded too many times and slid the axe back over her shoulder. Leather creaked as it settled into its sheath.

Ro tucked arrows into her belt, just in case she couldn't find enough of hers, then swept her hand aside. "Lead the way, Mademoiselle."

"I will then, *Fräulein*."

They walked to the barrier and stopped.

After a moment of eyeing Ro—and Ro trying to look completely harmless so the girl wouldn't change her mind—Odette sighed. "Help me line up these rocks."

24

Ro jumped to help. They lined up seven heavy rocks that had been scattered around, then Odette nervously swiped her hand to the side. A doorway opened in the barrier.

Ro's mouth fell open.

"Well?" Odette snapped. "Are you coming or going to stand there and gawk all day?"

Although her words were fierce, there was a tremor in them.

Ro forced her feet to move. Forced down every insult that came to the surface about the girl's insistence that they couldn't leave her homestead.

On the other side, Odette scanned the trees for a long time before hauling another stone close and propping it upright. It looked natural, but Ro could tell if the barrier wasn't there, it would tumble down.

A landmark so they could find the entrance again.

Odette seemed jittery outside the barrier, jumping at every sound, including her own footsteps.

Ro hurried over to where her bow lay, dug it out from the rotting leaves, and crooned lovingly to it as she inspected every inch. Even still strung—it should've been unstrung while not in use—it looked fine.

She drew, and the string didn't snap, the wood didn't give more than it should have—she blinked back tears, and before she knew it, she'd clasped it to her chest and was standing there like an idiot, hugging her bow, of all things.

Then she rolled her shoulder, realizing it had finished healing in the time she'd spent with Odette. Thank Dieu.

At a noise from Odette, Ro cleared her throat, flung her bow over her back, and set about gathering arrows from the ravine she'd tumbled down, what felt like a lifetime ago, careful not to touch the barrier that traversed it.

It wasn't as steep as she'd thought—but then again, she wasn't tumbling tail over teacup this time. Sigh.

After climbing back up the unimpressive ravine that had bested her, Ro brushed fallen leaves from her breeches and scraped mud from her boots.

Odette made an impatient gesture. "Ready?"

Ro nodded and started to follow, then paused after only a few steps, her eyes turning toward her grandmère's cottage. At least, to where she assumed it might be. She'd be lying to herself if she didn't admit she'd love some help right now. Liam, Olt, possibly her brothers.

As if sensing her hesitation, the girl spun on her. "You're going to bolt, aren't you?"

Ro lifted her chin a notch. "I brought others with me. They could help—"

"*Nein!*" Odette looked horrified. "Those who pass into this kingdom wander aimlessly, until the empress finds them. You would not reach them, nor they you."

Ro eyed the girl. How much could she trust a girl who talked to swans, really?

"I'm serious. The empress's powers—you shouldn't mess with them. We shouldn't even be out here."

"Then why are we?"

Odette fidgeted and glanced away.

"You must have some hope of success, else you wouldn't have let me out."

The girl ignored that. "If you see anything, anything at all, shoot first, ask questions later. Her spies are everywhere."

Reluctantly, Ro turned away from her grandmère's house. After a searching glance, just long enough to see Ro's nod, the girl led the way, and Ro didn't bolt.

She had a feeling she would regret this.

❧

After a good hour and a half of hiking, they came to a thicket of woods and underbrush. So thick and full of thorns, they could hardly pass.

Much different than the scraggly woods they'd just crossed.

Still, Odette plunged ahead, following an animal trail that made their journey slightly less horrible.

Branches and brambles reached out and tried to shred Ro's clothes, face, arms, and hands. Odette slipped through it all almost easily in her furs. Ro noted the thick tan leather gloves she wore and high collar and face covering she'd pulled up at some point meant that Odette was being far less mutilated than Ro.

Ro grumbled to herself. Odette could have at least *told* her she needed to cover herself head to toe in protective gear. Even if it was too warm to wear such things.

Just when Ro thought her cloak could never be repaired, a stench met her nose that had her gagging and trying not to retch. "What in all the realms—?"

Odette shushed her.

Almost as if it were jumping out to surprise them, suddenly a stone wall loomed before them, roughly stomach high, overgrown and mostly hidden in the tangle of forest.

Odette took a sharp right and continued down the trail right up against the stone wall, until they came to a wrought-iron gate. She pushed it open, and although Ro expected it to shriek at their trespassing, it was as silent as the grave.

Which they were now surrounded by.

Ro took in the church drowning in ivy and half hidden by trees before she noticed Odette had her axe out, half crouched, scanning the churchyard uneasily.

Ro removed her bow and had an arrow ready instantly and silently. Gravestones stuck out of the greenery, moss covered and trailing ivy.

Yet the stench persisted. Ro's eyes watered from it.

It didn't smell like death or decay, as one might expect in a graveyard, but it was so overpowering, Ro was half tempted to head back the way they'd come.

No wonder Odette had covered her face.

Apparently satisfied, Odette jerked her head at Ro, then crept toward the opposite side of the stone wall from where they'd come in. A thicket of summer-green plants stood between them and the wall, and Odette wove her way through them, careful to touch them as little as possible.

"Stinging nettle," she hissed.

Ro was careful to stay away from the plants too.

A clearing opened ahead, just on the other side of the wall, and Odette hunkered down in the overgrowth, still scanning the churchyard at their backs at intervals. Ro followed her lead.

They crept forward, briars tearing at their clothes and hair, leaving little scratches all over Ro's exposed skin, which stung like fire when they then brushed against nettle, until they reached the wall and a vantage point to look over. The wall was cracked and stones fallen out—or taken out—just enough for a person to slip through.

They peeked over and through the wall.

The smell hit Ro right in the face, and she just barely kept from gagging.

Mud, everywhere. Fenced off. Rooting and grunting pigs. One dirty ramshackle old hut, ready to fall over any second. All in a little valley that had been absolutely destroyed by the pig farm.

The hut's giant sliding door was barnlike, and Ro could see swine within the house, as well as cleavers and knives of all sizes dangling from the ceiling.

A man came into view: dirty, stringy hair ringed his head, with a bald patch on top. His potbelly hung so far over his trousers, it almost touched his knees, and his clothing was so threadbare and full of filth, it looked as though those had been his only clothes—for the past ten years.

And then he turned around. Ro gasped. He was disgusting!

It looked as if someone had taken all his facial features, twisted them until they could no longer do so, then twisted them some more, pulling everything out of proportion, then mashed it back in place haphazardly. She'd never seen anything like it.

Another strong blast of pig feces and rank odor smacked her in the face just then, and Ro turned to the side and heaved.

Odette clamped a hand over Ro's mouth, nearly crawling over her to do so. She'd never seen the girl move so fast.

"Don't," Odette commanded in a low voice. "He's killed for less. Whatever you do, do not gag, vomit, or let your disgust show. Follow my lead."

"What is he?" Ro gasped, certain he wasn't human.

"One of the fey," Odette said simply. "And although pig is a close second, human is his favorite meat."

Cold fear settled deep in Ro's belly.

Without warning, Odette shoved her axe at Ro. Ro

dropped her bow over her shoulder and took it in surprise, giving Odette a questioning look.

She kept hold of the axe. "You should be safe, because it's daylight, but there are…things…that live here in the grave-yard." Her eyes darted around and came back to Ro. "They live in the graves and in the basement, and although I've only seen them at night, this is their domain. We are trespassing. I wouldn't have brought you here, put you in this danger, if you hadn't insisted. You understand?"

"Um," Ro said. Non, she did not. "What are they? And what on earth were you doing here at night?"

"I have no idea what they are. And…the stinging nettle. I need its…medicinal properties. I can only harvest it at night, under a full moon, in a church graveyard." Odette's face burned under Ro's scrutiny. "The only way to kill the crea-tures is to lift their heads from their shoulders—but they never bothered me after that first time."

Ro's mouth was opening to ask so many questions when Odette released the axe and jumped to her feet.

"Now, stay here until I say it's safe, and try not to insult him." Without any warning, Odette climbed through the wall and called out, "Ho, neighbor! Are ya up fer some visitation?"

Ro's eyebrows rose at the lower-class accent that came from the girl's mouth. Ro put her back to the wall so she could watch Odette and scan the churchyard in turn.

The not-man looked up and grinned, his teeth half missing and the other half rotting out of his head. "I thought I smelled ye. Come fer a visit, ye have?" He tilted his head. "But I smell another. Bring me a present?"

He had a powerful sense of smell if he could smell Ro downwind—and past the reek of the pigsties.

Odette laughed and made her way down the muddy slope. Once she stood next to him, she placed her small hand on his beefy arm. Ro blinked. Now that she stood next to him, he seemed to tower above her, like a…

"Giant," Ro squeaked.

His head came up, and he looked right at the crack in the wall where Ro was hiding and smiled. It would most likely give her nightmares.

Ro had heard stories—so farfetched she'd dismissed them —about giants who would shrink to big, hulking men, take up jobs such as slaughtermen or woodsmen, then coworkers or a local family would go missing, and the giant would move on.

They were wily, cunning, devious creatures, and although they were not the brightest, that made them no less dangerous. Perhaps more so. Ro swallowed hard.

This was one particular fey creature she had yet to face. And her lore on how to defeat them or escape them was severely lacking.

Another waft of the pigsty hit her, and Ro covered her nose and mouth. How could she ever pretend that smell away?

The giant rubbed his hanging belly and scratched a few places. "Oh, I does miss me a good loaf of human-bone bread."

His frame seemed to stretch and grow a little taller, but Odette just gave a flirty laugh and leaned closer. "Oh, I'm afraid she's not for you, my pet. She's here to meet the empress." She turned daintily to the graveyard. "Huntress? You can come out now. Come meet my friend—and yours, too."

The giant seemed to shrink at that. He grumbled, "Well, if she has ta be my friend…"

She patted his arm. "I'm afraid she does, *mein Freund*." Her eyes met Ro's. "Come out *now*," she snapped.

Ro stood and did as she was told, breathing shallowly through her mouth. The taste of pig filth coated her tongue. She made sure her bow was secured across her back and Odette's axe tucked in her belt, present but not a threat, and dipped a curtsy, remembering fey creatures appreciated politeness. "Enchanté, Monsieur."

"Ah…" He closed his eyes and sniffed delicately. "French. Makes the lightest, fluffiest bread of all." His eyes snapped to Odette. "Are ye sure she's a friend?"

Odette just smiled and shook her head, as if he were a naughty child she found amusing. "'Fraid so. Now. This friend needs to meet the empress. Any idea of how to go about that? She'll need a weapon to penetrate her magics."

Muttering to himself, he ambled into his shop-slash-barn-slash-living area. Light flared, something hissed and popped, and he returned shortly with a pile of metal soldered together. A billet, if Ro remembered correctly from her time hanging out at the town's blacksmith shop while the farrier shoed her père's horses.

The apprentice blacksmith had been muscular, shy, endowed with dimples, and smiled often at her. It was no hardship to do the blacksmith runs.

He held it out to Odette. "Will this do?"

Odette leaned forward and inspected it closely. After a few moments of only the sound of pigs grunting and rooting around, a smile broke out on her face. "That'll do perfectly, *ja*." She straightened and bestowed a beaming smile upon him.

Ro didn't know what to do with herself. She was completely out of her element, breathing shallowly wasn't working, and she was mètres away from a giant who could spring to full size any moment, crush them, and then eat them.

He shoved the billet into a pocket in the center of his shirt. "I require payment. First."

Odette's smile turned brighter, like she was forcing it to stay on her face. "Of course."

And then they were kissing each other.

Like, trying to suck each other's faces off.

Ro's mouth fell open. How—? What—? *Why?*

She took a step forward, ready to tear him off the girl and

flee for their lives, but Odette flung up her hand in a motion to stop Ro, and the giant took the kiss deeper, with tongue, but blessedly kept his hands to himself.

Rage started to boil in Ro's head and overflow in a rigid stance, curled fists, and vibrating body as she wanted to know *why* she wasn't over there, teaching him a lesson in manners.

This was not right. There was no way Odette was truly willing for this to happen!

After longer than an eternity, they broke apart, Odette looking a little sick, and the giant leering at Ro suggestively. Ro glared and stepped forward.

Odette's eyes widened, and she swiveled the giant's head back to her. She tried to smile, but she was definitely struggling. "Was that payment enough?"

He burped, scratched his belly, and shrugged. "Eh. Just barely."

Odette nodded and stepped back. "We'll wait in the churchyard. At the border."

The way she emphasized the words stuck out to Ro.

He shrugged. "Suit yerself." And ambled away.

Ro couldn't be certain, but it looked like his features were twisted just a little less.

Odette made a beeline for Ro, grasped her arm, and hauled her away as fast as she could. Once they were back in the brush on the other side of the wall, Ro couldn't contain herself anymore.

"*What was that?*"

Odette fell to her knees and searched the ground for something. She came up with a handful of browning mint leaves and shoved them in her mouth. After chewing a bit, she spit them out and shoved in more.

Ro waited most impatiently.

Odette shuddered and drew her knees to her chest. She tried to act nonchalant, but she was shaking too much to be taken seriously. "He deals in kisses. Although you can see the empress's palace for miles, you can't approach it. Something cloaks it from wanderers. You can spend weeks circling the hill it rests upon and never access it."

Ro couldn't keep the disgust from her voice. "Kisses? Really?"

Odette ducked her head. "It—I had to. Although *Mutter* made a safe place for us in case we needed it, I barely survived the first few years." She shrugged. "I can't manage a garden, never learned how to put food back for winter. I can't hunt, and I couldn't bear to lose my few animals. I wouldn't have made it without him."

Ro growled. "I'd like to go down there and make sure he can never kiss anyone ever again."

Odette smiled a little. "You wouldn't make it two steps if you meant him harm."

Ro nodded. She'd figured. "So…what next?"

Odette looked small and fragile and very, very young. Though she had to be around Ro's age. Maybe older? It was hard to tell. "Now we wait."

Ro glanced around. "Are we safe here?"

"As safe as we can be in daylight. The empress's spies cannot come here, and *he* cannot enter the churchyard."

"Why not?"

She fingered the leaves all over the ground and surrounding them in thick stalks, running her hand over them without touching them. "The nettles are poisonous to him. He cannot come through here without swelling up in blistering welts. It doesn't take long for him to reach the brink of dying." She nodded to the gravestones. "Not only that, the creatures here would swarm him to defend their territory. He feeds them from his stock to keep them on their side of the wall, though they tend to only drink the blood and leave the meat behind. I have no idea why."

Ro frowned. "And that…works?"

Odette gave her a tremulous smile and took back her axe,

keeping her eye on the weed-infested yard at Ro's back. "It is part of their bargain, *ja*."

Ro swallowed. "Even in his…bigger form?"

Odette's smile turned strained. "The empress can't…touch him…if he remains in his human form. If he swells, she will then have access to his magic and suck him dry. There won't be anything left but a husk."

Ro squinted at her. "Are you sure we don't want that?"

Odette turned her face away. "I—I need him." She quickly amended, "Well, I need his help."

Ro wasn't so sure about that. "How long do we wait?"

Keeping the axe at hand, Odette curled tighter into herself, resting her chin on her knees. "Until it's done."

As if to punctuate her words, hammering began, the metallic sound ringing through the trees. The inside of the hut glowed red, and smoke billowed through the chimney.

After a few hours of hammering, silence, then hammering again, Odette pulled bits of dried meat from her side bag and offered some to Ro.

It was still hard to eat with the horrible smell, but Ro's nose had started to go numb, so she attempted it.

Until she tasted dried pig, and almost spit it out everywhere.

Once again, Odette clamped a hand over Ro's mouth. "Don't. He'll risk the nettle and the creatures over such an insult."

Ro choked it down and wouldn't touch any more. She'd never much cared for pig before; now she downright couldn't stomach it.

They took turns keeping watch on the churchyard at their back and the clearing before them.

After a full day of hammering, sizzling, and hissing noises, soon metal scraped against metal, releasing a melodious ringing into the clearing. Odette started nervously surveying the sky and churchyard in turns. Dusk would soon be upon them.

Then all went silent. Odette's head came around. Ro tensed. They waited, but no more sounds came from the pig farm. Odette took a deep breath and stood.

Ro clamped her hand around the girl's wrist. "Let me go."

"You can't. He didn't make the deal with you."

Ro thought she was going to throw up again. "You don't have to…make any additional payments, do you?"

Odette almost smiled at that as she handed Ro her axe once more. "*Nein.* But I appreciate your concern all the same."

Ro slid into a defensive position, then Odette was making her way into the clearing, the grossly flabby man making his way toward her.

He held twin long knives. Ro gasped. They were the most beautiful knives Ro had ever seen. She leaned forward, trying to pick out every detail.

Odette clapped her hands and cried out, "Oh, they're perfect!"

She started to reach for them, but he pulled away. "You know none but the knife wielder can first touch the merchandise."

Odette froze, her shoulders hunching up by her ears. "But…I can take them to her…if you wrap them…"

"No!" the giant roared. He lowered his voice, looked pleased with himself. "Only the blade wielder can first wield the blades."

Odette tried to smile at him, then looked back at Ro and bit her lip. Ro came forward, just a little, not entering the clearing just yet, wondering what had changed.

Odette spun back to the giant. "She is my friend. *Your* friend."

He gave a small nod, a vacant smile on his face. "Friend."

"Uh, she's your neighbor. *Our* neighbor."

His smile grew. "Neighbor."

Odette backed up a step, and whatever confidence she'd pretended earlier, Ro watched it ebb from the girl like a tide. Now she looked lost, scared, and far younger than her twenty-ish years.

Ro had no idea what was going on, but she was certain this was bad. Very bad.

Odette dropped her voice, but Ro didn't miss how it wobbled. "We made a bargain."

He bared his teeth and grinned now. "A bargain."

Ro did *not* like where this was going. And from the look on Odette's face, she didn't either. She looked at Ro helplessly. Ro straightened her spine, squared her shoulders, and made her way into the clearing. She fingered the axe at her side and met the giant's eyes steady on.

Odette shrank back, but Ro's confidence grew. She didn't know what was about to happen, but she was going to get them out of it.

He extended the knives. Ro stopped just out of reach—which would mean nothing if he grew to his normal size—and glanced down at them.

She almost melted into a puddle. Damascus steel. Hundreds of layers. Soft, supple leather-wrapped handles. Curvy, sexy, single-edged blades sharpened to gleaming points.

Ro had never seen such gorgeous long knives in all her life.

Her eyes lifted to meet his, and for a second, the pride of making such stunning weapons flashed there. Then the leer came back.

Certain it was a terrible idea, Ro reached forward and accepted the knives. They hummed a little in response when she touched them. The blades flashed with red light, for the briefest of moments, and Ro glanced at Odette to see if she'd seen.

But non, she was staring at the giant, her eyes glassy and starting to form tears.

His voice lowered into a deep, grating pitch, and his eyes gleamed with greed. "And my part of the bargain is fulfilled. And your *friend* is no neighbor of mine."

He exploded into a towering giant.

Ro dove straight for Odette and heaved her into the closest pigpen. She screeched and fell back into the mud with a squelch.

A wave of noxious fumes hit Ro in the face, but she kept sliding. She spun and faced the giant, who, in his enormous size, lumbered in a wide circle to come back at her.

Odette sat up a little, sobbing, her hair stuck in the mud and not letting her rise all the way. "You can't use the knives against him! They'll break if you do!"

Ro cursed. She hadn't known that. She shoved the knives away and reached for the axe at her belt. Odette's axe.

Odette could barely get the words out, but she managed to finish just as the giant was turning around. "And now that he's no longer hiding, the empress will come for him!"

Ro didn't think that was such a bad thing. "Kill two birds with one stone, non?"

"*Nein.*" Odette shook her head fiercely. "Then she'll take us too!"

The moment the giant turned, Ro dove again, changing directions at the last minute and throwing him off course.

"Hold still, measly human!" His voice rattled the ground, and Ro fell to her knees.

He turned to Odette, bending far over to pinch her between his fingers. She screamed and fell back, once again planting herself firmly in mud.

"Hey!" Ro yelled, right before his fingers closed around the muddy girl.

The giant paused and looked up, inches from his goal.

The axe swung, and one of his pigs fell at her feet, dead.

His face went pale, then bright red as he screamed at her. "No! Leave my pigs alone!" He stepped toward her, then visibly restrained himself. "You may tempt me with my own herd, but I'm feasting on human tonight, not pig."

She slit another pig's throat, and the giant visibly struggled.

"I do not want to, but I will kill each of your pigs until you no longer have any excuse to be here," Ro said calmly, though she felt anything but. "What happens when they're all dead? Ah, you can't let that happen, can you? Now, let the girl go." She quickly amended, "Let us both go."

He ground his teeth, the sound echoing through the forest.

"You have already caught the attention of the sorceress; I suggest you do not make it worse."

The giant considered the still-sobbing Odette. A few of the pigs came over to lazily investigate. A brief…something… flashed across his face, and he hesitated.

Then he stepped back, shrank in size, and jerked his head. "Go. Quickly. Before I change my mind."

Ro squished across the pen, climbed into the pen Odette was in, and tried to help her up. Muck squelched halfway up Ro's boots. And Odette's hair stuck fast to the mud.

Ro pulled one of her long knives to cut it free, but Odette went ballistic trying to get away. "*Nein!* You cannot cut it! Not even one strand!"

Ro glanced from the shrieking Odette to the giant, but he was still restraining himself. Just barely. She slid the knife away and dug Odette free.

"Can you stand?" she asked quietly.

Odette nodded, tears streaming down her muddy face, and the two slowly, carefully made their way out of the giant's earthly domain. He watched them go, an unreadable expression on his face.

Ro waited to speak until they were across the churchyard

and at the gate, ready to plunge into the forest. She grabbed Odette's shoulders. "I don't want you dealing with that creature, not ever again. I don't care how much you need his help."

Odette trembled as she attempted a wobbly smile. "I don't think that will be a problem. Not with you here."

Ro felt a pang at that. She wouldn't be here much longer, not if she could help it. Her focus was still Allura.

The women glanced behind them, just as a flash of green light suffused the area, and the rooting pigs fell silent. Ro pulled Odette to the ground and reached for her bow and an arrow, but her arrows were no longer there. Must've fallen out in the mud. Again.

She really needed to figure out a way to keep that from happening.

No other sound reached their ears.

"Was that the empress?" she whispered.

Odette's trembling became worse, her teeth chattering as she nodded. "I imagine so."

Ro started forward, knives clutched in her hands.

"*Nein!*" Odette pulled her back. "She will have gone already. She strikes fast and leaves, so she isn't caught by the many who hunt her. Besides, her form isn't…corporeal…out here. She cannot be harmed outside her fortress."

Frustration built in the back of Ro's skull.

"Your best bet is to go to her castle, to attack where she thinks she's safe."

Ro settled back, adrenaline still thrumming. "Can you lead me back to your tower? Without being seen?"

"*Ja,* just…we should hurry."

But Odette's eyes weren't on where the green light had come from.

Non, they were rooted on the church basement. Her expression horrified.

Not really wanting to look, Ro's gaze drifted that way, and

glowing silver eyes lined every half-buried window, peering out. Crowding each other to look.

The dirt over the graves, all freshly churned as if each body had just been buried, started to tremble and move upward.

Without a word, Odette scrambled to her feet and ran through the gate. Ro nearly trampled her to be the first one out.

"Close the gate! Close the gate!"

Ro and Odette fell all over each other to close the gate at the same time, and Odette wrapped a chain around it with shaking hands and left it looped there.

"Aren't you going to lock it?" Ro demanded as the girl started to run into the woods.

"The gate only needs to be closed. Come on! The empress's spies will be nearby."

Ro scanned the trees for birds, but none revealed themselves. Didn't mean they weren't being watched. A moment later, she realized Odette had left without her and bolted to catch up. The sun was slowly sinking, making it darker in the forest than it actually was.

Feeling a presence at her elbow, Ro glanced toward the wall she ran beside.

Dark forms that looked like shadows in the dusk lined the wall and watched them with glowing eyes. Silvery, as if they reflected moonlight.

One smiled, and sharp, fanglike teeth appeared in the shadowed face.

Ro squeaked and almost fell backward into the trees.

Then Odette was by her side, hauling her forward. "They can't cross the wall. Or…at least…they never have. Quickly!" She bit her lip. "I don't know what they'll do with a fresh scent. Or someone who doesn't have permission to be here."

Hardly needing an explanation to run faster, Ro and Odette clutched each other's hands and stayed as far from the wall as possible, which was difficult with all the undergrowth pushing them closer.

Ro nearly sobbed in relief when they reached the game trail that delved into the forest. Odette dropped her hand and sprinted away, Ro close on her heels.

They raced through the forest. Odette stopped briefly to take the axe back from Ro and slip it over her shoulder, then took off again.

"Hurry, we don't know how much time we have until she finds us!" urged Odette, her furs and double-headed axe bouncing on her back.

It was all Ro could do to keep up, even with her own long stride.

At once, they burst from the thick tangles and into the more sparse, dead part of the forest, where it would be much easier to run.

A flock of nightingales shot into the sky, startled at their appearance, and Odette grabbed Ro and tumbled them both back into the foliage. They rolled and lay still, even as a gray wolf shot past them both and tried to flee the nightingales.

But the birds saw what they thought had startled them, and they converged upon the wolf in a whirlwind of black feathers.

Ro and Odette held perfectly still, hardly daring to breathe.

When the birds moved away, they left nothing behind but bones, tufts of fur, and speckles of blood. Ro felt sick, and Odette took a deep, steadying breath, sounding close to tears. The dark cloud moved into the sky and away, making for the empress's pagoda.

Ro grabbed a rock and lobbed it into the open space, but no other nightingales scattered, and they didn't attack.

They exchanged a look, and at Odette's nod, they crept forward, then took off as fast as they could while keeping an eye on their surroundings.

Even though neither woman had left a visible trail, or the forest had wiped their trail clean, Odette somehow managed to lead them straight to the opening in the barrier.

Odette moved the stone, then stepped through as Ro stepped back. "Come on. We have to tell the swans…" Odette looked behind her just then and stopped. "What are you doing?"

Ro gave her a tight smile. "What I came for. I'm going after the empress."

"But—you're covered in mud. And it stinks." Her eyes flitted around. "And it's dark out!"

Ro glanced down at herself and sighed. "It's unfortunate, oui, but I must hurry. And I hunt best at night."

"But—how will you find your way back?"

"I may not."

Odette looked simultaneously scared and bewildered. "But—aren't you going to help us?"

Ro made sure the knives were secure in her belt, and checked her quiver. Where her arrows no longer were. She grimaced, wishing she had time to make more.

The knives would have to be enough.

"Hunting the empress will help you. Besides, I'm here for my niece. Now that I have a way to the empress, I have to do what I came for." She took off her bow and handed it to Odette. "Here, hang on to this for me, will you? I'd like to come back for it."

Ro scanned the trees, but her head came around at the half-sob Odette let out.

"You won't be able to find this place again if you leave! It isn't safe out there."

"Then come with me. Fight her *with* me." Ro's eyes blazed, and she took a step forward. "You don't have to accept what she did to you. To your family." She eyed the axe over Odette's shoulder covered in dried mud. "Take back your kingdom and rule it how it should be run. With fairness, unity, and open-mindedness, as never before."

For a brief moment, Odette's eyes flared to life. As if she were considering — as if she believed she could do it.

Then the light in her eyes went out.

Odette shied back, one step at a time. "I couldn't possibly. The empress. My swans. I have to stay here. If she were to see me…"

Ro felt a flash of annoyance but pushed it away. She nodded to Odette's safe haven. "Then go. Hide yourself. Care for your swans. Stay safe. Tell Odin goodbye for me."

Ro hated to admit it, but she'd gotten attached to the swan that followed her around like a favored pet.

The girl sniffled, looked like she might yank Ro in with her.

"And wish me luck." With that, Ro strode away, toward where the old palace and now the empress's pagoda rose on a hilltop above the Black Forest.

Hopefully the empress wouldn't smell her coming.

25

*R*o hated to admit it, but mud made great camouflage, even though she didn't run into any more of the empress's spies. Which set her on edge.

It was well into the night when she climbed the steep hillside the old family castle rested upon—and reached the pagoda atop castle ruins. If Odette was right and no one could get close to the empress's dwelling, Ro hoped the girl was also right that her new knives would grant her access.

Especially after the price Odette had paid.

The moon, which had been waxing bigger each night, shone bright in the sky and lit things just enough for Ro to see, but hopefully not enough for her to be seen as well. She took in the massive structure. The empress's dwelling, though it had only been here five years or so, according to Odette, was crumbling.

Stone had broken off the winged roof and tumbled down the long steps, either making it to the bottom or stopping partway and giving up altogether. Quite a few chunks were missing from the steps too, and cracks ran all over the structure itself.

She'd only seen such dwellings in storybooks of faraway lands. Lands she hadn't yet visited. Some in fairy tales.

Such as the one about the nightingale who sang the great emperor back to health. And the mechanical bird that had replaced it, only to be thrown out when the metal bird couldn't possibly compare to the real thing.

And here lay a similar palace, on the edge of Germany's Black Forest.

A chill skittered over her skin at the deadness of the place. Some places reflected their occupants. Some places were lovely in spite of their occupants. This place seemed to crumble under the weight of the evil it housed.

Ro pushed forward, sticking to the tree line, and made her way around the pagoda. Far taller than it was wide, its sides were too steep to climb, and brush, brambles, and crumbled stone crowded its base. The only steps, the only foreseeable access, was on the one side. The side that faced her grandmère's section of woods.

Ro was soon back to where she'd started, covered in scrapes and clothes torn even more by her fight with underbrush. She grumbled at having to repair her cape. Again.

Soon, there wouldn't be anything left of original cape her mère had made. Soon, she would have replaced it all, little by little. Would it still be the cape her mère gave her, then? Would it still hold the magic of a warm embrace she swore she could feel every once in a while? Or would all that fade as the fabric was made anew?

Worries for another time.

She was only distracting herself from her duty. And the steps. Thousands upon thousands of steps. (Probably hundreds, but it looked like thousands to Ro.) The only way in.

She checked the ties of her red cape, made sure it was settled firmly around her shoulders, and checked both long knives to make sure they were easily accessible.

And she was still standing there.

"Just go already!" she ordered herself, voice low.

She pushed her feet into motion. As she stepped toward the steep staircase, a slight pressure kept her from going any further. Ro slid out her long knives and sliced at the air. What looked like limp skin fell away, and she cut out a gap big enough to squeeze through, then glanced behind her.

The hanging flap was slightly visible, reflecting moonlight, but she'd best mark it lest it disappear. Ro snapped a branch, pointing toward the slice, then memorized where to walk back toward.

Tucking her knives away, taking a deep breath, she faced the stairs, then began the long, arduous climb. The steps were so steep, she had to heave herself onto each one.

"How in all the realms does someone get up here?" she groused.

Each step came to her waist, and as she heaved herself over each edge, she was exposed for a few precious seconds before she could crouch against the next step and its shadow to see if she'd been spotted.

She was perspiring before she'd gone a quarter of the way. Drenched halfway. Trembling near the top.

And spending far too much time announcing her presence on the exposed steps. She wished she had backup in the trees below, arrows ready. Not that they'd be able to do anything against a flock of nightingales swarming their prey.

Once again, she thought of Odette shrinking back, too scared to join her.

If only the fool girl were brave enough to come with her.

Ro stilled at the thought. That wasn't something she'd normally think. At least, not worded in such a way. Someone else talked like that...

Ro bit back a laugh as it came to her. Her grandmère. She was starting to sound like her grandmère, and she'd only just met the woman.

"Heaven help us all," she muttered, scrambling up the last few steps.

The moment she reached the top, Ro bent over her knees, taking in big gulps of air, knives out and eyes darting around for threats.

She forced her heart rate to slow, forced herself to take calm breaths, even as her lungs burned and begged for more sustenance. She scanned her surroundings, taking the heady scent of the forest and high mountain winds deep into her lungs.

A small building sat atop the structure with an open space before it. A walkway circled the building, narrow and treacherous and with no rails to stop someone from falling.

The moon shone on two blood-red doors with Chinese symbols, or kanji, if Ro remembered correctly, weeping paint. The doors were warped with moisture and wedged shut.

On either side of the doors, two circular stone enclosures stood sentry: one, a pond, and the other, a dead garden with bamboo shoots sticking out of it. A single black swan statue rested in the center of the scummy pond, neck curved gracefully and beak as red as the doors, but she didn't give it more than a passing glance.

There were statues everywhere. Namely, fierce dragons on the peaked corners and birds lining the tiled roof. Though most were the color of stone, except for that black swan.

Seeing no threats, Ro stepped forward to start hacking at those heavy, decrepit doors. She was getting in, and she was finishing this.

When she placed her foot just past the first planter, the black swan came to life and flew at her, slamming into her and knocking her over.

Her knives went flying.

Covering her head with her arms, Ro tried to protect her face. Wings, dark feathers, blade-sharp teeth, huge, biting.

Ro kept swinging, kept trying to fend off the creature, but

its long, snakelike neck snapped out again and again, biting her, tearing into her, leaving torn skin hanging and blood streaming down her arms. It was all Ro could do to keep it away from her face.

She'd give just about anything to have her leather arm bracers right now.

The thing barreled into her again and again, flapping, squawking, biting, eyes wild.

She tried to swat it away, but it tore another gash in her arm and hung on.

Ro couldn't hold back her scream.

As it hung there, biting down, latched on to her arm, Ro heard a woman's voice shouting, "Go back! Go back! You are not safe here. You're in danger!"

Ro shook the swan from her arm, the small, razor-sharp teeth opening another wound. The moment the swan released her, the voice snuffed out.

Lightheaded, Ro jerked back, eyes wide, and raised blood-soaked arms. But this time, the black swan didn't attack. It stood there, wings spread, not allowing Ro to pass. Giving Ro a moment to take in her attacker.

Black swan. Red beak. Silver circlet around its neck.

As if in response to Ro's glance, the swan tried to rub off the silver collar, first against the stone and then against its body and wing. It gave a pitiful little bleat.

Non. Ro refused to feel sorry for it. It had attacked her. Wounded her.

And she needed to get past it.

Ro readied herself. The swan crouched, made a hissing motion with its mouth, though no sound came out, and spread its wings farther. A good six-to-eight foot wingspan, soft, downy feather tips just touched the stone planters on either side.

And past this platform, nothing. A drop-off. One misstep…

Ro shook out her shoulders. She needed to get in. She needed to break this curse. Her niece's life depended upon it.

But something within her balked at killing the magnificent creature.

Some huntress she was.

Not wanting to take her eyes off the bird, yet afraid to move, she tried to catch a glimpse of her twin long knives. There.

She'd grab her blades, slash at it, and if that didn't work, wring its neck. But oh Dieu, she didn't want to. Its eyes were so sad. She readied herself. Crouched a little.

They moved at the same time.

The black swan charged; Ro kicked it straight into the pond. She got a split-second reprieve before it was flying at her again, spraying her with putrid green water.

She reached for her blades but didn't get a chance to grab them.

It drove her back. Toward the steps. Toward the expanse of nothing below.

It was just a bird! How could she not take down a bird? After punching its beak away from her again and again, she got low and scrabbled for her knives, trying to reach them with one hand while protecting her face with the other.

Panic tightened her throat, made it difficult to breathe. She tried to bite back the terror, but her childhood fear would not be silenced.

She'd just started liking swans again, too.

Her hand closed around one of the weapons, and she slashed straight up at the swan. It dodged her strike. Hit her full on the chest, moving past her attack as fluid as water. She swung again, clumsily, missed, was caught off guard as it nipped her hand.

The weapon went flying and clattered down the side of the structure.

At the same time a bell tolled, a massive clock ticked backward to six, and Ro staggered, trying to keep her feet *on* the little platform.

She tried to get away from the edge, away from the hundreds of steps below, but the swan used her distraction against her and once again slammed both feet into her chest, using its full weight to drive her back.

Ro shuffled frantically to stay upright, to gain some ground, but suddenly, there was nothing under her feet.

Without warning, she was falling backward, grasping for something to hold on to. The black swan watched her go with mournful eyes and silver collar winking in the moonlight.

Time suspended, horror fighting with consciousness for dominance, and she curled in on herself after hitting the first step.

Flashes of stone steps, a flash of bright light, intense pain, then nothing.

❧

Something nudged at her. Something important. Something she couldn't quite grasp.

Disturbed her sleep. Something she very much wanted to get back to.

Once again, a woman urged her of danger, the voice faint, oh so faint.

She groaned and pulled away from it. *Just leave me be!*

It nudged her all the harder. Told her to remember. To wake.

"Leave me alone," she mumbled.

It wouldn't.

Like a persistent, unwanted pest, a sense of danger kept intruding, forcing her toward wakefulness. She peeled open her eyes. To trees, forest, dim light. As if the moon was leaving and the sun was ready to burst forth into the sky.

Everything was hazy, disjointed. Far away. She tried to lift her head, but that hurt too much.

She touched her face. Her nose. Her arms. Blood, everywhere.

Ro groaned and tried to sit up. Everything hurt so much. Slowly, she moved her limbs. Nothing broken, everything in pain. Giant knot on her head.

She gingerly poked at it, wondering what could make a knot that big, and tried to look around her. Everything was bathed in ever-lightening darkness. She must've been out for hours. She was surrounded by a haven of wild plants.

What had she escaped? Some kind of…bird?

Just through the leaves she could see crumbling stone. Creeping vines. Moss and rot and encroaching woods. Her eyes went back to the dark stone. And followed it up, up, up, the structure almost invisible under all the greenery she was lying in.

She squinted. Hadn't there been some kind of creature up there?

At the top of the pagoda, far above, black feathers with a deep-red beak whipped out of sight, just barely visible in the almost dawn.

"I dare you to come down here for round two." Her mouth felt like sandpaper as her tongue stuck to the roof of her mouth and her words came out all garbled.

Ro laughed weakly at herself and tried to stand. Yeah, she was pretty sure she wouldn't survive another battle with the swan. She'd fallen, hadn't she? She shouldn't have survived that either. How had she?

As if in answer to her question, a little strength trickled back in. Her arms bled a little less.

Oh. Her healing ability. Of course.

A boon from the Queen of the Fairies, gifted to her after Trêve had married Cosette. Which, according to her grand-mère, had been there all along.

It was all so confusing.

She shook her head and instantly regretted it. Her hands flew to her skull as she waited for the throbbing to pass.

Planting both hands on the ground, one hand touched something cold and metal. Her fingers closed around it as she concentrated on standing upright.

It took far too long, but eventually she made it to her feet, though she had to hold on to a tree to keep it that way. She picked her way back the way she'd come, her eyesight lighting things, then sputtering out at intervals.

Then something resisted her, some kind of pressure, and Ro slashed out with the metal thing in her hand. It parted, and she pushed through.

She came to at different places in the forest, usually leaning heavily on a tree trunk, wondering how she'd gotten there. She was so thirsty.

How long had she lain there? Been unconscious?

She paused for a brief moment and almost tipped over. Gentle hands propped her upright and pushed her forward, but when she looked around, no one was there.

Gritting her teeth, she forced herself to keep going. Where, she didn't know, just that she needed to keep moving.

Ro didn't know how long it took her to get back to the barrier, didn't even remember there *was* a barrier until she felt the familiar snap that made her a prisoner once more, but she fell through it. And lay there.

Squawking. Flapping. Feathers.

Ro tried to claw her way back through the barrier. It was as impenetrable as ever, and she did *not* enjoy the jolt that rattled her teeth and flung her wounded arm away. But at least it woke her up a little.

Her tongue was thick, her body weak, her head swimming. Cool hands soothed her brow, her face. Heaved her upright.

Once she saw it was Odette, white swans—no black

feathers in sight—she gave herself over to oblivion, only waking to gulp the water being poured into her mouth.

"Come on. I can't get you up here by myself. You've got to wake up, huntress, and, ugh, *help* me."

Then she was dangling in the air, the girl directing from above, swans pulling ropes from below—she had to be dreaming.

Soon firm, insistent hands prodded her into a bed, tucked her in. Then a cool cloth bathed her face. Enjoying soft blankets instead of scratchy hay for once, Ro happily gave herself over to her dreams and drifted off into the most delightful slumber.

26

Ro cracked open an eye, instantly alert. Where was she? Why was she sleeping?

She had to get back through the barrier before the empress found her!

As she sat up quickly, the room spun.

When she could focus, soft colors met her eyes, as well as a round interior room made of light-gray stone. Pastel flowers adorned every surface, making the place look homey, comfortable—and way too girly. So much purple. And yellow. And green.

Where on earth was she? No doors, only one window…

Something swung into the room through the open window.

Ro cried out and fell off the bed, trying to untangle herself from the blankets cocooned around her.

The swan! The black swan was back!

She fought harder, but the blankets seemed to wrap tighter as the thing ran at her.

"Argh! Ack! Get away!"

Ro ducked her head, prepared for more biting, for the

massive thing to slam into her again. How to get out of these blankets?

"Ro! Huntress. It's just me! Calm yourself. You are safe. Here. With me."

Ro stilled. "Where is here?"

"My room. My tower room. You are safe."

Odette. It was Odette. Not a swan.

Ro suddenly felt very foolish. She poked her head out of the blankets, hair sticking out everywhere. She was half tempted to cut it all off again. "Your tower?"

Odette nodded and watched Ro with wide eyes, looking scared and concerned. Mostly scared.

Ro struggled some more, but she was going nowhere. "Think you can help me get loose?"

Odette ducked her head as she carefully helped Ro to her feet. "Um, well, you see, I had to go out, and I was concerned you might wake and be disoriented…" Her voice trailed off.

Ro stared at the girl gently forcing her to sit on the edge of the bed. "You mean…you tied me up?"

Odette wouldn't meet her eyes, just started unwrapping. It was impressive. The mummy-wrappers in Egypt could learn a thing or two. "I didn't want you to fall out of the tower."

Ro could feel her face getting hot. "And if someone came in here and attacked me? I thought that's what you were doing!"

"I'm sorry, but I didn't want you to get hurt."

Ro just glared. "Merci. Untie me. Now."

Odette fumbled with the blankets, her face bright pink.

Ro waited till she was free to shake herself loose and stand. The room tilted. Odette caught her, nearly going down under Ro's tall, willowy frame, and managed to aim her toward the bed. Ro sat down hard. Felt a cup at her lips. Drank, deeply.

"That better?" Odette asked.

"Much. Merci."

"*Bitte*." Odette didn't wait long to ask, "Can you tell me what happened?"

Suddenly, the weight of everything lay heavy on Ro's shoulders. She didn't like feeling weak. And foolish. And hungry.

"Perhaps food first?"

Odette jumped to her feet and raced around the room, soon coming back with a bowl of stew and a chunk of bread. She set it on a little table and pulled it close to Ro.

Then she leaned forward. "What did you do? The pagoda is gone! I can't see it from any direction. And the forest paths are even more twisty than usual. What happened?"

Between bites, Ro outlined what had happened, to the best of her memory. Odette seemed to pale further with every word.

"I don't understand why the empress didn't come after me. Or her spies," Ro said.

Odette chewed on her lip. "You say there was a black swan?"

Ro gave Odette a long look. "Oui. That's what I said. Among other things."

"Was it…well? The swan."

"Well? The thing attacked me! I didn't ask if it was *well*."

Suddenly, Ro panicked and felt around her waist. "The knives! Oh, Odette! I am so sorry. I'll go back and get them. How long have I been up here? And the better question: How in the world did you get me up here?"

Ro sent a significant look to where the girl had just barely hauled Ro's weight to the bed earlier.

"Three days. It's fine, I promise. We'll figure something else out. I'm not even sure you *could* find them with how the forest is misbehaving. But the swan…"

"Three days?" Ro stilled. "What about the swan?"

Tears filled Odette's eyes. "I didn't know she was still alive. I was hoping, but…alive!"

As tears spilled down Odette's cheeks, she buried her face in a handkerchief, giving way to deep, wracking sobs.

Ro watched the girl, horrified. Her sisters had pretended to cry to get their way—except Cosette, of course—but this seemed real. And Ro didn't know what to do about it.

"Uh, another pet of yours?"

Odette just cried harder.

Ro desperately wanted to leave. How far was it to the ground anyway? Surely falling out a tower window couldn't be worse than what she'd just gone through.

After an eternity, the torrent abated. "I'm sorry. I'm so sorry. I've just waited so long to hear anything…I'm so glad you didn't kill her…"

Odette blew her nose on the handkerchief. Loudly.

Ro had had enough. She plunked the bowl on the little table. It teetered on the edge and almost fell off. "Odette, what's going on? I can't help you if you're going to keep so many secrets from me. Why does the black swan mean so much to you? It attacked me, for heaven's sake!"

Ro's words only served to spark more crying. Ugh. She scrubbed a hand down her face, still sore, still weary, still wanting to get back to the others…and Olt…more than anything. Since when had she started thinking of him so much?

"Odette, please, you have to tell me. If things had gone differently, I would've put those knives right through that swan."

Apparently the girl could cry harder. Ro sighed. Odette was going to make herself sick.

"I wouldn't have known, all right? I wouldn't have known, because you didn't tell me. Anything. I've had to guess and assume and pull information from you as one pulls out a bad tooth."

Now Odette looked a little queasy. Ro couldn't blame her.

Bad nutrition and hygiene meant bad teeth, which she'd seen far too much of in her line of work.

Ro leaned forward, doing her best not to keep going and pass out in her bowl of soup. "The time for secrets is over, Odette. If you want my help, you need to tell me everything. Now."

Odette looked to the side, twisting her handkerchief every which way. "I don't know…"

"Non, that's not acceptable. You're going to tell me. I almost died! Does that mean nothing to you?" At her continued silence, Ro rubbed her temples. She didn't know how much more convincing she had in her.

Abruptly, Odette stood. "All right. *Ja*, I will tell you what you need to know."

Ro sagged, ready for more sleep. But she was going to stay awake to hear this.

"Once you're able to leave this tower."

"What? But—"

Odette lifted her chin, tears still swimming in her eyes. "It's better if I show you. Trust me. I can't explain…just show."

Ro shook her head, which hurt, then lay back on the bed. "I'll hold you to it, you know."

Odette came over to help her with the blankets.

Ro shot her a hard look. "No more tying me up, understand?"

Odette startled, then nodded far too many times. Then she hesitantly pulled Ro's blankets over her shoulders and jumped back the moment she was done.

The last thing Ro saw before her eyes closed was Odette sneaking over to retrieve her bowl. Ro couldn't help her smile. She'd never met anyone so skittish. And fierce. At the same time.

"'And though she be but little, she is fierce,'" Ro quoted to herself as she dropped off to sleep.

The next time Ro woke, she took in everything about the tower. Including the many details she'd missed on the first perusal.

Neatly woven tapestries in brilliant colors hung around the room to keep it warm and to break up the monotonous gray stone.

In front of five of the six tapestries hung elaborate frock coats, the pretentious ones worn by noblemen when presented to a king, with tails that reached the ground, high collars, sleeves that draped past fingertips, and enough material to fully cover the wearer.

Hoods had even been sewn into the shoulders.

Yet they were ghastly. All the same sickly green, all a rough weave, all something she would never, ever curse someone to wear.

Even if they did get progressively better in cut and style.

A spinning wheel sat under each tapestry, six in total, the horrible green thread on only one spindle, set under the only tapestry without a frock coat. A covered basket rested next to it, probably holding whatever dyed rough-weave wool or cotton the girl was using to spin out the thread.

A giant loom took up a huge portion of the space. How had it even gotten up here? Material was partially woven on it, the spindle empty, which was perhaps why more was being spun on the spinning wheel.

Unless she was spinning thread to sew the ghastly cloth together.

A worktable held a partially completed frock coat, of course made out of the same awful green material, surrounded by needles and thread and bobbins and pincushions.

So...the girl sat up here all day and made horrendous coats? What on earth?

A bed, a stove, and a small table for eating took up the rest of the space—everything neat and tidy and in its place. Something, for some reason, Ro had not been expecting.

Her elder sisters seriously needed to take "How to clean things so that they actually stay clean" lessons from this girl.

The room was spotless. Unlike the rest of the homestead.

The tower room was as circular inside as out, and curtains had been moved aside to display curved lattice windows evenly spaced around the whole of it to give plenty of sunlight—and to allow anyone in the tower to look in any direction.

Something Ro hadn't noticed the first time. Perhaps all but the one had been covered then? Ro struggled to sit upright. She wanted to look out them.

Instantly, her head started throbbing, the room started swimming, and she fell back on the bed. What was happening? Was her healing ability not working? Or was she more wounded than it could handle?

Cold fear clenched tight in her gut, and Ro made a strangled sound.

"Easy! Steady." Odette came bustling over from the other side of the room.

Something else Ro had missed when taking in her surroundings. She was seriously beginning to doubt her observation skills.

"Your head wound is much better, but you still aren't quite right, huntress."

Odette settled the blankets around Ro's shoulders, then gently pulled away the head dressings and prodded the wounds. "Now don't you worry about a thing—"

She gasped and drew back.

"What? What is it?" Ro asked quickly.

Odette was clutching the bandages to her chest, as far away as she could get from Ro while sitting on the same bed, staring at her with wide, horrified eyes. "Are you sure you're not a sorceress?" she said through bloodless lips.

Ro would've rolled her eyes at that, but her current

headache made that particular motion nausea inducing. "Your swan hasn't convinced you I'm not yet?"

When she could focus on Odette again, Ro was surprised at how much fear was on her face. She sighed. "Fine. What is it this time?"

"Your—your head. It was…kinda…caved in. Just a bit! I mean, there was this giant knot, true, but then this divot right under—I thought for sure you had brain damage—"

Now Ro was the one staring in horror as the girl babbled. Slowly, she lifted her hand to touch her head.

"Don't touch it!" Odette yelped as she batted Ro's hand away. "I mean, please. You don't want to do that. I think? The dent isn't still there, but after falling out of bed yesterday, and you were talking nonsense, I was so scared…" Her voice trailed off, and she shrugged helplessly. "I just…I don't understand…"

Ro closed her eyes, weary, but wanting to set the girl at ease. "I am my sister's protectress. My sister is the Fairy Queen's daughter. I think I told you that already?"

She peeked, but Odette shook her head, eyes wide.

"Oh. Long story short, the Queen of the Fairies hid her daughter in my family when she thought my sister, my true sister, had…died." Ro swallowed the lump in her throat and kept talking before Odette could ask questions. "I got beat up pretty bad once, and after Cosette married Trêve—now the king of France—the Fairy Queen gifted me with swift healing ability."

"Oh. That explains why you didn't die. You should have."

Ro would've left Allura to her curse, let Cosette down, and she never would've seen Olt again… Her throat was suddenly thick, her nose itching, her eyes burning. She needed to get Odette out of here before Ro did something humiliating like bursting into tears.

Oblivious to Ro's inner turmoil, Odette leaned forward and began wrapping Ro's head.

But then Ro said, "Odette, how am I going to defeat the empress? I couldn't even get past her attack swan."

Odette stiffened, then went back to wrapping. "I don't know."

Stubborn, stupid tears with minds of their own slid down Ro's temples and soaked her pillow. "I don't think I can do it. I don't think I can defeat her."

Odette had reached for a cup to give Ro something to drink, and she almost threw it when she flung her hands out. "That's what I've been trying to tell you!"

Ro closed her eyes so she wouldn't have to look at Odette. To see the disappointment there.

Odette's chipper voice intruded anyway. "Wait till the summer solstice. It's only a few days away. You can defeat her then. I'm sure of it."

A date on the calendar meant nothing if she couldn't get anywhere near the empress. Ro had never felt so helpless. She kept her eyes closed and didn't respond.

Odette carefully patted her shoulder. "Just you rest. We'll talk when you're feeling more like yourself."

Then she got up, went over to the spinning wheel, and soon a faint whirring noise was the only sound in the chamber as she fed raw material through to spin into that ghastly green thread.

Ro remembered she'd wanted to ask about it, but before she could, the whirring of the wheel lulled her to sleep.

A hunting horn pealed through the forest, and Ro sat up, wincing as she did so.

Odette pushed her back down on her way to the window. Apparently the girl hadn't much experience caring for the sick. At least, not stubborn ones like Ro.

Ro gritted her teeth and climbed to her feet. Although she was healing quicker than she should've after a fall like that, it wasn't quick enough.

Not that she could complain.

Gratefulness flooded her for the many gifts, including healing, the Queen of the Fairies had bestowed upon her (no matter what her grandmère said), a rare feeling that came and went with lightning speed.

She'd hand over her gifts with all haste if the Fairy Queen would come help Allura. Why wasn't she helping her granddaughter, when she'd been so protective of her, so doting over her?

Ro made it to the window and gripped the casing there as Odette gasped. Ro peered over the shorter girl's head.

There, in the clearing under the tower, gathered a group of

mounted soldiers in East Asian armor, red banner flying over their heads. Ro's eyes widened.

The leader, a stout man—though they all looked stout in the wide armor—slapped both hands together, one fisted and one open, and bowed from his seated position atop his horse.

He called in broken English, "We come in peace. We wish to speak to your Lady of the Realm."

Odette shrank back, but Ro hauled her forward, gritting her teeth against the pain. "That would be you, dearie."

"But I don't—how did they get in?"

Ro started wrapping her hands to descend. "I don't know, but I'm going to find out."

For a moment, Ro thought the girl would object, would try to make her get back in bed, but gratefulness flooded Odette's eyes. *"Danke."*

Ro nodded and grabbed the rope.

"Wait!"

Ro turned.

Odette bit her lip, indecision warring in her eyes. And a rather healthy dose of curiosity. "Perhaps I should…"

Ro sighed. "Perhaps you should come with me, see what they have to say. I'm happy to speak for you."

Ro didn't think the girl could possibly look more grateful than she had moments before, but she was apparently wrong.

"Oh, thank you!" Odette clasped her hands under her chin and looked all of twelve years old.

Ro did not roll her eyes—though she dearly wanted to— and readied herself to descend. The pulley system made it easier, but it was still a lot of work. For her. She went first, covering her dizziness by taking a moment to straighten. Odette's feet hit the packed earth behind her with a thump, but Ro kept her eyes on their visitors.

They slid from their horses, and now all the soldiers slapped their hands together and bowed from the waist, as if the move had been choreographed. The thunderous clap echoed through the trees.

Ro and Odette copied the motion as best they could, and their uninvited guests straightened.

The leader, once again, spoke to Odette in thickly accented English. "We have answered your summons, Lady."

Odette's eyes were as wide as the saucers the barn cats drank out of. "What summons?"

Ro wanted to sigh. The girl needed to learn some confidence. She was a princess, for heaven's sake! And if her father were dead…she might be queen.

Ro couldn't step forward without tottering, so she crossed her arms and nonchalantly leaned against the tower, putting steel in her voice. "Who are you and how did you cross the barrier?"

The leader flicked a surprised glance her way but directed his words to Odette. "Does your second-in-command speak for you, Lady?"

Odette stuttered, and Ro sent her an impatient look. Odette swallowed. "She does."

He nodded respectfully at Ro. "We are warriors of the great Qing empire, from the Middle Kingdom, here to serve our…emperor. We have sought the enchantress far and wide, and our search has led us to your lands. Have you news of the woman called the Nightingale?"

Odette and Ro exchanged glances. Ro spoke hesitantly. "There is an enchantress here, but she calls herself an empress."

Anger filtered through many eyes. "We do not recognize her claim as our empress."

"She—she's our empress. I mean, she forced her way into our royal family." Odette looked as if she might faint. "She's my stepmother."

The men exchanged glances, and the commander said in a

surprised, disgusted, and somewhat apologetic tone, "She's my stepmother as well."

Ro's eyebrows climbed her forehead. Now that she hadn't been expecting.

"We received your query and came right away." He gestured to the men behind him. Ro counted twenty. "My men are at your disposal and are willing to fight. Might we discuss battle plans?"

Odette looked helplessly at Ro.

Ro closed her eyes briefly. "That would be just fine."

The commander glanced around the clearing. "If my men can set up camp here, we can plan our attack for first thing in the morning."

Odette looked to Ro, who nodded, so she turned back to the soldier and nodded.

A hint of a smile graced his face. "Perhaps my second-in-command can brief your second-in-command? After supper."

The commander's second—young, handsome, and strong—stepped forward and bowed. Ro steeled herself and bowed back, but this time, Odette floundered for a moment before settling on a curtsy.

At the mention of food, of not being expected to make battle plans, Odette seemed to come to life. "Of course, sir. I will get a meal ready for your men."

The offer was generously given, but Ro couldn't help but notice the quick frown or fleeting glance she tossed at her tower, as if anxious to get back to something.

The only thing Ro had seen the girl do nonstop was make those awful coats. She wasn't passing up a way to defeat the empress—or the Nightingale, rather—for some material, was she?

The commander bowed and said graciously, "We accept your offer of hospitality, but we are more than happy to provide the meal in exchange for your time."

Odette wilted at that. "*Danke.* I mean, thank you kindly."

The handsome commander seemed to be hiding a smile. "It is my honor."

He nodded at his second-in-command to proceed. He then began directing the men where to hobble their horses and pile supplies.

Ro glanced around for the swans, but they seemed to be off foraging. Wouldn't they be surprised when they came back and found their home invaded?

The thin-framed soldier approached Ro and did the same bow thing. Ro nodded back, more than ready for bed, knowing it was now hours away. It was taking so much longer to heal than normal. She couldn't wait to feel like herself.

Odette, who'd climbed the tower the moment the commander's attention was elsewhere, threw down the crutch she'd crafted out of a walking stick, and Ro looked at it helplessly. If she bent down to get that, she might fall over and just lie there.

The second-in-command retrieved it and offered it to Ro with both hands, head lowered but eyes steadily on Ro's face. Ro took it and nodded her thanks.

They made their way toward the barn.

The young man started speaking quietly. "We will need to know your plan of attack, how many men you have—"

"It's just the two of us."

The second-in-command stopped walking. "Surely not."

Ro just looked at the soldier. She didn't lie, and she rarely repeated herself.

The second-in-command shot her an incredulous look. "You were not planning on attacking her with only two?"

"Non."

The second-in-command breathed out a sigh of relief.

"Just me."

Stunned, the officer couldn't seem to come up with anything to say to that.

Ro offered a smile. "I've been through worse."

"You haven't." It was said simply.

The men were well on their way to setting up camp, so Ro showed the second-in-command what she could in the barn, which was almost nothing. Just a wall of tools that had been scavenged, cleaned of rust, and arranged in neat rows.

Ro had piled supplies along the curved stone wall of the tower.

The young soldier stared at the tools in horror. "Where are your weapons?"

Ro sighed. "Long story. But I really miss them."

Her axe was in the lake, her bow wherever Odette had hidden it, and her exquisite long knives at the base of the pagoda somewhere.

The officer said matter-of-factly, "I shall see about outfitting you with a bow and a sword."

Ro felt like hugging the soldier. "Merci beaucoup. I cannot tell you how much of a relief that is."

The second-in-command nodded once. "We haven't many extra weapons, but I'll see what can be spared." Then, eying Ro carefully, "Will you be able to fight?"

Frustration spilled into Ro's voice. "I certainly hope so. I had weapons—two long knives—that let me get close to her tower. I lost them when I…fell. Down the steps."

Wide eyes took her in from head to toe. "Your ancestors must have been watching over you."

"Something like that," Ro muttered.

"Very well. You shall lead us, but if you are in no condition to fight, please stay back. The Nightingale is our problem that we unleashed upon the world. There is no shame in letting others do what you cannot."

Ro's jaw tightened. She'd be fighting, her body would be ready by then, or else. "I would like to hear more of her, s'il vous plaît."

"And you shall, but it is my commander's tale, not mine."

Ro nodded her agreement, and the two fell silent.

While they were standing there, still in the barn, Ro casually mentioned, "You are welcome to stay in here. With me. If you need or want to."

The second-in-command froze, turned shuttered eyes on Ro. "I'm not sure what you mean."

Ro met the soldier's gaze, unflinching. "You do."

That's it. That's all she said. She waited.

"I…" The soldier's gaze darted all around the barn, as if looking for escape.

"Ah. They don't know."

Now fear touched the soldier's eyes.

"Does the commander?"

The girl disguised as a man didn't answer, but Ro could see the truth in her eyes. *Non.*

"Then why—?"

The second-in-command dropped her voice, even though they were far away from anyone who could overhear. "My father had no adult sons, and my little brother was too young. And my father is injured. From an old wound. When the call to battle came, I could not—I must bring honor to my family since I cannot"—shame swept her features—"however I can."

Ro nodded.

"Will you—will you tell anyone?"

Ro was certain her surprise was clear on her face. "It's not my secret to tell."

Intense relief swept the girl's features, then resolve. "My twelve years of service are up in two months. I do not know what is tradition in your country"—her eyes swept Ro's hunting clothing, though not in a judgmental manner—"but it is not acceptable for women to fight, to engage in battle, to dress as men, in mine. I cannot stress to you the importance that no one knows until my father receives my commendation and I am released from service to the emperor."

"I give you my word, not a soul will hear it from my lips."

"Good. Then we shall not speak of this matter again." She

deliberately began discussing the small army's needs, though they were few. Mostly restocking some supplies.

Ro couldn't help her curiosity. "What is your name?"

"Han-Xu."

"Non, your real name." Ro said it softly.

The young woman flushed, just a little. "Mulan," she whispered, as if she relished saying the name, "but please. Han-Xu. It must always be Han-Xu."

"But of course, Han. What can you tell me…"

Mulan shook her head with a laugh. "No, huntress. My name is Xu; my family name is Han. We say our family name first to honor our ancestors."

Ro's mouth hung open for a moment as her own flush suffused her features. "I see. And I apologize. Do you prefer Xu or Han-Xu?"

"Xu is just fine. Han-Xu is more formal."

"Got it. And you will tell me if I make any more faux pas?" At her confused look, Ro amended, "Any more mistakes?"

Mulan smiled kindly. "You will not offend me, huntress."

Ro could have fallen over from relief. "Bon. Because I tend to do such things quite often, it seems."

"And you? What is your name?"

"Ro LeFèvre, huntress for King Trêve of France. Though most people shorten that to huntress. Or Ro."

"It is my honor to meet you, Ro."

"You speak English well."

"That is indeed a compliment. A few officers from noble families were trained in preparation for our quest. Our instructor made it seem that it was the most important language to learn, due to extensive trade attempts from that country." She made a face. "It seems that advice was not always correct."

Ro laughed, drawing looks into the open barn, but no one approached.

She lowered her voice. "If you will forgive me for asking,

and I know it's none of my business, but why? Why can't you tell them who you are? Twelve years…that's a long time for a secret such as yours."

Just then, the commander walked by, and Mulan's eyes tracked him.

"Oh." Ro thought she understood, just a little.

Mulan turned a fierce gaze on her. "It's not like that. My service was up in six years, but then I received a promotion from foot soldier to officer, with the promise of a commendation if I served another six years. It would free my family from further service. Forever. At first I joined to protect my family's honor, to protect my father's life."

Ro nodded, encouraging her to continue.

"But I stay to protect the men, my fellow warriors. You see, there are things that hunt them, things that seek to destroy them, that only I can see. I am the only one who can protect them." Mulan frowned, looking troubled. "I thought I would be able to return home by now. But I cannot. Not if I want them to live."

"I understand. You're doing the best you can with what you've been given. It takes a brave soul to do so."

Mulan gave her a grateful smile. Ro returned it.

Surprising herself, Ro laid her hand on the young woman's shoulder. "But if you need anything—tell me."

She'd changed it from a question at the last minute, realizing her little sister Cendre never would've asked for help, and most likely, this young woman wouldn't either.

Mulan hesitated, then nodded.

Ro dropped her hand as a shadow filled the barn door.

"Commander Qing-Zhu." Mulan did the hand-clap-bow thing.

Ro's mind scrambled. That would mean his name was Zhu, and his family name was Qing. But she hadn't been given permission to use Zhu, so Qing-Zhu or Commander it was.

She sincerely hoped she remembered that. She was terrible with names, but these were just interesting enough, perhaps they would stick in her mind?

"A meal is prepared. If it is convenient, huntress, we can discuss our plans for removing the Nightingale from your lands."

Ro wanted nothing more.

She followed them out of the barn.

After food had been distributed—a thin, salty broth with floating white chunks and deep-green herbs, as well as some kind of clearish-white pastry stuffed into little handheld balls and warmed in steam baskets—Odette, Ro, the commander, and his second-in-command all sat in a circle to discuss taking down the empress.

PART IV

THE EMPRESS'S PAGODA / LA PAGODE DE L'IMPÉRATRICE

"The Ballad of Mulan"
La Ballade de Mulan
Unknown

I step outside to see my comrades-in-arms;
They are all shocked and astounded.
"We traveled together for twelve years,
"But we never suspected that Mulan was a woman!"

Je sors pour voir mes compagnons d'armes ;
Ils sont tous choqués et stupéfiés.
« Nous avons voyagé ensemble pendant douze ans,
Mais nous n'avons jamais soupçonné que Mulan était une
femme ! »

Qing-Zhu's tale was perfunctory, factual, and said with little emotion, as if to shield himself from how painful the subject surely was.

He did not know English as well as Mulan, so as he spoke in his native tongue, Mulan translated, her grasp on the language phenomenal.

Qing-Zhu was the emperor's second son, the first remaining at the palace to help the country recover after the emperor's brutal murder at the hand of the Nightingale. She called herself Lim Wei-Yip, after her master Lim-Qi, whom they had not known was a sorcerer until it was too late.

"My father trusted him. Yet when the emperor fell ill the first time, this little brown nightingale alighted on the branches outside his window and sang him back to health. Lim-Qi was furious, though we did not know it, and not long after, this mechanical nightingale showed up at the palace, a gift from the emperor of Japan. Or so we thought."

Ro tilted her head. Something about that sounded familiar, but she couldn't quite remember what. Oh, right! That fairy tale she'd read.

"It was made from pure gold, encrusted with jewels, and

the loveliest tune came from the gears within. The court was enchanted, but my father still loved his plain little nightingale best. Until one day it flew away, and my father was heartbroken.

"Little did we know Lim-Qi had caged it, hidden deep within the palace.

"My father soon fell ill again, and he couldn't bear for the mechanical bird to leave his side. He requested it be played over and over. He was so pale, so ill, so near death—my brother was prepared to become emperor as soon as he had passed."

Qing-Zhu paused, grief suffusing his features. Mulan put her hand on his shoulder, and after a moment, he nodded at her and took up his tale once more.

"We did not know Lim-Qi was planning to overthrow the kingdom. That he was using the metal bird to siphon the emperor's life force into himself, to give him enough power for his revolt.

"Somehow, the nightingale, the real one, got free and flew to my father's side, dashing the mechanical bird against the floor. The moment it shattered, up rose a beautiful woman from the broken pieces, only now pulling my father's life into herself, sucking it into a jade stone around her neck.

"My brother and I couldn't move. Couldn't raise our swords against her. She looked like...just like...our dead mother, only wrong. More beautiful. Too perfect."

His eyes widened. "Not that our mother wasn't beautiful! She was. But in a normal, quiet way. Only this woman... this...copy, couldn't possibly compare to the real thing.

"Lim-Qi burst into the room, furious, and tried to kill our father. And us.

"My brother and I had not left our father's side, and we both wished we had acted sooner, for when we tried to stop the sorcerer, he thrust us aside as if we weighed nothing. As he advanced, the woman stood between him and my father.

"I—cannot explain what happened next." He and Mulan exchanged glances, and she nodded, as if encouraging him to continue. "But after a burst of light, Lim-Qi was dead, the woman had brought our father back from the grave, and the little brown nightingale was gone.

"She—she forced our father to marry her"—his hands clenched into fists—"taking over his will when he refused. Again, something we did not know until it was too late.

"She had fallen in love with him as she sang to him at his bedside, but it was not long until we could see her obsession had turned to madness. Anyone who disagreed with her was soon listless, compliant to anything she suggested. Serving maids and young messenger boys disappeared from service faster than we could replace them.

"Everything was seen as an insult to her honor, and fear swept the palace as consequences became more dire.

"As we were discovering the extent of her treachery, we found those she'd trapped asleep in caves, piled everywhere, their life force keeping her in power, especially children. We think it is because they contain the most vibrant life within themselves."

Ro's fists were clenching tighter the longer the man spoke. All she could think about was Allura, trapped in the same sleep these other children had suffered, her life force being drawn from her to sustain the creature in the pagoda.

Ro was ending her, here and now. And she would show no mercy.

"Any enemy who resisted her or could not be intimidated or enchanted to obey her was soon asleep. I never knew, and may never know, why my brother and I were not enchanted, but perhaps our father somehow protected us.

"The emperor began to resist her, to express his displeasure at being ensorcelled, and the perceived rejection broke what little hold the woman had on sanity. She put everyone at the palace to sleep. We escaped her rampage but barely, and my troop and I hatched a plot to rescue my father."

His quick glance to Mulan, and her solemn nod, spoke volumes.

"We freed the palace, we were able to break the sorceress's hold on some of my soldiers—she had stretched herself too thin—and we gained the inner chambers."

Qing-Zhu stopped, unable to go on.

"We found the emperor brutally murdered," Mulan said in a quiet voice. "The sorceress was bent over him, weeping, blood on her hands. We would have killed her—"

"But she escaped our clutches," Qing-Zhu finished, his voice stronger. "She pulled some kind of green mist toward herself, and when we could see again, she was gone."

Mulan said, "We have heard tales of her deeds throughout many lands, including demands of marriage to the ruling monarch, curses cast after a deep offense of honor, and children falling asleep and not waking, before she moves on to the next."

"We had just heard of the little princess in your kingdom, huntress," Qing-Zhu said to Ro, "and were on our way to investigate, when we received your missive, Lady," he then said to Odette. "It is the first we have heard of where she might have hidden herself, so we came right away."

"I sent no missive," Odette said through pale lips.

They looked as surprised as Ro felt, especially since Odette hadn't denied it earlier.

The commander said something to one of his soldiers that Mulan did not translate, and a man rushed over with a satchel, from which the missive was carefully unwrapped and presented to Odette.

"It has passed many hands," Qing-Zhu said apologetically, "but we preserved it as best as we were able."

A dirty, wrinkled letter lay in his hands, penned neatly in

elegant, slanting letters that were just the slightest bit blocky. As if the writer were unsure of them.

Odette frowned. "That's not my handwriting. I mean, it *looks* like my handwriting, just a little, but it's not quite right...Odin!"

She took off her slipper and threw it at the bird, who'd apparently joined them at some point during the commander's tale. The flock huddled close to Odette with all the soldiers milling about.

"Like I can't tell whose handwriting that is!"

Ro sighed. Just when Odette was starting to act somewhat normal, she had to go and accuse a bird of writing a letter.

Odin squawked and flapped away, and confused looks were exchanged all around.

"I do not understand—" Qing-Zhu started to say.

Odette cut him off. "It doesn't matter. I didn't send it, some meddling person did, but you're here, and now we have to deal with it." She folded her arms and looked cross.

"Lady, we do not wish to offend, but we must find the Nightingale now, before she discovers we are here and escapes our grasp. We need you to lead us, to take us to her right away. We cannot find her hiding place. It is shielded from us."

Growing more agitated the longer the commander spoke, Odette was shaking her head by the end of it.

He and Mulan exchanged glances. "Am I not being clear? Perhaps my second can explain better."

Odette was looking fierce by now, and Ro had gotten to know her just well enough to realize that meant she was desperately holding back tears.

"*Nein. Nein, nein, nein,*" Odette said. "You have to wait till after the summer solstice. You can defeat her then. After my brothers are free."

Ro highly doubted that a celestial event would be enough to wake Odette's brothers from a sleeping curse.

Ro cleared her throat. "Odette, there's a chance you can't free your brothers if she isn't defeated first."

Now Odette spun on Ro. "You don't know that. You don't know how she works. How *any* of this works!"

Ro tried to keep her tone reasonable. "I do know that most curses can't be undone if the curse wielder is actively keeping them in place. If she draws power from her victims, that in turn makes the curses stronger. And impossible to break while she's still alive."

Odette's jaw dropped, and she sat there, stunned, staring at nothing.

Speaking English, Qing-Zhu went on, carefully, as if being sure of every word. "When the Nightingale attacked the emperor, may he rest with our ancestors, and fled, she left many still sleeping. We have been unable to wake them, and many have died."

Ro felt the words like a punch to the face, and she sucked in a breath and fought off welling tears. Mulan gave her a questioning look, but Ro ignored it as she wrested her emotions under control.

"We are hopeful that if we defeat her," Qing-Zhu continued, "our healers can wake any survivors. We cannot delay. We must fight her now, before your summer solstice"—the two words were said with care—"and before we lose any more of our people."

Ro came to her feet, ready to fight the empress *now*. "Then why wait till tomorrow? I can help you find her pagoda. I've been there before."

Not that she'd been able to see it, either, after her fall.

Qing-Zhu and Mulan stood as well. "Excellent, huntress. That is just what we were hoping. My men need rest, but I appreciate your enthusiasm. We will leave at first light."

He nodded to Mulan and walked away.

Ro turned to Odette. "Do the forest paths still open to you? Like how you were able to find your way back here after the…churchyard?"

Odette was standing now as well, fists clenched, nearly vibrating with tension. "I can't leave this place."

"Then can I do it?"

Odette shook her head. "I told you. The empress controls the forest paths. Now that you no longer have the knives, you'd become just as lost as anybody."

"But you can do it?"

Odette glanced away and refused to answer.

Frustration built in Ro. Her niece didn't have time for this! "Just help us reach her, Odette! Then you can scurry right back here and do whatever is more important than actually setting your brothers free."

Ro regretted the heated words the moment they'd left her mouth.

With a cry, Odette spun and ran for the tower. A soldier walked into her path just then, so she turned, sprinted for the barn, and slammed the door behind her.

Mulan looked between the barn and Ro with wide eyes.

Ro sighed. "Perhaps I should go apologize?"

At no objection from the warrior, Ro trudged away, wishing for once she'd *think* before words came flying out of her mouth like flaming arrows.

"Wait." Mulan's quiet voice stopped her in her tracks. "Have you asked her *why* she cannot leave? What keeps her here?"

Ro looked over her shoulder. "Many times."

Mulan gave her a hint of a smile. "Perhaps you are not asking the right question."

At a flash of frustration, Ro said, "If you figure out what that is, let me know."

She stomped to the barn. What question could she possibly ask that would get her a direct response?

Ro heaved open the barn door, her energy spent after the mild activity.

That was going to make any battle tomorrow about a thousand times more difficult.

Odette was hunched over by the tower wall, heaving aside sacks of flour Ro had piled on crates there to get them out of the middle of the floor. It apparently had been covering a secret entrance to the tower, one Ro hadn't seen before, which was partially open but not yet wide enough for Odette to slip through.

Ro tried to speak reasonably. "Odette, you're the only one who might be able to get us in. Especially since I lost those knives. I'm assuming that war axe works differently for you than it does for other people? Or can I use it?"

"*Nein*, you can't use it. And I can't leave! My brothers' lives depend on it, all right?"

More likely, her brothers' lives depended on Ro and the Chinese warriors. Ro leaned against the wall and tried to take Mulan's words to heart. "What do you suggest?"

The girl spun around and jabbed a finger at Ro. "Suggest? I suggest that you not go at all. I suggest that you wait until after the summer solstice. But will you listen?" She paused long enough to spear Ro with a glare. "Of course not. You'll sprint straight into danger without a thought for your life, and the witch will claim yet another victim. Do you not remember that you almost *died*?"

Ro leaned forward with a growl. "My niece's life is at stake. I'll sprint into that and worse if I have to."

The girl just blinked, like she was trying to figure out what to say. For all her bluster, Odette had a softer, sweeter, quieter side that came into play when Ro startled her or she let down her guard.

"Help me," Ro said. "Help me take these warriors in there to defeat her. Then you can come right back here after."

The girl studied her a long moment. "You're serious, aren't you? No matter what I say—you're still going."

"Oui. Completely." Ro held her gaze. "And now we have help. Help I desperately need. I can't let this opportunity pass me by, Odette. Children are dying. My niece is dying. I have to do *something*."

Precious seconds ticked by. "I will help you if I can, but I cannot go with you," she said fiercely. "I'm sorry."

Ro clenched her jaw but forced herself to speak calmly. "If that is what you wish."

"It's not what I wish—it's what I have to do." Odette hesitated outside the hidden door she'd uncovered, not climbing up to the tower right away.

"Why, Odette," Ro said softly. "*Why* can't you leave this place? What has you so scared?" Before Odette could make more excuses, she jumped in with, "You said you'd tell me the moment I got up. Well, I'm up. Will you keep your word?"

As she was speaking, the six white swans waddled into the barn, most likely concerned by their raised voices—again— and formed a half-circle around the two women.

"Because of them," Odette said quietly.

Ro raised an eyebrow. "What about them? For all that you love them, Odette, they're just swans. What about your brothers? Don't you want to wake them?"

Odette blinked rapidly and opened her mouth, but nothing came out.

Ro tried again. "You haven't told me what the summer solstice means for you. For your brothers. Why you think it'll break a sleeping curse."

"My brothers aren't asleep!" burst out of Odette's mouth.

Now it was Ro's turn to blink. "What? But you said the empress cursed them…"

"The empress can do more than put people to sleep, huntress. Like—" Odette clamped her mouth shut and looked away. Such pain crossed her face that Ro winced on her behalf. It must've been something truly awful.

And that reminded Ro of her conversation with Olt, that his family had been cursed by the empress too. Had he been worried about something other than a sleeping curse?

"Then what happened?" Ro asked.

"The witch, she—she cursed my brothers. She—she

turned them all—she turned them all..." The girl choked and buried her face in her hands.

"Odette..." Ro stood there for several awkward seconds, trying to decide what to do.

A rustle sounded, right next to her, and Ro reached out and stroked Odin's neck, comforting the creature as she waited.

Odette was staring at them.

Ro looked between her and the swans, several times, as an inkling of a thought dawned on her. "You don't mean..."

Now Odette and the swans—the swans, for heaven's sake—were all staring at her, waiting for her to continue.

But she couldn't. Because what she was thinking was just ridiculous.

Her eyes returned to Odette. "Explain. Now."

Odette swallowed, hard. "That witch seduced my father. She wanted to rule my kingdom, wanted the Black Forest for some reason, wanted my six brothers and me out of the way."

The way she emphasized six brothers set Ro's stomach to roiling. Her eyes drifted to the swans. She counted them. Six. Non. It couldn't be. She tore her eyes away when Odette started talking again.

"She cast her spell and tried to turn us all into...to turn us into..."

"Swans?" Ro said it weakly.

Tears filled Odette's eyes and spilled down her cheeks. "Swans."

Ro let that soak in a moment. "But not you?"

She huffed a bitter laugh. "Oh, she tried. It didn't work. I'm not even sure why, but she was furious. My brothers all ran as the curse chased them down, but the witch trapped my sister-in-law, caged her for her transformation, and I escaped."

"How did she—how did it happen?"

Odette scowled. "My stepmother threw a big celebration

for my father's birthday, invited us all to come. We knew something was wrong, but we went anyway." Her head fell back, and she shouted at the ceiling. "We were so stupid!"

One of the swans squawked and flapped its wings.

Her gaze snapped to the swan. "We were all stupid and you know it, Oberon! Now your wife is trapped up there, with the witch, has been for almost six years, and there's nothing any of us can do about it. I want Odile back as much as you do."

The swan settled and hung its head, making a low keening sound.

Ro scrunched her forehead. She knew she'd heard that name before… "Odile?"

"My sister-in-law. My younger brother, Oberon—the eldest of all my brothers—married her." She gave a deep and heavy sigh. "I told you some of this, but she was my best friend from childhood, and he had the biggest crush on her for the longest time, could barely speak two words in her presence, but then he grew up and she noticed." A wistful smile found her face. "I've never seen either of them so happy. They'd just returned from their wedding trip when my stepmother threw the party."

One of the swans squawked again, and Odette shushed it. Him.

Guess Ro had to think of them as people now. Which was just confusing.

"But—what about your père? The king."

Odette's expression turned to stone. "What about him?"

Although Ro knew exactly how she felt, or at least, had an idea, she couldn't help asking, "Don't you care what happened to him?"

Odette's hard look didn't crack. "He was the fool who married the witch in the first place, just to keep peace. Didn't even fight it. Why should I care what happened to him?"

Ro could relate. She really could. The only thing her père

hadn't done was marry a witch after her mère died, just a hard and cruel woman with two spoiled brats for daughters. And Cosette had been forced to live with them.

Had Ro known…well. She would've broken Cosette out of there. If Ro hadn't been trapped in the beast's château then, of course.

But still. "Surely the Nightingale must've spelled him to do what she wanted. Don't you want to know if he's still alive?"

Odette gave a firm shake of her head. *"Nein."*

Ro glanced to the swans. They shifted, looked away, appeared mournful—if Ro had to guess, they didn't agree with their sister. But how on earth could she ask a swan?

"Could you, uh—" Ro faltered when Odette turned her still-stormy gaze on her. She swallowed. "Can you introduce me to them?"

Odette swiped at her eyes and tried to pretend she hadn't been crying. "Sure. Why not?" She pointed to each of the swans. "Oberon, Odysseus, Odwin, Olov, Orbart, and Odin."

Nope. She'd still never be able to keep those names straight. But she'd had no idea the first time Odette had introduced them that Ro was meeting the girl's brothers.

Each swan, in turn, either ruffled its feathers, nodded, squawked, or, as the last one did, gave a sweeping bow, to the heckling of the others.

That put a phantom of a smile on Odette's face. "Odin is the youngest, as you've probably guessed, and the clown of the family."

Ro gave him a warm smile. She'd grown quite fond of that particular swan over the course of her stay. Of course, he was the one who'd led her here and gotten her trapped, but at least he'd kept her company ever since.

Even slept at her side most nights.

Now that she knew he was a person under all those white feathers… A sudden flush suffused her face. You know what? She wasn't going to think about that.

Once he was human again, they were having words.

"Those are…interesting names," Ro said, since she couldn't think of anything else to say.

Odette nodded. "My mother was obsessed with names that started with 'O.' Whenever she read us a story when we were little and came across another—especially a strong character with heroic feats—she would scribble down the name for later." She glanced at Odin and grinned. He backed up a few steps. "But when she read us Norse mythology, she ran into a bit of a hiccup."

Odin backed all the way behind his brothers, and Odette's grin spread.

"She fell in love with Loki's mischievousness, and Thor's strength fascinated her, and Odin was such a leader, sacrificing himself on that tree. The physicians had already told her the child she carried would be her last, and the rest of us already had names that started with 'O.' What was she to do?"

Ro wanted to know why this girl thought she cared about this particular story, but she nodded to be polite while her mind wandered. A bit. If she were being honest.

Now Odette's grin looked more genuine—more older-sister teasing. "Why, name him all three names, of course!"

Ro blinked, realizing she must've missed something. "Pardon?"

Odette rolled her eyes. "Odin Loki Thor? But Odin hated it. Something we couldn't stop teasing him about." She smirked.

The bird called Odin squawked and flapped its wings, more agitated than Ro had ever seen him.

But Odette would not be stopped. She was enjoying this far too much. "Insisted we call him Olt. Wouldn't let us call him anything else—"

Ro spun toward him the moment Odette said his name. Even though he was trying to hide, his brothers kept pushing him forward and pecking at him, exactly how she'd imagine her sisters would do were the situation reversed.

Olt! The swan was Olt?

Her heart pounded, her head spun, and she felt sick. Everything collided in her mind at once, and it finally made sense. All of it.

His reluctance to return. His overly carefree manner. The way he stared at the forest as if it would eat him. The pain he'd kept so well hidden before their journey. And she'd made him come here. She'd forced him to turn into a swan.

And he'd come anyway. For her. For Allura. Even though he knew what would happen. Tears filled her eyes.

Odette was still talking, but Ro didn't hear another word.

"Olt?" Ro whispered. "Is that…you?"

The rest of the barn got quiet, but Ro didn't notice, she was so focused on the swan.

"Olt?" She could barely speak around the lump in her throat.

He ducked his long neck and huddled his head under his wing, still trying to hide. Ro followed. Got to her knees. And wrapped her arms around him.

The warm bird body trembled in her arms.

"Oh, Olt, I'm so sorry," she whispered. "And you came anyway."

She put her head down as silent tears soaked into his feathers.

And the giant white swan snaked his long neck around her and held her.

30

Mulan came into the barn as Ro was wiping away the last of her tears. She hesitated at the door, but Ro waved her in, even though Odette seemed reluctant to keep talking.

"And the black swan?" Ro asked.

After a moment, Odette nodded to the biggest white swan, the one that tended to boss the others around. "As I said, Oberon's wife, Odile. My best friend from childhood."

And Ro had almost stabbed her. Ro felt weak. Now she understood Odette's relief at the black swan's survival. Thank goodness she hadn't killed the creature.

"But…the swan attacked me. Has the witch turned her? Is she evil now?"

Oberon let out a low, mournful sound and flattened his head on the ground. Odette squatted down to stroke his back. "It's possible, I suppose, but I hope not." She squinted up at Ro. "Did she have a band around her neck? Silver or gold, perhaps?"

Ro snapped her fingers. "Oui! A silver band. One of the few things I noticed before she hurled me down the steps and tried to kill me."

Odette winced, and Ro regretted her words.

"That wasn't kind. Désolé." Even if it was the truth. Ro looked around, taking in the birds. "D'accord, new plan." Her eyes settled on Odette. "You take a few soldiers, rescue the black swan, and bring her back here, while the rest of us break into the empress's lair and defeat her."

Odette was already shaking her head stubbornly. "I can't leave here. I told you that."

Before Ro could strangle her, Mulan said quietly, "The Nightingale turned people into swans?"

Odette's eyes went huge. "Oh, please don't tell anyone!"

"Even if it's important?" Mulan asked.

Odette was on the cusp of tears. Again. "I don't want anyone to hurt them. I have to protect them. If the wrong people found out…"

"I think it's important for the soldiers to know," Mulan said kindly. "We hunt and eat what we can, but if the Nightingale is turning nobles into birds—well, it would explain the many birds we thought she had imported to the palace."

Odette paled and swooned on her feet.

Ro nodded at Mulan. "Please let your commander know. Ask him to…discreetly…inform the others."

After a quick glance at Odette for her begrudging nod, Mulan bowed and hastened out of the barn.

Ro startled when she found Odette glaring at her. "I swear to *Gott*, huntress, if you've cost me one of my brother's lives…"

A little of her own temper made itself known. "Would you be more upset that the soldiers knew, or to wake up one morning to find them roasting one of your brothers over a spit?"

Odette gasped and made a broken sound, and the swans surrounded her, simultaneously hissing at Ro and trying to comfort their sister.

Ro rubbed her face. "That didn't come out how I meant it.

But please. They are safer if the soldiers know. If for that reason only."

Odette looked away.

Turning, Ro studied the swans, all princes…

Which meant Olt was a prince. Once his curse was broken, he wouldn't look twice at her. Just like Trêve. She'd lose another friend. Another…more than a friend.

Her heart stilled. The pain was cutting, sharp. Sinking deep into a place Ro was reminded at the worst possible times still wasn't whole.

Whatever. She didn't care if Olt no longer pursued her. It was a relief, even.

And she'd tell herself that until she believed it.

Edging away, Odette interrupted the absolute maelstrom flinging itself around inside Ro. "I'll just go back to my tower, then, shall I?"

That got Ro's attention. Right. Focus on what was in front of her, not a future she couldn't control. "We're still going to need your help."

Odette froze. Then began emphatically shaking her head. "*Nein.* I can't."

Ro's temper started to climb. "Odette." She propped her hands on her hips. "No. More. Secrets. Why not?"

Odette said, "When the empress cursed my family, she missed me. If she catches me…"

"I'll protect you. Or better yet, you can protect yourself. By fighting her. Taking your kingdom back. Uniting it under your rule."

"You don't understand. What if the witch catches one of my brothers before the summer solstice? They have to *be* here for it to work."

Ro cocked her head. "For what to work?"

"Never mind. I can't risk my brothers!"

Ro looked around at the swans. They all stood a little taller. "Then they can fight her too."

"What? Nooooo…" Odette stared at them, fear in her eyes.

"Seriously? Have you been bit by one of these things? I'd be proud to fight with giant, scary attack birds at my side." Ro hooked a thumb over her shoulder. "They have rows of teeth in their mouths. And on their tongues. One pushed me off a *building*."

"But they can't…we don't…"

"Can they lead us to the empress?"

"Well yes, but…"

Ro shrugged, the move very French. Made her miss her mère. And home. "I think it's time to stand up to the empress, don't you? She can hide in her fortress all she wants, but it's time for us to breach it and take her down."

Odette just looked angry. "You'd be taking them away right when they need to *be* here!"

Ro threw her hands out at her sides, her temper rising. "And if breaking the curse depends on the empress's defeat? Odette, I know in my gut, deep in my bones, that my niece isn't going to survive much longer. I need to defeat the empress now!"

Ro was shouting, and she didn't even care. She'd been trapped too long, anxious for escape, and now she had a way to escape *and* to defeat the empress.

"You can't wait *one day* till the summer solstice?" Odette demanded.

"Not if we have to defeat her first for whatever you're doing to even work!" Ro shot back. "What does the summer solstice have to do with anything?"

The swans surrounded them, unsettled, squawking, flapping, as agitated as the two girls facing off.

Odette kept arguing as if Ro had said nothing at all. "I'm not about to sacrifice my brothers while you go get yourself killed! Or lost. Not when we're *this close*."

Olt waddled forward, bumped Odette's hand, then made his way to Ro's side, turning to face his sister.

Odette's mouth dropped open. "You can't possibly be thinking of going with her!"

The rest of the swans moved to Ro's side as well.

"Fine. Go get yourselves killed. See if I care." Odette choked on a sob as she spun away. "You'd best be back by the time the moon rises tomorrow, or I'll strangle each of you myself," she called over her shoulder.

"*Why*, Odette?" burst out of Ro's mouth. "*Why* must they be back at the summer solstice? What ceremony are you performing? What are those awful—um, *eccentric* frock coats you're making? What aren't you telling me?"

"You don't understand. *I can't tell you*," Odette growled.

As Ro started to argue, a memory struck her: the conversation she'd had with Olt at her grandmère's cabin. "Odette. The sorceress lied to you. If you truly can't speak of it, you'll be under a compulsion and won't be able to form specific words. But sorceresses don't have as much power as they claim they do to monitor every word you say. *Say it.* Stop giving in to fear. Tell me what's really going on. Your silence only empowers her further by keeping you trapped in your own fear. Tell me. Help me *break this curse*."

Fists clenched, Odette took a deep breath, keeping her back to Ro. "If I don't finish the last coat by the summer solstice, my brothers will remain swans…forever."

Ro's mouth fell open.

"And because of *you*"—she shot Ro a dirty look—"I'm much further behind than I should be. So *nein*, huntress, I am not joining your little hunting party. And nothing you say will change my mind. They come first."

Ro stepped between the swans and laid a hand on the girl's shoulder. "I said I would help, and I'm going to. I will do all in my power to reunite you with your family."

Tears filled Odette's eyes, and this time, Ro didn't mind.

"While I appreciate the sentiment, huntress, that won't mean much if I can't complete my task in time."

The girl shrugged off Ro's touch and disappeared into the hidden staircase, shutting the part of the wall that swung inward behind her. It blended into the stonework perfectly. Ro moved to where she could see the tower.

Soon a lamp was lit and the girl's shadow bent over the final frock coat.

No wonder Odette spent so much time in that tower. No wonder she'd been so upset when first Ro then the warriors had breached her barrier, taking up even more time she didn't have.

Ro was going to find that witch, break each curse, and get back to Allura. As swiftly as she could. No one should be placed under a curse. No one should be held against their will. Whether in sleep, to another form, or by a promise they never made.

Apparently it was up to Ro to set the captives free.

Ro eyed the swans. "Sleep well. First light comes early."

A somber procession trailed out of the barn, disappearing to wherever they slept at night. Ro's eyes lingered on Olt, but the moment he was out of sight, she turned back to the tower.

She needed sleep too, but first, she was going to see what she could do to help Olt. Hopefully she'd get a little rest before tomorrow.

With a sigh, certain she'd bothered the poor girl enough for a lifetime, she decided to explore the hidden staircase for herself. A second escape route was never a bad idea.

Ro flung open the trapdoor in the middle of the tower's floor, chest tight, breath coming in short gasps. A rug slid off in a pathetic heap, but Ro didn't care. The only way she'd take that route again was if her life was in danger.

Apparently she didn't care for small spaces either.

Ro hurried to the open window, breathing deep. She'd gladly climb the tower's flimsy ropes every time if it meant never going in that dank passage again.

"Hey. I locked that," Odette protested.

Ro turned and noticed a splintered section of the trapdoor, where she'd broken it in her panic. She gave the girl an apologetic look. "I'll fix it."

Then Ro closed the trapdoor, shoved the rug in place, and propped her hands on her hips. "Tell me what to do."

Odette straightened from her sewing table, bending and twisting her back. "You can't."

Ro's jaw went hard. "Oh?"

Odette held out her hands, covered in welts, scars, and mounds of blisters.

Ro winced. "What on earth?" Then she spied skin-toned gloves resting next to Odette on the work table. Ro blinked. Had Odette worn gloves this whole time?

"There are many things you don't understand, huntress. I must weave the frock coats from stinging nettles grown in the old churchyard. I must do it with my bare hands. I must complete one coat a year, milestones reached at a certain time, or the magic unravels and I have to start all over again. This is not something you can do."

Ro couldn't even begin to form a response. The nettles had not been kind.

Also, now that Odette had discovered she *could* talk about this, it appeared she was in a hurry to get it all out as fast as she could. As if it were a relief to say the words.

"I will suffer for my brothers, not you," Odette continued. "It's how it has to be."

"I'll do it. I heal quickly."

Already she was feeling better. Perhaps focusing on others instead of how awful she felt was helping? Then a thought hit her. She felt better each time the moon came up, and the summer solstice was bringing in a giant moon, hanging low in the sky and close to the earth. She bit back a groan and rubbed her shoulder.

She couldn't forget that time in her life fast enough.

"*Nein*. It won't work unless I do it." Odette looked around nervously. "In fact, I'm not even sure you should be in here. Now that you're not recovering."

"Why in the realms not?" Ro demanded.

"The…information…I received on breaking the curse was very specific. I have to keep the room spotless. Not a speck of dust can touch the frock coats. I alone have to do all the work. If you help…I don't know if that will negate the magic. I imagine it will."

Ro started to argue. Paused. Rethought her protest. That sounded different than an arbitrary "you cannot speak of this" directive. "Are you sure?" she asked.

Odette raised an eyebrow. "If it were your brothers, would you take a chance?"

"Non, I would not."

Odette went back to stitching cloth together with pulpy strands.

Ro eyed the room. Five complete frock coats, with tails, hoods, and buttons twisted out of nettles, all the same drab green. That she got. But the six matching spinning wheels… "Why six?"

Odette startled, as if she'd forgotten Ro was even there. Unfocused eyes settled on her even as her hands stayed busy. "What?"

Ro gestured to the equipment. "Why six of each?"

Odette's eyes drifted over the room, taking in her entire purpose for the past five years. She sighed. "You're not going to leave me alone till I tell you the whole story, are you?"

Ro just smiled, crossed her arms, and leaned against the curved wall of the tower room, near the window. "As long as it doesn't interfere—but oui. I'm curious. Also, I need as much information as possible before a hunt."

"All right. I can work and talk." Odette bent back to her task. "No matter who I asked, what information I sought, I couldn't find a way to break my brothers' curse. Then I heard of a woman who deals in breaking curses. I'm not allowed to say who—"

"Madame LaChance?"

Odette pricked her finger on her needle. She yelped and sucked on her already-raw skin, and Ro was nearly bowled over by a swan flinging itself through the open window.

Ro went down, rolled away, and came up on her feet in time to see the swan fussing over Odette, nipping at her fingers as if trying to see them.

"I'm fine, Olov, really!"

The swan wouldn't let up, so Odette sighed and held out her hands. The swan tilted his head over them, and soon tears were dripping onto her hands.

Ro's eyes went wide. What was even happening right now?

As each tear fell, a hissing sound filled the air, little curls of steam rose, and the wounds smoothed over and closed, leaving more puckered skin.

Odette opened and closed her hands and sighed in relief. "Thank you, Olov."

The swan honked and was out the window in a flurry of wings. Odette went over to the washbasin, poured cool, clear water, and started washing her hands.

"I can't get blood on the coats," she said by way of explanation.

Ro instantly felt horrible. "Oh. Désolé."

"It is nothing. I shouldn't have been so jumpy."

"The information was that detailed?"

"It was that detailed, and my…source…was so sure of it, she'll take half of my payment after I have my brothers back."

Ro's eyebrows shot up. That wasn't how Madame LaChance worked. Normally she requested mounds of gold to even *consider* helping someone. Apparently Madame LaChance was changing how she did business.

Odette patted her hands dry and went back to the workstation, threading a string of nettle through her needle, plunging it into the collar she was currently working on, attaching a hood.

The coat was still missing both sleeves.

"I had to make one coat per year, paying attention to all the details of a ceremonial frock coat. The nettles must be ground into pulp, dried, then woven into a continuous strand. Each piece of cloth must be made from an unbroken strand."

Ro's eyes widened with each monotone addition to the list, as if the girl said it to herself in her sleep. Which she probably did.

"It breaks, I have to start again. I don't make the cloth big enough for the entire coat, I have to start over. Each coat must be made on its own brand-new equipment—that's why there are six spinning wheels—but I couldn't fit more than one loom up here, so I've had to tear it down each year and build a new one."

Ro repented of every time she'd been frustrated with the girl for locking herself away in her tower for full days at a time.

"The final coat must be finished before the seventh year begins, and each thrown upon my brothers' backs at the rising of the full moon, before it leaves its zenith, on the night of the summer solstice."

Ro started pacing just thinking about it. There was so much that could go wrong! Surely she could help somehow.

"What do you have left to do?" Ro asked, glancing around.

Odette laughed. "Go feed the swans, make sure the animals are put up—or whatever will keep you from pacing all night—get some good sleep, and leave me to my task. That is help enough for now."

Ro nodded and opted for descending the tower instead of going through that horrible small space again. She swung out onto the pulley system, started lowering herself, and paused. "One more thing."

Odette looked up expectantly.

"Your hair?"

Odette flushed the brightest shade of pink she'd seen on the girl's face. "I—can't cut it. The whole six years. It… moderates the magic so I don't use too much or too little in the coats." She ducked her head. "It grew rather longer than I expected."

Ro bit back a laugh. "I'll say."

Odette scowled and shooed her off with a hand. "Go. Make work. Get all that energy out of your system so you'll be of some use tomorrow."

Shaking her head, Ro went back to lowering herself.

She could use some good, hard work to keep her mind off all the things that had to happen just right. Then she'd fall asleep exhausted and wake up ready to attack the Nightingale empress at first light. Rescue the black swan.

Turn Olt back into his handsome, normal self.

In the meantime, she'd pray Odette finished that coat in time, and she'd do everything in her power to make sure the swans were back in time as well.

So many things could go wrong.

31

Mulan led her soldiers out through the barrier as easily as she'd led them in, something Ro was trying very hard not to be salty about.

The troop moved silently through the trees, the only noise coming from the swans when they rustled their feathers or investigated something in the brush. With the swans leading the way, they found Ro's trail easily enough.

It wasn't long until something metal glinted in the underbrush.

Ro cried out, seized her treasure with fierce joy, and held it aloft for the others to see. The knife! The single long knife she'd used to escape the empress's barrier, the one she'd dropped. Now they didn't have to find the spot she'd sliced through before.

The soldiers just looked at her, uncomprehending, but not daring to make any noise. Ro clamped her mouth shut, hid the knife carefully away, and hurried toward the empress's pagoda even faster, no longer carefully searching.

The soldiers matched Ro's speed toward their destination. They swiftly climbed the hill the palace rested upon, eyes lighting as this time, they were able to get close to it. As they approached the pagoda, the swans stayed back. They all paused right outside the barrier and hunkered down to take in the sheer massiveness of the structure.

"How did it even get here?" Ro asked quietly.

"I have no idea," Mulan responded, eyes wide and lips tight.

Qing-Zhu added, "We must pray this doesn't mean her powers have grown beyond what we can fight."

Ro adjusted her borrowed arm bracers. Dressed in leathers, hunting gear, and her red cape, she felt ready for the hunt. The soldiers wore the same elaborate armor as yesterday.

Ro kept fingering the bow across her back, the fletching of the arrows at her side, the long sword the soldiers had lent her, and now the knife tucked at her waist.

She never wanted to be without weapons again.

And she especially loved how this quiver could turn upside down and not a single arrow fall out, yet if she drew one, it came out seamlessly. Smiling, Mulan had said she could keep it when Ro had nearly swooned over it.

Ro kept her voice low. "The only way up is this staircase. The black swan, the guardian, is at the top. It wouldn't let me pass, but we need to get to the doors behind it."

Oberon flapped his wings and honked.

"Shh!" Ro and Mulan said at the same time. Then Ro said, "But he's right. We need the swan alive, to bring it back with us."

Oberon settled at her words.

As Ro crouched there, Odin came close and rested his chin on her thigh. She absently rubbed his head. Then the bird gently gripped her cape and tugged.

Ro ripped it from his grasp with a scolding glance. If this really was Olt, he knew how much her cape meant to her. How it protected her.

Still, he bleated quietly and tugged.

"What do you want, you silly bird! We need to be quiet, in case she doesn't already know we're here." She said under her breath, "Which is doubtful with all the ruckus you made getting here…"

The swan waddled away, came back, waddled away again, then came back, only to tug at her some more.

"He wants you to go with him." The smile in Mulan's voice was unmistakable.

Ro looked to the pagoda and back. "But don't we need to start climbing? It's going to take a while."

"Maybe we should see what he wants first?"

Ro grumbled a little, but she shoved to her feet and picked her way through thick brush after the swan. The soldiers followed.

She had no doubt Odin was truly Olt. He was just as annoying as a bird. Didn't make her miss him any less, though she'd never admit it out loud.

But it was also really hard to call him Olt in this form.

Ro wanted to scream when the swan took them away from the pagoda, well past it, then deeper into the wood. They never came up against the barrier.

At an especially thick part of the forest, Ro and the soldiers were forced to stop. They spread out and began looking for another way through.

Odin gave a gentle bleat and pressed right into a thick clump of brush and disappeared.

"Han-Xu, we should probably go back—" Ro said to Mulan.

Trying to see where he went, she placed her hand on what she thought was a solid tree branch. The dead wood snapped, sending her tumbling into the brush, into darkness, into— rocky soil and a shallow stream.

Mulan and the rest of the soldiers pushed through the curtain of hanging vines and brush. Ro scrambled to her feet, boots and cloak half wet.

They were in a cave opening of some kind, shielded by an overhang. Growth crept over an opening on two sides, where the stream and rock bed entered and left.

"Where are we?" Ro asked, but of course no one knew.

The soldiers immediately spread out, inspecting every inch of the rock formations.

One of them called out, near the rock wall in the back. Qing-Zhu translated for Ro. "A passageway. Leading into a system of caves."

"A back way into the palace?" Ro questioned.

Mulan said, with excitement in her voice, "Hopefully."

"The empress somehow placed her pagoda over the palace. Palaces often have an escape route for the royal family. Perhaps how Odette got out?" Ro mused.

Odin squawked and flapped his feathers, so Ro followed him to where the soldiers had found an opening. Ro peered into the dark, and her eyesight flared, illuminating the rocks slightly. The tunnel seemed to delve deep into the rock.

"The Nightingale tends to gravitate toward cave systems," Mulan said. "Where she can hide her victims as she draws life from them."

Ro clenched her jaw. "Let's go get her."

Torches were quickly assembled from the surrounding forest, and flint sparked as soldiers lit them and passed them out.

"From here on in, no speaking unless absolutely necessary," Qing-Zhu said.

Ro and Mulan nodded their agreement as the instructions were repeated in his language for the soldiers.

With a deep breath, Ro drew her knife and led the way in.

❧

Apparently the cave bypassed whatever protective barrier the empress used, because Ro never had to cut through it.

She crept down the tunnel with Mulan and Qing-Zhu behind her, swans in the middle, and soldiers bringing up the rear. As they made their way deeper into the cave system, the ground slanted ever so gradually downward.

Ro had never been more grateful when the tunnel came to an end and opened around her into a large, cavernous space. She felt weak and shaky, and a trail of sweat slid down her temple.

She wasn't as recovered as she'd hoped.

A little section of rock made a rather convenient bench, so she sat. Taking deep breaths, she tried her best not to sound breathless while she took in the space lit with torches as the soldiers fanned out.

Odin was there immediately, his concern flickering as much as the torchlight as he fussed all around her. She stroked his feathers to comfort him.

The cavern was big enough for everyone in the palace to make their homes here and be comfortable.

On the far side, torchlight fused together and was sucked into a wall of stone the color of pitch. Soldiers converged upon it, talking in quiet voices, examining it closely. The wall stretched the length of the cave and extended far overhead.

Ro pushed herself to her feet and joined them.

"Do you recognize the stone, huntress?" Mulan asked quietly.

Ro leaned close and sucked in a gasp. The stone wasn't black, but a green so dark, it was hard to differentiate the two colors. "It's the same stone that makes up the pagoda outside," she said just as quietly. "Incroyable."

Not only towering overhead, the smooth jade wall had also buried itself deep, with jagged stone crumbling at its base from where it had plunged itself into the rock.

It was hard to imagine a sorceress having so much power to do something like *this*.

Strangely, two portions of the smooth wall crossed each

other at a slant, much like how each side of Ro's robe criss-crossed each other before she tied them shut.

Ro was going to live in that thing for a week after this hunt was done and over.

"Is there no way to get in?" Mulan asked.

Ro's eyesight lit the wall as if with candlelight, edging the crossed section of the wall. As she studied it, an idea formed in her mind. She moved toward it, feeling the size of an ant compared to what she was standing next to, and placed her hand on the wall.

It thrummed with energy, but it didn't respond to her touch. As if Ro were shielded from it. She rubbed her mère's cloak, gratitude suffusing her.

She moved to the crossed section and leaned over to see behind the front portion.

There. A gap between the two walls, large enough for their group to travel single file. Ro smirked, waved them over, then shimmied down into the crack by bracing her feet on one side and her back on the other.

When she reached the bottom, she turned to the group peering down at her and whistled softly for them to join her. The soldiers silently descended, as graceful as dancers, and the swans fluttered down in what looked like a controlled fall.

Ro looked ahead. The crack seemed to hold for a good distance, but it was smaller than she'd thought. She just hoped they wouldn't get stuck and couldn't turn around…

She shuddered and eyed the soldiers' armor. If they removed it, they could fit with their slight frames. Her? Not so much. She wasn't big-boned by any means, but she was tall, and her frame was larger than any of her companions.

They conferred in their beautiful language, then removed their armor and tied it in packs to carry. Their torches cast ghoulish figures all over the walls.

Ro turned to Mulan. "Ready?"

"I rather feel like the whole thing is just waiting to fall on us." Mulan scanned the rocks they'd climbed down and into the small crevice.

Ro immediately tried to put her at ease. "However the walls were shoved so far down here, the structure looks solid. Everything seems to have settled. The walls split just enough, not to make the structure unsound, but for ants to get in."

"Ants?" Mulan tilted her head.

Ro chuckled. "Don't you think we look like ants compared to the size of that wall?"

Mulan took in the wall. "Ants are easily crushed. We are not."

"True. But ants are resourceful and get into places they shouldn't. We've found the crack in her defense, and now we're getting in a way she won't be expecting. See? Ants."

Mulan nodded, sharing a grin with her. "Ants. That then swarm her and eat her."

Ro bit back a laugh. "That's one way of looking at it."

"Huntress?" Qing-Zhu said in a low voice. "Shall I go first?"

Ro shook her head and quickly stepped forward. "Non, merci. My abilities allow me to see dangers in the dark. Let me go first, s'il vous plaît."

She and Mulan both, but she wasn't about to say that.

"Then please, lead the way."

Ro took a deep breath, turned sideways, and slipped into the crack.

Ro was about one hundred and fifty paces in when the walls grew apart, allowing her breathing room. She tried not to collapse with relief, but it was a near thing.

No more than twenty more steps—and she was counting—and Mulan could've walked next to her, though it would've been a tight fit.

She took a few more steps and stopped.

"What is it, huntress?" Qing-Zhu asked in a low voice.

The soldiers at her back immediately tensed, growing still and even more silent. If that were possible.

Ro held up one hand. After a moment of inactivity, she motioned that she was going ahead and for them to stay.

Qing-Zhu relayed the motion to his men, and they kept their torches low and off to the side. Mulan gave her a firm glance that said, "I'm coming with you."

But Ro was already moving, leaving the light far behind. Her eyesight should work better in the pitch black. Alone. Without distractions.

Mulan followed her, their steps nearly silent.

A figure stood partway down the tunnel, his back to Ro, large spear in hand. He easily had four feet to Ro's already tall frame. He was monstrous!

Ro crouched, ready to flee, to fight if need be, wondering how she could get the birds and soldiers back out the crevice with this giant chasing them. Though, it wouldn't take long for him to get stuck.

She eased just a little closer. Mulan flanked her. Both had their bows drawn.

He still hadn't moved. The walls kept going past him, the split above their heads stretching on and up, no end in sight.

She stayed crouched against the wall, praying. *Creator, what do I do? I don't know if I can protect those with me against that. Please don't let them be harmed.*

She'd been doing it more and more ever since she'd traveled across the great ocean with winter nipping at their heels. Thinking she was going to meet her Creator at any second for three months would do that to a person.

Do not be afraid.

Ro took another deep breath. Of course not. He was only a giant. Of course, she'd learned of the shepherd boy David in

Mass. If he'd faced a giant, unafraid, so could she. Just like she'd done with the other giant. Mostly.

She moved forward as silently as she was able, arrow nocked and bow aimed. Mulan matched her movements.

They rushed him. Ro let an arrow fly.

A metal sound rang out in the tunnel, bouncing away down both ends.

The giant didn't even flinch.

Ro frowned, moved close enough to poke him, then let out a relieved breath. It was just a metal statue!

Soldiers and waddling feet came rushing down the tunnel. As they surrounded the statue, Qing-Zhu assessed the situation in an instant.

Ro spoke in a low voice. "It looks like we found the reason the wall split here. I think the statue is the only reason we got in."

She studied the walls above her. The pagoda had hit the statue just right, cracking it in such a way that the empress had a weak spot she didn't even know about. Ro hoped.

She glanced at the statue's face. Strong, masculine, handsome, a crown on his head.

Something about him reminded her of Olt and Odette, in a way she couldn't describe. Had Odette's father been turned into a statue? Or was it crafted in honor of him? She wouldn't know until she asked Odette. If they got back in time.

The thought spurred her steps on.

Ro glanced back once to find the swans fanned around its base, staring up at it in a way that made Ro's heart go out to them.

She walked on. Standing here wouldn't change anything, but taking action—that she could do. It wasn't long until footsteps, and the shuffle of webbed feet, followed.

Soon a huge pile of rubble blocked them. Soldiers rushed forward and started pulling broken stone away. A yawning black space opened into a tunnel, the only place they could go from here.

Ro stopped, for some reason not wanting to go any farther. As she stared into the darkness, cold fear washed over her as if a bucket of water had been thrown over her, head to toe. What if she failed as spectacularly as she'd done with the guardian swan?

Mulan was instantly at her side, looking worried. "Huntress, are you well? Do you need to rest?"

Qing-Zhu made a slight noise, reminding them to be quiet.

Ro took a deep breath. Shook her head. And climbed into the tunnel.

32

They stepped out into a castle dungeon.

As they traversed the dank space, they came upon two sleeping sentries no longer guarding the dungeon's exit. One of Mulan's soldiers snatched up the keyring and, after several tries, slipped the right key into the locked door.

They made their way through an eerie castle, void of life. Cobwebs decorated every corner like forgotten lace, and dust coated everything in a fine powder. They found sleeping maids and cooks in the kitchen, guards and courtiers in the hallways, and, finally, partygoers filling a grand hall.

The king was slumped over on his golden throne.

The swans rushed the throne, bleating and poking at the king's trousers with their beaks. Their orange webbed feet tracked long trails in the dust. Ro herded them away in case they harmed him in his slumber.

So he was still alive! If they could break the sleeping curse, that was.

Light-green mist rose off each person and streamed away, as if being drawn elsewhere. Ro sucked in a breath. Had the same thing happened to Allura? Was it still happening? She hurried forward to inspect it.

Cobwebs strung from candelabras to platters, and food had moldered or rotted away entirely. But the mist didn't come from everyone.

That's when Ro noticed several skeletons seated among the courtiers—those who'd fallen asleep in their food and been unable to breathe, or perhaps had given up, or been drained entirely. Ro felt sick.

They swiftly moved on, the swans subdued and huddled at the back of the procession.

They cleared the entire castle and found not one person awake, nor did they find the empress holed away in a forgotten nook or cranny. The German castle was thick and blocky and seemed to favor function over French elegance, comfort, and fripperies, so it took less time to explore than expected.

Next, they came out into the castle courtyard to find the interior of the great pagoda stretching above their heads. Far above their heads.

Everything glowed with such a deep-green light—light that rippled and shivered in the walls, as if alive—Ro felt like she was standing inside an emerald.

Below, the pagoda's walls had been smooth to the touch, but so dark it was hard to tell its color. Here, the walls glowed slightly transparent, as if with sunlight, lighting everything in a rich green shade, and Ro realized—

"The Nightingale's fortress is made of jade," Mulan said.

Ro nodded, in awe despite who'd put it here.

If Qing-Zhu's story was accurate, how might that amplify the empress's powers? Especially if her powers came from— or were stored in—the jade necklace she wore. And what of the object stored deep in the pagoda that Odette had told them of? Perhaps the pagoda *was* where she stored her power.

Ro took a deep breath, and strength seemed to flow into her. The air smelled sweet, of flowers, trimmed greenery, and that fresh scent after a rainstorm.

At a word from the commander, the group snuffed out their torches.

As soon as they did, Ro could see light-green mist trailing out of the castle, and from the sleeping guards stationed around the castle's wall, into the pagoda itself. Even more trickled down the walls from somewhere outside and up high —possibly from those the Nightingale had put to sleep in other kingdoms?

Enough speculation. Time to find her.

They hurried to a portion of the castle wall that hadn't been smashed by the pagoda, turrets at regular intervals, and moved around sleeping guards. They climbed to the parapet to get a better view.

Above their heads, a winding staircase circled up the inner walls, completely open, shafts of jade stone jammed into the wall to create each step. It ended at a layer of stone that might've been the floor of the little room far above or its roof.

If it were the roof—

Her stomach dropped. She would've hated to fall all that way.

Little quivers of green light shimmered down the walls, in no discernible pattern, but all going somewhere. Ro followed one down to the open space in front of the castle.

Outside, the pagoda crowned the top of the mountain it rested upon, but here, on the inside, the castle didn't cover the entire mountain. A village lay sprawled before it, only all greenery had been torn up, and only sandy pathways remained. Ruined structures created a labyrinth, a rounded building with a sharp point rising in the exact center.

Yet that sweet scent remained, and Ro found herself taking deep, soothing breaths. Her head cleared, her body ached less, and she stopped putting effort into remaining upright.

The soldiers rappelled down the castle fortifications and

spread out, all over the labyrinth, Commander Qing-Zhu staying high so he could direct them with hand signals.

"Clear," he repeated, for Ro's sake, when they all reported in. "Nowhere to hide in any of the buildings, and the dome in the center has no apparent entrances."

Ro flushed. When this was over, she was doing them the honor of learning their language. Until then, she appreciated their kindness.

She looked at the staircase above their heads. Dangerous, treacherous, no handrails whatsoever. "We're going to have to climb that, aren't we?"

"I believe so, huntress," the commander replied.

Ro made it to the top, not out of breath as she should've been. Perhaps she was drawing magic from her surroundings; she didn't know. But she was suddenly hopeful she'd last through whatever battle lay ahead.

Although the plan had been for the swans and two of Mulan's soldiers to return to Odette as soon as they reached the black swan, the treacherous stairs changed that. Not willing to risk their lives, Ro had insisted the swans stay below, guarded by Mulan's soldiers. They'd figure out the rest after they faced the empress.

At the top of the winding staircase stood another set of red doors with golden handles, messy black kanji painted on them in dripping characters. The warriors at her back hissed and made warding-off signs.

Ro wanted to ask what the symbols meant, but one of the doors was ajar. Drawing her bow, she hurried forward.

"No, huntress, wait," said a muffled voice behind her, one that sounded as if it were speaking through a pillow. The words held no meaning for her and flitted away almost immediately.

Ro pushed open the door the rest of the way with the tip of her arrow.

"Come in," called a voice in another language—one that untwisted in her mind and became clear, just as the sirens' language had done.

Unease slithering through her like a serpent, Ro stepped into the square room. Wild twists of bamboo engulfed her, sprouting out of squat square pots. Overgrown and haphazardly trimmed bonsai covered tables, and a golden throne rested on a vibrant red dais. It looked as if it were being slowly eaten by all the greenery.

A sickly sweet fragrance slammed into Ro, and her eyes watered. It smelled as if rot, decay, and filth had been doused in perfume, and it wasn't up to the task. She fought off a gag.

As she took a second step toward the empty throne, scanning for the source of the voice—and the smell—the door slammed shut behind her, cutting off the warriors.

She suddenly stood in a cavern deep, deep underground.

Ro staggered and went down on one knee, disoriented. It felt as if the weight of rock above her head were crushing her. As if the mountain were crushing her.

She gasped and stared at the ceiling. Domed. Far above her head. Plenty of room to breathe. Solid, no cracks, several stories high—her fear didn't make sense.

A single beam of light came in from the side of the dome and shone down to the opposite side of the room. She tracked it, still dizzy, and tried to focus.

It shone on a completely silver throne. Non, it only looked silver in the light. It was more a dark metal, once perhaps silver, now tarnished to a dark gray, almost black in places.

Ro squinted, and as her eyes adjusted, a tree came into view on the other side of the beam of light. A completely silver tree. Grown straight out of rock. Though it too was tarnished a darker metal color.

On the tree were hundreds of birds. Maybe thousands.

The tree took up the entirety of the space above their heads, twisting and growing against the ceiling, as if there was no more room for it, yet it kept pushing onward.

The ceiling looked very much like that domed building at the bottom center of the pagoda. Yet there hadn't been an opening, had there?

Woozy from being sucked someplace else entirely, Ro staggered to her feet.

This room smelled dry, dusty, like the sand under her feet, with a funk that came of birds housed in one space for a long time, without great airflow.

At least the scent of decay was gone. Though this could hardly be called an improvement.

The tiny birds perched on its branches were pitch black, with black beaks, black eyes, black feathers. So dark it felt as if they sucked in every color nearby, giving off none of their own. The way they voided the light reminded her distinctly of the wolves plaguing the Black Forest…

Then she felt it. A gentle breeze at her back. A waft of decay from upstairs. She spun around.

"What do you think of my birds?"

A shriveled Chinese woman came around from the back of the throne that was a tarnished mirror of that above. Dressed in all black and with an authoritative air, she wore an elaborate headdress, glittering with black jewels. Her face was painted snow white with red dots on her cheeks and a blood-red stripe from her lips to her chin.

She stood there placidly, her hands folded in front of her, and waited for Ro to speak. The throne dwarfed her.

Rage filled Ro. This was the woman who'd cursed her niece? Who'd killed the emperor from the Middle Kingdom? Who'd made Odette's life a living hell? How dare she!

Ro drew back her bow, pointed her arrow right at the woman's heart, and shouted, "What have you done to my niece?"

Her French words were immediately twisted into whatever language the woman spoke. It sounded similar to the language the warriors spoke, but not quite the same. As if magic infused the words themselves.

Ro was pretty sure whatever she was speaking to wasn't human.

The ancient woman twitched. "Niece? You aren't here for the black swan?"

Ro blinked. Well, oui, she was. But later. After she'd defeated the creature before her.

Hopefully a few of the warriors had grabbed Odile, if they were able to, while they were up there.

Then the old woman laughed. "Ha! This is even better than I'd hoped. What have I done to your niece? *I* have done nothing."

Ro gave her a hard look, but try as she might, her gaze kept returning to the hundreds upon hundreds of perfectly still nightingales perched on bare silver branches above their heads. Were they asleep? Were they dead?

But, non. Every once in a while, one would shudder or twitch.

The empress followed Ro's gaze. "Ah, my nightingales."

"Where did they all come from?" Ro had never seen so many in one place. And never in this color. Most were light brown with cream-colored chests.

Although they may have been rare in Mulan's country, they were quite common in Angleterre and the southern part of France.

"Where did they come from? Fool! What does that matter? My nightingales have the most beautiful, haunting song known to man, and they serve only me. That is all that matters. You should be thankful they are singing to someone else right now and not to you, else you would be unable to resist."

The empress glanced at Ro's bow and arrow, ready to fire

at the slightest provocation, then dismissed the weapon with an unconcerned glance.

Bon. Let her underestimate Ro's skill.

Then the empress tilted her head. "I have an enchanted border around this kingdom of mine." Her eyes traced Ro's form. "I wonder how you of all people got in?"

Ro couldn't help a grin that was all teeth. "Dumb luck?"

The empress snarled. "In this place, only *I* wield luck. She serves only *me*."

Great. With Ro's luck, she was probably talking about another enchantress.

Ro's gaze returned to the birds. A chill swept through her. She didn't know why, but she hated those things. They sent dread bouncing like spiked balls throughout her stomach.

The diminutive woman's smile grew. "I suppose I can spare one for you."

She flicked one curled nail—her fingernails nearly the same length as her fingers—and one of the birds roused itself and flapped its wings, as if awakening from a trance.

Then it started to sing.

Ro's eyes slid closed, and without really thinking about it, she released her draw and let the weapon's tip drop away as her feet moved closer to the beautiful music.

The woman just laughed and beckoned with her long fingernail. "Yes, little one. That's it. Surrender to the magic of my nightingales."

Green light started to stream off Ro, at first a few tendrils, then more as the bird's song deepened.

Something glowed from the empress, and Ro's gaze slid away from the nightingale long enough to see a pulsing jade stone, about the size of a fist, suspended from around her neck. It had blended in with her dress until it began to glow.

The empress drew in a deep breath, sucking Ro's light into herself and the emerald-colored necklace. "My, but you are a sweet one. I'm glad to add you to my collection. And almost as powerful as a child, too! How interesting."

That sickly sweet odor filled the air, with just a hint of rot. Although part of Ro screamed to wake up, to get away, to stop walking *toward* the monster, the singing lulled Ro further into complacency.

A small part of Ro fought against the nightingale's call, a part that was growing distant. The witch didn't seem to notice Ro struggling to raise her bow—or if she did, she didn't perceive it enough of a threat to care.

The song grew sweeter, the woman's laugh rose to the domed ceiling, and Ro's control slipped away entirely. Her eyes started to slide shut.

"Yes, my darling, come to me. Surrender yourself. Give yourself over entirely to my sweet, sweet song and go to sleeee—"

Just then, a bell tolled, a clock ticked to five, and the power of it shook the nightingale's hold loose.

With a cry, Ro broke the remaining strands of music that held her listless, and with one fluid motion, raised her bow and sent an arrow clean through the nightingale's throat.

The empress shrieked as the bird fell dead at her feet. "My nightingale! My song! My pretty little bird! What have you done?"

She fell to her knees and gathered it into her hands. Above, others trilled and flapped their wings and sang a mournful song before falling silent once more.

But not all of them.

Several staggered under the little bird's death, eyes closed, gently swaying on their branches.

Ro panted from the exertion of freeing herself, of that clock growing more insistent each time, but she had another arrow ready and pointing at the witch. Green light immediately snuffed out all around her.

She was no longer feeding the witch her life force.

After a slight hesitation to ensure she aimed true, Ro loosed her arrow at the enchantress.

A bird dove from the tree and fell dead at the empress's feet, Ro's arrow sticking out the other side of the little creature.

The woman cried out again and swooned, as if momentarily weakened, then staggered to her feet and screamed at Ro. "Come in here and kill my birds? Desecrate my sanctuary? You will not leave this place alive! Let's see how you fare against a full *chorus*."

And she raised both hands and flung them at Ro.

Bright-green light boiled off her hands and barreled straight toward Ro.

At the same time, birds exploded from the dead tree overhead. They flapped around Ro, tried to entrap her with strands of music, tried to pull green life threads from her.

As the empress's power engulfed her, Ro realized the stench seemed to be coming from the light itself.

Through the euphoria that kept trying to entangle her, it felt like slivers of hot metal were being pulled from her, leaving a burning cold and a fierce ache in their wake.

But the bell's tolling had already broken the first strand. As the rest of them slipped around her like satin ribbons, each of them painful while trying to lull her to sleep, she tore them from her like sticky web.

Ro took out bird after bird after bird, and they fell with wet, sickening thuds.

Such a waste. Such a horrible, heartbreaking waste. But they were of the witch's design—or in her thrall—so down they must come.

The woman's shrieks grew shriller with each fallen nightingale. Most still slept in the tree, and although Ro didn't know why the witch didn't send them at her all at once, she was grateful. It was all she could do to keep up with the ones attacking her.

As nightingales fell to Ro's arrows, the empress vibrated with rage. "How dare you? Kill the huntress! Kill her!"

Another flock shook off their trance, lifted from the branches, and dove toward Ro, heaving the weight of whatever burden they carried on their already overburdened companions.

Ro stepped back, raised her bow, and downed the first one.

The way to the empress was past these nightingales, and by Dieu, she was going to thin them out until the empress had no protection left.

Let her call them all.

33

Suddenly the room was full of warriors and white swans. They dropped from the ceiling, through the hole that streamed light, hacking and slashing with swords and long bladed pikes. They ran up walls and did other impossible feats to rid Ro of the attacking nightingales.

All were focused on reaching the empress.

Elation at someone having her back, fighting with her, swept through Ro, and she shot arrows faster. Any arrow Ro sent flying at the empress was intercepted by a nightingale sacrificing itself for her.

No matter. Ro would find a way past them.

Torches flared to life, and the warriors threw them to the edges of the room, lighting the entire space. Ro had to admit to surprise—couldn't they see with all the green light coming from the empress?

A swarm of nightingales broke off the attack and cycled around the empress, hemming her in and the others, out, in a cyclone of feathers, talons, and sharp beaks.

Ro went cold as she thought of that gray wolf.

Then Mulan was at her side. "We have the black swan,"

Mulan said, earning a startled jerk from the empress. "Do what you came to do."

Just then, Ro raised her bow and shot an attacking nightingale out of the air, right before it struck Mulan. She nodded her thanks and slashed a few more out of the air herself.

"Huntress, here!"

In Mulan's hand, her second lost long knife. Ro's eyes widened, and she snatched it from Mulan's grasp and joined it with the other at her waist. "Merci."

Mulan nodded and spun away. Ribbons of music held one of the soldiers captive, holding him still so nightingales could tear at his flesh, so Ro ran over and slashed them away, releasing him from the empress's enthrall.

Mulan cried, "Huntress! Behind the throne."

Ro fought her way closer, to see what the warrior had. Behind the throne, steps led down to the back wall, where a giant crack split the stone, like an upside down lightning bolt zigzagging up to the ceiling.

There, glowing from the crack, was the same green light that trailed after each nightingale as it flew, that boiled from the empress's hands, that shone from the jade stone around her neck.

The swarm surrounding the empress grew, making it almost impossible to see the empress past them all. The nightingales on the tree hunched and shuddered under their renewed burden.

Ro nodded at Mulan to show that she'd seen the crevice and would act, then threw herself into getting past the empress and her nightingales. She just needed an opening.

Mulan sent up little bursts of force between slashes, stopping the birds mid-flight and sending them crashing to the ground, some with broken necks. Arrows flew as fast as Ro could shoot them.

And suddenly, the way was clear.

"Go, go, go!" Mulan cried.

Ro ran straight for the crack in the stone, but before she could reach it, a surge of power from the empress caught her off guard, and the ground bucked and threw her off her feet.

Like oozing sludge, thick green tendrils wormed their way out of the crevice and fed into the necklace. The empress's laugh echoed all around them. Then she raised her arms, clenched her fists, and pulled both hands straight up.

All the dead birds at her feet came to life, wings broken, necks twisted, and arrows still in some of them. They heaved themselves into the air and threw themselves at the warriors with greater fervor.

Even the birds with missing heads.

One flung itself at Mulan, winging past her defenses, and tore into her cheek with its sharp little claws. Green mist rose out of the cut, and Mulan's wide eyes met Ro's.

"Go!" shouted Mulan, hacking at the newly risen birds. "We've got this."

Ro rushed toward the narrow crack, her footsteps loud in the cavernous space. She plunged her hands into the green light, trying to take hold of it, stop it, something, but it just parted around her and kept streaming toward the empress.

And there was that sickly sweet rotting smell again. She hated how every time she breathed it in, she felt renewed.

Now she just needed to stuff her body into this child-sized crevice.

Ro rolled her shoulders. Then glanced at her bow. She felt the full weight of the arrows on her back and the sword at her side. Her weapons wouldn't fit. She had to leave them behind.

Except for her long knives.

She set the rest on the ground, next to the crack, and tried to steady her breathing.

She'd never been scared of heights—not until falling from the mast while hunting the sirens, anyway—but she'd never particularly cared for small spaces. She forced back a shudder and her body into the crevice, crouching and turning sideways to fit.

She had to take a few more deep breaths in order to take the first shuffling step.

Bleak stone pressed on either side, crushing her, drawing the air from her lungs. It was cold. So cold. So tight. It felt like there was no air. What if she got stuck?

Her heartbeat sped up, and sweat glided between her shoulder blades and under her arms. It didn't matter how sweet the air smelled; this space was *tiny*. And the underlying rot reminded her too much of a grave.

If she got out of this alive, she would never, ever climb into another small space of her own free will.

She finally broke free into an open space, the green glow blinding her to what lay beyond. She stumbled to a halt and bent over her knees, gulping deep breaths.

Please oh please may there be another way back, she pleaded silently.

It felt as though the Creator just smiled.

She grumbled at Him, then straightened and kept going.

After a few steps, she stood before solid stone. On all sides. A dead end.

Her heart crashed against her ribs, and she blinked back tears. It couldn't end like this. It couldn't! But then…where was the light coming from?

When she turned around, green tendrils streamed away from her, faster and faster, as if the empress was pulling it toward herself in a frenzy.

Ro turned back with determination. She was *going* to find a way through. Somehow.

Placing them on the stone wall, her hands met empty space, and she stumbled right through the wall and landed on her knees in sand.

The space brightened at once.

Stacked crypts hemmed her in at all sides, but in their center, a glowing green ball hovered midair, grasped within a golden dragon statue's claws. Its slow spin was in direct contrast to the angry whirl inside, like it was filled with boiling dark-green ink.

The power source Odette had told her about!

And finally she knew where the pagoda walls were feeding the jade-green tendrils of light. They traveled down the length of the dragon's spine and poured into the glowing orb.

Ro climbed to her feet and ran, straight for the jade stone.

It pulsed with light, shooting power from it in waves as the empress called it to herself, into a chunk of the same jade around her neck, to replenish her nightingales, to make her unstoppable.

Ro stopped inches from her goal, looking for ways to destroy it. She wished she had her grandmère's axe.

There, in the center of the orb, was a hollow, the exact same shape and size as the jade stone around the empress's neck. The sphere pulsed with a deep glow, almost like a heartbeat, but not. Perhaps many heartbeats?

She eyed the dragon, but it stayed still. Just another golden statue.

Ro reached for the globe, but a clear shield, like the one around the pagoda, wouldn't let her anywhere near it.

Ro drew out her long knives and cut through the barrier. It fell away like an apple peel. Then she brought the blades down on the slowly rotating orb, but they sparked and flew from her hands.

She cursed and opened and closed her hands, working out the pain. She reached for her knives, then froze. They had melted into slag, a pile of liquid metal that looked nothing like the gorgeous knives they'd once been.

Her head fell back, and she let out a deep groan. Not her knives! Those weren't just weapons—they were exquisite pieces of art!

No wonder Liam had once teased that keeping her in

weapons would bankrupt the kingdom one day. She was starting to believe him.

Only one thing left to do.

Ro plunged her hands into the wash of power and started to pull the heavy orb the size of a melon away from the dragon pedestal. Without warning, the dragon's claws clamped around her hands, piercing skin and crunching bone and drawing blood.

Ro screamed, panic overtaking her senses for half a heartbeat. She cut herself off mid-scream, the sound echoing in a way to suggest the crypt was absolutely humongous.

Pain pulsing through her, she stayed still, silent, hands trapped, and forced herself to *think*. Even though the dragon was incredibly lifelike, the flickering light making it appear to undulate in serpentine waves as if it swam in water or wind, nothing but its fist had moved.

And then she smelled it. That sweet, decaying scent, and drew it in. Some light diverted from the ball and into her nostrils.

Her skin took on a reddish glow. Not green. Red.

Ro's eyes widened.

It changed color when it touched her. Unlike when it was being drawn from her. This close to the power source...she could see it. She was drawing on the same power. And it felt...incredible. And so very wrong.

It came from *children*, for heaven's sake.

Unable to move, she drew power from the ball itself and used the red tendrils to wrap around the dragon's talons. Then she pushed out with all her might.

Slowly, ever so slowly, the dragon reluctantly released her, and the ball hovered in the empty space once more.

With a cry, she kicked it away and stumbled back the moment it was clear.

The dragon's talons clamped into a tight fist and stayed

still. Nothing else moved. The ball hovered midair next to the crypts.

Blood streamed down her hands and dripped into the sand, but even as she watched, a red glow suffused her hands, fractured bones knit back together, and her skin wove itself closed.

Something she would freak out about later.

She ran to the ball, snatched it out of the air, and threw it straight down, her healing hands protesting the movement. The moment she released it, it just hovered there, not smashing to the floor as was her plan.

Ro groaned, and when she grabbed it, gravity returned to it.

Hefting it in her hands, hardly able to bear its weight, Ro dropped to her knees and smashed it against the stone base of the crypt, over and over, grunting with the effort. It was like trying to move an object in water while the current was fighting to push it the other way.

Cracks spread up its face and deep within the stunning green orb, and a high-pitched whistling built in Ro's ears. With a sharp pain, her ears popped and blood dribbled out, yet she still fought to lift the stone and smash it to pieces.

The cracks spread, and with a final crunch of glass, power was sucked back into it, then out, and it exploded into a fine powder. Ro shielded her face, but she was doused with a powdery mist anyway.

The power traveling over the lifelike golden statue started to build with a hum, circling madly as if it had nowhere to go. It started to glow brighter and brighter. A deep trembling in the earth began, and the statue started to vibrate.

Then it started to undulate and writhe as if it were…alive.

At the same time, the crypts started to rattle.

Just then, the golden dragon turned and looked straight at Ro. Its lips curled back from its fangs in a hiss, and it dove right at her.

Ro rolled out of its way just in time, and it crashed into the stack of crypts, splintering them and sending a wave of broken wood flying into the air, only to crash back down in pieces.

Then bony arms and legs reached out of opening crypts, and skeletons sat up. Green light swirled around the bones, creating tendons and muscles made of light, and green balls of light hovered within empty eye sockets.

Suddenly, as if a puzzle box had snapped open, revealing its secrets, everything made sense.

The empress wasn't just draining the living. She was stealing power from the living to feed the dead.

Ro felt sick. None of the nightingales out there were alive, were they?

But, if that were true, the dragon…was it real? Or…had it once been so?

Her eyes pinged away from its golden scales.

Nope. Only one earth-shattering revelation at a time, thank you very much.

The skeletons clambered out of their resting places and came toward her, ancient weapons clutched in their fingers. At the same time, the dragon untangled itself from the destruction it had caused, rose into the air, and caught sight of her.

It roared—how it did so without lungs, Ro would never know—and undulated toward her, writhing like a serpent in water.

Time to go.

Ro staggered to her feet and bolted for the crevice. She was terrified to go back in there, but she was more terrified to stay.

More crypts slammed to the ground, bursting open and spilling their contents.

Ro didn't bother to watch the skeletons coming free.

Non, merci. She was done with this place and the so-called empress.

Just then, a skeleton got between her and the hidden exit. She rolled to the side just in time, and the dragon slammed into the wall, rattling the whole cave.

It met solid wall. The one Ro had run through to come in here.

Her heart dropped. Was it sealed off now?

Once again, the dragon took a moment to untangle itself, and Ro fisted her hands as skeletons glowing with green light turned toward her new position. How could she fight creatures that weren't even alive? Without any weapons?

One skeleton lunged, trying to grab her, and she twisted away, but not quickly enough. Ice cold trailed where bony fingers touched, and her arm went numb. Green mist rose off the skeleton.

But as she spun back and kicked it with her boot, Ro sucked in a breath and drew in all of its mist. As if a puppet's strings had been cut, green light winked out, and the skeleton dropped straight down. Its bones broke apart in a jumble when it hit the ground.

As if in answer to her wordless cry for help, a memory hit her. Of fighting an enchantress who called herself Magic. Of power barreling toward her, then Ro grasping that power and using it against the witch.

She sucked in a breath, a reaction to the memory, yet more green light streamed toward her, lessening on the not-dead creatures in the room.

The dragon caught sight of her once more.

With a cry, Ro used both hands and *pulled*, drawing the light toward her with all her might. It barreled toward her, faster and faster, then cut out.

Bones rattled, metal clanked, and the skeletons and dragon fell to the ground, lifeless.

And power writhed around Ro, no longer green, but a deep, vibrant red.

Thrown off balance, yet desperate to get back, Ro staggered to the wall, using…herself…to light the way. She easily passed through what had been solid wall to the dragon, and once again, stood before the crevice. It was all she could do to make herself go back in there.

I am with you.

Ro nodded once. "I know."

The words gave her courage to dive in, and she began the excruciating journey back.

And then…it happened again. The bell tolled, the walls shook—though Ro couldn't tell for the life of her if it was in her head or from whatever she'd done in the crypt—and the clock ticked backward. To the four.

Ro cried out. Not knowing what it meant. Having an idea. Hoping she was wrong.

She was running out of time to help Allura.

Rocks and dust crumbled over her head and shoulders as she scrambled down the length of the crevice, proving the tremors weren't all in her head. At some point she had to drop to her belly and crawl.

Was it getting smaller? It felt like it was getting smaller.

Ro stifled another cry, biting her lip until she tasted blood. *You* are *getting out of here, you* will *get to Allura in time, and you* will *see Olt free of his curse!* Ro growled to herself, trying not to weep.

A few tears slipped down her cheeks anyway.

She finally had enough room to scramble onto her knees, and she burst from the crevice just as the tunnel collapsed behind her.

34

Ro scrambled free just in time, and her eyes caught on Mulan's. She relaxed, giving Ro a firm nod. Ro gasped several deep breaths before she could nod back.

Demonic, high-pitched wailing met her ears, and it took Ro a moment to focus on it.

The empress's voice was joined by the birds winging around her head, whose beautiful music had turned ugly. The jade stone around her neck was cracked in places, pulsing with light, struggling to hold the power shoved at it from the destruction of the bigger stone. But at least it didn't seem to be drawing in more power.

Dead birds once again littered the floor.

One of the soldiers above—perhaps so they'd have a way out?—called through the hole in the ceiling. "The pagoda! It's vibrating and starting to crack!"

Ro blinked. She could understand him!

Not important right now.

The power must be building with nowhere to go. Would the pagoda shatter like the orb? Ro's heart picked up its pace. They had to get out of here.

"Is anyone awake? In the castle?" Ro yelled up at the warrior. "Can you check?"

He immediately looked to Mulan, more in surprise than for a translation.

Calling rapid-fire orders, Mulan now wielded a long pike that ended with a monstrous curved blade, with a red tassel on one end and a wicked spike on the other. Flashy, gorgeous, deadly.

Ro had to get herself one of those.

One of the warriors disengaged from the battle, grabbed the black rope still hanging from the ceiling, and pulled himself up it, hand over hand, at an incredible speed.

Ro stared, mouth open. She kept herself in good shape, oui, but even she couldn't do something like that.

With the replacement guarding the exit, the soldier above ran for the castle.

A nightingale dove at her, and Ro scrabbled for her abandoned sword and slashed it out of the air. Then she reached for her arrows and groaned at her mostly empty quiver. There were too many birds and too few arrows. She had to conserve them. Reuse them. Ply her sword, for now.

Chinese warriors jumped through the air, their movements so swift and graceful, it almost looked like they were flying. They bled from open wounds, cut down nightingales, and tried to get close to the empress. Several soldiers lay unconscious or wounded around the room, their companions protecting them from being further ravaged by the birds.

Ro had to help them, had to use their help to her advantage.

Slamming down the terror building alongside the growing vibrations, she took a steadying breath and focused. Her niece, Odette's family—every person the empress had harassed and enchanted—depended on Ro.

She slashed out with her borrowed sword, fighting for an opening to the empress past the flocking nightingales, snatching up every loose arrow she came across and shoving it into her quiver.

She pressed forward, not retreating, no matter how many sharp beaks tore at her skin. She was putting an end to this. Now. Before the woman could hurt another soul. Before she could destroy Allura. Or any other child.

Before that clock ran out of numbers.

Mulan fought to her side, and they put their backs together. Blood streamed down Ro's arms from new cuts. Mulan's only visible wounds were on her face, as she was covered from head to toe in armor.

"Whatever you did, it's working! She can't regenerate the birds anymore. Once they're dead, they stay dead!"

Ro grunted and kept blocking, slicing, stabbing—putting her sword training to good use.

"I have to get close to her," Mulan said.

"Together?"

"Together."

They crept toward her with every swipe of their blades, but the empress kept a flock of birds around her like a whirlwind, and the birds rose en masse to push them back. But the warriors were making progress, centimètre by centimètre.

"We have to get through that swarm," Mulan said, drawing Ro's attention.

Ro took in the room, trying to plan. Trying to come up with something that would work. Her eyes fell on the six white swans, fighting with all their might, tearing nightingales from the sky with their vicious orange beaks.

"We have to distract her." Ro nodded at the swans.

Mulan's wide eyes met hers. "Do you think that will work?" Then, without giving her a chance to answer, "I will follow your lead."

"We're going to rush her."

And they did.

Swiping birds aside with every cut, they barreled toward

the empress and the living barrier she'd placed around herself. The sting of beaks and talons and feathers felt like a thousand blades against Ro's exposed skin.

Even though Mulan slashed and stabbed with her bladed pike, she just as often sent up little bursts to stun the creatures. Yet Ro could tell she was holding back, trying not to reveal her secret.

Well, one of them, anyway.

Ro caught her gaze and nodded. With a fizzle of sparks, Mulan shielded herself and pushed past the barrier, past the empress's guard, and stabbed at her. Ro darted in the same opening and thrust straight out with her sword.

The empress blocked both attacks with a fan sporting wicked blades as its ribcage. Then sent a wash of power barreling into them that flung them both back.

The cyclone of birds pushed out, surrounding all three, cutting off the other warriors.

Ro lay sprawled on her back, sword out of reach, as the empress advanced.

"You have tainted my forest, slaughtered my birds, and mocked me for the last time, huntress. And you!" She swiveled to Mulan. "My own countryman. My own soldier. Showing me the greatest dishonor of them all. I shall not go lightly on you, warrior. You should be serving *me*. I am your empress!"

Power swirled around the sorceress's hands in that deep-jade color, bouncing off her face and her dark dress, giving her eyes an even wilder look. Her headdress hung askew and hair sprouted from it.

Movement at the empress's back had Ro smiling. "Oh, I think you're the one who's finished, witch."

And the swans stalking the Nightingale, the ones hidden behind her throne, the ones Mulan had allowed to slip through while distracting the empress, attacked as one, coming up and over and around the throne, driving the ancient woman to her knees.

They swirled around her, biting, tearing, pinning her to the ground. Ro rolled away, swooped up her bow, and when she couldn't get a clear shot at the empress, began firing at the birds in the air.

Her eyesight lit each nightingale with a reddish hue, and her arrows steered clear of the swans. Each one trailed a line of red, as Ro used what power she'd taken in to direct her arrows exactly where she wanted them to go.

She pushed out, just a little, and the red glow rose above her skin, keeping the birds from scratching her. Mulan's eyes widened for a brief moment before she threw herself—and her blade—back at the false empress.

Ro could've wept at the reprieve from burning pain.

The empress wasn't so lucky. Although her nightingales dove at the swans, they tore the smaller birds out of the air and slammed them to the ground, snapping their necks with brutal orange beaks. And they bit the empress every time she tried to get away.

Ro fought harder. Straining to get to the empress. To get a clear shot. She didn't want to harm the swans. Failure was not an option.

Nor was giving the empress an opportunity to kill any of the swans.

The empress screamed as the swans kept worrying her—like a savage dog with a fox or rabbit—tearing skin, hair, and jewels from her. Her hair stuck up all around the headdress, which now tilted forward instead of to the side. Jewels scattered at her feet, and blood ran from bite marks along her arms and face.

The empress thrashed wildly, and the swans began to scatter, unable to land every attack.

And then a thrumming. A swell of power. Coming from the jade stone.

"Non!" Ro held out a hand, grasped the jade power coming from it, and stole it for herself. She then sent a wave of heat, a deep, dark-red color, straight at the empress.

It slammed into her and knocked her down. Her head bounced off the throne, and she hit the rock floor with a cry.

The jade stone's vibrations snuffed out, but some power was still there. Pulsing. Expectant.

Waiting for someone to call it.

Ro dropped to a knee as energy drained from her core, from what made her a huntress, a protectress, and left her weak and shaking.

The swans surrounded the empress and hissed at her. She curled up into a ball, dazed and whimpering. Ro knew exactly how she felt—but cruelty was a choice. She'd brought this upon herself.

Trusting her instincts, Ro raised her hands and felt for the power that hummed just past her fingertips. She could touch it, as she'd been able to do in the cave, but she didn't like its oily feel. Didn't like where it came from: those trapped in sleep, life draining from their bodies, their souls.

But she could use it. Briefly. Better her than the empress.

Somehow, Ro reached out to the pagoda, and it gave her what she sought. Light wisps streamed green and glowing to her, trailing through the ceiling's opening and into her hands.

Yet not one of the warriors looked at it, as if they couldn't see it.

But Mulan tracked the light with wide eyes.

As it passed through Ro's hands it turned apple red, the same shade as her cloak, and changed somehow, no longer able to be wielded by the empress.

How she knew that, she'd never even begin to explain.

But she listened, reached out with her instincts, and did what felt right for the situation. She did the best she could with the non-information she had.

Oui, she definitely needed to be trained.

Ro sent a wave of pure energy to scatter the flocking birds overhead, then drew it into herself. The birds fell from the sky all at once, their life force drained instantly. The life that wasn't theirs to begin with.

Then, as if trying to plug a leaking barrel with her bare hands, Ro tried to stop the flow from the pagoda above and shove every bit of power back to wherever it had come from. To keep it from draining any more victims.

She had no idea if it worked, but the pressure, the sickly sweet odor, lessened.

Ro sat back, exhausted, and nodded at the swans.

They could end the empress. It was their right. She'd stolen their kingdom, their family, their happiness, and it was time for them to take it all back. Time for them to bring this nightmare to an end.

The swans hissed but left off their attack.

Ro's gaze riveted on the nightingales still perched on the silver tree, hunched over, feathers ruffled, trembling as if sick or in pain. Weary, arms still shaking, she retrieved her fallen bow.

"Enough! Enough!" the empress pleaded. Her cries fell on deaf ears.

Mulan's pike had fallen out of reach, so she drew her sword and short sword, both curved with red tassels on the ends, and stood guard over the empress.

The warriors previously outside the barrier rushed in, creating a wall of armor the empress couldn't escape.

"My babies. My poor, precious babies," the woman sobbed.

Ro walked over to the silver tree. The birds on its branches swayed, the weight of whatever they were carrying too much without the others.

Ro pulled an arrow, sighted it on one of the birds, and let it fly. The nightingale fell with a poof of feathers, then sank into a skeleton with dull feathers spread around it.

The empress shrieked with each fallen bird.

Ro winced. She hated killing things that couldn't fight back. Yet she knew, deep in her being, that those creatures weren't alive, not really, that they were still harming someone, somewhere. She had to end it.

Some of the warriors drew their own bows and joined her. They shot until only one bird was left.

It began to physically twist and bend, its bones breaking and turning out at impossible angles, as it fought to hold on to whatever it was doing in its mind.

The warriors lowered their weapons. Stopped shooting. Mulan whirled toward Ro, her now-untied hair splaying out in slow motion. The swans grew still midair, facing the empress as she started to rise.

A voice touched Ro within. "You don't have to do this, you know. It's just one little bird. What harm is one little bird?"

Mulan tried to swing a sword that was stuck in nothing but air and called, "Ro?"

Everything around Ro stilled completely, even as the empress moved.

Ro trembled, guilt overwhelming her. Look at what she'd done! Those birds were just sitting there. Singing. Making beautiful music. And she'd killed them in cold blood.

"Huntress!" someone cried from far away.

But even Mulan's desperate voice couldn't pull her from her trance. From staring in horror at all the birds at her feet. Even the thrum of the jade stone swelling with power did nothing to capture her attention.

Somehow pushing through what held the others, Olt came to her then, leaned against her side. Nudged her till she looked at him.

Don't listen to her voice in your head. Don't let her distract you. I believe in you, Ro. I always have, and I always will.

Time snapped back in place, his voice snuffed out, and the

empress started to laugh. She was on her feet, away from those guarding her.

Ro sagged to her knees as the sludge-like feeling released her, yet left her muddled.

"It's too late. Don't you see? It's too late! And you will all die for showing me dishonor, as is your fate!" With a swell of power, the empress gathered every scrap left in her necklace, then pushed it out in a broiling green wave.

Ro fumbled to grab it, but it slipped through her fingers like oil, now protected against *her*.

Finding her quiver empty, Ro scrambled for a fallen arrow as power shot from the empress, straight toward her, Mulan, the swans, and all the warriors.

A little brown nightingale, chest creamy tan, flitted through the hole in the ceiling past the warriors and barreled right for the empress.

The bird caught the stream of power and shoved it away from its targets, right before it would've slammed into Commander Qing-Zhu, pulling the rest of the strands to herself as well, as if capturing them in a net.

Ro could've sworn a voice screamed, "You shall not have him!"

But Ro ignored it and pulled back in one smooth motion and sent her arrow through the last nightingale perched in the silver tree.

It fell, releasing the last of its power into the stone around the empress's neck, and she screamed a terrible, high-pitched sound that made the dome rattle overhead.

"No. No. *No!*"

As the empress raged, Ro searched for the little brown nightingale, in case it was a threat, too. It lay crumpled on the ground, not far from the tree, the only spot of color in the midst of midnight. Tendrils of green smoked from it.

Ro spun and cried out to Mulan, who was closest, "Destroy it! Destroy the necklace!"

Mulan raced toward the empress. Her fingers closed around the jade stone, and she yanked it from the empress's neck.

The moment Mulan touched it, before she could smash it as Ro had the orb, power drained from the jade and shot into Mulan, as if choosing where to go next.

It threw everyone else in the room back. Ro fell, heavily.

The empress, sprawled on the ground with the rest, held out a hand. "No! Don't leave me. Don't leave me!"

Although it felt as heavy as the globe she'd just smashed, Ro lifted her head in time to see Mulan study the necklace, now cold and dark and void of light, and then slip it into her pocket.

Its existence winked out of Ro's mind the moment it was out of sight.

The empress fell back with a sob, wailing and making an ungodly racket as she begged the stone's power to come back to her.

Without hesitating, Mulan hefted her sword, and with one swipe, should have lifted the empress's head from her shoulders.

Instead, her blade clacked against her neck and bounced off, flinging Mulan to the ground. Her head cracked on the stone floor, and she lay still.

The empress pulled the fan from her waist, flicked it open to best show each sharp and deadly blade, clasped the knot, and drove it straight down at the dazed Mulan.

Olt jumped over her and splayed his wings, taking the brunt of the attack meant for the warrior. The spikes came down on one wing, hard, and delicate bones snapped. The swan screeched in pain.

"Olt!" Ro screamed. She jumped to her feet and ran for him, her head throbbing with every step. She did not run in a straight line.

Ro wanted to gather him up, to cradle him in her arms, but she had to focus.

She held an arrow. Two steps, and Ro pressed against the empress's neck.

The woman just laughed, even as the sharp wedge indented her skin. Skin that was…tough. And didn't feel right. "Do you really think that will work on me?"

"Non, but I think this will." Ro drove a second arrow up and into the shriveled woman's side, just below her ribs.

Shock and horror converged on the woman's face, and her eyes bulged as her hands went to her stomach.

Ro followed the woman to the ground, keeping the iron deep in the wound, not giving it a chance to heal. She'd hit a vulnerable spot, and if she could just keep it there long enough…

The empress coughed up blood, once, twice, and the spray hit Ro full on the face. She didn't even flinch.

Mulan and Olt both lay unmoving at the edge of Ro's sight. Ro wanted to go to them with all her heart. But she wouldn't be able to help either of them if the empress lived.

The moment the empress grew still, Ro left the arrow in place and rushed toward Olt. Commander Qing-Zhu already cradled Mulan.

She should've known better.

She'd just touched Olt, gently, when the empress began chanting. A rush of sound filled the space behind her. Ro spun, but she was too late.

Instead of shooting power at them, now the empress drew it into herself, draining everyone in the room of their life force, all at once.

It was clumsily done, nowhere near as potent as when she had a place to store her power, but it was still effective.

The empress's outstretched hands shook from where she lay, but the pull was relentless, and everyone sank to the floor, weak and tired and unable to resist.

Ro tried to react, to fight as she'd done before, but she couldn't quite figure out how. So she gave up. What was the point?

She was so very tired all of a sudden, and she just wanted to *sleep*...

In the midst of everyone else sinking to the floor, lying over like they were going to snooze right there, Mulan sat up. Ro wasn't quite sure—she blinked several times, but everything was just so darn fuzzy—but she *thought* Mulan raised an unfamiliar necklace over her head, slipped it on, and tucked it into her armor.

A necklace that glowed with a black light at its heart.

The empress didn't notice as she cackled like a deranged hyena.

Mulan rose to her feet, her gaze focused, intent on the empress. The commander's arms fell away, and Olt tumbled off her and lay still.

"Stop!" Mulan shoved out her hand with the word, and something...happened.

Ro didn't feel quite so tired all of a sudden, but she also couldn't do more than watch.

The empress laughed. "Come back for more, warrior?" Her voice turned strangled. Strained. Mechanical. "What? No! What is happening to me?"

She rushed Mulan and raised the fan for another blow, but before the empress could strike, she glistened with an unnatural light...and shrank. The fan fell to the ground. Her jeweled monstrosity of a dress caved in on itself, and out hopped a little mechanical bird, carved from gold and covered in jewels. Its eyes glowed green.

It spread its wings, uttered a high-pitched squawk, and ran straight at Mulan.

Mulan heaved her sword above her head. The mechanical bird made it only a few steps before Mulan's blade came down on it, again and again. It shattered into cogs, gears, and precious gemstones. The light went out in its eyes, and it lay still.

The warriors in the room crawled to their feet, shaking their heads and doing their best to remain upright. One of the soldiers hurried over and started gathering every gear, cog, and jewel, shoving them into a burlap sack he carried.

And the rumbling that had tapered off began anew, low growls in the deep that hinted at more to come.

Ro's sole focus was Olt, when the strangest thing happened.

With a sigh, the little brown nightingale spoke. "My son. My beautiful, strong, handsome boy."

Qing-Zhu stood there, stunned, for half a heartbeat before he flung himself toward the crumpled creature. "Mother? No!"

He fell to his knees next to the nightingale, gathered it gently in his hands, and wept. Soft whispers rose from the soldiers, and Mulan went to Qing-Zhu, limping. She laid a hand on his shoulder and comforted him. And then they bent their heads and seemed to be having a conversation…with the nightingale.

Shaking off her lightheadedness, Ro knelt next to Olt, looking for the best way to help him without hurting him further. He lay there, wing splayed and bent at unnatural angles, weakly bleating.

"Oh, Olt." Using an arrow tip, Ro ripped off a length of her tunic and began to work.

Carefully, each bleat of pain wrecking her heart, Ro popped brittle bones back in place as best she could, making sure they were set well enough to heal. Olt stopped making pitiful noises at some point and went limp, so Ro worked faster. She wrapped his wing, then folded it against his body, binding it so it wouldn't move.

"Please, let me speak with the huntress. I haven't much time," came a soft, quiet voice.

Her head came up to find Mulan and Qing-Zhu motioning her over.

Settling Olt down gently, Ro hurried to them. Qing-Zhu kissed the little bird's head, then passed it to Ro. She cradled it in weary hands.

Unsure of what to do with the small brown creature, its breast beating rapidly as it gasped short, fast breaths, Ro glanced between Mulan and Qing-Zhu, but their eyes were fastened on the nightingale.

Then it spoke. "You have saved my sons, huntress. Thank you."

"Um…" Ro had to take a moment to mentally prepare herself for this conversation. "Who are you? Where did the empress go?"

The bird lay there, panting, staring at Ro with one eye. "I—I watched the false empress for many years, huntress, as she learned at the side of her master, as she grew more powerful than he, as she seized his power and made it her own." The little bird's voice caught. "As she stole my husband and then tried to steal my sons."

At this, the commander sucked in a sharp breath and spat, "Never!"

Thankfully, Ro could still understand their language with all the residual magic in the air.

"You are a good boy. The best of sons," the nightingale crooned.

Ro hated to take even a moment away from them, but she needed to know. "How do I save my niece? Is everyone awake now that the empress is defeated?"

"You must first destroy the mechanical birds. They bind the curse to each child. Only then will those she trapped be able to be freed."

The words slammed into Ro with a jolt.

Allura had such a mechanical bird, at her bedside. A gift, one that never left her side.

One they had taken to the summer château to keep at her side. To comfort her.

Ro had *helped* keep her trapped.

Energy thrummed through Ro, but she forced herself to listen. To listen and not fling the dying bird aside and race to Allura as fast as she could.

How had she not realized when the commander told his story? When the empress had turned into one? Then again, she'd barely given Allura's music box more than a passing glance. It was the first thing she was smashing to pieces.

Mulan asked, "How will we find them all? How many did she trap in enchanted sleep?"

"You—you will be led to them. The necklace…it will guide you. But do not be seduced by its power. It serves no one but itself."

Ro's head came up at that, but Mulan stiffened and kept her eyes on the nightingale. Ro took a deep breath and let it go. Without realizing she'd done so.

Ro's eyes slid over to the Prussian princes huddled around Olt. Who were all still swans. She dropped her gaze to the nightingale in her hands. "How do I help my friends? And why are they still swans?"

"I—I do not know, I am sorry. Lim Wei-Yip and her sorcerer master used powerful magic, most of it stolen. Magic even I never understood."

Something Ro had far too much experience with, unfortunately.

The bird struggled for breath. "Lim-Qi trapped me. Turned me into this creature of song, all because I would not be swayed by his false words, because I tried to send him away. Instead, he gave me as a gift to the emperor, my own husband."

Qing-Zhu put his head down, and once again, Mulan offered comfort.

"I had to watch as he built that creature out of metal and jewels, imbued it with unnatural life, and replaced me with it.

"Only he did not know what he had done.

"When he tried to kill the emperor, when I tried to save him as Lim Wei-Yip stole her master's power, when she transformed from a mechanical bird into a woman, I thought all was lost. But then you came."

The dull-brown nightingale turned to Mulan with those words.

"I have seen you watch over my sons, warrior. The things you do for them, the things no one else can, have not gone unnoticed. You are powerful in your own right, and I have nothing to fear with you by their sides. Serve your emperor, fight by my second son's side, and you will bring much honor to your family."

Ro's eyes drifted back to Olt, who lay in an unmoving heap on the floor. She asked quietly, "And how do I—we— break the sleeping spells? After destroying the music boxes?"

The bird's eyes closed. "You must unravel them, huntress. Like a finely woven tapestry, you must unravel them thread by thread."

Despair filled Ro's heart. She didn't want anything to do with spells. She didn't want to become enslaved too. She didn't want to hurt those she loved most.

But that's all she seemed capable of doing.

Using the empress's power was heady, exhilarating— something she could get used to. And it scared her.

But she had to put her fears aside for now. Allura first.

Ro nodded once. "I will."

"I will as well," Mulan agreed.

The bird trembled. "I know you will, huntress. And you too, my warrior. Thank you." The little nightingale struggled to speak, its life draining away drop by drop, its body broken and crumpled. "Now come, I will show you both what you must do."

Mulan reached out and held the bird with Ro.

Heartbeat fluttering rapidly, the nightingale began to sing, putting every last bit of herself into the song. Ro stilled as the joyous melody filled her, strengthening her, showing her the way to unweave the spells. Then she sang of faraway lands and emperor's palaces and forests, showing her love for her country and her sons more powerfully than mere words ever could.

Ro's eyes filled with tears at the vibrancy of every image the little bird placed in her mind through its song.

And from the stillness of the other warriors and the tears on Mulan's and the commander's faces, they were seeing the same things. A love of a mother for her family, the love of a true empress for her emperor and country and people, and the lengths to which she'd go to ensure her sons were free.

The last note faded away, and the little brown nightingale grew still.

Ro gently handed it back to Qing-Zhu. As she did, a silver band, much like the one on Odile's neck, glinted on the nightingale's foot. Ro fingered it, and with a ringing note, the power from the song burst out of her fingers and shattered it to dust.

At the same time, a second bird seemed to leap from the still body, flitting around the room in joyful song, before flying straight up and going into a second beam of light that shouldn't have been there.

Ro blinked once, and it was gone.

Mulan gathered up the limp body, and one of her men came hurrying over with a length of cloth. They wrapped it carefully, put it in a box, and handed it to the commander.

One of the swans came near and squawked at her.

She brushed off her hands on her trousers. "Come, we have to get back to your sister."

Just then, the floor gave a mighty heave, lifting them and dropping them back down. The warriors staggered, and some fell. Giant cracks splintered up the wall, all the way to the top of the dome, and resounding booms said the same thing was happening outside this chamber.

And Ro was running. She had to get to those asleep in the castle before the pagoda fell down around their heads.

The warriors began the impressive climb out of the cave, hoisting up their wounded. The swans didn't have enough room to become airborne, so they had to be carried out as well.

But Olt was the only one still unconscious.

35

$\mathcal{A}$s they came out in the ruins, an explosive roar under their feet rattled the entire pagoda and sent them staggering. Cracks split the sides of the structure, letting in light from outside. They ran for the castle.

The moon was rising, full and large and heavy, its rays piercing the jade walls and lighting them another shade of vibrant green. More cracks appeared, and silver rays stabbed through at a sharp angle, shining on the party fleeing for their lives.

Climbing the ropes left on the castle walls, since the gate was buried under rubble, they hurried as the pagoda shook overhead, green tendrils of light writhing madly, as if they had nowhere to go.

Huge chunks of stone rained down all around them.

Ro carried Olt the whole way, even when he woke and gave a pitiful bleat and struggled to be put down. She wasn't about to lose him.

They dove into the castle to find mostly everyone awake, befuddled, and huddling in the great hall.

The warriors took in the situation, then came over and spoke quickly to the commander and Mulan.

374

Mulan turned to Ro. "They are too weak. They will never make the long climb out through the caves. And the emperor of the German kingdom—he did not survive the waking. Many did not."

Ro sucked in a breath through her teeth. Not only would she have to break that news to Odette later, but he hadn't survived the waking.

He hadn't survived. Waking up.

She had to compartmentalize that. Think about it later. Or she wouldn't be able to go on. All she knew was Allura would survive. She'd make sure of it.

Mulan's eyes were wide. "What do we do?"

To underscore the danger, the ground gave a mighty heave.

Ro met Mulan's gaze. "We have to try. We have to try to save them."

Mulan gave a sharp nod, then she was off, barking orders to her men. Qing-Zhu stood off to the side, eyes glassy, staring at nothing—in shock.

It took some convincing, but they got everyone up and moving. And although it took more time than Ro feared they had, they got everyone into the dungeon, through the still-open tunnel, and up into the cave. Including the wounded soldiers.

Once they were in the giant chamber, the quaking intensified. The ceiling rattled over their heads and the ground trembled beneath their feet.

Ro pulled ahead, Olt in her arms. Yet Olt hissed and insisted on waddling on his own two orange feet. Ro put him down the moment his nipping came too close to biting.

As the ground heaved and rocked beneath them, Ro ran in a drunken line toward the exit. Then she paused and looked back at all the people behind her.

The warriors hustled emaciated and weak people after her, but they were much slower with their burdens.

"Go!" Mulan cried. "We'll see them safely out. And we'll bring the black swan!"

Ro had forgotten the black swan in all the excitement. How had they managed to capture her, anyway? A question for another time.

Still, she hesitated. Should she…stay? Help them?

But the six swans…and Allura…

Mulan limped over and laid a hand on Ro's shoulder. "Go, huntress. We unleashed the empress on the world. We will clean up her mess. It was an honor to meet you."

Ro wrapped her in an impromptu hug. "The honor was all mine."

She pulled back to see Qing-Zhu staring at the ground, his hands in his hair, tears in his eyes.

Ro tilted her head in his direction. "You should tell him, you know."

Mulan looked at him fearfully, but with such longing, Ro couldn't imagine it wouldn't be long until something came of it. "Perhaps. After my honorable discharge is in my hands and my commendation is in my father's. Once my father is free of any obligation to the empire. Perhaps then."

Ro's eyes slid toward the exit. She needed to go.

"But I will look after him. I promise." Mulan smiled. "Now go. Set that little girl free."

They clasped arms, and Ro turned and ran for the forest, the swans at her heels.

After Ro climbed out of the caves, past the barrier that was no more, and on to the next hill over, she felt a hum build behind her. She cast a glance over her shoulder.

Green light writhed over the outside of the pagoda, streaks of emerald driven to a craze, its hum growing deeper in pitch until it practically growled. Then all at once it shattered—green light shooting over the forest and riffling the trees as the tower crumbled into jagged shards and fell straight down.

Ro threw herself on the ground, covering Olt, before the wave hit them. A gust of wind swept over them and threatened to tear Ro's cloak from her shoulders. Dust and debris shot by, stinging any part of Ro it could reach. She tucked Olt closer and hid her face, making sure every bit of him was covered.

With it came a jolt of energy. One final gift from the empress. Whether she meant to or not.

The moment the wind died down, Ro leaped to her feet and stared at the great ruin in the distance, no part of the tower left standing. Guilt and horror instantly flooded Ro.

Dieu, may they have escaped unharmed, she prayed.

The warriors, the people she'd left behind—she swallowed—and the black swan.

A bleat from one of the swans roused her, and Ro looked up. The moon was high in the sky, clouds parted around it, not long from reaching its apex. Half an hour, at most?

At her back the swans squawked and flapped their impressive wingspans.

She turned to them in a panic. "We have to hurry. It's almost too late."

Ro took off running, the swans flocking after her, all but one.

"Come *on*, Oberon," she called. "We'll go after her if we need to, but after you get changed back to human, all right?"

He hissed at her threateningly, but at least he joined them.

"I consider myself warned," Ro muttered.

The moment they came to a clearing with enough space to run until they could lift their heavy bodies into the air, the swans took to the skies. All but Odin, who waddled after her as quickly as his orange feet would take him.

Ro hefted the bird in her arms and ran, racing the moon to its zenith.

Ro burst into the clearing. The swans arrived just then—as if Ro had flown over the ground as quickly as they'd flown in the sky—and came in to land on the far side of the lake. They sailed across the water, waddled up the shore, and gathered at the base of the tower, all in the time it took Ro to round the lake.

They began making the biggest racket below Odette's window.

Odette and all her blonde hair appeared in the open window. She stared blearily at the swans, then up at the moon. With a squeak, she disappeared.

"Hold on, I'm coming!" came her muffled voice.

Ro ran all the way to where the swans waited, set Olt carefully down, and called, "What can I do to help?"

Odette poked her head out once more, saw Ro, and wilted in relief. "You're here! Quick, help me." She disappeared and was back in seconds. "All those coat racks in the barn? Set them up, there in the clearing. Hurry!"

Ro ran for the barn.

One of the many odd things stored there, these coat racks had circular bases with a hole in the center, a tall staff to place in the middle, and two shoulder-width wooden prongs to hang the coats upon.

Ro had all the pieces out in three trips and set them up faster than anything she'd done in her life.

"The coats!" Odette shouted. A bundle of pale-green woven tweed appeared on the window ledge. She leaned out over the coats. "Quick! Help me lower these."

Ro caught the rope Odette tossed down and lowered the bundle quickly.

"Don't let it touch the ground!" Odette shrieked.

Ro gritted her teeth and stopped them at the last second. "What shall I do with them, then?" she asked as she held the burden less than a mètre off the ground.

"Oh! I'll just, um. Be right there!" Footsteps raced away from the window, something heavy swung open, and it wasn't long until Odette was running out of the barn and the secret passage there. "Hold them steady!"

Ro did as she was told, the swans flapping around them both uselessly, as Odette unbundled coats and hung them up. Her flesh sizzled as it came into contact with the material, and she winced in pain.

Ro reached out to help.

"Nein!" Odette gasped. "Only I can touch them."

Ro dropped her hand, wishing she could help. "But they're dried out," she said helplessly.

"Like magical things care," Odette grumbled, even as she shook from pain.

Ro bit her lip. It was so hard not to do more.

Odette grabbed the rope to the tower and stepped into the looped end. "Pull me up, huntress. There are more coats."

They repeated this process twice more as Odette set up in the open space between the tower and barn and lake, not letting Ro anywhere near the frock coats.

Odette was crying as she hung the final coat on the rack. "I'm sorry. I'm so sorry."

"Your hands..." Ro said, wishing she could share her healing ability.

Oberon was already moving toward his sister. He craned his long neck over the girl's hands and turned his head to the side, letting a few tears fall. Then he turned his head the other way and let a few more tears fall into her other hand.

Magic washed over her palms like a tide, washing away the hurt, if not the evidence that it had been there. Odette's skin still looked marbled and waxy and slightly melted, but no longer blistered and welted.

Odette knelt and wrapped her arms around the bulky swan. "Oh, Oberon, thank you! Just a few moments more, and you won't have to do that ever again."

The clearing brightened, and Ro took in the moon, easing its way ever closer to the sky's apex. "Princess! It's time."

Odette whirled, gasped, and shooed the swans toward the stands. "Places. Get in place!"

The swans obliged, standing in front of their coats, eldest to youngest, if Ro had her guess right, and Odette babbled as she flung out instructions.

"Remember! Hold still. Keep your entire body under the coat. Just like we practiced with the blankets. Hurry!"

Ro could feel it, the moon sliding into place. It was the strangest sensation. The clearing brightened, everything crisp and clear, and Ro's entire body hummed with awareness.

"Now!" Odette cried to herself, and raced to the first coat. She flung it over Oberon's back, covering the swan's entire head, then repeated the action for each of her brothers, ending with Olt.

Only...she froze when she came to Olt's coat, staring down at it in horror.

Ro's eyes went to the moon. "Odette, now!"

"But I didn't—"

"Now!"

With a choked sob, Odette flung the last coat over her

youngest brother's back and pulled up the hood as the moon bathed the area in blazing silvery light.

The moment she was done with Olt, Oberon moved toward her.

"Nein!" Odette cried, hands raised and shaking. They were puckered with welts worse than before. *"Nein,* don't move the jacket, not even for me."

If a swan could look pained, that one did.

"Now, tuck back under."

Oberon hissed a little, but he obediently put his head back under the nettle coat.

Even from where she stood—as close as she could without being in the way—Ro could see the angry red blisters had burst and were oozing blood and clear liquid.

Ro wished the girl would let one of her brothers cry on her hands one last time.

The moon settled into its apex. Ro couldn't have said why, but it seemed to hover there—as if it had settled into a groove, content to rest directly above them.

Odette cried out, jumped up and down—and spun to face her brothers.

Six swans stared back.

The dismay on Odette's face matched what churned in Ro's gut.

They waited a few more heartbeats, breaths held, but… nothing happened.

Odette started wringing those hands, oblivious to the pain. "I don't understand. Nothing's happening. Why isn't anything happening?" She spun on Ro. "The witch is dead? You saw this?"

Ro gave a fierce nod. "Oui. The witch is dead. Her nightingales are no more. Her power has been shattered."

Odette stared up at the moon, then at her brothers. Then again at the moon.

She cried out, covering her cheeks with her hands and

looking from brother to brother. "I don't understand. I don't understand! Why didn't it work?" Again, she spun on Ro. "Did you touch them? The coats?"

Ro shook her head.

"Did you let them touch the ground? Drop them? Spill something on them while I wasn't looking?"

Ro held out her hands. "Non, I promise you. I knew what was at stake."

Angry tears coursed down Odette's face. "How could it not be you? You are the only one who showed up here, came here—you are the reason it didn't work!"

Odette took a step forward, but the swans shrugged off the painful material and converged on her, blocking Ro. Odette crumpled to the ground, sobbing, and the swans twined their necks around her and held her. Giant tears splashed down the swans' faces, all of them crying together.

Oberon made sure his tears fell on her hands.

"Odette? Odette!"

Ro jerked upright as a stranger's call rang out in the night. A man stumbled toward them, dressed in rags and covered in filth.

Ro reached for one of the discarded coat racks to use as a weapon.

Odette's head shot up. "Hans? Hans!" She held out her hands to him, not bothering to get up. As if she were too weary to make the effort.

He ran for Odette, but his smell hit Ro first.

She staggered back and covered her nose.

He smelled…just like…pig filth. A sty.

Ro's eyes widened. The pig farmer?

He grasped Odette's hands and knelt before her, and they leaned their foreheads together.

"Oh, Hans, you're here," Odette said. She looked him over, as if checking for wounds. "However did you escape? What of the villagers?"

Shame filled his face. "The empress killed them all. All but me."

"Oh, Hans."

Malnourished and filthy, Hans wasn't much more than rags and bones, and although his skin was no longer warped like his face was melting, it was pockmarked as if hundreds of beaks had torn into him, and scratched as if talons had gouged his skin. He was also now normal human size.

"They're still swans." Odette sobbed. "It didn't work, and my brothers are still swans."

"Shh, my love. I'm here. I'm here now." Hans pulled her into his arms, and then they were kissing. As if they couldn't get enough of each other.

Ro looked away, dropped her makeshift weapon, and shoved her hands deep in her pockets. She felt so helpless. Almost as if it were her fault, though she didn't know how.

Something soft brushed her fingertips, and Ro strained her fingers toward whatever it was. Maybe she shouldn't have had such deep pockets sewn into her trousers.

She grasped whatever it was and pulled it out.

Two swan-wing combs glinted in pearlescent colors in the moonlight, a rainbow of colors dancing within its creamy luster. And suddenly she knew.

Knew why the siren had let her have these.

Knew why she'd never turned them over to Madame LaChance, even though the businesswoman had paid for them.

It was for this moment in time.

"Put them back on," Ro said.

Odette lifted her head, then her eyes riveted on what Ro held. "Where did you get those?"

Ro tore her gaze from the swan-wing combs. "Put them back on. Put the coats back on the swans!"

Odette rushed to obey, falling down twice in the process. She rescued the nettle coats from the ground, shook them out, and settled them just so on the swans' backs. Hans helped, even though he winced each time he touched them.

"They touched the ground…" she fussed. "And—" She flicked a glance at Hans but didn't say anything more.

Ro didn't answer. Either it would matter or it wouldn't.

The swans all faced Ro, their backs to the moon, and Odette stood trembling behind them. Ro motioned Odette forward. She moved toward Ro, entire body quivering, tears trembling on her cheeks, eyes wide with hope.

"Odette, you have watched over your brothers faithfully. You have toiled endlessly to set them free. You saw to it no harm came to them if you could help it. You were faithful."

The words came to Ro unbidden, and she took a deep breath to ease the pressure in her chest. She couldn't get them out fast enough.

"Your Creator has seen. He has heard. And He has loved you all the more for it. He is a rewarder of the faithful. Of the diligent. And it is His pleasure to reward you to the fullest. Come."

Odette came. She knelt on the ground. Not to Ro—in honor of the Creator.

And Ro swept back one side of Odette's thick blonde hair that stretched to the ground, held back in multiple thick braids—not once cut while her brothers were imprisoned— and settled one comb firmly there. Then Ro swept back the other side.

At once, light burst from Odette, and the most glorious swan Ro had ever seen, bigger even than Oberon, stood before her, shining. A crown of gold, silver, pearls, feathers, and wings perched above her head, in the air, and her swan's body was covered in feathers of the richest crème.

She turned, and the brothers shrank from her. She stretched out her neck, spread her wings and flapped them, then honked a deep, resonating noise that swept the forest in a wave of pure energy.

Then she spoke, and her voice had changed. Grown deeper, more commanding. "My brothers, come. Shake off your curse and follow my voice. Follow your queen."

And the light flowed from her and into them.

Each swan stretched and lengthened and transformed into a human shape, the nettle frock coats disintegrating into ash around them.

It was almost too bright for Ro to see, but she strained to catch a glimpse of Olt.

As if shielding the private moment from her, the light swelled in heat, in intensity, and at the end of the swell, Odette stretched back to her normal human height.

Still, the crown rested on her head, and a cape made entirely of swan feathers rested around her shoulders, a glistening white dress replacing homespun.

The light faded by degrees, but it stayed in her eyes, otherworldly and powerful.

The moon moved out of place.

And six brothers and one queen stood in the clearing.

Ro approached Odette cautiously. It was her, but it wasn't. Self-assured, quiet, calm—it was as if someone else had replaced her. And little tendrils and motes of golden light still danced around her. "Odette?"

The girl—the woman—glanced up, and Ro stopped. Her eyes. Her eyes looked as though she carried all the stars in the heavens within them.

Odette reached up and fingered one of the combs, then tilted her head regally at Ro. "Huntress."

Before Ro could say anything else, one of the brothers, his form so dim compared to his sister's that he seemed to be in shadow, strode forward and took his sister's hands in his. "Your hands," rumbled a deep, concerned voice.

She smiled kindly at him. "They will bear my scars. A reminder of my sacrifice."

Oberon—at least, that's who Ro assumed it was—tore the hem of his tattered shirt and gently, lovingly wrapped his sister's hands. "You have sacrificed so much for us…"

"And it is your turn to sacrifice for me."

Ro readied herself. This wasn't Odette. Odette would be

sobbing, falling all over her brothers, crying her eyes out and making a general mess of herself.

This person—who was this creature in Odette's place?

Her eyes settled on Ro, and although her features were the same, gone were the homespun and furs. Now a pearl-white dress, shimmering a rainbow of colors, and a crown that fanned around her head like wings, spreading from the combs themselves, gave her an otherworldly look. "I am in your debt, huntress. Thank you."

Ro nodded, not liking the sinking feeling in her gut. Had she defeated one sorceress only to create another? Yet…the Creator had orchestrated this. Hadn't He?

Be at peace, a quiet voice spoke to her spirit.

Five brothers converged on their sister, but they held back. It wasn't the happy reunion they'd so long dreamed of. They were wary. Concerned. As if they knew something had changed, but they weren't sure what.

Something Ro very much wanted to know herself.

One thing Ro was thankful for? That she wasn't about to question? All the brothers seemed to be in the same clothing they'd worn when they'd turned into swans, if the outdated fashions were any indication, but torn and soiled.

"Go," the new Swan Queen said to Ro, startling her. "Your niece can be woken now. But you must hurry." She frowned. "The magic does not wish to let her go."

Ro's heart dropped low in her belly, yet it stoked a fire there. Well the magic couldn't have her niece.

"Perhaps you'd like your axe? You may have need of it."

The Swan Queen waved her hand, and the lake started to broil. A moment later, Ro's axe popped to the surface. Then, impossibly, it drifted to the edge of the lake and bumped against the bank.

One of the brothers fished it out and brought it to her, dripping lake water.

Ro thanked him, but she stared down at it, unseeing. Unsure if she should leave. Something still wasn't right here.

Oberon spoke again, a pleading note in his voice. "Please. Odile."

Turning her galaxy-gaze to him, Odette said, "*Ja*. You are right. We should free your wife now." She tilted her head. "Yet she is on her way to us, even as we speak."

As if her words had called him forth, one of Mulan's warriors burst into the clearing, the black swan clutched in his arms. "Huntress!"

Ro turned at the interruption, grasping it like a lifeline, allowing it to keep her here just a little longer, to observe. To make sure the others were safe with this queen.

The black swan didn't look so good.

Oberon cried out and moved toward them, but Odette stopped him with a raised hand, even as she waved the warrior forward. "Come. Place her here."

The warrior did as asked, then stepped back and bent over his knees, sucking in deep breaths.

Odette ignored him. "Huntress, the collar."

Ro stepped over to the listless swan and tapped the silver collar. The nightingale's song swelled out of her, and it burst into powder, all over her hand. Ro tried to wipe it off on her trousers, but it smeared there like graphite.

Odette swept the length of her swan-feather cloak over the limp bird and intoned, "Odile, hear my voice and come forth. You are no longer bound to that form."

Unable to see exactly what was happening under all those feathers, Ro noticed the shape underneath swell. A dark hand pushed the cloak aside, and Oberon cried out in joy.

He ran for her, pulled her into his arms. Her skin was so beautifully dark, as if from the deepest midnight, that Ro caught herself staring. No wonder her feathers had been so richly shaded.

But she didn't dwell on that long.

Oberon's cry was echoed by another of the brothers, only it wasn't joyful.

Ro's eyes widened, and she spun to find…one of the brothers lay crumpled on the ground.

Whenever there was danger, she was able to dismiss everything around her and concentrate on that danger. If it wasn't right in front of her, she couldn't see it. If it didn't pertain to the situation, it didn't exist.

It was wonderful in a fight. In a hunt. Unless there was another opponent, and unless a second predator was stalking the huntress.

But right now, concentrating completely on the new queen, Ro didn't notice or consider anything else that wasn't brought to her attention.

Including Olt.

Who was writhing on the ground in pain.

Ro's heart dropped right past her toes. She threw the axe and pushed into the gaggle of brothers, staring down at the form clutching his arm. An arm…that didn't look right.

Broken and bent the wrong way, in several places, lumpy and misshapen — Olt was almost insensible from pain.

"Olt!" Ro skidded on the ground next to him, past all the brothers crowding him, and turned his face gently toward her, trying to assess for injury.

He moaned, eyes closed, face a rictus of agony.

"Olt, what is it? What happened? Where does it hurt? Are you all right? How can I help?" Insensible questions, but she was panicking here.

She reached for his wrist, to start assessing damage, but her hand brushed silken feathers. Ro froze in horror. Her eyes drifted down to find feathers poking out of his linen sleeve.

Slowly, not wanting to at all, she lightly ran her fingers over his shoulder, where thick human muscle morphed into a lightweight avian wing, the wing that had been destroyed by the empress's bladed fan.

He moaned again, a deep, painful sound that shook Ro to her core, and she jerked back.

"It hurts. Ro, it hurts." He was clutching at his shoulder, trying to stop the pain in a broken arm that hadn't changed with the rest of him.

Tears filled Ro's eyes, and she smoothed back the hair falling over his forehead. It settled back into place as it always did. "Shh. I've got you. I'm here, Olt. I'm here."

Even though she'd done it earlier, her brain shut down on how to splint a wing on a human body. She felt Odette come up behind her.

"What happened to him?" Ro asked in a broken voice.

The lofty voice held none of the warmth of before. "I told you. I did not finish the coat. I said my help would cost you, and it has. It is most unfortunate."

Ro dropped her head, every pant and groan coming from *her Olt* breaking her heart. She wanted to take all the pain from him, to feel it herself, to make it stop hurting—she'd do anything.

"What…on the coat…didn't you finish?" Ro whispered.

"I believe it was one of the sleeves," Odette mused.

"Can't you help him? *Please?*" Ro begged.

"Very well." Odette—or the Swan Queen, or whoever this creature was—bent down and ran her fingertips over the splayed wing. "I believe I can…there."

With a shiver, the swan wing vibrated, then vanished, leaving…nothing…in its place. Nothing but an empty sleeve.

Ro cried out, and the brothers all made similar noises of protest. Olt groaned, still writhing and barely conscious.

Ro stared up at Odette in horror. "What did you do?"

She looked at Ro as if she were a pest asking a ridiculous question. "I took away the part that wasn't human." Unspoken was her *duh*.

"But…then…why is he still in pain?"

The Swan Queen dusted off her hands. "Who knows? I'm afraid that's all I can do. Can you make him comfortable?"

Ro climbed to her feet, glancing into the faces of the brothers—at least they looked horrified—before her hard gaze settled on Odette. "Fix it. Fix it now."

A hint of sorrow entered the new queen's eyes. "I cannot. I am Queen of the Swans"—she tilted her head, as if listening to something or someone—"all creatures of flight, it would seem, since the former queen stole her position and did not do her job properly, but I cannot change the human world. I am sorry."

"You couldn't have *transformed* his arm instead of taking it away?"

Odette shrugged. "If it helps, the wing was shattered beyond repair. He never would've been able to use it, even if he hadn't already used up all the magic in the frock coat for the transformation."

Ro's fists clenched.

Odette's eyes tracked the movement. "I would be careful if I were you, huntress. You don't yet know the extent of my powers."

Ro stepped close. "And you don't know mine."

"*Fräuleins*, please," Oberon interrupted. "Odin lies before you in agony. Can we not see to him first and figure out every-thing else later?"

Ro nodded, her eyes still on Odette, promising retribution if she did not *fix this*.

Hans, who'd remained unobtrusively in the background until this point, came close and reached for Odette, but she brushed him off with a disdainful look. "Bathe yourself, human. You are not fit for our company."

Hurt flashed on his face as he withdrew.

Before Ro could figure out how to respond to *that*, four brothers surrounded Olt, lifted him, and carried him into the barn as he clutched his shoulder, sweating profusely. Ro hurried past them, threw her cloak over the hay where she slept on rainy evenings, and waved the brothers over.

"Place him here."

She tore open his sleeve to find the skin at his shoulder puckered but closed. No open wounds, no sores, no remaining feathers.

Outside the barn, she heard Odette say to Oberon, "Come, I must speak to you and your wife."

Ro hovered over Olt, unsure how to help. She was thankful when he passed out from pain. Someone brought a basin filled with cool water, and she took it and wiped down his clammy skin.

Footsteps roused Ro from a light sleep, and she jumped up to check on Olt, then bathed his face with cool water again.

"Huntress."

Groggy, Ro turned to the speaker and wiped her eyes. "Oui? Um…"

He bowed. "Olov, *Fräulein*."

She nodded.

His eyes went to his brother briefly. "The Swan Queen says since your Allura can be released from her sleeping curse, you should return and break the enchantment without delay. You are…pressed for time."

Ro studied the sturdy, handsome young man. He reminded her of Olt, the way his hair misbehaved, though a lighter shade, and the way he stood, though shorter and thicker. "Is any part of your sister left?"

He swallowed and looked down. "She may yet…return to us…when she has set right all the empress has made wrong."

Ro's jaw hardened, and she turned to Olt. "Has she taken over ruling your kingdom now that your father no longer lives?"

"Oh. *Nein*, not at all."

Ro's head whipped around at that.

"She wants Oberon and Odile to rule, as is their right now

that she is no longer one of us, and she asked them to unite the kingdoms. She said she has much to do…elsewhere."

He looked as though he was having as much trouble accepting his words as Ro.

Olov nodded to his brother. "We need to move him to the tower."

Ro's hands tightened around Olt's remaining hand, squeezing harder than she meant to. He would have to learn to use it alone now. "I have to watch over him."

Olov shifted uncomfortably. "She says you need to leave."

Ro's head whipped up, and he raised his hands in a calming gesture.

"Not because she is forcing you. Because your family needs you." He gentled his tone. "Odin is our brother. Our family. He is in good hands, and we will watch over him."

Ro ducked her head to hide the sudden onslaught of tears that filled her eyes. "Give me a moment?"

Olov bowed. "Of course, *Fräulein*. Thank you for all you have done for my family. And for me."

Ro nodded, unable to look up. When his footsteps faded, Ro dropped her head on Olt's chest, her heart aching so hard it must be physically breaking. "Oh, Olt. I don't want to leave you. But I have to. I have to go to Allura."

She looked up, searching his still face.

"You'll understand, won't you? You won't…hate me for abandoning you while you're hurting? While you're healing?"

Her eyes drifted to his arm that was nothing more than an empty sleeve, and her gaze darted away, as if she were rude to look.

She cupped his face in her hands. "I'll come back for you. I promise."

And then she kissed him. Pouring all her heart and soul into the kiss.

He didn't respond.

Choking on tears, Ro fled the little barn.

Swiping up her axe, Ro sprinted down the path that had first brought her to this place. And this time, the barrier didn't stop her as she ran toward her grandmère's house in the woods.

It was time she went home to Cosette. It was time she helped Allura.

She'd come back for Olt later.

PART V

THE CASTLE OF THE BLACK ROSES / LE CHÂTEAU DES ROSES NOIRES

The poor Emperor could scarcely breathe; it appeared to him
as though something was sitting on his chest; he opened his
eyes, and saw that it was Death, wearing his golden crown. …
All at once the sweetest song was heard from the window; it
was the little living nightingale who was sitting on a branch
outside—she had heard of her Emperor's severe illness, and
was come to sing to him of comfort and hope.
—Hans Christian Andersen, "The Nightingale"

And soon the six swans, flying toward her, alighted so near
that she was able to throw over them the nettle coats. As soon
as she had done so, their feathers fell off and the brothers
stood up alive and well; but the youngest was without his left
arm, instead of which he had a swan's wing.
—Jacob Grimm and Wilhelm Grimm, "The Six Swans"

Laura Hollingsworth

Ro crashed through the Black Forest, her heart left more firmly behind her with every step. With Olt.

But Ro needed to find her brothers and—she gulped—Liam. Whatever he'd tried to create between them, she was going to have to end it. If she even knew what it was or how to do it.

When Olt had kissed her, had revealed the deepest part of his heart to her, her heart had responded, whether she'd meant it to or not. Although she truly didn't like to think of it, any of it, she'd never responded that way to Liam. Not once. And she couldn't lead him on.

Her heart now belonged wholly, irrevocably, to Olt and no other. And she had to admit that to herself.

She gasped against sobs, trying to stuff them deep, trying to ignore everything she was feeling. A few tears leaked down her cheeks anyway.

No crying! She could give in to her emotions *after* Allura.

As if she wasn't desperate enough to get back to Allura, the bell gonged once more, knocking Ro off her feet, the loudest it had ever been. The clockface ticked back to three, looming in her mind long after it had faded from view.

Ro scrambled to her feet and ran even faster. She surged out of the forest belonging to Olt's family, her senses fully alert, her instincts leading her straight to her grandmère's house, where she hurtled up the steps and burst into the cabin, causing a commotion that nearly took off her head.

Her brothers jumped up from bedrolls, and Liam swung his sword, stopping just shy of Ro's neck. She pushed the flat side down and turned to her grandmère. "The source of the curse is gone, Grandmère. We must go to Allura, right now. We must wake her."

Her grandmère didn't move from her rocker, still puffing away on her pipe, eyeing Ro shrewdly.

"Oh, that's typical, Ro," cut in Claude. "No 'How are you?' or 'Here's where I've been the last few weeks.' Oh no, just bursts in like she owns the place and demands we do exactly as she says."

Liam eyed the dark night past Ro's shoulder as he sheathed his sword. "Can it wait until morning?"

They were all thinking it: wolves.

Ro shook her head. "Non. We must leave now. She hasn't much time."

That stupid, stupid clock. Only three ticks left. Guilt swamped her for the extra time she'd taken at Olt's side—and for leaving him there. What would he think when he woke? That she'd abandoned him at the first sign of trouble?

She shook away the thoughts. Later. She'd think about that *later*.

Liam moved past her. "I'll saddle the horses."

Pascal pulled on clothing over his sleep attire and moved to help, stopping briefly to touch her arm. She gave him a small, pain-filled smile, and the concern in his eyes deepened.

Claude started to sit back down.

"Go help 'em, you lazy arse!" Grandmère barked.

Clause shot to his feet and tried to stroll nonchalantly toward the door, but that was difficult to do when he was quite obviously trying to stay out of reach of her cane. He too gave Ro a look that said he was glad she was back before grabbing his own clothing and disappearing into the night. Ro turned to follow.

"*Nein.* Help me pack."

Ro took a deep breath and faced her grandmère. The old woman watched her still.

"Where is the boy? And your mère's red cloak?"

Tears filled Ro's eyes, and she turned away, but not before she saw a hint of compassion touch the old woman's face.

"He…couldn't come with me," Ro said, not wanting the crone to think he was dead, but still salty at being left in the forest while this woman just sat here and smoked.

Even if it had led to Ro defeating the empress.

"And…someone else needed it. The cloak."

Neither of them spoke again, and soon they'd packed their bags, banked the fire, and were riding as quickly as they dared through the dark forest, straight for Allura and the summer château.

Ro stood to the side, impatient as her grandmère took time to stretch after dismounting, drink something, and light her pipe, only now walking along the invisible gate to Trêve's summer château, inspecting the spell Ro had placed.

"Very good," she muttered. "Impressive. Intricate and delicate, with a finesse not oft seen with the untrained."

Although the words themselves were flattering, the way she said them wasn't, and Ro was impatient to have her niece back in Cosette's arms, alive and well.

"Very good indeed."

"Well?" Ro demanded, unable to take it anymore. "Can you help me unravel what I did and return time to this place or not?"

Ro had already tried once and failed, to her horror. She couldn't understand *why*. Hadn't she placed the blasted thing in the first place? Her foot tapped the ground, arms tightly crossed, to keep her from slamming her fists into the thorny vines in her frustration. She should be able to do this herself!

A few puffs of smoke drifted into the blue sky before her grandmère spoke. "Non."

Ro threw her hands out to the heavens, imploring them for patience a split second before impatient words came pouring out. "Then why are we here? Who *can* help us? Would Mulan be able to do it?" She'd told her grandmère about the warrior on their journey. "If killing the empress wasn't enough, then why did we waste our time coming all the way back here—"

Ro stumbled to a halt as her grandmère's twinkling eyes met hers. "But I can do it with your help."

Ro wilted. "Good heavens. Why didn't you just say that instead of letting me go on?"

Liam smirked, and she shot him a glare. He held up his hands and backed away, pretending to soothe an unruffled horse. Her eyes went to Olt's unmounted horse, which they'd used to carry their packs, and she immediately looked away.

It hurt too much.

"One day you'll learn to hold your tongue. Humility does that to a person, and you need it in spades."

Ro ground her teeth. "Help me wake Allura, and you can teach me whatever you want."

Her grandmère's eyes flew to hers. "Is that a promise?"

Ro blinked, jolted by the intensity of her grandmère's gaze. Ro considered before she answered, knowing instinctively that her answer was important. "Oui. It is."

Satisfaction filled the old woman's gaze, and Ro regretted everything. "Bon. I will hold you to it."

Ro had no doubt she would.

"Now, come here."

Ro obeyed, not enjoying being barked at. And she just knew Liam was enjoying every minute of her discomfort.

"Feel that? You can touch the edges of the spell, like a woven tapestry. Grasp the right ones, and it will unravel. What are you doing? Pay attention!"

Ro yelped as the old woman slapped her hands. "Ouch! What was that for? What did I do?"

Grandmère reached out in a sudden motion. "If you would just—"

Ro jerked away. "Stop hitting me!" she yelled, cutting off whatever her grandmère was about to say. "Non! I am not some young girl to be bullied into whatever you want me to do. Not that a young girl *should* be poked and slapped and degraded, but still. I am a woman grown. And you will stop hitting me, right now, or I'm done. I will walk away right now."

The old woman raised an eyebrow. "You would give up on helping your niece?"

"I'll figure it out on my own." Not that she'd been overly successful thus far.

Her grandmère sniffed. "In my day, young people respected their betters."

Ro lifted her chin. "Then give me something to respect."

Absolute silence from everyone in the clearing, including Liam and her brothers.

Although Ro tried not to burn with humiliation that they'd overheard, this *needed* to be said. She kept expecting someone else to stand up for her.

It was time she stood up for herself, let her grandmère know that Ro wouldn't accept being slapped or berated or belittled constantly. No one should accept that.

The old woman eyed her for another minute. "Very well, then. Come back over here."

Ro hesitated, so she grabbed Ro's arm and yanked her over. Ro sighed. One step at a time, non?

The old woman glared. "Back to what I was saying. You pulled away. You can't do that if you don't want this to rebound and hurt a lot of people."

Trying to pivot from their previous conversation, Ro stared at her, baffled. She hadn't pulled away—she'd stood perfectly still. Not a muscle had twitched, she was sure of it. A second passed before Ro yelled at the top of her voice, "I didn't even move!"

"You can pull back in more ways than one, Demoiselle, and right then, you yanked away from the spell and threatened to snarl the whole thing before we'd even begun. What were you thinking?"

"I did nothing of the sort. I don't even know what you're talking about."

They matched each other, glare for glare, until the old woman called to everyone else in the group. "Leave us! It'll be a long day, and perhaps night, and the 'mighty huntress' has a lot to learn."

The men in the group didn't move, their eyes shifting to Ro for permission.

"Go!" Grandmère barked. "I need her cooperation. Better without spectators."

Ro couldn't imagine why they still looked to her, but she nodded once. She was willing to work with the crabby old woman. For Allura.

But surely no one this grumpy could teach her anything.

As soon as they had gone, her grandmère turned on her. "What? What is it?"

Ro just stared at her blankly.

"Why did you pull away from the spell?"

Ro didn't know how to answer. She hadn't pulled away. Had she?

The old woman sighed. "I need to know. If not, you could pull back when it matters, and little what's-her-name may not survive this." She grumbled, "Neither may we…"

Ro swallowed, hard, and wracked her brain. If she'd pulled back, which she wasn't entirely convinced she had, then what could make her do it?

She shrugged and shook her head, at a complete loss.

The old woman eyed her for an age. Then she snapped away her gaze and tottered to an old log.

Ro sagged as the weight of that gaze left her. The woman was excruciating to be around.

"Come. Sit."

Ro looked between the old woman and the château in disbelief. "But…what about Allura? What about the spell?"

She patted the log next to her. "I need to know more about the spell I'm working with, and these old bones don't like to hold me up for long spans at a time."

Yeah right. The ancient woman was spry, hunting wolves in the forest, riding horseback as if she did it every day, and keeping up with them as no other woman this old could've done. Was everything she said a falsehood?

Ro grumbled as she took herself over to the log and sat. She rested her hands on her knees and glared at the old woman. "Can we help Allura from here?"

"Where did you find the spell?"

Ro almost didn't answer, out of spite, then decided to get this over with as fast as she could. She took a deep breath and blew it out slowly.

"Trêve had a similar curse placed on him. I found it in a… book of spells. Latin. For mundane things. Like making life easier. Making your hair grow faster. Then I started noticing a pattern. Marie—that's the witch who cursed France—cobbled bits and pieces together to trap the prince. I needed to do that, but on a lesser scale. I needed to stop time and create an impenetrable barrier. So I came here and did it."

Guilt swamped her. She'd used dark magic, tainting her soul just as Marie had, making it that much easier to use the empress's unholy power.

The old woman's eyes widened. "Came here and did it yourself."

"That's what I said, isn't it?" Ro knew she sounded defensive, but she felt so guilty, her entire being ached to make it right.

"I see. How did you work the magic?"

Shame washed over Ro, and she almost couldn't answer. "I just…once I figured out what Marie did, I copied it, but smaller and stronger with more limitations and…"

"Stop."

Ro did. Gladly. She hadn't wanted anyone to know what she'd become.

"And you copied it. Just like that."

"Oui."

"Then why does guilt and shame and regret surround you like a cloud?"

Ro couldn't look at her, but she answered anyway. "Why do you think? I came here and created the very curse the sorceress used to plunge all of France into despair. I worked the same dark magic, for the same reason—to save someone I love—and cursed myself in the process. I'm no better than any of the sorceresses I fight."

"That's what you think, is it?"

Ro's eyes flew up at the surprise in the old woman's voice. "Oui. I do." She couldn't understand why the old woman was looking at her so askance. "Shouldn't I?"

A heartbeat, then the old woman exploded. "Of course not! Do you think you could've worked an enchantment so beautiful, so exquisite, so protective, if you hadn't the Creator's giftings and help?"

Ro's mouth fell open.

Her grandmère tapped her chin closed, her eyes intense

but her voice gentle. "You are a protectress. It is within you to do everything in your power to aid those in need. To work with the powers given you by the Creator."

Ro couldn't comprehend it. "But I—I did exactly what Marie did. I followed her example. I used dark magic. Evil magic."

Her grandmère's voice gentled even more, something Ro didn't think was possible. "Oh, dearest, no wonder you look so heartbroken every time a curse is mentioned."

Ro glanced away, not comfortable with all the feelings being dragged out into the open.

"Magic in and of itself isn't evil. It's the *source* of that magic —what you do with that magic—who strengthens you and whom you follow. Look around you! The stars that fill the night sky, the bud of a new seed, the creatures that prowl this green earth—those that are supposed to prowl it, anyway. All magic. All too wonderful to comprehend.

"This particular magic"—she tapped her cane in the direction of the château—"happens to come from the Realm of the Fey, entirely commonplace to them, yet just as magical as new life or the sun that rises in the sky to us. Only because their world is bleeding into ours can we sense it, and for a particular few, wield it.

"It is not evil, child. And you are not evil for harnessing it and making it your own."

Ro wasn't convinced.

"Did you not feel the Creator's help every time you needed it?"

Non, not really. She felt desperate and like He was just waiting to punish her for every misstep. Though He *had* been rather persistent in His pursuit of her...

"Did you not find the right thing to do—freeze time as only the most powerful of the fairies can do—just when you needed it?"

Ro wasn't aware it was a fey trait. But it made sense.

"Did you not answer your calling, to save and protect those given to your care?"

Finally, something she could agree with.

A gnarled hand covered her own and pulled it toward the gate. "Feel this."

Breathing deep, Ro obediently stretched out her hand. Warm light reached out and touched her hand, and Ro could see it—in her mind—stretching away from them in a web. Intricate. Beautiful. And powerfully strong.

She started to shake. She hadn't been able to see it before.

Her grandmère held her hand even tighter. "It is pure light. Not a thread of darkness. Can you not feel the Creator in every strand?"

Tears filled Ro's eyes. She could. "Oui."

"Do not shy away from this. You did not enact a curse, filled with deep, dark magic writhing with evil, coming from evil, and filling all those near you with darkness. You used your creative abilities under the power of your Creator and weaved a tapestry as only He can. You created *with* your Creator."

Tears spilled onto Ro's cheeks. "But...what about the empress? Her magic—I-I used it. That which she stole from the living to give to the dead. It felt...wrong. Oily. And I used that too."

Her grandmère chuckled. "Know you not that He uses all things for good? What happened to the magic when you touched it, when you wielded it?"

"It"—Ro blinked—"changed. Turned from green to red. Apple red. And she couldn't use it anymore."

"There you have it. Now you just need to accept what I've said and stop believing the lies. You *are* good enough. You *are* being used for His glory. You *are* changing this world for the better. And if you let Him, He'll keep using you to do so."

She'd never heard anything so beautiful in all her life. She hadn't messed up. She hadn't ruined someone else's life. She hadn't failed.

She'd done exactly what she needed to, when she needed to do it, and it was exactly what the Creator wanted her to do.

He had done it *with* her.

Ro started to cry, and the old woman pulled her into her arms and held her like her mère used to. Which only made her cry harder.

When her tears were spent, she sat up and wiped her face with her sleeves, gulping oxygen as a fish breathes water. Her face burned, but she tried to push away her embarrassment.

She'd never felt so cleansed—so free—before. The sweet forest smelled that much sweeter, the bird song that much lovelier—every color brighter.

She hadn't messed up every moment of her life since she'd been on her own. It was absolutely freeing to realize such a thing.

She peeked at her grandmère. A toothy grin met her glance.

"Now, are you ready to wake up this little girl?"

Ro gave her a true smile. "Oui."

The old woman cackled and heaved herself to her feet. "I hope you have some energy left after all that crying. This is going to be the hardest thing you've done in your entire life."

Ro groaned and followed her. But of course it would be.

39

The moment the spell fell, Ro staggered and dropped to the ground, weary down to her soul. Exhausted, head reeling, and breathing hard, Ro tried to make the world stop spinning.

Working spells was brutal. Well, un-working them, anyway.

"There we are!" The old woman, fresh as a newly unfurled flower, happily pushed open the now-visible gate, free of rose vines and thorns, leaving Ro on the ground in the dirt. Covered in sweat. So gross.

Stars were beginning to show themselves in the still light-blue sky, and Ro was thankful they'd only spent the day unraveling the spell, not the oncoming night as well.

Darya turned to Ro and frowned. "On your feet, girl! We don't have time to laze about."

Liam helped Ro stand. Just then, the clock started chiming over and over, urgent, insistent, as if warning her the deep toll was about to sound.

Grandmère's eyes widened, as if she could hear it too.

The clock appeared to Ro, larger and more solid than ever, and the hour hand clicked from the three, to the two, and started moving toward the one, as if Ro had used up all her time at once.

"What are you waiting for? Go, go!" her grandmère shouted. "Get in there and wake that little girl before it's too late!"

Liam boosted Ro up in her saddle and handed her the reins, and she pretty much fell over Fairweather's back as he took off.

Righting herself, she galloped through the gate and down the crushed-shell drive, making a beeline for the sprawling château partway hidden behind orderly rows of orange trees, the clock the only thing she could see.

Now that time had been released, she could feel it. The curse, pressing down on little Allura, increasing pressure, trying to crush her. As if in revenge, one final push from the dead empress, from the magic she'd bound to the mechanical nightingale.

Ro urged her horse faster. Once she got to the château, she launched herself from Fairweather's back and pushed through the front doors. Ro's eyes lifted, and she took in the grand staircase that split in the middle and led off to the east and west wings.

The translucent clock rested there, and a minute hand appeared, spinning madly, pushing the hour hand from the one toward the twelve.

Allura was out of time.

With a gasp, she ran up the sprawling staircase, and as she reached the split, a human-looking hand reached out of nowhere and grabbed the minute hand, stopping it seconds before it would have pushed the hour hand over.

Ro scrambled to a halt, staring.

The hands struggled against each other, the human hand squeezing tighter and tighter until light-blue blood ran from it, dripping down and disappearing.

Go, a weak female voice said.

The last thing Ro saw was ice spreading over the clock-face, freezing everything into place, including the hand stopping the clock.

She bolted the rest of the way up the stairs, down the hallways, and to little Allura's bedroom. She burst into the room and froze, gulping air. A mist had settled over Allura, greenish in hue, pressing down on her, again and again.

The little body jolted with each push.

Ro dashed forward. Part of the mist separated, came for her.

Dodging its tendrils, she ran past Allura, confusing the mist. It swirled in place a moment before following her new trajectory.

It was just the time Ro needed.

Snatching up the little jeweled nightingale, she raised it above her head and threw it straight down. It shattered against the marble.

With a scream that rivaled the empress's, the mist shattered into nothing. Ro took the poker from the fireplace and slammed it down on the music box again and again, until nothing was left but cogs, jewels, and twisted metal.

Just as Mulan's warriors had done, Ro gathered every piece, tied it in a pillowcase, and took it over to the rose still hovering in its glass and iron dome.

She held out the pillowcase. "Take this and bury it deep."

Unfurling from its metal cage, crafted from the wrought-iron table, a rose vine reached out, snatched up the broken nightingale, and sucked it away and out the window.

Ro peeked out at its progress, until it was sucked deep into the ground and buried.

The moment the vines returned to the earth, leaving nothing but one rosebush behind—its vines trailing from the ground to Allura's window, grown from the rose she'd brought—Ro returned to her niece.

Taking deep breaths, Ro collapsed on the bed, smoothed

back Allura's hair. Her love for her niece swelled, bringing tears to her eyes, but Ro didn't fight it.

She would need everything she had to call Allura Aurore back, to keep her from wandering off forever. And still that frozen clock loomed in the background.

"Allura? Can you hear me? You need to come back, sweetheart. You need to follow my voice. You need to fight. Your maman, your papa, they need you. I need you. Please come home, sweet one. Open your eyes."

Ro kept smoothing her hair, kept speaking to her, kept searching for that spark that meant Allura heard her.

The smothering pressure was gone, dead with the anchor, but still Allura slept.

Footsteps echoed down the hall, rushing toward Allura's room. Liam burst into the room, Claude and Pascal stopping at the threshold.

Ro lifted tear-filled eyes to Liam, and he swiftly came over. "What can I do?"

"Pray," she whispered, and bent her head over her niece, calling for her again and again, coaxing her back from the darkness. "You are not going anywhere, little one. It's not your time yet. Follow my voice and come back to me."

And burly, strong, gruff Liam knelt beside the bed, clasped his hands, and lifted his face to the ceiling. "Notre Père, qui es aux cieux, que ton nom soit sanctifié…"

As his steady voice murmured next to her, repeating the Lord's Prayer over and over, Ro fought the hardest battle she'd ever fought. For her niece's life.

Exhausted, Ro and Liam were close to falling asleep, voices hoarse from speaking for what felt like hours. Dusk was slowly blanketing the room in darkness, and someone had lit candles.

Allura was still asleep. Ro frowned. What else did they have to do to wake her?

"Try true love's kiss, girl."

Ro startled at her grandmère's voice. She hadn't even realized she'd entered the room. Then what she said soaked in, and Ro stared in horror. That was a real thing?

Her grandmère rolled her eyes and pointed at her own forehead. "Right there, you simpleton. If you truly love the girl, it should work."

Ro focused on Allura. She blocked everything around her —the pressure of others waiting, the weight of her grand-mère's unrelenting stare, the ice starting to crack on the clock-face—and leaned over the little girl.

"Please, Allura Aurore. Listen to my voice, come back to us. For your mother. For me. We all love you so." Ro choked a little, wanting her to wake more than anything.

Then she closed her eyes and placed a gentle kiss upon Allura's brow.

The clockface shattered instantly with a dissonant, resounding gong from the clock and a quiet sigh from whoever had been holding it back. For Ro. For Allura.

Ro's eyes flew open, and she peered into the little girl's face eagerly.

Calm blue eyes stared back.

"Allura!" Ro grasped the girl and almost strangled her in a hug. Belatedly remembering she was a stranger and Allura was most likely weak, she dropped her niece back on the bed. "Oh! Je suis désolé! I am so sorry! I am your tante—your aunt—and this is Liam, whom I'm sure you remember—"

Allura's bell-like voice rang out clearly. "I know who you are," she said, still looking at Ro.

"Oh! Really? D'accord. All right. That's—anyway, we're at your family's summer château, but the moment you feel up to it, we can take you back to Paris, to your parents—"

"Huntress, I already sent runners," Liam said quietly, and a fair bit wearily.

"Or! You can wait right here till your maman and papa get here." Ro smiled, worried she'd made a fool of herself and had scared the poor child senseless.

She wasn't good at this whole aunt thing. Yet.

But she'd get there.

"I'd like to go now, s'il vous plaît."

"Of course!" Ro jumped to her feet and looked to Liam. He shook his head with a scowl. She quickly backtracked. "But, um, wouldn't you rather wait until the sun comes up? We can go at first light."

Allura sat up and swung her feet out from under the covers. "I am quite ready to leave now." She tilted her head. "But perhaps something to eat first?"

Food. Food! Why hadn't Ro thought of food? She looked at Liam somewhat desperately.

He just smiled. "I think that can be arranged."

"On it." Claude and Pascal disengaged from where they'd apparently still been lurking and hustled off for supplies.

That's when Ro was startled by a snore, and peeked over to see her grandmère fast asleep in a rocking chair in the corner. Seriously? She'd fallen asleep that quickly?

Ro bit back a laugh and eyed her niece, who folded her hands and perched on the edge of the bed, waiting patiently. Rather well spoken for a three-year-old. And well behaved.

Of course, had she expected anything less from Cosette's daughter?

Pascal and Claude were soon back with provisions. They sat right on the floor and had a picnic in Allura's room, then Pascal gently woke their grandmère while Claude went to ready the horses.

"Huntress, I must protest leaving now, as night has fallen," Liam said, winding up to go on for a bit. "Wolves, riding in the dark, being set upon unawares—it really would be better to go in the morning."

Biting her lip, because he was right—of course he was—Ro didn't get a chance to say anything about Liam's opinion, which was clearly against a nighttime trek with the kingdom's most beloved treasure. Nor did Liam get a chance to continue.

Allura said solemnly, "Maman needs me soonest. I'm not afraid of the dark."

Ro couldn't argue with that, and apparently Liam wasn't going to either.

His eyes crinkled in that not-grin he oft wore. "As you wish, ma princesse."

Ro raised an eyebrow. Amazing how quickly he'd changed his stance. Ro had a feeling they would've spent the rest of the night arguing otherwise.

She tried not to hover *too* protectively over Allura. "Shall we take you back to your mère, then?"

The little girl stretched out her arms, and Ro lifted her and held her close.

All the way back to Paris.

40

Ro almost sobbed in relief when Paris came into view, three days later.

She'd barely slept since waking Allura. Before that, even. When had she last rested more than a few snatched hours?

Didn't matter. All that mattered was placing Allura back in Cosette's arms.

Unfortunately for Ro and her impatience, Liam had them wait outside the city until it was dark enough to enter without notice. He got them past the gates with his rank and his taciturn "private business with the king" before riding hard for the palace, Allura hidden deep within the folds of Ro's borrowed drab brown cloak.

He led them straight to a rarely used and enclosed porte cochère to a secret back entrance, used only for the king's business. Taking Allura from Ro with one arm, he then helped Ro off her horse with the other, holding her close a few moments past strictly necessary.

Ro hardly noticed. But she didn't collapse to the ground when her knees buckled, so that was a plus.

She stretched out her arms for Allura, but Liam kept hold of the girl. "Allow me, huntress."

She didn't object. But as they moved toward the secret entrance, her grandmère didn't follow. In fact, she headed in the opposite direction.

Ro paused. "Aren't you coming in too, Grandmère?"

The old woman's jaw clenched. "Non."

Ro blinked. "Then where are you going?"

"Why, to visit my grandchildren and great-grandchildren, of course." She pointed a finger at Claude and Pascal. "You two can take me. I'll stay with each of you in turn, then with your sisters."

Both brothers didn't cover their horror very well, and Ro hid a smile behind her hand. Finally, someone else would be terrorized besides her. And each of her sisters would get a taste of their own hospitality.

She wasn't excited about that. Not at all. She only wished she'd be there to see it.

Yet it still didn't make sense. "But...surely you'll join us first. Don't you wish to see Cosette?"

"I'm off to see family. *Real* family," she said, hobbling away, attached to Claude's and Pascal's elbows and pulling them along in her wake.

A trace of fury lit Ro's insides and cleared her head. "She's your granddaughter too, Grandmère."

"Non."

Ro stepped back at the low growl, the fierce look on the old woman's face.

"That usurper's kin will never be mine."

Without another word, she hobbled right outside, and Ro didn't try to stop her.

Of course. Cendre was Ro's blood sister, and she was now under the ocean half a world away.

Cosette was the Fairy Queen's daughter, hidden in Ro's family, taking Cendre's place, but...that was no reason not to make an effort to love someone in your family, whether they were born to it or not.

Anger and hurt filtered right back in.

Why didn't the Fairy Queen help Allura? Surely she was powerful enough to break a sleeping curse. Enough! Ro *would* find the Fairy Queen and she *would* demand answers, but for now, Cosette needed her daughter.

Turning resolutely toward the palace, she didn't hide her hurt quickly enough, for Liam was waiting for her and saw it. He gave her a gentle expression full of sorrow, and Ro glanced down. Straight at Allura.

Ro sucked in a breath as somber blue eyes stared back, the girl having woken at some point. Had she heard every ugly word?

From the look on her face, oui.

Fighting back fury, Ro marched up to her and gently took the girl's face into her hands. "She shouldn't have said such things. I'm sorry you heard that, and I'm *proud* to have you in my family. She'll apologize. You'll see."

Or Ro would make her.

Allura didn't answer, and Ro smoothed back her hair with a loving gesture before nodding at Liam and following them both inside.

How could her grandmère say such cruel things in the girl's hearing?

One thing was certain: they'd be having words the next time they saw each other.

Trêve was pacing madly when they were shown into the king's private office—the one he hid in when he needed to be away from prying eyes and gossipy courtiers.

With a cry, Trêve raced toward them and swept his daughter into his arms. He crushed his little girl to his chest in a fierce hug, then kissed her cheeks, over and over again.

Ro strained to look past him. "Cosette…?"

Trêve choked on his tears. "I could not tell her. I could not. In case…"

He couldn't say another word.

Ro swallowed against tears and looked away, not wanting to intrude on such a tender moment.

Trêve pulled back from the hug and gave his daughter a warm smile. "Shall we go tell your maman the good news?"

The barest of smiles touched her face, and she gave her father a single nod. "Maman needs me," she said solemnly.

He instantly carried the three-year-old girl from the room.

Leaving Ro behind.

Suddenly weary, Ro dropped into an armchair and went right to sleep.

She didn't notice when Liam covered her with a warm blanket, banked the fire, and closed the door gently behind him. She slept the whole night through and well into the next day, dead to the world.

❦

The moment she woke, Ro sat straight up. Where was she? When had she fallen asleep? Allura…

Her eyes riveted on a cheerily blazing fire, and memories came flooding back. With a relieved sigh, she sank into the chair and pulled the blanket up over her shoulders.

Even with a full night's rest—or however long it had been—she was weary to her core. She'd been going so long and so hard, all she wanted to do was sit here and stare into the fire. For days, possibly.

As if someone had been watching for her to wake, the door opened, and servants bustled in, adding logs to the fire, setting a tray next to her chair, and filling it to the brim with steaming food, cool water, and a café service.

Then she was left alone again, and she dug in, ravenous.

The moment she finished, everything was cleared away

and a servant stopped before her and curtsied. "Bonjour, Mademoiselle. The royal family requests your presence in the nursery."

Heart pounding wildly, Ro jumped to her feet and followed the servant. Too many emotions swirled through Ro that she dared not let one loose or she'd stop in the middle of the hallway and sob.

They reached the nursery door. The servant pushed it open and bobbed another curtsy, gently urging Ro through when she didn't move.

Ro emerged upon a scene straight from a fairy-tale painting. A mop of stunning golden curls bounced in a stream of sunlight as Allura played a rousing round of—something—with her dolls.

Ro nearly fainted with relief. She was all right. She was all right!

It hadn't been a dream.

Next came her sister's beaming face as she launched herself at Ro.

"Oh, Rose, I can't thank you enough!" Cosette said. "You brought my daughter back to me! As I knew you would. Did you get enough rest? Something to eat?"

Ro's heart was too full to even speak. She just held her sister, trying to choke back her emotions. She barely noticed as Trêve passed by, briefly placing a hand on her shoulder, and closed the door behind himself and Liam.

When Ro could finally speak, she said, "I was so… worried. I thought…I thought…"

And she burst into tears. Not wanting her sister to see, she covered her face and cried harder. All of it caught up with her. All of it.

The stress of her journey. Olt's loss, even if it was temporary. Especially if it wasn't. Her mère's cloak left behind. Fighting so hard for Allura's life, wondering in the back of her mind if it was too late.

That stupid clock counting down at the worst possible times.

Months—years—of stress came out in a torrent, and Ro might've felt bad had she been able to control its release in any way. As the torrent ebbed, Cosette bent slightly, another body joined them, and small arms wrapped around Ro's neck.

Ro jerked back, startled out of her tears.

A serious little face returned her stare, even more cherubic in such a picturesque setting. "Tante Rosette, ça va?"

Ro blinked, her mouth forming an O and staying that way.

Cosette gave her a warm smile and cradled the little body close. "Your aunt is just fine, ma petite chérie."

Little darling was right. Had there ever been a more beautiful child?

Ro still couldn't string two words together.

"Darling Rosette, meet your niece. Allura Aurore, this is your tante."

"I know," the little girl said simply. "I met her already, Maman. Elle est très belle."

Ro flushed, though she had no idea why. Beautiful? Her? She'd never been described that way before. Well, except by Olt.

Whom she was not thinking about right now.

"Wouldn't she?" Cosette prodded.

Ro snapped out of her thoughts. "Pardon?"

Cosette gave her a patient smile, one that warmed Ro. "You would love to see the rest of her dolls, oui?"

"Oh. Ah, oui."

Cosette set her daughter down, and the little girl clasped Ro's fingers and pulled her across the rugs, chattering the whole way. Ro could hardly keep up with what she was saying, but soon Ro held the dolls she was allowed to play with, while the setting and the script were laid out in great detail.

What was happening right now? How had the little girl so

thoroughly wrapped Ro around her finger, so much so that she'd gotten Ro to play *dolls*?

A dizzying thirty minutes later, Cosette laughed and held out her hand to Ro. "Enough, ma petite chère. It is my turn to hold your aunt's attention all to myself."

Ro had never been more thankful in her life. She'd never cared for dolls as a child, and being told what to play, how to play it, and exactly what to say was a whole new experience.

Allura smiled prettily and went back to playing by herself, allowing Cosette to pull Ro into a chair next to her own. They talked quietly about everything and nothing, sticking to safe topics. Which, in all honesty, was exactly what Ro needed.

Then Ro leaned forward and dropped her voice.

"Has she said anything about—you know?" Ro tilted her head toward Allura, not sure how to finish. How to ask without saying too much.

Cosette shook her head and moved closer. "I haven't been able to get her to tell me anything. Not that I'm pressing! Not yet, anyway. She'll tell me in her own time, that I'm sure of."

As if they hadn't been whispering at all, Allura spoke up from the far side of the room. "Oh, but I had such pleasant dreams while I was asleep, Maman."

Heads together, Cosette and Ro looked up at the same time. Cosette frowned slightly. "What was that, my darling?"

The little girl continued to play with her dolls. "A beautiful fairy came and sat with me, and we played games together."

"Games?" It was Ro's turn to frown, although Cosette had already smoothed away the wrinkle-causing expression.

"Oh yes, all kinds of lovely games. And she held my hand when I was scared. We were surrounded by a lovely wood, and the birds kept calling and asking me to come play, but she told me to stay right next to her and wait for my tante to wake me up."

Knowing instantly who she was talking about, Ro could only stare, stunned. While feeling horrible for being furious with the Queen of the Fairies. But why hadn't she told either of them she'd been with the little girl the whole time? Why let them worry so?

"Did you…know who was with you?" Cosette asked. "In the dream?"

Allura shrugged and raised a cup to her doll's mouth, carefully feeding her the pretend drink. "She was very nice, and she would hold me and sing to me when I cried."

"But why were you crying, ma chère?"

The little girl still played with her dolls, but her face turned serious and took on some of the fear she must've felt in her dreamworld.

Or wherever she'd actually been. The Realm of the Fey, perhaps?

"The birds wouldn't stop asking me to come play, and sometimes they told me I was mean for not going with them."

"Why didn't you?" Ro asked.

The little girl answered matter-of-factly. "She said if I went, I would not see my maman again for a very long time or get to meet my tante, who was fighting so very hard for me, so I stayed."

Ro and Cosette exchanged glances.

"And what frightened you, my darling?" Cosette asked.

"During one of our games, while she was telling me a story, the birds' song changed."

"Changed how, my love?"

The little girl shrugged, concentrating harder on her dolls. "They started screaming. Falling to the ground and dying, arrows sticking out of them."

Cosette's hand flew to her mouth. Ro just sat there, stunned.

"She held me, turned my face away. Sang to me. Rocked me. Rubbed my back and told me not to look. That it was going to be all right."

Then she looked straight at Ro, as if she knew.

Ro swallowed, her throat burning. "Did the beautiful fairy tell you anything else?"

She bit her pink tongue between small, evenly spaced teeth and thought a moment before brightening. "Oh! Not really. But she hurt her hand, and she wouldn't let me see. And when the birds all went away, she wiped my tears, kissed my forehead, and gave me the most glorious smile. Then I woke up to find you leaning over me."

Her eyes shifted toward Cosette, then widened. "Why, Maman, whatever is the matter? Why are you crying? Did I do something wrong?"

Visibly distressed, the girl clutched a doll to her chest.

Cosette choked on a half-laugh, half-sob and opened her arms wide. "Non, ma chérie, you did exactly right. I am so proud of you."

Allura launched herself into her mère's arms, but her little face was still distressed at the tears streaming down Cosette's cheeks.

Cosette stroked her daughter's hair. "I am just so happy to have you back with us, my darling." She held Allura gently a moment before saying, "Be a good little girl and ask Cook for some pastries?"

Allura brightened and ran off, not giving either of them a backward glance.

"Take Chantie with you!" Cosette called.

"Oui, Maman," came her sweet little voice, then she was gone.

Cosette sighed. "She has been so serious since she woke up. Now I understand why. What she's been through!" She stood, dabbing at her face with a lacy handkerchief and laughing self-consciously. "Excuse-moi, but there is someone I must thank. Right away."

Ro nodded, but she doubted that Cosette saw as she flitted off to thank the Queen of the Fairies—her mère—for staying with her granddaughter and protecting her while she slept.

Protecting her more than Cosette even knew. Stopping a clock, perhaps?

The door closed behind her, leaving Ro in blessed silence. She sat quietly. And, thankfully, Cosette knew her well enough to have the servants leave her alone and let her process.

"Merci beaucoup," she whispered to both the Fairy Queen and the Creator. She had no doubt both heard and each knew to whom she was thanking for what.

Only then did Ro notice her own tears and swiftly tried to do away with them. But more tears came, and Ro allowed them.

It wasn't a torrent, a wild storm, such as earlier, but a gentle cleansing, washing away the last of her worry, heartbreak, and even frustration when she couldn't save those she loved.

Because this time…she had.

And the darling little girl was now with her parents, just as she should be, and the witch was dead, just as she should be, and Olt's family was free, just as they should be.

All was as it should be.

Except for her heart.

That still hurt very much.

41

Ro paced her room, unable to get used to being back in Paris. The crowds, the sedate lifestyle, the utter ease of everyone else in the world except for her.

It wasn't fair.

She also might be feeling the slightest bit sorry for herself.

Ro settled into a chair facing the street, chin in hand. Wagons, carriages, and hackneys rumbled by, while people with bright parasols and dapper frock coats strolled on the other side of the street, enjoying the parc Cosette had planted for anyone's use.

Not one of them was worried about curses, swans, magical queens, or missing someone until every part of them ached...

Ro jumped to her feet and paced madly. Well of course she missed Olt! The last she'd seen him, he'd lost an arm and was being hustled away to recuperate with his long-lost family — while she was running in the other direction, toward her niece.

A letter from his family had snuffed out any idea she had of going after him.

They'd asked to care for him, for her to give him space while he healed, all while thanking her profusely for services

425

rendered to the royal family. She didn't know if it was solely his family's request or Olt's as well, but the message that Olt didn't want to see her came through loud and clear.

Even if she longed to saddle Fairweather and go after him right this very minute.

A sheaf of papers caught her eye, as well as a full inkpot and a trimmed quill. She flipped through the papers. All deliciously blank.

She wouldn't put it past her sister to have left this here specifically for her, knowing she needed to vent. Silently. Instead of at people.

Unable to stand being alone with herself another minute, not wanting to seek anyone else out to be miserable with her, Ro pulled the sheets toward herself, sat down, and removed the cap from the inkpot. Then she dipped the quill in and wrote across the page in elegant, looping letters, ending with a flourish.

La Belle au Bois Dormant, or The Sleeping Beauty—

She chewed on the end of her featherless quill. She didn't want the girl placed under a sleeping curse to be a child—it was too soon for that—but each time she'd experienced something, something she needed to process, it came spilling out in story.

Perhaps little Allura Aurore would want to read it one day.

What was a good fictional name? Persinette? Or should that be the name of a girl locked in a tower, only able to raise and lower guests by her ridiculously long hair? What of the six swans? Or should that be a separate fairy tale altogether?

Non, non, non. She was getting ahead of herself. *Sleeping Beauty* first, *then* other tales. What about naming her Briar Rose?

Ro scribbled madly, liberally changing details, making the story more fanciful and beautiful than what had actually happened, bending it to how she'd wished events had taken place, not how they actually had.

And it freed her from worrying about Olt for a blessed day and a half.

Until Cosette interrupted by marching in and handing her a leatherbound book. Without saying a word.

"What's this?" Ro turned over the slim volume. It was beautifully bound, with a lovely gilded cover tooled in rich burgundy leather. She glanced up when Cosette didn't answer.

A mysterious smile played about her lips. "Read the title, ma chère."

She flipped the book open to the title page and scanned what was printed there.

La Belle et la Bête by Madame Gabrielle-Suzanne Barbot de Villeneuve.

That sounded familiar...

She froze. Eyes wide. Gaze flying to Cosette's.

Cosette's smile deepened, revealing dimples. "Surprise!"

"Did you—what did—is this—what is this?"

Cosette looped her arm through Ro's and made her leave her room for the first time in days, practically dragging Ro along as their footsteps echoed down the hallway. "I read the whole thing in a snap, and I loved it. Loved it, Ro! It reminded me so much of when we'd stay up late and you'd tell me your wild, fanciful tales."

Ro couldn't help her small smile. And Cosette had still believed her when she'd claimed to see a castle in the woods that no one else could. Incroyable.

Cosette shrugged, the motion so lovely and French, it reminded Ro of how much she'd missed her sister the long years she'd been away. She held Cosette's arm just a little tighter.

"What can I say? I passed it to my Mesdemoiselles-in-waiting. They loved it as well, so I sent it to a publisher."

Ro gasped. "You didn't!"

"I most certainly did."

Ro went to cover her face with her hand and ended up smacking herself with her book. "Ow!"

"Rosette! Are you all right?" Cosette's eyes were sparkling as she tried desperately not to laugh aloud.

Ro tucked her book—her book—her book!—under her other arm and rubbed her face. "I'm fine, it's just—Cosette, but of course they published it since you sent it to them. You're their *queen*."

Cosette laughed, the merry sound bouncing down the hallway and making everything in her gorgeous palace that much more charming. "But of course I thought of that!" She winked. "That's why I didn't tell them who sent it."

Ro groaned and wanted to sink onto the nearest chair. Cosette, seeming to know her every want or need, had led her in a giant loop of palace hallways back to her own room, letting her clear her head then returning her to solitude. She led Ro to the nearest window seat and settled her there without Ro even noticing.

"But, Cosette, they would've seen the return address."

Cosette's eyes twinkled. "I had someone deliver it."

"But, but…" Ro couldn't wrap her mind around it.

Cosette just laughed. "Are you not pleased to see your book in print? To hold it in your hands?"

Ro couldn't say. She just stared at it, mixed between feeling like it was a snake about to bite her and a present she wanted to tear open and revel in for hours.

A soft kiss landed on her temple. "I will leave you to it, my darling. Simply ask François where to find me when you're done."

Ro didn't even notice her float away. She inspected every page leading to the first chapter, and once she was there, she lost herself in the book.

A tale of a beautiful maiden winning and taming the heart of a beast.

A story she'd written.

&

Ro found herself standing outside Cosette's chambers, hand poised to knock.

The door opened, and Ro startled.

Cosette's personal maid stood there, nightcap on, bleary smile on her face.

"Her Majesté said to come right in."

Ro stumbled into the room. When she entered Cosette's sitting room, Cosette was bundling herself in a wrap and settling on the settee.

"Come in, my dear. Margot, please send for a little café?"

Margot curtsied. "I shall make it myself, Madame et Mademoiselle."

Cosette sent her a thankful, absent smile before turning back to Ro. "Well? What did you think?"

"It's…it's magnifique. I—I can't believe I wrote that. At all. Are you…sure I wrote it?"

Cosette beamed at her. "Well done, chérie. I am so proud of you."

That mischievous smile was just too much.

Tears filled Ro's eyes. "How could you?"

At the dismayed look on Cosette's face, Ro wished she could take the words back. Yet she meant every syllable. What was Cosette thinking, putting her work out like this?

"I wrote this for you. Only you. It's a ridiculous little story, nothing but fluff, no substance whatsoever, and now it's out there for everyone to see. Why would you do this to me?"

And she burst into tears.

For the love of all the saints. What was wrong with her? Ugh.

"Oh, Rosette!" Cosette gathered her in her arms and let her cry.

Words came pouring out as fast as her tears. "What if everyone hates it? What if it isn't any good? What if other people"—and by other people she meant Liam. Claude. Pascal. Trêve. And oh good heavens, Olt!—"find out I wrote this silly, nonsensical piece and tease me for the rest of my life!"

"Ro…"

Ro could hear the smile in her sister's voice, and it made her cry more bitterly. She had been wronged. *Wronged.*

"Aren't we being the teeniest, tiniest bit dramatic, my darling?" Cosette asked gently.

Non, she most certainly was *not* being dramatic. Besides, she was on a roll here.

"What if the only reason they published it is because it came from the palace and they were too scared not to?" She gasped and sprang up, nearly knocking Cosette in the chin. "Oh my merciful heavens, have they sold any copies? Has anyone else read it?" Her hands flew to her face. "Has anyone talked to you about it? What did they say?"

Cosette laughed and settled Ro's flailing arms in her lap. "Stay here. I'll be right back. I have something to show you."

And she danced out of the room, leaving Ro to her misery.

Ro dropped her head in her hands and groaned. How could this have happened? Everyone in her family hated her stories. Hated them. Ridiculed her for them. Cosette only listened because she was the kindest person—fairy—half-fairy?—whatever she was, she was the kindest—in all the realms.

Cosette danced back into the room, and Ro felt a fresh wave of despair. How could her own sister be so blissfully happy about her misery?

She held out a slip of paper triumphantly. "Regarde!"

Ro squinted at the paper, her bleary eyes working hard to read it. She rubbed them. What time was it anyway?

"You read the night away."

Ro squinted up at her. Had she said that aloud? Come to think of it, she was rather tired... Cosette grinned, and Ro noticed for the first time that Cosette's hair was quite perfectly tousled, she was in her night wrap, and it was dark out.

"Dawn will soon peek over the horizon, dearest."

Ro gasped. "And I woke you..."

"Never mind that. I was expecting you to." She nodded at the scrap of paper again. "Read it. Go on."

Ro did. And gasped again at the number of livres written upon it—with the false name she'd used for the story. "What —what is this?"

Cosette bounced on her toes. "Ro, everyone loves it! Your story is selling so many copies. The publishers have inquired if the author has written anything more." Her smile turned positively feline. "You have written more stories, haven't you?"

Oui, something ridiculous about mermaids. And then that latest bit about a sleeping beauty. Just for fun. But *those* would never see the light of day.

Ro couldn't in all good conscience answer, but something in her face must've given it away.

"Aha! I knew it!" Cosette gave an excited, yet still ladylike, little dance.

Ro had no idea how she managed it, but everything Cosette did was ladylike.

She pounced onto the settee next to Ro and leaned close, her words pouring out in her excitement. "No one need know who's writing the stories. You can write to your heart's content, then give them to me, and I'll make sure they get to the publisher. Put a different name on each one, if you like." She nodded at the paper still in Ro's hands. "And I'll make sure you get those. Nothing to it."

She grinned mischievously.

Ro blinked. Nothing to it? She may have written the first story in one sitting—once she'd started, she couldn't stop—but it had completely drained her, and she'd slept for a week after. It was exhausting. Yet exhilarating. She didn't know what to say.

Someone lightly knocked on the door.

"You may come in, Margot."

The outer door opened, and the maid entered with a tray. Ro paid little mind to what was on it, but soon Cosette was handing her a steaming mug.

"Here, chérie. This will warm you and help you think."

Ro just stared into the lightly colored brew as Cosette sipped hers.

Cosette chuckled. "Margot, will you see that my sister makes it back to her room? And that she's not disturbed for any reason tomorrow until she wishes it?"

"But of course, votre Majesté."

Ro's head swirled as Cosette helped her stand and walked her back to her room. Cosette saw that she was tucked in—which made her smile—dropped a light kiss on her forehead, and left with the servant.

Apparently Cosette wasn't the only one who had trouble letting servants do everything for her.

Ro finished her café as she watched the sun rise, then slipped under the blankets and fell into a fitful slumber.

Her last thought was of the sirène manuscript she'd written on her voyage and tucked into her satchel for safe-keeping.

She was terrified Cosette would find it and publish it before she'd even had a full night's rest.

42

Ro came into the room and halted, staring in shock. Grandmère sat with Cosette, easy as you please, both of them sipping café, with a halfway plundered plate of pastries between them.

Ro forced herself not to stare at the delicate pastries, but she didn't bother doing the same with her grandmère.

"What are you doing here?" she blurted.

"Rosette, please," Cosette chided. "Is that any way to welcome your grandmother?"

The old woman cackled and got heavily to her feet. "No matter. I came to train you, as I said I would."

Ro crossed her arms and jutted out her chin. "Non."

"Non? Going back on your word already, are we?" the old woman said lightly, but her eyes flashed.

"Rosette, *please* be kinder, if only that she is your elder…" Cosette rubbed her temple.

"Apologize first," Ro said, not looking away from her grandmère.

Both women startled and looked at each other, then back to her. "I beg your pardon?" Cosette asked.

Grandmère said nothing.

433

"Have you? Apologized?" Ro persisted. "Because I'm not going anywhere with you or placing myself under your tutelage until you *make this right*."

The elder and younger LeFèvre glared at each other, neither budging, and Cosette wisely kept silent, watching them in turn.

"And if I don't?"

Ro couldn't speak for half a moment, so blinded was she by the injustice of it. She stepped forward and spoke quietly, urgently, so that Cosette couldn't hear.

"She heard you. She *heard* you, Grandmère. Those are the kinds of words that bury deep and torment you for the rest of your life. You *will* go to her, and you *will* explain yourself and apologize, or we are done. Forever."

A scraggly eyebrow rose. "You would throw away the family you only just found, just like that?"

"To protect Allura? In a heartbeat."

Cosette frowned. "What are you saying?"

She apparently wasn't used to being unable to overhear conversations, especially those happening right in front of her. Ro had somehow cloaked her and Grandmère's words. On purpose.

Ro stepped back and released whatever she'd done.

"Shall I escort you back to your cabin, Grandmère?" Ro asked with forced politeness.

"Oh, very well. Have it your way." She plunked herself down in the chair she'd vacated. "Bring the child to me. These old bones don't work like they used to."

Cosette looked between them, but she went and got Allura herself. The child's smile dimmed when she saw the old woman, and she wouldn't let Cosette put her down. Cosette settled her daughter in her lap, and Ro moved to stand protectively at their side.

Grumbling a little, Grandmère plunged right in. "Now see here, girl. I might've maybe said some things that I ought not.

Think you can forgive a foolish old woman for being tetchy at the end of a long ride?"

Allura just stared at the old woman without a change to her expression, but Cosette looked up at Ro with wide eyes. Ro kept her gaze where it was, urging the cranky old lady to continue and do this right.

"All right. How to say this so you understand? You know how your tante here is my granddaughter, but your maman ain't? Well see here, your grandmama, the Fairy Queen, stole my granddaughter, who your maman replaced, and I had to go get her back, see?"

Cosette's lips grew thinner with every word. She reached for Ro's hand, and Ro clasped it tightly.

"Well, I got something against the Queen of the Fairies for that, but I shouldn'ta taken it out on you. So for that I apologize."

Ro's grandmère sat back with a grunt, as if she'd just completed an arduous task.

Allura gave a solemn nod, and Cosette rose in a flurry of skirts. "Time for a nap, my love, wouldn't you say?" She headed straight for the door and said to Ro in an aside, "A word?"

Ro followed her out. Cosette spun on Ro the moment they were out of earshot. "That woman is *never* to come near my babe again, do you hear me? Never."

Ro blinked, unsure of what to say. Didn't Cosette want someone who had said such things to her daughter to apologize?

"Don't be mad, Maman. She lost everyone, just like you did once, only she didn't handle it so well." Allura patted Cosette's cheeks in a sympathetic manner. "And she never got most everyone back, like you did. Well, not till now."

Cosette choked on a half-laugh, half-sob. "Out of the mouth of babes…"

Ro was horrified that she might've made the situation

worse. "I'm sorry, Cosette, truly. I—thought I was doing the right thing. That I was making *her* do the right thing." Ro scuffed her boot on the thick runner. "I never would've insisted otherwise."

Cosette sighed. "I see. Well, perhaps I spoke too hastily." She glanced at Allura, and at her encouraging smile, said, "Perhaps she can stay for dinner?"

Ro immediately said, "Oh, I have no problem asking her to move on. There's no way she could've visited all our sisters in…how long has it been? Two months?"

And still no word from Olt.

Cosette laughed. "Two weeks. And if she has truly been staying with our sisters, perhaps that is punishment enough." She rose to her tiptoes and kissed Ro's cheek. "I'll see you at dinner." Cosette turned a beaming smile upon her daughter. "Come now, my darling. Let's rest those pretty eyes of yours."

And Allura went off quite happily to be put to bed, making Ro absolutely certain she had fairy blood instead of Reynard roots.

Ro waited till they rounded the corner before returning to the receiving room and her grandmère.

"Decided not to send me away, have you?" her grandmère said grouchily.

"It was a near thing." Ro reached for a pain au chocolat, pretending not to notice her grandmère's startled expression. "Allura spoke for you."

"I see," she finally said, a touch of chagrin in her voice for the first time.

Ro bit into the pastry, nearly moaning aloud as chocolate drenched her tastebuds. She could easily eat this every day, for every meal.

"You sure you're not needed back home?" she said around a mouthful, without heat.

"Naw. Old man Gustave can take care of things for a bit.

Give me a stretch of a break. Besides, you need to be trained! Might as well do that. You've got lots to catch up on."

Oh joy. Ro tried very hard not to grumble, but she might make herself scarce in the coming weeks. Then again, she did want to know how her magic worked…

She sighed. She'd just have to bear it as long as she was able.

"Oh, quit your huffing and puffing. You'll thank me when this is all over, you'll see."

Ro very much doubted that, but she'd force herself to. If it was actually helpful. Maybe.

"Now, show me this book of supposed spells you used for the little one, and I'll tell you if we need to burn it or can use it." Grandmère looped her arm through Ro's and pulled her out of the room.

Ro stared longingly at the pastries they were leaving behind. "What was all that talk about the source? Magic being inherently good and whatnot?"

Grandmère tapped her nose. "We gotta see if the book itself is a good source, or if the writer has tainted it with necromancy, divination, and other rotten things not to be used. For instance…"

Grandmère hobbled off while she waxed eloquent about the dos and don'ts of their craft, Ro waiting patiently next to the right corridor whenever she hobbled down the wrong one, and eventually they found the library, Grandmère in the lead the whole way.

Her eyes brightened as soon as they rested on the tome. "Ah! Good old Matilda's handiwork. If that ain't good old-fashioned fey magic, I don't know what is."

And she plopped herself in King Trêve's chair behind his desk and started outlining the finer points of fey magic, and how a select few humans on earth could wield it.

&

"The family is in the portrait gallery," François said in imperious tones, when Ro asked where she might find them.

Ro's heart sank. Where on earth was that? The Parisian palace was just so blasted monstrous.

"Shall I show you?" François asked, still the perfect maître d'hôtel, or master of Trêve's household, after all these years.

Ro's entire being relaxed. "Oui, s'il vous plaît," she said in relief. Then she glanced over her shoulder. "But, uh, could we hurry? And if…anyone…tries to find me, perhaps you could take them the long way around?"

Then again, every part of the palace felt like the long way to Ro. François tilted his head and led her away at a fast clip.

Ro never thought she'd be happy to escape the library, but there she was, barely a week into her training with Grand-mère, desperate to join the family a few hours before dinner, just to chat.

Trêve raised an eyebrow when she came in, and she gave him a look that said, "I know, I can't believe it either," even as Cosette rushed over with hands outstretched, face glowing.

"Rosette! You decided to join us." She kissed Ro's cheeks and squeezed her hands, still smiling as if Ro had just come from across the sea, not from elsewhere in the palace.

Ro mustered a smile for her sister. "Oui. I, uh, had the time."

Claude snorted. "More like she's escaping Grandmère, I imagine," he said, then grunted when Pascal elbowed him. "What? You know it's true."

Glancing over her shoulder, Ro sent a smirk her brothers' way, but just then, Liam moved into her line of sight and caught it instead. He smiled at her, obviously thinking she was glad to see him.

Cosette had already started to move away, but she must've caught a whiff of some kind of drama happening nearby, for her head whipped around. She eyed both Liam and Ro in turn, looking for all the world like she was up to something.

Ro nodded stiffly at Liam and glanced away.

He sidled right up to her anyway. "How fares our sweet princess?" he asked, far too much hope in his voice.

Ro shrugged and took the offered champagne from a servant a bit desperately. "You would know better than I," she said, somewhat grouchily. "You spend all your time protecting her, and mine is wasted, I mean, *spent*, with my grandmère."

She gulped her drink, realized what it was, and spit it right back out into her glass flute. Then she froze and peeked at Liam.

His eyes danced with laughter. "I take it your training is going well, then?"

"Oh, yes, hmm. I guess so," Ro said, handing her champagne back to the waiter, who took it with a look of disgust.

Just then, François announced someone, but Ro didn't catch what he said because she turned her head.

And her eyes met Olt's.

She gasped. What was he doing here? He looked like he was going to fall over any minute!

A little pale, a little shaky, his empty sleeve wrapped around his waist and pinned to the opposite side, Olt searched her eyes, desperately, like he wanted to say something.

Mouth suddenly dry, Ro hurried over, dread growing like a leaden ball in her stomach with every step. She'd been vulnerable, told her secrets to a stupid swan *because* he couldn't talk. She'd had no idea she was baring her heart to Olt every time.

She stopped before him, and they stared at each other, neither saying a word. All Ro wanted to do was throw her arms around him and tell him how much she'd missed him, how glad she was to see him, but her courage failed her. Anxiety filled her.

And he did *not* look encouraged by whatever colors he could see over her head.

"Ro, I had to come…"

The rest of the party crowded them, exclaiming over Olt and asking after his well-being. He smiled politely and gave short answers, peeking at Ro every chance he got.

At a lull, he said, "Actually, I came to return this."

Olt pulled Ro's red cloak, perfectly repaired and somewhat freshly laundered, from his satchel.

Ro gasped, snatched it from his hands, and held it close. It smelled like him.

Something inside her settled at having her mère's cape back. She'd felt unclothed without it, constantly reaching to run her fingers along its silky satin edge only to find its comforting presence missing.

"Is that the only reason you've come?" Cosette asked in an impeccably innocent manner, though even Ro could hear the glee in her voice.

Olt flicked a glance at Ro, but said, "My family would like to open talks between our kingdoms. I…agreed to represent them."

Trêve beamed. "It is good to hear from our neighboring kingdom. Perhaps our new ambassador would also like to choose a townhouse nearby while we discuss terms? Though you are welcome to stay at the palace as long as you like."

Olt flicked another glance at Ro, but she just stood there, frozen, unable to respond with so many watching. Especially her devious sister.

"That would be…good." Olt deflated a little, but he kept the polite smile plastered on his face while he shook the king's hand.

Feeling a thousand times the fool for thinking he'd come back just for *her*, Ro let the others widen the distance between them as conversation resumed.

Just then, Liam settled at Ro's shoulder like a thundercloud, glaring at Olt like he was staking a claim.

Oh good heavens.

When Cosette informed Olt that Allura was awake and

well, he gave Ro a melting smile. "I'm so glad," he said in a low voice that rumbled its way through every nerve in her body. "I knew you would do it. How have you been?"

"She's been just fine," Liam said, crossing his burly arms. "Busy settling into the palace, taking up her duties here. She's very important. To us. Here."

Ro scowled at him. What duties?

Before she could hotly inform him that she could speak for herself, Cosette spoke right over her. "Rosette, take a turn with me about the room, s'il vous plaît?"

Cosette held out her elbow.

"I, uh, sure." Ro hastily tied on her cloak, and although she felt absolutely ridiculous doing so, she took Cosette's arm and strolled alongside her in a wide loop around the gallery. Massive portraits loomed over their heads.

Seriously, had one of them tipped over, Ro didn't think they could escape fast enough, they were that big.

Ro growled a little as she watched Liam and Olt glare at each other, though Olt's wasn't as fierce. What in the world was he doing, traveling all this way so soon after his injury? And he needn't rise to Liam's bait.

She waited to speak until they were out of the men's hearing—she hoped. "What in all the realms is wrong with them?"

"Why, they're both in love with you, dearest."

Ro yelped and nearly fell over. She spun on Cosette and gave her sister her best scowl. "Warn a person before you dump such news upon them, will you?"

Cosette just smiled. "And miss a reaction such as that? I don't think so." She winked.

Ro sniffed and turned away, hoping Cosette would let it be. She should've known better.

Cosette claimed her arm once more and casually observed the two men making fools of themselves—over Ro. "So tell me, which one do you prefer?"

Ro's gaze swung back to Cosette. She was certain her expression was positively horrified, as was the rest of her. "Which one do I *prefer*?"

"Olt or Liam. You hold both their hearts. Who holds yours?"

Ro crossed her arms. "I don't do love triangles."

Cosette's merry laugh bounced throughout the vast chamber, drawing everyone's attention. She was enjoying this far too much. "Of course you don't, dear, but you happen to be smack-dab in the middle of one."

Now Ro had three people she wanted to strangle. She waited until everyone had turned back to whatever portraits they were perusing to speak. "Look, I kind of want to ignore everything and hope it goes away. Is that too much to ask?"

Cosette tugged Ro's arms free, looped her arm through Ro's, and continued their slow circuit around the vast room. "Do you truly think that will work?"

Ro grumbled a little under her breath.

"What was that, dear?"

Ro sighed. "Perhaps not."

Cosette patted her arm. "That's what I thought."

Ro tried to tug her arm away, but Cosette held on, unhurried and without a care in the world. Well of course. She was only Queen of France, and Ro, a lowly huntress with men problems. Plural. Ugh.

"May I offer some advice, dearest?"

"Only if you say it quickly then promise never to speak of this again."

Cosette's pearly teeth gleamed too bright and her rosebud lips were far too perfect for anyone's good. Or her own. "You know I won't."

Ro grumbled.

As they came to a stop under a portrait that took up most of one wall, Cosette gently turned Ro to face her. "Do not lead them on, my darling. Confess your feelings to the one who holds your heart, and respect the other enough to let him know where your heart lies. Lend him the strength to move on."

Ro could only stare, horrified. Like she was ever having *that* conversation.

"Or," Ro pointed out helpfully, "I don't have to decide. Nor do I have to speak to either of them about this. Ever. We can all just go on as we are. Friends and confidantes and companions. All good *friends*, specifically."

As if Ro hadn't uttered a word, Cosette said, "Believe me, it's best to put them out of their misery right away. Then we'll have no more of…whatever that was."

"What happened to your earlier advice of letting them figure out what they want?"

Cosette led her once more in an easy stroll. "I think you're far past that, Rosette. Watching those two vie for your attention—it isn't right."

Ro wholeheartedly agreed. "Tell me about it."

Cosette studied her. "Perhaps neither holds your heart?" Ro didn't respond. "You know, two particularly fetching noblewomen have been badgering me to introduce them to Olt and Liam. Well, before Olt left, anyway. Perhaps you'd like me to do so?"

"Olt? Interested in someone else?" Lightheaded, Ro could've sworn the room spun as her stomach took a freefall like she was once again plunging from the mast of a ship.

Ro composed herself and turned a suspicious gaze upon her sister.

She looked no less satisfied than the cat that practically ran the palace. "I see." She stretched up on her tiptoes and dropped a kiss on Ro's cheek. "Then I suggest you think about what I said, then perhaps speak with Olt?"

Ro's head reared back. "Olt? What do you mean, Olt? To discourage him or encourage him? What about Liam?"

Ro lifted a hand to her forehead. Why was this so confusing?

Hunting. She needed to go hunting. By herself. For several months. Years, even.

"Vos Majestés," came François's dry tones from the main doorway. "Dîner is served."

Cosette grinned and squeezed her sister's hand, then moved to her husband's side.

Ro stared after her, feeling more frustrated than before. How could she possibly talk to Olt when all she'd done was push him away? When he'd only come back to be an ambassador? *Especially* after abandoning him in the Black Forest.

And Cosette thought Liam loved her too? Well that was just ridiculous. Attraction, maybe. Love? Hardly.

She had half a mind to take Captain Red up on her offer and run away to be a pirate with her and travel all over the Caribbean.

Ro eyed the men, and Liam caught her eye and winked. She spun on her heel, face flaming, wishing she hadn't chosen to join them for dinner.

Perhaps going back to the library and her grandmère's incessant "Non, *this* way" wasn't such a bad idea after all.

❧

Why wouldn't Cosette stop *talking*? That's all she did, prattle on and on about everything and nothing at all.

And Liam. He hadn't left her side. He'd even wedged himself between her and Olt at the dinner table. She sent a growly look his way.

All he did was stare back, defiantly, like he was challenging her to do something about it. Or to tell him his attention was unwanted.

She refused to think Cosette might be right.

All she wanted was a word alone with Olt. Was that too much to ask?

Ro watched his every move. Just to make sure he was all right, of course.

Not because she couldn't soak him in fast enough.

But every time Olt's eyes met hers, she flushed and looked down, unable to say a word for the entire meal, completely ill at ease.

Although he'd been peppered with questions, he'd grown quieter and quieter, the hopeful look fading from his eyes the more he watched Ro's avoidance and Liam's frustrating behavior, and Cosette increased her chatter to a frenzy to make up for how awkward the meal was growing.

Until Ro had a headache the size of the château's ballroom.

Which they were currently in, because Cosette wanted their opinion on the upcoming ball she was throwing in someone's honor. Ro hadn't caught whom. She'd been too busy trying not to stare at Olt nonstop. While avoiding him.

But what could she do? She didn't know how to navigate any of this. Romance was for other people. Not her. Evidenced by how dismally she'd failed at it so far in her life.

Feeling suffocated by Liam's looming presence, she looked away.

In time to see Olt's retreating back, headed for the stables. Because that's the path she'd take to escape for a ride. His gait was awkward, his steps halting, as if he were still in pain.

Cosette's words faded as Ro hurried across the ballroom after Olt.

&a.

Ro chased him all the way to the stables. She came across him attempting to saddle a horse, his saddlebags hung over the stable wall next to him.

Instantly, Ro knew how he felt when he found her preparing to leave without him the day she'd received Cosette's plea for help.

She swallowed. "Going somewhere?"

His hand froze on the horse's bridle a moment before resuming his task. "*Ja.*"

"Back to your family?"

He gave a brief shake of his head. "*Nein.* They don't need me…"

His "either" hung in the air, unspoken, between them.

"Besides," Olt continued. "Olov wanted to come—he's better at this negotiating stuff anyway—but I insisted. Should've listened to him."

Ro stood there, heart breaking. "Are you…mad at me? For making you go with me to the Black Forest? When you didn't want to?"

He'd lost his arm because of her, after all. First, she'd made him go. Second, she didn't understand when he'd tried to warn her about the empress. And third, she'd distracted Odette when she should've been finishing his frock coat.

Even if not one of them had been clear about the consequences, it would make sense if he couldn't forgive her.

Olt laughed, but it had an exasperated edge. "I didn't want to go because I'd turn into a swan, not because I didn't want to be with you. And I didn't *know* I had to return for the curse to be undone. If you hadn't made me…" He shrugged. "It all worked out."

"Oh. Um, I see." Ro decided to take a risk. "I'll miss you."

His shoulders stiffened. "Will you?"

"Oui. I will." She moved to help him.

As she reached for his saddle, he said, "Don't. I have to learn to do these things for myself."

Ro's heart ached at the bitter words, but she stepped back and let him heave it onto the horse's back. "Surely you want to stay and rest? You just got here."

He bent to cinch and buckle the saddle straps. He grunted, and sweat lined his brow. His movements were awkward, unsteady, and he kept moving like he was trying to use both hands, then remembering he couldn't.

It broke Ro's heart to watch.

"I'm off to Angleterre to sign on to another ship. I can rest on the channel crossing."

She sucked in a breath, stricken. He really had no problem leaving? Just like that?

He had to turn toward her to grab his saddlebags, and his flinty look met hers. It felt like a sucker punch. Olt turned away and tossed the bags over the horse's back, tying loops one-handed to secure one side, then the other.

As if picking up the conversation they'd left off, he all but muttered, "At least you'll have Liam to comfort you."

She almost left. She could walk away, let him think what he will. Button up her feelings. Her heart would never be vulnerable again.

But this was her opportunity, maybe her only opportunity, and she wouldn't waste it. Not again. He deserved her honesty. Even if she never saw him again, he deserved to know the truth.

Ro took a deep breath. "I don't want Liam."

He froze.

"I want you."

The words sent him into an almost frantic motion, making his loops sloppy and his movements jerky. It almost made it easier to talk to him. Almost.

"Olt, I'm sorry I haven't said it before. I'm not good at sharing my feelings. Any feelings. You are my rock. My safe harbor. And when I found out you were that swan and might never be anything else…"

His hand went still, his back to her.

"I couldn't bear it. When I thought I'd lost you, I didn't want to go on. And when you kissed me…"

Stupid tears threatened, and, throat burning, Ro swallowed to try to stop them.

Her voice turned decidedly husky. "When you kissed me, I knew I never wanted anyone else to kiss me for the rest of my life. Even if you leave right now, even if you break my heart as I'm sure I've wounded yours, I just thought you needed to know."

He hadn't moved.

Ro's voice turned rather small, and she felt foolish and childish, all at once. "I understand if you want to leave. I do. But I couldn't let you without telling you my heart is yours. Always. Even if it's hard for me to show it."

Ro moved slowly toward him, reached out to rest her hand on his. Opened her mouth.

Doubt, fear, uncertainty assaulted her. What if it was too late? What if she'd just pledged her heart aloud only for him to throw it back in her face?

"I just thought you needed to know," she choked out.

Turning, she did the one thing she swore she'd never do again. Flee from someone she loved.

He didn't follow.

❧

Ro had just come out of the garden maze, two steps from one of the many back doors closest to her chamber, when she felt someone at her back. His familiar scent drifted on the breeze. She sighed.

She *really* didn't want to have this conversation right now. But Cosette was right.

Even if Olt rejected her—even though he practically *had* rejected her—she couldn't be unfair to Liam. She couldn't give him hope when there was none.

Her heart was spoken for.

"So he's gone, then," rumbled Liam's deep voice, with far too much satisfaction. And a fair bit of gloating. Ugh.

Ro took a deep breath. She could have this conversation like a normal, rational person, no matter his attitude. "Oui," she said simply.

"Did he ask you to go with him?"

Ro glanced at him in surprise. "Non. Did you think he would—?"

He let out a gust of air. "I was hoping he wouldn't."

"Oh." Ro frowned. "Liam, look—"

"Ro, if you would just—"

Both chuckled nervously and fell silent.

Ro took a deep breath and spoke before he could. "Liam, it just wouldn't work between us."

His jaw got that stubborn bent, and his eyes went flinty and hard. "You don't know that."

Ro tried to remain calm. "I do." The look in his eyes gave her an idea. "You're like flint, and I'm the spark. When we're together, forest fires rage and homes burn to the ground."

She bit her lip. She hadn't meant to be quite so dramatic.

Amusement and something dark leaped into his eyes. "Passion and fire. It's not a bad way to live, Ro."

"It is when we leave destruction in our wake," Ro grumbled.

"I prefer to think of it as…living life to its fullest."

Ro sighed. "We argue nonstop."

Again, Liam's jaw was doing that clenching thing when he was trying not to get frustrated with her. Or when he was well past it. "That's because you won't see reason. I could be good for you. We could have a good life."

A tremble went through Ro's hands. He'd never put it so…bluntly. She wasn't ready to hear this. Any of this. She opened her mouth.

"It's because of him."

Ro forgot what she'd been about to say. "Him who?"

"Olt." Liam ground his teeth at the name that caused Ro's heart to leap. "It's because of him, isn't it?"

Ro wanted to argue, but she couldn't keep lying to herself. Or anyone else. She sighed, glanced away. "Oui. I suppose it is."

Fire leaped into Liam's eyes. "Ro, he isn't good for you."

Ro's spine went ramrod straight. "Not good for me? Excusez-moi? Who do you think you are to tell me—"

"He isn't who he says he is!" exploded out of Liam's mouth.

Ro's own mouth hung open for a split second. He'd raised his voice before, sure, but he'd never yelled at her like that, right in her face. She didn't like it.

Ro ground her teeth, and her own voice came out louder than intended. "What? That he pretended to be a sailor—was a sailor—while he hid from the enchantress who cursed his entire family, killing half of them and turning the other half into swans? Is that the deep, dark secret you're so afraid I don't know?"

Their raised voices had attracted attention while they stood outside the château's door shouting at each other, so Liam gritted his teeth and pulled her past the maze and into a gazebo overhanging a small pond, yelling for the gardener trimming vines there to get out.

He fled, as any sane person would.

Ro's eyes went wide as the garden settled into silence and Liam stepped far too close for comfort.

"That's not what I meant and you know it. He's hiding something, something big, and I'm going to figure out what it is. I don't want you to get hurt." He dropped his voice. "Princes' pasts aren't all perfume and palaces. He's hiding something…ugly."

Ro's mouth was still parted when she saw red and her temper exploded. She shoved him right into the pond. He went down, squelching into muck at the shallow pond's edge.

As she turned to storm away, he bounded to his feet and came after her, splashing water and mud everywhere. He climbed up the bank as Ro skittered past.

Liam swiped for her arm, but she jerked it and her cloak out of reach. "Non!" She pointed at him. "Don't touch me. Even if there was no Olt, I wouldn't choose you, so just stop!"

She regretted her harsh words the instant she saw the hurt he tried to hide behind a hastily thrown-up scowl.

"I'm sorry. That was…cruel. I shouldn't have said it that way." She lowered her voice. "But don't you *ever* say anything against Olt in my presence again, unless you have *proof*."

She stomped away, leaving a dripping Liam standing there, seething. She clenched her fists and seethed even harder than Liam. Olt wasn't who he said he was. Ha!

But the damage had been done, and doubt swept her afresh. Could she trust Olt? Really?

And would it even matter if he'd chosen to leave?

A few minutes later, Ro stared out her window as Olt rode his horse out of the stables and away.

She stood there a moment, stupefied. He'd left? After she'd bared her heart and soul to him? Had he even *tried* to go after her? He'd certainly waited around long enough before riding away.

Ro stumbled over, locked her door, and cried until she couldn't breathe.

Why on earth hadn't she let him know how she felt sooner?

Why had she let him know at all?

And why did it feel like a hole was being carved out of her chest and whatever was doing it was still digging?

43

Ro kept obsessively checking the window, hoping he'd come back. Knowing he wouldn't. It had been several hours, after all.

Her face burned as she paced her room. Had she really said all those things? Out loud? And had he truly left anyway?

She groaned, from deep in her soul, heart splintering into a million pieces all over again. This. *This* was why she didn't share her heart. This was why she was better off alone. Why say things that could be buried deep instead of splayed out for others to judge and ridicule and reject?

Ro dropped her head into her hands, tears threatening all over again. Non. She wasn't going to cry. She wasn't! She'd done nothing *but* cry lately.

So she decided to distract herself by grabbing the closest thing to read, which happened to be a newspaper. She was instantly engrossed.

Not because it was a suitable distraction from Olt. Oh no. Because her name was plastered all over it. Nothing less could have held her attention.

Ro chewed on her lip, brow furrowed, as she clutched the

Parisian Weekly: A Journal for the Discerning Monsieur in a death grip and scowled.

"Rosette? Dearest?"

Ro yelped, jumped half a kilomètre, and threw the broadsheet. "Cosette! Sneaking up on people now, are we?"

Cosette smiled, but her bright eyes searched Ro's face a little too keenly.

To distract her sister from her puffy red eyes, Ro glanced past Cosette and put on the fakest of smiles. "How's my niece? I'm surprised she's not with you."

Except for late dinners that were well past the little girl's bedtime, Cosette was rarely seen without Allura at her side.

Cosette's smile was warm and authentic. Well of course it was. She hadn't just had her heart dragged through muck and briars and horse manure. Her heart had been restored to her with the return of her child.

Ro's smile gentled. She couldn't begrudge her sister's happiness. It was more important than her own heartbreak anyway.

Cosette fluttered a hand in the air. "Oh, she's resting. But she wakes a little when I poke her."

Ro's eyes widened. "Cosette!"

Cosette looked sheepish, but her grin couldn't be stopped. "It's a lovely change from before."

Ro laughed, the sound a bit thick. "Of course it is."

Cosette just smiled, a mischievous sparkle in her eyes, and nodded at the paper, which Ro had completely forgotten. "Did you enjoy the write-up about you in Gérard's journal?"

Ro's scowl came back with a vengeance. After retrieving it from the floor, Ro folded it with more force than necessary. "It's not true. Not a word of it."

A small smile hovering about her mouth, Cosette held out her hand and waited patiently. Ro sighed and handed it over.

Cosette unfolded it and scanned it. "I thought it was a lovely piece."

Ro couldn't look at her. "I didn't save France; you did."

Cosette made a disgusted noise. "Rose, if you hadn't insisted you could see a castle no one else could, if you hadn't uncovered that the prince was the beast—not that a beast had murdered the prince—none of us would be here right now."

Ro still wouldn't look up. "Oui, but you are the one who broke the curse. I couldn't—I couldn't—" She swallowed against the burn in her throat. "I couldn't love him like you did."

There. She'd said it. Even her saintly sister couldn't forgive that Ro had almost married Cosette's husband. Out of duty, but still.

She apparently couldn't love anyone well enough to choose her.

For heaven's sake! There she went, feeling sorry for herself again.

Cosette came forward and took Ro's hands. "I know, dearest."

Ro's head flew up, eyes wide.

Cosette smiled gently. "I could tell you were so focused on freeing France, no matter the cost, that you would do whatever it took to make it happen. I could tell you didn't want to marry him."

"But, but…" Ro couldn't get her thoughts to come together properly.

Cosette led her to the window seat, and they settled upon it together. "You see, my darling, you were so focused upon your task, sacrificing everything to make it right, I had to do my part. To make him love me. Marry me, the sister who could flirt—don't deny that you can't—and who loved things such as luscious gowns and the gossipy French court and all that came with being queen. That wasn't you, dearest, and I couldn't stand to see you unhappy."

Ro's eyes widened. And just like that, the weight of years

of guilt slid off her shoulders, and she clutched Cosette in a fierce hug. "Oh, Cosette! I thought you must hate me."

"Never, my darling," Cosette said just as fiercely. "Never."

Cosette rubbed her back and murmured soothing French nothings their mère used to say when they were distraught, and more importantly, she didn't rush Ro or make her feel less than.

After far too long, Ro sat up and rubbed at her face, which was surprisingly wet. Ugh. Not again. Cosette handed her a lace handkerchief, so Ro wiped her eyes and blew her nose.

"Merci, Cosette."

Her sister smiled. "Always."

Ro had barely taken a shuddering breath when Cosette clapped her hands and bounded to her feet. "Now! The reason I came in here."

Ro startled. "Can I…help you with something?"

Cosette just grinned and tugged her to her feet. "Help me? Why, my darling, you have done more for me than I can ever repay." Cosette winked and pulled her toward the door. "But I intend to try my best. I do believe there's someone who would very much like to see you right now."

Ro's heart plummeted. Liam. Not again. Had he seriously gone to her sister for reinforcements?

She pulled back. "Cosette, I just can't. Not now, please? I'm not interested in him, all right?" She had a feeling her eyes were saying more than she wanted to. Stupid tears tried to spill over, but she was sick of crying, so she blinked them back with a vengeance. "Please, just let me be."

Cosette just smiled. "Oh, I have it on good authority that you're going to like this very much."

Ro scowled. "Whose authority?"

Cosette winked again. "A little birdie told me."

With how kind Cosette was to animals and people alike, she didn't doubt that could be completely true.

Ro rubbed her temples. "Cosette, I don't think I can take any more of this right now…"

Cosette poured water into a basin and held out a towel, not giving Ro a choice. Ro gave her sister a dirty look, but she obediently washed her face and patted it dry.

And then Cosette launched into what she did best: trussing Ro up in a ridiculously lovely dress that draped over her willowy frame fetchingly, adding the barest hint of rouge to her cheeks and lips, and brushing Ro's shoulder-length dark hair until it shone.

Which had Ro sweeping down the hall with her chin held a little higher than normal, if she were being honest. Which she wasn't.

It was all wasted effort, anyway. She'd still be telling Liam *non*.

As she was hauled into the deep recesses of the palace, she marveled at how Cosette could get her to do just about anything, whether Ro wanted to or not.

Three hallways and two staircases later, Ro wanted to object all over again. Cosette or no Cosette.

The cooler air of the lower floors wafted over them, and Ro grumbled at the low stone ceiling. Everything was off-putting today, even though she normally liked coming down here during the heat of the day.

"Cosette, please…"

They rounded a corner, and suddenly, Olt was there.

Ro stopped so fast, she jerked Cosette to a halt.

His eyes widened as he took her in from head to toe. "Wow, Ro, you look…wow."

He quickly shut his gaping mouth, and Ro tried to beat a hasty retreat.

Having none of it, Cosette pushed her forward, not even a little gently, disentangling the arm Ro had seized. "Go, talk to him."

As if Cosette wasn't even present, Ro and Olt just stood there, staring at each other. Something tumultuous writhed in his gaze.

Ro's heart dropped to the rough-hewn stone floor. He was angry. He was going to take everything she said and throw it right back in her face. She deserved it, after how long she'd pushed him away, but she still didn't want to be present for it.

She frowned. But then why was he here?

Ro started to back up. "I think I'll just…"

He came toward her then, his steps sure, steady—eyes full of intent.

She wanted to cower, flee, run far and long, but she squared off with him. She'd never backed down from a challenge, and she wasn't about to start now.

Let him say what he will.

But the intensity of his gaze was too much for Ro's fragile heart. Tears, those stupid, stupid things that showed up when they were least welcome, made everything go blurry.

"Olt, I—"

He grabbed the back of her head and covered her lips with his.

She stood there, mouth parted, completely frozen, as he kissed her. Firm, insistent, decided. He wasn't backing down, and he wasn't asking permission.

He was telling her how he felt.

Then he gentled his touch, taking the kiss deeper, and Ro responded. Although she had no idea what she was doing, she melted against his firm chest and kissed him back, trying to show him everything she couldn't say, all at once.

I'm sorry. I didn't mean to hurt you. I will always be there for you, so help me Dieu.

And…dare she think it?

I love you.

His kiss said it right back.

They broke away at the same time, gasping, and stared at each other.

Olt ran a thumb over the corner of her mouth. "Yes. *Yes.* I want you too."

A laugh burst out of Ro's mouth. She couldn't help it. Joy

bubbled up inside her and tumbled its way free, unable to be contained.

She threw her arms around him, holding him tight.

"I'm so glad you came back," she whispered.

He held her just as tightly. "Me too."

Ro suddenly pulled back, self-conscious. She glanced all around them, but Cosette had gone.

"Your sister left as soon as she pried your grip from her arm." He grinned, his look teasing and light and oh-so-achingly familiar. "That was a feat of magical strength, if I do say so myself."

Ro laughed and wrapped her arms around his waist, resting her head on his chest. "I will always remember this as the best day of my life, not the worst." She drew back, searching his eyes. "Where did you go?"

He grasped her hand and led her toward a bench. They settled there together, and he pulled her close.

"I had to think. In my wildest dreams, I never imagined you saying such things to me. Return my kiss, maybe, but bare your heart like that? I didn't know what to do."

Ro's smile was rather frail. "A kiss right then and there would've been nice."

He grimaced. "In retrospect, that's exactly what I should've done. But you—after Prussia—I thought I'd never win you. I finally heard the no you've been saying since I met you."

Ro winced. She was rather abrasive like that.

"But then you handed me everything I'd ever wanted, all at once, and I didn't know what to do." He took her hand, kissed her knuckles. "I couldn't wrap my mind around it. I needed to think. It was a fragile and precious gift, and I didn't want to mess it up."

Her eyebrows climbed her forehead. "So you let me think I'd lost you and cry for three hours instead?"

Olt pulled back, eyes wide. "You cry?"

And those stupid tears decided to make an appearance right then to prove just how human she truly was. Ro swiped at them angrily.

He immediately looked horrified, and Ro realized he'd been teasing.

"Oh, Ro." He tugged her close and held her tightly with his arm. "I am so sorry. I didn't think. And I shouldn't have teased just then. I made a mess of things, didn't I?"

Neither said a word for a while, Ro taking deep breaths to conquer the traitorous things. "I saw you ride away," she said in a small voice.

Olt rested his chin atop her head. "I rode to the forest to think, but that wasn't right. I wandered the city, but everywhere I looked, I just thought of you. Then I went to see your sister —"

Ro tensed unconsciously.

"—and she took one look at me and told me to come down here and not move a muscle and she'd get you right away."

Ro relaxed. It was insane she'd thought for even half a moment that Cosette would steal Olt, too. She apparently still had some healing to do in that area.

"I love you, Rosette. You, always you, and no one else, ever."

Ro sighed. Of course her body would betray her insecurities like that. She pulled back and met his gaze. "And I love you, Olt. Truly. I don't know why it took me so long to figure it out, but I do."

He smiled. "I know. Well, I know that *now*, I mean."

Glancing over her head, Olt's smile widened till it looked like it might split his face. His eyes sparkled as he leaned in.

She sighed right before his lips touched hers. "All right. Spill. What colors are you seeing over my head right now?"

He grinned and nuzzled her neck and whispered in her ear, "You're shining like a diamond."

Ro gasped, and he took that as an invitation to show her just how happy that made him. Ro didn't mind one bit.

When they came up for air, their breathing ragged, he gave her a self-deprecating grin. "There's…just one thing."

Ro tilted her head and waited.

"Now you have to decide if you want someone with one arm."

"Olt!" Ro couldn't help her scowl. "That doesn't matter to me. You know it doesn't."

Although his relief was palpable, he rested his forehead against hers and said, "You're adorable when you scowl like that."

Which of course only made Ro scowl more. She was not *adorable*. He'd soon figure that out. Best to ignore it, for now.

Then another worry struck her, and she bit her lip.

"What? What is it?" Olt asked.

"That is, if you can forgive me…for letting it happen in the first place."

He frowned, and the silence stretched on a little too long for Ro's liking. She began to sweat. Would he say what he was thinking already?

"What are you talking about?" he finally asked.

Tears filled her eyes, and this time, she didn't try to stop them. "I—it's my fault. If I hadn't forced you to go, if I hadn't distracted Odette so she could finish your coat…"

"Oh, my love. My sweet, sweet love." He kissed her tenderly. Then he sat back and held her chin firmly. "It's not your fault." He cut off her protests. "It's solely the empress's for placing the curse and being a raving, murdering lunatic.

"If I hadn't followed you, my brothers would still be swans, I'd still have a curse waiting for me at the border of my kingdom, and I wouldn't have known Odette had found a way to make us all human again. Which still wouldn't have happened without you and your brilliance, so I should be thanking you for making me go home. In fact, I am.

"*Thank you* for making me go home." He gently kissed her eyelid. "*Thank you* for forcing me to face my fear." He kissed her other eyelid. "*Thank you* for restoring my family to me." He kissed her nose. "*Thank you* for stopping that old windbag who thought she could ruin our lives." He kissed her chin. "*Thank you* for being who you are."

Ro was a weak mess by the end of it, clutching at his shirt and trying to remember what he was thanking her for. "How did you escape it? The curse."

She was pretty sure that was something she'd been wanting to know.

He grinned, thoroughly enjoying the way she clung to him. He continued to sprinkle kisses over her face and neck as he explained.

"When she cursed us, it wasn't easy for her. Not like other things she did. Once she sent a curse toward one of us, in billowing green smoke, she'd start whipping up the next. We all ran, but one by one, my brothers were changed into swans." He broke off the kissing to duck his head. "Odile was caged, I lost sight of Odette, and like a coward, I ran and didn't look back."

Ro made a noise of protest. "You are *not* a coward. But you can keep kissing me. If you want."

He laughed and happily obliged.

"Why did she choose swans instead of nightingales, do you think?" Ro asked a bit breathlessly.

"Ah, well, yes. You see, my father liked to serve roasted swan at his banquets, cooked and then dressed once again in its feathers for an elaborate centerpiece."

Ro pulled back with wide eyes.

Olt winced. "I know, right? It offended her, and she let her opinion be known. Quite loudly. I honestly didn't know if my family lived or died after my escape, just that my step-mother's curse chased me all the way to the border, where it stopped, pacing and prowling and waiting for me to return. I could feel it watching me. I knew I couldn't go back, and I couldn't get word from anyone in my kingdom, so I assumed she'd…changed them and killed them, to punish us for offending her."

His hold on her tightened. "I couldn't go back. I just couldn't."

"Oh, Olt. I'm so very sorry." She laid her head on his chest, wishing she could take such awful memories away.

Something within her revolted at that thought, and she frowned, remembering what her grandmère had said about her own memories being altered. Non, she couldn't wish that on anyone.

Olt stroked her hair a moment, deep in thought, before straightening and giving her a brilliant smile. "But that no longer matters. My life is with you now, I love *you*, and you have absolutely nothing to apologize for. I'll take you any way I can get you." His gaze turned hooded. "But I'll understand. If you don't…you know…you don't *have* to…"

Olt's eyes smarted, a flash of vulnerability and heartache there, and he gestured to his missing arm a bit helplessly, as if it pained him to mention it.

Feeling brave, wanting him to know *how much* he meant to her, Ro leaned over and kissed his shoulder gently, not wanting to cause pain.

"I don't care, Olt. You are perfect for me, just as you are. You are enough, just as you are. I don't regret a thing about you." She kissed his mouth, then whispered against his lips, "I'll take you any way I can get you, too."

After a stunned moment, he returned her kiss fiercely, and Ro couldn't have told anyone how long they remained in the lower levels of the Parisian palace.

But every second with Olt was worth it.

"We should probably get back, non?" Ro asked lazily. She didn't know how long they'd been down here, and frankly, she didn't care.

But she also didn't feel like being interrupted in the midst of getting to know each other better. No one needed to see that. Ro was so new to this whole kissing thing, she couldn't imagine it looked anywhere near as nice as it felt.

"Naw," Olt said just as lazily, more satisfied than Ro had ever seen him. "I have a feeling your sister would happily run people off for us all day, if necessary."

Ro laughed and threaded her fingers through his. "So how does this work now that I know you're a prince?" A cold thought slammed into Ro. As Liam's warning came back to her, coupled with her grandmère's story. "Uh, your family wouldn't happen to own a seaside palace, would they?"

Ro felt like the entire world held its breath, waiting on Olt's answer.

She'd *kissed* him, for heaven's sake. Many times. They weren't…they weren't *related*, were they? Surely not.

A small furrow dug itself between his brows. "No, I don't believe so. At least, not last time I checked."

Relief flooded Ro and soothed all the places that had twisted into knots in the seconds it had taken her to form the question. She sagged against his side.

"Where did that come from?" he asked, rubbing her arm, still sounding confused.

She couldn't even begin to explain how the possibility of being related to Olt would have killed her. Dead on the spot.

"No reason." Quietly, Ro muttered under her breath, "Thank Dieu."

"Oh. The palace by the sea. The one your grandmère's prince lived in?"

Ro went still, but her face flushed to new levels of red.

"Would've been disappointed if I turned out to be your long-lost half-brother?" he teased, a smile in his voice.

She elbowed him. "Hey now. That would be my long-lost second cousin, or something."

"Or something." He frowned and pretended to think. "Might've made things awkward at the wedding when both sides of the family showed up, hmm?"

She did a double take, then scowled. "We are not there yet. Not even close."

He laughed and pulled her close, the smile that lit his face radiant. "Understood. May I kiss you again?"

"Please."

He wrapped his arm around her, and Ro had half a thought that Cosette had planned for this very thing, ever since she'd first laid eyes on Olt, before Ro wasn't thinking at all.

Grandmère dropped her bowl, a faraway look in her eye. "I have to go."

Everyone at the long table paused at her pronouncement, waiting for the old woman to elaborate, as she was so fond of doing, but instead, the Reynard matriarch rose to her feet and stumped out without another word.

Ro and Olt exchanged a glance, and he shrugged. Ro went back to eating, unease sliding through her gut. Should she go after her? Find out what was wrong?

"I hope she means to go back to her forest," said Bernadette out of the side of her mouth, her lowered voice pitched just right to reach everyone at the table.

Yvette snorted. "And stays there."

Ro wiped her mouth with a napkin to hide her smirk. It seemed Grandmère had sufficiently terrorized her grand-daughters—Ro included—and would be sorely missed.

Decided, Ro stood. "I should see if she needs help."

Olt gave her a smile meant just for her and touched her hand. She gave him one in return before tracing her grand-mère's steps.

Ro found her in the barn, saddling her horse.

"Leaving so soon, Grandmère?"

Ro held out the bridle, which the old woman swiped and slipped gently over the horse's head.

It really wasn't all that soon. The old woman had traveled from home to home, spending weeks with each granddaughter and forcing her to work—whether she had servants or not.

"Don't be impertinent, girl."

Ro hid a smile. "So suddenly, then."

"It wouldn't be sudden if you'd smelt what I did."

"Smelt?" Ro frowned. "What did you, uh, smell?"

"Something's wrong in my forest." Her grandmère cinched the saddle tight and used a stool to clamber onto the horse's back. Then she seemed to stare at nothing. "Something is moving through my forest that shouldn't be there. I shouldn'ta left Gustave to watch it alone for so long."

Ro handed her the reins.

Before Ro could ask who Gustave was, Grandmère's piercing blue eyes settled on her. "I could use your help."

Ro squirmed a little and was saved from answering by a servant girl rushing in with a small bundle.

"Your things, Madame."

"Took ye long enough!" the old woman snapped. "What, did you search the whole palace? It ain't like I got much."

Ro shot her grandmère a reproving look and the servant an apologetic one. "Merci, Arletta, for your help."

The girl gave a brief curtsy and fled.

"Help these days," Grandmère groused. "Almost as lazy as your sisters."

"Grandmère…" Ro hoped she sounded somewhat reproving. That might apply to some servants, but definitely not Arletta, Chantie, or Margot, all survivors of the beast's curse and hard workers.

Grandmère sniffed. "What? You know it's true."

Ro took a deep breath, hardly able to believe what she was about to say. "Just because it's true doesn't make it kind."

A real smile touched the old woman's eyes, a rare sight. She touched Ro's cheek. "You reminded me of your mother just then."

Ro ducked her head as her throat swelled and she couldn't speak. Kinder words had never been spoken, and she would treasure them for the rest of her life.

"I meant what I said."

Ro composed herself and looked up. Grandmère was staring at her strangely.

"Come live with me. Hunt with me. I'd train you further. Teach you everything about your powers that you want to know, and more besides."

Without thinking, Ro glanced at the palace.

Darya chuckled. "You can bring your young man." At Ro's gasp, the old woman shook a finger at her. "Just marry him first. I don't run a brothel."

Ro choked, her face on fire, then burst out laughing.

Grandmère grinned, the look erasing years. Then she gave Ro such a gentle, kind look, Ro almost couldn't believe this was the same woman who'd mistreated and berated her all the way across Prussia and France.

"But…what will you do, Grandmère?"

She straightened her bent shoulders. "Why, travel this great big wide world, o' course. I ain't got to see most of it before I had your mother, helped her raise her babes, then hid myself away with your sister."

Ro's heart gave a pang at the mention of Cendre. She'd give just about anything to see her again, to know for herself that her sister was happy in her choice to live at the bottom of the sea. That she was still…herself.

"I mean it, Rosette. I would love to have you. You and your man could lead a quiet life. I could build elsewhere or go see the world. Up to you. Just—think about it, all right?"

Ro nodded, too overcome to speak. Family. Home. Love.

All of her own making. Away from everything and everyone else. It sounded like heaven.

They wouldn't be expected to dine every evening at the palace. With his siblings or hers. The location was ideal. For her, anyway. What would Olt think?

"That's it. I've decided. I'm leaving the cabin to you." Grandmère nodded once, as if satisfied with what she saw on Ro's face. "I trust the two of you to take care of it."

Ro's cheeks flamed. Sure, she and Olt had kissed, but he'd hardly proposed marriage.

Well, hinted at it, maybe.

Ro pushed back her shoulders. "Merci, Grandmère. I will consider your offer, then I will let you know what I decide."

And there was Darya's world-famous glare. "If I said you'd have my cabin, then I meant you'd have my cabin. What need have you to decide on anything? It's yours!"

Ro's jaw tightened. "I—cannot make such a decision on my own. Not if it involves Olt. He'll want to have a say."

Grandmère sniffed but didn't press further.

And Ro wasn't comfortable bringing it up anytime soon. She might as well get down on one knee and propose herself, and she was in no way ready for that. They'd just started kissing each other, for heaven's sake!

Besides, if—*if*—there were ever a proposal, a secret part of her wanted Olt to do it.

"Well, I'm off, then."

Ro jolted herself out of her thoughts, face burning, and her grandmère reached down and squeezed her hand before Ro could move away. Then the old woman nudged her horse out of the stable yard.

"Think about it!" she called behind her.

Ro raised her hand in a wave. "I will!"

The old woman urged her horse into a canter, then a full gallop as she rode through the palace gates and across the bridge, soon out of sight. Ro dropped her hand.

Going with her grandmère was so very tempting. Oui, she had another cabin in the woods, one that had once belonged to the Mesdemoiselles of the Mountain, but Hamish and Clement had more than earned it by caring for the hungry of France these long years.

She had no right to call it her own. Not anymore.

Deliberately, she turned away from the open road and looked up at the palace. Perhaps she would join her grand-mère. Perhaps she wouldn't.

But right now, this very moment, she was doing what scared her.

What filled her with such happiness, she thought she would burst.

She smiled and made her way inside…to Olt.

And the future she'd chosen for herself.

THE END

Ro's story continues in

Slay the Wolf

Book Four of the Beast Hunters.

Available Now from L2L2 Publishing.

THANK YOU!

Thank you for reading this book!
Did you enjoy *Quell the Nightingale*?
Please leave a review!
It helps more than you can possibly know.
Thank you so much!

~Michele Israel Harper

ACKNOWLEDGMENTS

Ahhh! Another Beast Hunters book is finally done and ready for someone else to read other than me. I hope you loved it!

First of all, thank you, dear reader, for spending your valuable time on my stories. It means the world, and I can't wait to hear what you think. While you read this, I'll be working on the next book!

As always, there are so many wonderful people who worked with me to make this book much, much better.

Beta Readers: Alicia, I treasure your intuitive comments and questions, and I look forward to your feedback every single time. You are magic! Cathrine, I absolutely love your no-nonsense approach and the way you see story. Thank you for your invaluable insight! Stephany, you had so many wonderful insights, and I am so grateful you took time for my book. TJ, you really helped me wrangle some of these characters into behaving, and I'm so happy with your comments. Thank you all for reading my book when it was such a mess!

Editor: Oh my word, I can't even tell you how much I loved working with you! Your comments were pure gold, and the best changes to this book were because of you. I loved squealing with you over Olt, and every time you enjoyed a part of this story gave me a jolt of pure happiness. Thank you!

Endorsers: Annie, Cathrine, Connie, Emilie, Jasmine, Ronie, Savannah. It is terrifying to ask for endorsements, and the fact that you gave me such lovely ones humbled me and honored me and thrilled me in ways I can't even begin to express. Thank you from the bottom of my heart for such kind words! I will treasure them always.

Sara Helwe: Oh, Sara, I love your covers so very much! Thank you from the bottom of my heart for working with me. You are so patient and kind, and I am so grateful for you and your skill. This one is so beautiful!

Rebecca P. Minor: Ahhh! Thank you so much for creating these lovely sketches of scenes from my book! :D I have always loved your art, and I am so thrilled to be able to include some in this book.

Laura Hollingsworth: Your art blows me away every single time! Thank you for bringing my characters to life, then working with me to create the special edition hardcovers. I squeal every time I see a new piece of loveliness from you!

Naomie: Thank you for your help with French translations! Those tenses were killing me, and you swooped in like an angel and saved the day. Merci beaucoup!

Ben: Did you like the dedication? It was so hard to keep it a secret! I wanted to show you *so* many times. I meant every word, and I'm so incredibly grateful I can pursue this writing passion of mine with you at my side. *L'Chaim!* To life!

Blaze, Maverick, and Gwenivere: I love each one of you more than I can possibly say. You are my heart, and I'm so glad God chose you for my family.

And most importantly, thank you Father God, Jesus Christ, and Holy Spirit for giving me such a love for stories. I'm so honored to be writing my own!

With all my heart,

~Michele Israel Harper

ABOUT THE AUTHOR

Michele Israel Harper spends her days as an acquisitions editor for L2L2 Publishing and her nights spinning her own tales. Sleep? Sometimes . . .

She has her master's degree in publishing, is slightly obsessed with all things French—including Jeanne d'Arc and *La Belle et la Bête*—and loves curling up with a good book more than just about anything else.

Author of ten published novels (and more on the way), Michele prays her involvement in writing, editing, and publishing will touch many lives in the years to come.

Visit MicheleIsraelHarper.com to keep in touch or to learn about future books!

Michele loves to hear from her readers! Follow her on social media, check out her website, or drop her a line to let her know what you thought of Quell the Nightingale. *Happy reading!*

www.MicheleIsraelHarper.com
Facebook: @MicheleIsraelHarper
Twitter: @MicheleIHarper
Instagram: @Michele_Israel_Harper

Join her newsletter for bookish news and an ebook copy of
The Lost Slipper!
MicheleIsraelHarper.com/My-Newsletter

FRENCH AND GERMAN GUIDE

Below is a quick guide to the French and German words I used in this book. I tried to ensure they were self-explanatory, had a translation close to the word used, and were only a light sprinkling upon the story itself.

But in case you have questions, the meaning should be explained here. It was so hard not to use more!

I adore absolutely everything French, and I hope my love for this exquisite language and beautiful country and lovely people came through a little. Bon voyage!

- Angleterre: England
- Arrête: Stop
- Bienvenue: Welcome
- Bon: Good
- Bonjour: Good morning / good day / hello
- Ça va?: You good? Are you all right?
- Ça va: I'm good or I'm fine
- Château: Castle
- D'accord: Okay (But since "okay" wasn't around in the 18th Century, it means "all right" here.)
- De rien: You're welcome or it is nothing

- Désolé / Je suis désolé: Sorry / I am sorry
- Dieu: God
- Enchantée: Nice to meet you
- Excuse-moi: Excuse me, familiar
- Excusez-moi: Excuse me, formal
- Frère: Brother
- Grandmère: Grandmother*
- Incroyable: Incredible
- Livre: French money
- Madame: Ma'am
- Mademoiselle / Mesdemoiselles: Miss / Misses
- Magnifique: Magnificent
- Ma Reine: My Queen
- Merci: Thank you
- Merci beaucoup: Thank you very much
- Mère / Maman: Mother / Mom
- Mon ami: My friend
- Mon amour: My love
- Mon Roi: My King
- Monsieur / Messieurs: Sir / sirs
- N'est-ce pas: Is it not? Isn't it so?
- Non: No
- Oui: Yes
- Pardon: Pardon me
- Parfait: Perfect
- Père / Papa: Father / Dad
- Regarde: Look
- Rien: Nothing
- S'il vous plaît: Please—literally, "if you please"
- Sirènes: Sirens or Mermaids
- Sœur: Sister
- Tante: Aunt
- Vos Majestés: Your Majesties
- Votre Majesté: Your Majesty

GERMAN:

- Bitte: You're welcome
- Danke: Thank you
- Fräulein: Miss
- Gott: God
- Ja: Yes
- Mein Freund: My friend
- Mutter: Mother
- Nein: No
- Vater: Father

*Note: Technically, it should be "grand-mère" in French, but in all honestly, I just don't like how it looks. Since English is closed construction, I took the liberty of using "grandmère" in this series. I hope you'll forgive my changing it to match my preference!

THE LOST SLIPPER

COSETTE'S STORY

Did you know I wrote a story exclusively for my newsletter subscribers? May I introduce to you: *The Lost Slipper*!

Set between *Beast Hunter* and *Kill the Beast*, this novella from Cosette's point of view takes two beloved fairy tales, twists them together, and unravels them into a fractured new addition to the Beast Hunters series.

If you want it, all you have to do is join my newsletter—the ebook is completely free for anyone who wants exclusive updates. (But you can also find the paperback at your fave bookseller.) Enjoy!

Every day is the same for Cosette. Get up, clean, make breakfast, and meet her stepmère's and stepsisters' every demand.

That is, until an encounter with a fairy of the forest—or is she a witch?—and an invitation to a fête in honor of Monsieur Gautier promises Cosette's life is about to become the beautiful fairy tale of her dreams.

Or so the story should go.

Except her fairy godmère demands a high price for her help, one Cosette isn't willing to pay. Her stepsisters are as afraid of their mère as Cosette is. Can she truly leave them to their fate? And the handsome Monsieur Gautier hides a dreadful secret, one she's desperate to know—if only she can get close enough.

Cosette is faced with a choice: Should she feign ignorance and accept her happily ever after? Or dig deeper to find what may be lurking beneath?

"*The Lost Slipper* is a retelling of two fairy tales that could have easily been enough to carry the story on their own, but the addition of 'Diamonds and Toads' to the Cinderella narrative brilliantly escalates the tension and increases our poor heroine's suffering. A thrilling, emotional tale for anyone who ever thought, 'Cinderella had it too easy.'"

—C.O. Bonham, author of *Runaway Lyrics*

"*The Lost Slipper* is a short but satisfying read about grace and kindness when beset with cruelty, creatively combining two beloved fairy tales into a new, complex fable."

—H.L. Burke, award-winning and bestselling author of over twenty eclectic fantasy novels

"As someone who enjoys every Cinderella iteration I've ever come across, *The Lost Slipper* blends my favorite familiar elements of the story with unique twists—such as who the Fairy Godmother really is and the behavior of the stepsisters. With allusions that bring to mind *Ever After*, *Ella Enchanted*, and *Into the Woods*, readers will enjoy how Harper weaves this story and will be left wanting more!"

—Alicia Grumley, poet, Cinderella aficionado, and cohostess of Diversity Is Lit Book Club

Get it now at: **bit.ly/lostslipper**

More from L2L2 Publishing
Read the Whole Series so far!

French huntress Ro LeFèvre chases fairy tale creatures across France, Angleterre, Prussia, the Caribbean, and more, to protect those she loves. Join her as she's hired to kill beasts, hunt sirens, break curses, depose queens, and negotiate peace, all to end the fey's destruction across the human realm. The Beast Hunters series is sprinkled with many beloved fairy tales, full of frightful creatures, and complete at seven books. Stop the Snow Queen and End the Fey coming soon!

WHERE WILL WE TAKE YOU NEXT?

Devour *Beast Hunter*,
Hunt with *Kill the Beast*,
Sink into *Silence the Siren*,
Reread *Quell the Nightingale*,
and Discover *Slay the Wolf*.

All at
www.love2readlove2writepublishing.com/bookstore
or your local or online retailer.

Happy Reading!
~The L2L2 Publishing Team

www.ingramcontent.com/pod-product-compliance
Lightning Source LLC
Chambersburg PA
CBHW050947210726

48287CB00004B/1173